THE AGENCY

Ian Austin

THE AGENCY

Original cover art by Sallie Clough

Acknowledgements

Some of the best times of my life so far were during my police career. It is a job like no other requiring ordinary people to be extraordinary on a daily basis. I worked with some truly amazing officers and formed lifelong friendships which continue even though I am now on the other side of the world. This book is dedicated to them, the friends who literally saved my life.

I first heard the phrase, "You are only limited by your imagination," from one of them. The truth of this is contained in the next few hundred pages.

If you ever thought about running a marathon but are yet to do it, I cannot recommend the experience highly enough.

Ian Austin.

PROLOGUE

Southern England. Summer 2001

The garage was cool, the car smelled of pipe tobacco and cleaning products. She felt the need to whisper without being sure why.

"What about Kitty?"

"It's her I'm thinking about most," her husband replied. "She's making something of her life; she's turned into such a wonderful girl, hasn't she, despite all the things we have never been able to give her. It's us holding her back now."

"Are you sure you really want to do this?"

"Yes dear; tomorrow doesn't bear thinking about otherwise," he was already resigned.

"She will understand, won't she?"

"She'll be fine; I'm sure she will be just fine. I love you, pet. I'm so sorry it could not have been better for you both."

"Oh Norm, don't. You are the best either of us could have wished for. Come on, sit with me in the back. God forgive us and look after our precious girl." She began to pray as he settled next to her.

Operation Lime. 16:45 hours 14 March 2004

Detectives Nick Hetherington and Dan Calder were into the forty-first hour of their covert observations. Unusually, it followed straight on from a sixteen-hour mobile surveillance job because the subject had deviated significantly from what their original information was.

The subject, Robert Alexander Pittock, had driven north from London in his new Audi convertible and not stopped until he arrived at the remote location they were now watching.

The rest of the team remained hidden away, ready to move up to prearranged points and continue the surveillance if and when Pittock did move, or to make an arrest if Dan and Nick called them in. They were the lucky ones, able to have breaks, take on refreshments and also sleep. Dan had volunteered himself and his partner for the unenviable task of OP—observations post—which is how they came to be in the foul-smelling, rat-infested outbuilding close to the edge of some allotments on the outskirts of Manchester.

Pittock went into a house two hundred metres away almost two days before and had not emerged since. Nick and Dan's impromptu use of the red-brick shack was essential, being the only place within half a mile that gave a view of the narrow lane, house and driveway while affording them some cover.

Right now Nick would have happily traded the brick box for some fresh air, and his partner for anyone else on the team. As usual Dan could read his partner like a book. He knew it was only a matter of time before he would have to vent his feelings of misery once more, a fact Dan took constant delight in. He did not have to wait long.

"Tell me again why it is you always have to put your hand up for an OP? No, *our* hands?"

"Come on, this is the best part. Any time now, he's going to come out with a case full of crack, and we're going to be the ones to call the strike." Dan grinned without taking his eye from the powerful telescope.

"You're certifiable; you know that, don't you?" Nick went on. "I've been sitting here for the best part of two days, and so far

I've written sod all in the log because absolutely nothing has happened, and you're as happy as a pig in shit."

"We can always swap places if you want me to do the writing—you can do the watching for a while." Dan grinned again.

Nick changed the subject. "Have we got anything left to eat? I'm starving."

"No, *you* finished the last of today's supplies an hour ago, now we both have to wait until tonight when they'll deliver us some more."

Nick grimaced. "There was hardly enough to feed a bloody mouse last night. I'm going to phone Mick and tell him to make sure he gets twice as much—"

He was interrupted by Dan, who grabbed the covert radio set and urgently transmitted, "Stand-by, stand-by, stand-by!" without taking his eye off the house.

Nick switched into work mode instantly; glancing at his watch, he wrote down the time and his partner's code number in the logbook margin. There was silence for a moment. Dan took a breath then coolly continued into the radio.

"Subject is leaving the premises via the front door on the white side. Subject is wearing a black tracksuit top and bottom, shiny black material, full length zipped top, no hood, three white stripes across the shoulders the length of the arms and also the length of the trouser legs. White training shoes.

"Subject is carrying a black briefcase, yellow metal fittings; briefcase is leather or has the appearance of leather."

Nick wrote down what Dan said.

"Subject is approaching vehicle one; that is the vehicle he arrived at this location in.

"OP to Alpha 6; please advise."

A kilometre away, Detective Inspector Michael Swann picked up his in-car microphone. "Alpha 6 to OP; the information and intention are still as per the operation order. It's all yours to call."

"OP yes, yes," Dan replied in the same calm voice which betrayed his inner feelings. "OP to all units, the subject is in play. I repeat—the subject is in play. He is at the rear of the vehicle and has opened the boot and is placing the briefcase inside the boot. Boot is closed. The subject is into the vehicle, driver's seat. Stand by, stand by."

Nick checked his watch again and continued writing. Unseen by them and unbeknown to Pittock, who was at that second fastening his seatbelt, eight unmarked police cars were on the move.

"From OP, vehicle one is moving forward towards the premises' gates; Alpha 2 make ground."

Over the radio colleagues replied. "Alpha 2 yes, yes."

Dan continued. "From OP still towards the gates; Alpha 3 make ground."

"Alpha 3 yes, yes."

"From OP vehicle one is at the gates, the subject is the only occupant. The gates are opening inwards. Alpha 2 position?"

"Alpha 2 yes, yes."

"Alpha 3 position?"

"Alpha 3 yes, yes."

"From OP, vehicle one with the subject on board is at the gates and it's a left, left, left towards you Alpha 2."

"Alpha 2 yes, yes."

"From OP, all units make ground. Alpha 2 has halted in the roadway forty metres ahead of vehicle one. Vehicle one is slowing and it's a stop, stop two metres from Alpha 2. Strike! Strike! Strike!"

The narrow lane prevented Pittock from passing the stationary police car. A seasoned criminal, it took him no time at all to realise what was happening. The contents of the briefcase were a one-way ticket to a long prison sentence. He needed to be as far away as he could from it and the car.

As he was making that decision, police cars were converging on the lane to seal off the area and detain one of the most active drugs dealers in the country.

Dan kept the telescope on the incident as it was unfolding and the radio to his lips. *This should be the end of a five-month operation, if we've all done our jobs properly*, he thought.

"OP to all units; subject is out of vehicle one and is running on a return route towards the premises and towards you, Alpha 3."

"Alpha 3 yes, yes."

"From OP, Alpha 3 is approaching the subject. The subject is attempting to climb the hedge and fence on the opposite side of the road to the premises."

Silence.

Dan watched. Nick continued writing.

More silence.

"From OP, Alpha officers are approaching the subject."

Yet more silence.

"The subject is detained. Alpha 6 acknowledge."

"Alpha 6 yes, yes. OP shut down and extract. Good job boys, the first pint is on me."

As they wandered back across the allotments soon after, Nick talked animatedly about which locally brewed beers he hoped to be available to make up for their time spent in the isolated shed. As was his way, Dan was already ruminating over the just completed operation, downloading the facts into his brain so he could recall them again in detail at any future time. When the grass and earth of the allotment finally gave way to asphalt, the change brought about a change in his thinking too. He had put off telling Nick his latest news for too long already and decided now was as good a time as any to tell his partner he was leaving the unit.

Nick was completely taken aback. "Why? I mean why now, or why at all? This job is tailor-made for you and you for it."

"Time for a change, that's all. I'm going to remain as the Force Training Officer for Surveillance and also as a visiting trainer for National Crime Squad, so it's the best of both worlds for me."

"I'm gutted to see you go, mate, even with the OPs. Where are you going to?"

"Garstone."

"When?"

"Two weeks. Sorry, I was going to tell you before."

PART ONE

THE HUNTER

"The guilty one is not he who commits the sin, but the one who causes the darkness."

— *Victor Hugo*

CHAPTER ONE

London, England

Edwina Jacobs sat nervously in the small, well furnished room. Over the past week, she tried and failed to visualise this day.

When she rang the unmarked doorbell moments before, a familiar yet nondescript voice through the two-way communication box attached to the wall invited her inside.

"You are right on time," the voice had said. "Please wait a moment and the door will open. Come up to the first floor and make yourself comfortable; someone will be with you directly." Then the door clicked open to reveal a short passageway and a staircase of polished dark wood. At the top of the stairs, another door, also dark wood, displayed a brass plate: 'The Agency. Please wait inside.'

The room was as nondescript as the voice. Neutral colours on the walls, new grey carpet, a small coffee table and two comfortable-looking tub chairs in leather as dark as the staircase and door. And that was it.

Edwina was sixty-five years old and until recently thought herself reasonably fit and healthy. She was therefore shocked by the diagnosis of an advanced and inoperable brain tumour after what was supposed to be a routine hospital visit, but then a priority specialist appointment to investigate her headaches. Shock was slowly replaced by a resignation to her fate and a series of 'What life could have been like if …' thoughts which became routine—until an afternoon coffee and gossip with her friend Valerie.

Being able to control one's exit from this world had always appealed to Edwina. She remembered years ago a dinner conversation with friends about how you might choose to die if you could. That was before her husband Richard died after a long and painful illness. He'd said he wanted to die performing some heroic act, and their friend Michael just wanted to go in his sleep without any warning when he felt he still had years left in him.

When Mary asked Edwina, she'd nearly told them the truth but was too embarrassed and said something about wanting to know if God really existed just before it happened instead.

Edwina met Valerie Stenning at a flower show nearly a year before. Since then Val, a conveyancer in nearby Trowbridge, helped her out when she was selling the big house and buying another smaller one nearby. She was a real godsend and was always available for a chat or an evening in front of the TV when Edwina needed some human company to supplement her little dog Oscar. Younger by at least twenty years, maybe more, Val was initially an unlikely friend. She was, by her own admission, quiet and plain, with very few friends of her own.

Such was her quiet character that Val completely amazed Edwina when she gave her the number for The Agency. They were in a dimly lit bistro one evening, enjoying an early supper soon after Edwina was given the news about the grievous nature of her illness.

"A friend of mine used them. He wasn't supposed to tell anyone, but he did tell me in case anything bad happened. In the end, it must have gone exactly how he wanted, and the papers reported it so well that his family will always believe he died fighting overseas," Val whispered.

How the friend got to hear about this mysterious Agency in the first place, she did not know.

That was a month or so ago. Edwina kept the number in her bag for several days before calling—though she took it out and looked at it dozens of times.

When she finally telephoned, it was the same nondescript voice who answered the telephone at that time. She wasn't sure if it was even a man or a woman on the other end of this most odd conversation.

"Hello, how may I help you?"

"I understand you may be able to help me with some arrangements. Is this The Agency?" Edwina added, suddenly worried she might have dialled a wrong number.

"It is, and yes, we can help, I'm sure. Please tell me what it is you would like us to facilitate for you?"

She found herself taking a long, deep breath, in spite of all her mental preparation, before continuing. "I'm dying. I only found out recently and there's nothing anyone can do about it. I don't want to have to go through a painful ordeal or put my friends and relatives through it, either." She paused and prepared to continue, but the person on the other end cut in.

"We understand completely and you need not explain further. Tell me how you want it to be?"

Edwina was in a phone box near to Waterloo railway station; Val's instructions were explicit about not calling from home or from anywhere other than a public call box somewhere in London: "It's what my friend had to do. The only way to get in touch with them, he told me." Val said.

The journey to London was Edwina's first to the capital since Richard died. Nevertheless, she found herself looking around to make sure no one was watching or standing outside listening, before going on. "You won't judge?"

The voice was calming. "No, you can tell me anything, ask anything and request anything. Have no fear."

There was a silence between them until Edwina spoke, confession-like. "A mermaid; I want to be a mermaid. I have always wanted to have the experience since I was a little girl."

She could hardly believe she had said it. *Oh my God*, she thought, *what have I done?* She blushed and loosened her silk scarf as her neck suddenly grew hot.

The voice replied with an ease that made Edwina think for an instant she had not said it or had been misunderstood. Clearly, she was perfectly understood though.

"And would you like to go as a mermaid or just have the experience before becoming yourself again and passing then?" the voice asked.

"Go as one!" she exclaimed, unable to contain herself. After another look around, she covered the mouthpiece with both hands and whispered, "I could go as one?"

"Most certainly; no job is too hard or too big. It is your life, and it is definitely your death."

A few more seconds passed. "I never thought about dying like that, but I think … maybe … if it were possible?" she whispered.

"When is convenient for you? Do you have particular dates in mind or shall we make all those arrangements and have it as a surprise?"

If this conversation were not so deadly serious it could have been the stuff of fairy tales. Edwina flushed again and fanned her face with a trembling hand.

"As I said a moment ago, it really is all up to you," the voice gently reminded her.

"I think I'm going to need some time to decide, a few days at least."

"Of course. When you do decide, you need only telephone on the same number and we can discuss the final details then. If you prefer, there is an address where you can visit us."

Edwina gulped. "And payment, you haven't mentioned that."

There was a hint of laughter in the smooth reply. "Naturally; I can give you a reasonable idea now and a definite figure when we next speak, if you would like. The cost will be entirely based on your personal programme. I should say in the region of two hundred and twenty thousand pounds. No more than two hundred and fifty."

While that amount of money wasn't really the issue to Edwina—she had been more than comfortable for many years—it was still a very large sum, more than she'd ever spent on any one thing other than the big house years before. The staggering figure made her feel slightly faint for a moment. Regaining her composure, she said, "If I wanted a summary of the costs?"

The voice on the other end did not waver. "I am more than happy to tell you all you wish to know, and I can also write it down for you to see. I am afraid you will not be able to keep that written notation though. The Agency's existence relies on absolute discretion and our ability to do what we do without drawing attention to ourselves or our clients. If a document of our activities were ever made public, we would cease to be. I am sure you will be satisfied with our calculations based on what you want to happen. None of our costs will be hidden from you, and we will never ask for a penny more than the quotation."

"It might be better if I can see. This is not something I would have ever considered. It's difficult for me to understand; coming all this way to make a phone call and now to hand over all that money without even meeting you. I'm not usually this adventurous."

One or two further arrangements were made until they were both happy. Finally, she was given an address in Islington, and they agreed on a date and time.

"Please say nothing of this to anyone. The confidentiality of this venture is entirely in your hands. If you do not speak of it, I guarantee it will remain secret. Until the fourteenth. Goodbye."

A week passed since she made that call and on more than one occasion Edwina considered forgetting about it altogether before changing her mind again. It seemed stupid now, but she took half an hour to decide what to wear this morning just because the whole situation was so alien. As she sat picking at the loose fluff on her blue and green woollen skirt, she considered again whether she should just get up and leave.

The picking changed to brushing with her palm, as if trying to iron her skirt flat, and she was still working aggressively at it when the door opened quietly and a man entered, stopping her mid-brush.

He smiled and took the chair opposite. He had a strange look about him—a certain quality or a bearing, even. He glided across the carpet on the short journey from door to chair with no real discernible movement of limbs clad in his mid-grey, double-breasted suit. He seemed to take a moment to get comfortable; not physically comfortable, but ready to say whatever it was he was going to say.

His eyes plugged into hers as soon as he came in, and they still held her now. Edwina stared back but said nothing.

It could have been any amount of time before he spoke. When he did, it was in a quiet, authoritative voice, perfectly in keeping with his appearance, and devoid of any hint of an accent.

"Welcome to The Agency," he began. "My colleagues and I have a range of skills that guarantee success. As we told you on the telephone, no job is too complex, no job is too big. I can briefly outline what we have in mind for you based on your earlier enquiry." His voice was like syrup.

Edwina nodded, still saying nothing. Their eyes remained locked.

"Thank you again, by the way, for the details you provided before. We appreciate that it has been a slightly, let's say, unusual way for you to get in contact with us, but in these circumstances, I'm sure you will agree it is entirely necessary, and without as much detail, we cannot provide the precise service you want," the man continued, crossing his legs in an almost feline way.

"You are obviously restricted by time due to your circumstances. That shouldn't be a problem for us. If you like, we can still start in two weekends' time and it will be finished by the following Tuesday morning."

He paused, but only for effect.

"We thought Scotland, an early misty morning, you and your dog walking along the shore. It may be his barks, but something will alert you to movement in the water. At first you can't make it out, but then you see him fishing and playing around a few rocks close in.

"When he sees you, he swims away, but he comes back. He's smiling. Although it's cold, you will think nothing of it and go down the bankside steps and into the water too. You will be drawn to him. Oscar will have to stay, but we'll take care of all that," he said matter of factly, and then continued in a flawless oratory. "A lovely time, really lovely. I shan't spoil it all by telling you everything we have planned for you, unless you want to know the details.

"Spend the next day with him from as early as you like; all day if you wish. You can make your telephone calls or write letters to friends and family later in the evening, if that is still your intention."

Edwina was stunned by the way he was relating to her what could be her last few moments on Earth. She wanted to speak, but he was so captivating she could not utter a word.

"We thought of him being able to come to your cottage; a once in a lifetime ability for such people, a whole day and night out of the water in human form. You can spend the whole night together that way and be ready to go in the morning. We'll take care of Oscar, deliver him back to whomever you want with your note and that will be that.

"When you swim away together, you won't feel or know a thing about it. You will not be found—ever, if that is still your wish.

"I think that covers it all," the man concluded.

Edwina coughed. It all sounded so simple, so unreal, so unlike her.

The strange-looking man never took his eyes off her as he described the full range of services available to her; not even for one second.

The fact that she was sitting in this small room, in a small building, in the middle of London, with a man whose age could be anywhere between thirty-five and sixty, whose height she had not noticed, whose hair seemed to change colour in the light coming through the dormer window in the ceiling, and who, if she was asked tomorrow, she would be completely unable to properly remember or describe was inconsequential at that moment.

Even his eyes, which were still focused entirely on her, could have been blue or green or grey.

"You wanted to see the programme of events and confirmation of expenditure. I have them here for you to look through." As he spoke, he reached a delicate hand inside his jacket and removed an expensive-looking white envelope.

Edwina took the proffered stationery and removed a piece of folded matching paper from inside. The man reached forward indicating for the envelope, which she returned, and he replaced it inside his jacket.

On the paper was an itinerary and a list of amounts in pounds, all handwritten in a flowing script in black ink. Edwina was taken aback at some of the suggestions on the itinerary and looked across at the man a couple of times as she continued to read. When she was finished, he held out his hand again, revealing a glint of gold on his wrist. After she handed back the sheet, and it joined the envelope in his pocket, the man said, "I hope it is all to your satisfaction."

Edwina's heart fluttered when she replied. "Is it all possible, you can do those things for me?"

"If you want anything else instead or in addition, please, just say."

"No it's … it's beautiful, simply wonderful. I could never have imagined half of those things."

"We were sure you'd approve. You can see where the funds are required to enable your experience to be complete."

"Oh yes, quite."

"Can I take it then, that you are happy to proceed? If so, I just need to know when," he said it as if the decision was already a foregone conclusion.

Edwina took several deep breaths. "I don't need to put it off. You mentioned before about the weekend after next?"

The man blinked—the first time she was sure he had done so in all the time he had been with her.

"Very well. In a day or so, you will receive a letter saying you have won a competition; all the details will be inside that letter. In the meantime, please be good enough to transfer this amount to this account?" With two fingers, he removed a small card from the breast pocket of his jacket and gave it to her.

"You will receive the letter in any event, but we will only proceed if you have transferred the funds before the weekend arrives. You will not hear from us again, but rest assured all will be well."

As the man rose to leave, Edwina extended a hand, thinking he might shake it, but he merely glanced down and smiled.

"But I don't even know your name."

"Walter Terry," he said. And as easily as he had arrived, he departed and closed the door behind him.

Terry collected his new calfskin briefcase, which he left outside the door before meeting with the Jacobs woman. The brass plate and wireless intercom box had been secured with double-sided tape and came away easily, leaving no marks. He placed them safely inside his briefcase and clicked the lock shut.

Fortunately there was a taxi passing as he left—but then there were always likely to be taxis in Islington at that time. When the driver dropped him at Waterloo, he paid in cash and made his way to the toilets underneath the main concourse. With time to spare before his train was due, there was no need to rush to change into the vacuum packed casual clothes he also carried in the case. When he emerged back onto the platform, he was dressed in jeans and a lightweight fleece jacket and carrying a large brown paper bag from one of the big department stores with the case now inside.

Alone again in the small room for the second time in ten minutes, Edwina looked at the card. The numbers on it were obviously a bank's sort code and account number, but instead of being written or typed, they were embossed.

She did not look back at the doors of the room or the building when she left. If she had, there would be no brass plate or intercom box present anymore as both, recently removed, left no trace of The Agency ever being there.

When Edwina boarded the train and took a seat at the front of the carriage, she still had a few minutes to spare before departure time—before she left London behind for the last time and headed south and west to her home town of Melksham. She tried reading a gossip magazine, but it was no use. Her mind was full from the meeting with the strange man and the prospect of her imminent death. She was feeling ashamed about what she was about to do.

For most of the journey, she kept her hands inside her handbag on her lap and continually ran her fingers over the embossed numbers on the small card she held. There were a number of other people in the carriage, all probably going back to their west country homes at this time of day, but she was oblivious to all of them; even the young man who was sat in the seat behind her, with a big paper bag in the luggage tray above his head.

CHAPTER TWO

The following morning, Edwina woke from a fitful sleep.

When she got home the previous evening, she left a message for Valerie to see if they could meet for coffee sometime in the next day or so.

Val had previously made it very clear when she gave her The Agency's number: "I don't want to know anything more about it. Not even if you telephone them."

In the middle of the night, when Edwina was still wide awake, she decided not to burden Val with the knowledge of what she was now doing and resolved to remain silent about it when they did meet.

After breakfast and still feeling tired, she took Oscar out for a walk to the nearby park. Richard brought the little black collie-cross home one night after work about eleven years before, and from the moment she set eyes on him, they became best friends. Oscar would lay across her feet when she sat on the sofa watching television in the evenings. They had more or less gotten old together.

The leisurely stroll around the park suited them both. He was not at all interested in running and chasing the other dogs around, and she was still very much focused on the events of the previous day.

By the time they reached the wooden exit gate, it was just after 9:30 and all the shops in the little town centre were open. Oscar patiently waited for her to attach the lead to his collar and then they crossed the road before making their way along the narrow path towards the bank in High Street.

She absent-mindedly waved back to Douglas Tanner in the butcher's shop, who called a hello as they passed his open doorway. On another day, she might have got Oscar a hard bone, but today she just wanted to get done what was needed and go home.

After attaching his lead to a rail outside, she pushed open the big glass door and entered the tranquil space of the Wiltshire and West Bank, relieved to see it was empty of other customers.

The three cashiers were stationed behind the enclosed counter like greyhounds before the start of a race. They looked up expectantly as she approached, and as one, gave her a cheery corporate smile. She deliberately chose the eldest of the three, a middle-aged man on the left, and the other two went back to sorting paper.

"Good morning, how are you today?"

Edwina half-heartedly smiled back as she took her purse out of her handbag. "Can I transfer some money from my savings account, please?"

She took out her bank card and a piece of paper with The Agency's account number written on it. Feeling something akin to guilt earlier, she had copied the embossed numbers down, as if presenting the card at the bank may have been too incriminating.

She slid her card and the paper under the grille and waited.

The cashier picked up the card and swiped it through the electronic receptor. "Right-oh, Mrs. Jacobs, how much are you going to transfer today?"

The moment had come. Edwina tried her best to make it sound blasé. "It's rather a lot, two hundred and thirty-eight thousand pounds."

The cashier stopped tapping on his keyboard and his smile flickered off and then returned. "It certainly is, better make sure I don't type too many zeros for you," he chuckled.

Her heart leapt around inside her chest as she watched him go through the transaction process, all the time waiting for an alarm bell or other security measure to be initiated in front of her and stop the movement of the money dead.

An uneventful moment later, he benignly passed her card and the piece of paper back through the grille with a receipt for the transaction and the modest balance left in her account.

"Will that be all, or is there anything else we can help you with today?"

"No not today," she replied, unable to look him in the eye.

She felt short of breath as she undid Oscar's lead once outside again. He licked her hand and wagged his scruffy tail.

When she felt the touch of a hand on her shoulder, she nearly screamed.

"Hello," Valerie said. "I got your message, sorry I didn't reply. I was going to call you anyway. Oscar darling, how are you today, boy?"

Val stroked and patted the dog as he nuzzled into and around her legs. Edwina's heart was performing acrobatics now, and it took a short while for her to be able to settle herself and reply.

"Goodness, you gave me a start."

Val smiled and, still patting Oscar, said, "So, coffee. How about it? I've just finished one appointment and I have another later this morning. Let's go mad and have a sausage roll too."

Edwina was glad to see her friend, and a return to something much more familiar was a blessing. They walked arm in arm down to the Penny Farthing Café, where they knew Edwina's old friend Eileen would let them sit in a corner with Oscar.

"Two coffees with the chocolate on the top and two warmed-up sausage rolls, please," Val said as they stopped off at the counter on the way to one of the tables near the back of the quaint café.

Eileen smiled broadly as they entered. "Morning girls and pup. Give me a couple of ticks and I'll bring them over."

Once seated and settled with Oscar lying contentedly under the table, Edwina and Val caught up with the usual mixture of gossip and news.

"I'm thinking about going blonde again," Val said after a while. "Years ago I was like Marilyn Monroe, really I was. I might not go that far again, but it might be fun, don't you think?"

"I can't see you as a blonde; you were before? I could never have guessed."

"I'll have to show you pictures one day. What do you think the partners in the firm would say, though? It might raise a few eyebrows to say the least. They are a bit set in their ways."

Eileen set the drinks and food down in front of them and moved away. Edwina picked up her coffee in both hands and took a small sip.

"Are you alright? Not quite yourself today, by the look of things." Val said, reaching over and touching the back of Edwina's hand.

"Oh you know, a bit of a bad night. Oscar woke me up early too," she lied.

On hearing his name, Oscar looked up to check everything was alright and seeing nothing to worry about, laid his head back down on top of Edwina's shoes.

"I'm going to Birmingham next Monday—well, Sunday evening—for the whole week. Meetings with some new clients," Val said later when the coffee and the sausage rolls had been consumed and her hair colour was decided upon.

Edwina immediately saw the deeper meaning of what her good friend innocently said. This was going to be the last time they would talk or share a coffee. A lump the size of a tennis ball materialised in her throat, and she felt as though she might burst into tears. She picked up her napkin to wipe around her mouth and use up enough time to regain some composure. She desperately wanted to tell Val everything, but suppressed the urge.

"Well I hope they put you up somewhere nice."

"One of those Travel Lodges, I expect, but I am going to drive up so I can do some shopping as well at the new centre. A girl's got to make the most of her opportunities."

"Good idea, I wish I was coming with you, dear," Edwina answered, with more honesty than she expected—and more than Val could have possibly realised. Despite all the years between them, she did feel a real connection and kinship with Val.

Val settled the bill and they left the café together. On the street-side of the door, she went to give Edwina a hug. Edwina held her close and tight.

"Are you sure you're okay?" Val asked, looking directly into her older friend's eyes for confirmation.

Edwina straightened and smiled. "Yes of course, just lovely to see you. I … I … You have a good time in Birmingham."

"I will. We'll have a proper girls' night in when I get back, alright?"

"Yes, that sounds lovely."

Val touched Edwina's arm again and then gave Oscar a pat on the head before walking off towards her next appointment.

Edwina watched her go until she turned the corner back onto the High Street. Feeling downcast, she turned the other way and started off in the opposite direction. There was one more place she had to visit before they could go home, and she was desperately trying to think of how she was going to explain it to Richard before they got to the cemetery.

CHAPTER THREE

Auckland, New Zealand

The sky was a heavy ominous grey this June morning, but the air was as still as could be, forcing the seagulls to soar and swoop entirely under their own power.

Pounding along the footpath: open ocean to his right with the dim morning sun struggling to hold its position among the slate clouds, he tried to concentrate on his cadence and breathing. As with most things Dan Calder took on, he quickly became dedicated, if not addicted to the marathon training, which was now an extremely important part of his daily routine.

The fact that on some days it was much more than that, he kept buried deep inside.

He was largely ignored by other runners and walkers, which was just how he liked it. During his police career, his *ability* to go unnoticed had been his greatest skill and asset. It was a natural tendency, but also one he worked very hard to perfect. As a covert surveillance operative, to be seen but not noticed was as precious a gift as gold or diamonds. He was an average looking man, of average height and build and was so difficult to remember and describe that on one occasion during an exercise for trainees, he was likened to John Wayne, Bob Geldof and the then Prime Minister Tony Blair. In actuality, he had unusual eyes which were halfway between brown and green and contained tiny yellow flecks like gold dust, a complexion more olive than most of his colleagues due to his four grandparents being of four different nationalities, and a wiry but athletic physique, which depending on his choice of clothes and stance, he could manipulate so as to appear to be anywhere from a malnourished drug user to a slightly overweight stockbroker.

He generally ran first thing. After a large glass of water and a stretching routine, he always set off from home down the narrow lane that led to the seafront and then turned left onto the well-maintained footpath.

Calder had been a policeman most of his working life, a career constable first in uniform, and then a detective. Promotion was always a non-issue for him: the further up the ladder you went, he always said, the further away you got from real policing, preventing and detecting crime, locking up the bad bastards and helping those who suffered at their hands.

He resigned in 2008 after twenty-five years of service with a certificate and a smallish pension. His whole life changed since then. Three years and half a world away later, he had recently thrown himself into running and writing to keep himself occupied in his new home until he found something else more permanent to do with his time and mind.

He had always been fit and healthy and didn't like the idea of not being so. Now having the time and living by the sea, he decided he was going to run a marathon and had been in training for a few months.

He was five ks into today's effort and was feeling pretty good. Running was so much easier in light or no wind, better to have it rain than be windy.

When he first decided to run the marathon, the thinking was that four hours and twenty minutes would be acceptable for his forty-four years; now, after a few months into the training, he was determined to break the four-hour mark.

He was running twenty kilometres every other day; and maybe once every two weeks he was doing a longer run of up to thirty-five ks. He was thoroughly enjoying the whole experience now. On the non-running days, he made himself do dozens of sit-ups, jamming his feet under the heavy leather couch in the lounge each time he was passing between rooms.

Dan also thought he'd make a stab at writing another book. In his previous life, before he joined the police, the thought of being able to write well at all, let alone being able to write a book, would never have even occurred to him. His literary talent only surfaced when his duty reports and statements, then later training packages and lesson plans were received with ever increasing admiration. If truth were told, all his abilities could be traced back to when he joined the force. Prior to that he was a lost soul in every regard. He gained tertiary qualifications and in time became the Force Training Officer for Covert Surveillance and was also acknowledged as the best interviewer and Tactical Advisor for other interviewing officers.

The first book was a tortuous experience and was written with a feeling he was serving a penance. It came about when he was advised to write down his experiences and feelings by a counsellor he met at a meeting for people with depression. Once he started, he could not stop, even though it was painful, and he still found no pleasure in any of the three hundred-plus pages when he looked at it from time to time.

There was one chapter in particular he still kept hidden from the rest and secret from everybody. He often thought if he could write something else which did not hurt, it might somehow offset the first book.

A few minutes later and the dreaded seventh kilometre loomed. The seventh kilometre was always more uncomfortable than the six now behind him; breathing harder, legs heavier. It seemed to be longer than all the others for some crazy reason, but he also knew if he felt reasonably okay as he started the eighth, it bode well for the rest of the run.

His new Brooks running shoes were performing very well. It was quite a learning experience seeing on the shop's video the difference a decent pair made. In his old ones, his lower legs and ankles bowed outwards, putting pressure on all the joints be-tween feet and lower back. In the new ones; his lower legs and ankles were back in a vertical line as if by magic, and he bought two pairs on the spot.

The sea air was clean and fresh and although the road was only a few yards away, the running here was literally a world away from the grim streets around his old English home or even around the country park where he used to go to when he was exercising in the past.

The colour and movement of the water and the sky here still made every day a fresh picture and a new experience—free ther-apy. In the early weeks of his training, before he was properly bitten by the running bug, this was the single best thing that maintained his interest and enthusiasm.

He ran all the way down to the Viaduct Basin, where a small number of Auckland's rich moored their ego extensions. Keep-ing his pace steady all the way to and around the ten kilometre brass marker, he mentally checked his physical condition and headed on a return route towards St. Heliers and home.

Stepping through the door from the integral garage into the kitchen, Dan automatically checked the time on the oven clock. "Okay," he said to the empty house.

He quickly downed a litre of water and half a litre of cran-berry juice then went to shower and change before going back to the kitchen for cornflakes, a banana and skimmed milk. As he wandered through to the lounge with his bowl, he noticed through the large French doors his neighbour Shelley hanging washing out on the rotary line in her garden. She and her hus-band Paul were Dan's closest New Zealand friends. They had made the point to meet him when he moved in and the friend-ship developed easily from there. Paul was the manager of a men's clothes shop in the centre of Auckland and constantly urged Dan to pay him a visit having seen the sparsely populated

wardrobe in Dan's bedroom one day when he was helping remove the old carpet.

When Shelley saw him, she waved and mouthed something he
could not understand; he opened a door and took his bowl out.

"Hi, how are you?"

Shelley grinned back. "Good. Been running?" She had the gift
of looking good without trying, claiming her hourglass figure
was a gift from her mother.

"Can you come over for drinks tonight? About eight."

"Okay, thanks. How's the job hunting?"

Her smile became wider, emphasising her pretty face and perfect teeth. "Not so good. Social workers are obviously not a
valuable commodity, but I'm trying to stay optimistic. Anyway,"
she continued, "now you've said yes to tonight, I can tell you
I've got a friend I'd like you to meet; she's lovely."

Shelley appointed herself Dan's life coach months before on
another drinks night when she had jokingly interrogated Dan
on his lack of female visitors. The wine-fuelled encounter ended with Dan reasserting his belief that women made some of
the best police officers. "You're much better at diffusing violence and you are all born nosy."

"Ambushed again. Don't you ever give up?" he replied rolling
his eyes upwards.

Shelley was triumphant. "Never. Paul said don't forget about
the pub at five either," she called as she turned and headed back
to her house.

Dan's computer was on the upper floor, adjacent to his bedroom in a space that was originally designed as a walk-in wardrobe. Since his entire clothes collection fitted comfortably into
the small free-standing pine wardrobe and chest that took up a
corner of the bedroom, this free space was ideal for his study.
It was about three metres square and had a window overlooking
the back garden. After moving in a couple of shelves, a desk

with a decent lamp and a comfortable leather swivel chair, he was he was ready to create his masterpiece.

The sun now filtered through the window, and the small room was bathed in its soft light. Dan opened it and settled down in the chair. He checked his email first and then looked through a few pages of news and sport on various sites before opening up the folder and then the document which was his new book.

He didn't have a title for it yet, although he was a hundred pages into it. The last couple of days had been difficult, and he only managed a few pages between them. He reviewed the last ten pages, to build up a train of thought and gather some momentum.

The first book was about many of his life experiences from childhood through to his latter years in the police. This one was based on one single incident and experience. The idea to write about the time when he spent over two days alone in a covert observations van, and the mental journey he went through in that time seemed like a really good idea and suited his style of writing sensory experiences in great detail. On good days, he could work on the book while running and new lines or ideas would come to him, or he could sit in the leather chair and let the story simply unfold. When things weren't as good, like today, the computer took on a new, menacing life of its own. Right this second, he didn't have a single word in his head. *How is it you could draw a blank about what to write when you were writing a story based on your own personal experiences?*

He glared at the monitor. "Fuck you!" he said, really meaning it.

He reached for the giant-size coffee mug that an old work friend had given him a few years ago, which saved him from having to get up and make another refill quite so often, but now was one of those times it needed replenishing.

When he returned, his mind was still elsewhere; somewhere in the past rather than on the job at hand. As he sipped and continued staring at the mostly blank page, he desperately tried to conjure up a next line. After still further inactivity, he looked out of the window. The garden was small and neat, but lacked colour at this time of year, unlike Paul and Shelley's which always seemed to have flowers in bloom. Two or three native mynah birds chirped to each other on a skeletal lemon tree, their chatter earnest as their little heads bobbed up and down. Across the top of the tree, he could see the back of another house in the adjacent street and into what must have been a first-floor bedroom where there was a middle-aged woman applying make-up to her face.

She was looking into a mirror that he could only see the back of, puckering her lips and tilting her head for a better view. To him, it appeared she and the birds were performing some strange synchronised act. On another day, it might have brought a smile to his face.

Empty mug in hand, he headed back down to the kitchen again where French-roasted salvation was waiting.

The radio had been playing a continuous stream of inoffensive easy listening tracks since he turned it on when he got back from running. It occurred to him that something a little louder might give his mental block a much needed kick start. As he fingered the tuning dial of the retro-styled device, sounds of one unacceptable channel after another, separated by static hiss, filled the room until he gave up and hit the off button a little too hard.

In the past, he might have brought forth some equally dark thoughts about failure to achieve or meet expectations. Immersed in silence, Dan looked unsuccessfully into the black of his coffee for inspiration. For a while, he hoped a new start in a new country might end them, but was proved wrong. He was as disappointed by this latest arrival as he was angry and would have had to deal with it if at that precise moment the phone had not rung.

"Hello," he said non-committally into the handset.

"It's me again," Shelley's voice was clearly dejected. "You're off the hook for tonight at least. My friends' cancelled on me; a family thing she has to do with her brother. I am going to find you a wife though. I've made it my mission to save you."

He could not help a small smile and the feeling of relief. "Oh shame I didn't know I needed saving. Shall we make it another night too?"

Shelley's dejection did not last long. "No way, when you see Paul, can you ask him to grab some Chinese on the way home; you bring wine and I will tell you more about my plans for you Mr. C." She laughed.

Dan met Paul at their local pub at 5.00 p.m. He got there first and ordered two pints of Celtic ale but had not reached the table before Paul walked in.

"Thank God for this, it's been a crap day. Cheers."

Dan raised his glass. "Cheers. Why crap? No first things first, Shelley said to get Chinese on our way back."

"Okay thanks. Did she mention her latest job interview by any chance?"

"No."

"That sounds ominous; I think she's starting to get really down about not having work at the moment."

Dan understood very well how long periods of unemployment could start to play tricks with your mind. Paul did not dwell on the subject and returned to Dan's earlier question.

"Today has been so slow and there was a strange smell in the shop all day, like a homeless person slept in there overnight; probably the drains. What's new with you?"

"Nothing, I ran this morning and failed to write this afternoon."

"Ah my literary-challenged friend. Why don't you join the real world and get a job? You might not be so miserable all the time then."

Dan spluttered his drink. "Bloody hell Paul, thanks for the vote of confidence."

"You know what I mean." He laughed. "I know you've only told me a fraction about your old life in 'Pomgolia' and I understand how shit it can be to break up with a girl."

Dan held his hand up, just as he had done many times before on their regular pub meetings. "Okay."

"Come on, why such a long face today?"

Dan took another sip. "You know me moving from England to New Zealand was manna from heaven after the breakup with April?"

"Yes, you said."

"Well, she was the last in a number of failed family, personal and work relationships. I allowed myself to love her despite a warning from my best friend that she had a reputation for getting bored with her partners without any warning and leaving a trail of destruction in her wake.

"In the first few years, she seemed all I wanted, and we even shared a passion for the outdoors and travel. When April dropped the bombshell at the start of year four that she had met someone else and was leaving, she blamed me one hundred percent, citing my troubles with dealing with the past and my inability to communicate with her. I was so dumbstruck, I did nothing to try and stop her leaving. I just watched on as she packed her things and walked out."

April was the last person Dan shared a secret with and his abiding memory of her departure was that he would never be so stupid as to share another secret with anyone else.

"The next day, Monday, I went to work as normal and ended up volunteering for a lone two day-plus stint in an observations van. It was one of the times I look back on a lot; during that solitary time, I'm sure I suffered a sort of mini breakdown and went quite mad." He paused and looked into the bottom of his glass. Giving Paul snippets of his history was not unheard of but a detailed story like this was a real rarity. He took a gulp of courage before continuing.

"I reckon I self-treated myself and returned to sanity again before the Thursday morning when Nick opened the van doors to end the job. Today is the anniversary of her leaving."

"Oh right," Paul said.

"I wear my heart on my sleeve more these days, believe it or not."

"I wouldn't have before."

"That's why most of the time I keep my thoughts to myself."

"You know Shelley likes to give you the third degree as well? She means well and not knowing stuff like that might make it more difficult for her to understand you. You should talk to more people like you just did to me."

"Maybe one day, but until then we have beer and the cricket is starting in a minute." He pointed to the wall mounted TV as the intro credits appeared on the screen.

CHAPTER FOUR

When the letter arrived three days later, Edwina knew it was the one straight away. The large monogrammed envelope belonging to the prestigious Purple Heather Resort at Loch Fyne contained a thick, glossy brochure, as well as the covering congratulatory letter.

"Loch Fyne," it said in introduction, "is located in the Argyll and Bute region of Scotland, extending more than forty miles inland from Bute and connected to the sea through the Sound of Jura. The scenic beauty of the area around Loch Fyne, combined with the sight of dolphins and seals in summer, is one that will remain in your memories long after your visit has ended.

"The Purple Heather Resort at Loch Fyne, previously known as Castle Kenmore, opened in 2002. It is conveniently located near to the village of Tarbert on the shore of the loch itself and is surrounded on other sides by superbly maintained gardens and native pine forests. The resort complex offers top quality accommodation for guests and their canine pets as well as conference facilities and a world class spa and wellness centre.

"The castle has a range of beautifully appointed character suites including the famous Laird's Suite. Along the loch's edge are four luxurious solid wood cabins for two to six occupants.

"The Purple Heather Resort at Loch Fyne is most delighted to congratulate you, Mrs. Edwina Jacobs, on winning a four-day, four-star, all-inclusive holiday break and looks forward to welcoming you on Friday 24 June."

Edwina and guest—it was a break for two—could also look forward to being utterly pampered for their entire stay and enjoy all the amenities the resort had to offer.

"Starting with your chauffeured transportation to Bristol Airport and subsequent travel all the way to the castle gates, you will experience the benefits of being a Purple Heather traveller. Your driver will arrive to collect you at 1:00 p.m. on Friday 24 June and by 6:00 p.m. you can be drinking champagne on your private verandah looking out over the tranquil beauty of the loch." The letter was signed by Gordon Davidson, General Manager.

After a while, Edwina was still sat at the kitchen table, aimlessly flicking through the brochure. "It's all for the best," she said, looking into Oscar's upturned face.

The following days were a strange mixture of solemnity, peace, anxiety and a multitude of other feelings that Edwina rode like a hapless novice surfer.

She fell into tears and remorse often and constantly talked to Richard as she moved around the house, cleaning and tidying every room until the whole house sparkled. She took Oscar out to the park every day and sometimes they walked several circuits quietly together, unaware of how long they had been out.

She also thought about Val, who was up in Birmingham, and she wondered what on earth she would think when she came back to find her gone for good. She desperately hoped for her friend not to be unhappy or, worse, feel at all guilty.

In the evenings, she watched television and Oscar watched her. She was tempted to telephone friends and relations, but every time she picked up the phone, she knew that there was nothing left to say to them when they answered.

When Friday the 24th finally arrived, she had had her bag packed for days. After breakfast, she took Oscar to the park for the last time, and for the rest of the morning, she sat at the kitchen table looking at old photo albums and telling Oscar all about the life she had lived.

At five minutes to one, Oscar sensed the car outside before she heard it. Edwina moved the net curtains so she could better see the big black Jaguar which had pulled up next to the gate. She intended to have one last look around the house, but at that very last moment knew there was no point.

The doorbell rang, and through the frosted glass, she could see a figure dressed in black on the other side. She expected the driver to be male, so the gorgeous young woman smiling broadly at her came as a shock.

"Mrs. Jacobs. Good afternoon. I'm here to take you to the airport."

She looked like a model or a film star. Dressed in a designer black trouser suit with a white blouse and complementing black silk tie, she was easily six feet tall, although the perfectly tailored trousers concealed the exact height of her heels. Her smile was radiant, set off by bright red lipstick and the whitest teeth. She also had perfectly styled platinum hair tied into a single thick plait and held in place with a silk ribbon that matched her tie.

Taking all that in, Edwina couldn't help herself. "Oh my goodness, I was expecting someone else," and then, "No, not someone else, I knew you were coming, but I expected you to be a man. You're not; you're lovely."

Oscar had no similar difficulties. He sat at the chauffeur's feet looking up at her like an old friend, expectantly waiting to be petted.

"Thank you so much. I get that a lot," the driver joked. "I am Charlotte. May I take your bags if you're ready?"

"Oh yes, thank you here it is, I just have one small one."

As Charlotte reached down, she stopped.

"Actually can I use your bathroom before we go? I'm sorry to ask but I was feeling a bit funny earlier."

"Of course, it's just at the top of the stairs. Can I get you a tablet or something?" Edwina asked, concerned.

"No thanks, I'm sorry to be a bother. I'll only be a minute."

Five minutes later and Edwina was a little worried. She wanted to go upstairs and knock on the bathroom door to ask if
everything was alright, but stayed at the foot of the stairs.

When she called but got no reply for the second time, she became even more concerned and decided to go up. She listened
at the door, but heard nothing.

"Are you okay dear?" she asked through the closed door, tapping it gently.

When there was no reply, she opened the door a crack but
couldn't see anything other than the empty bath. She had to
open the door fully to see the rest of the room, and when she
did, was unable to comprehend why the driver was sitting on
the closed toilet seat filing her polished red nails with one of
Edwina's nail files. She had taken off her jacket and rolled up
the cuffs of her blouse.

Charlotte looked up. "Well it's about time, I really didn't want
to have to come and get you, but I was starting to think I might
have to."

Edwina was baffled; she took a step into the room. "I thought
you might have fallen or something. What on earth are you doing?"

The driver stood slowly at first and then, with cat-like speed,
she struck out at Edwina with a clenched fist to her stomach,
making her simultaneously gasp and buckle forwards.

She grabbed the collapsing woman effortlessly and propelled
her into the bath, where the plug was already in the plughole.
She then turned on both taps fully.

"If you don't struggle, it will soon be over," she said, taking
a steak knife from her trouser pocket with a freshly manicured
hand.

Edwina was still gasping to get some air back into her lungs
and had no comprehension of what was happening. The bath
was filling with pleasantly warm water when she felt her wrist

being grabbed. When she looked, the woman was holding a knife close to her lower arm.

Edwina's senses were reeling—yet she noticed there was something very odd about the knife: it looked just like one of her own, from a set she had in the kitchen drawer. In fact, she thought there was one missing several weeks ago, after she had a friend around to dinner.

After she had Val around to dinner.

The newly sharpened knife sliced easily through the layers of Edwina's skin and into the veins in a deliberate vertical line maximising the bleed out, hastening the inevitable end. She was so shocked that she did not resist at all when the young woman repeated the action to her other wrist.

Charlotte dropped the knife into the reddening water and firmly held both Edwina's arms under the surface.

"Please do try and relax," she said flatly in a voice Edwina now recognised as her friend Valerie. "Trust me, drowning would have been far more painful."

Edwina wanted to struggle, wanted to speak, wanted to do something. But all she managed was to silently open and close her mouth like a goldfish tipped out of its bowl.

The last words she heard before things became quiet and dark and she joined her beloved Richard were, "I decided on the Marilyn blonde after all. I think it really suits me."

Valerie was calm; she maintained her grip and waited patiently until she was certain Edwina Jacobs was dead. The warm water helped the blood flow from the older woman's body, but it still took several minutes.

She had previously planned on undressing her afterwards, but as she stood up and dried her hands on one of Edwina's flowery towels, she decided against it. She refastened her sleeves and put the silk jacket back on before one last check in the mirror of her faultless makeup. Then she closed the bathroom door behind her and went downstairs again.

Oscar looked at her and then passed her for Edwina, but when Val gave him a good pat all over he relaxed.

"Sorry I didn't say hello properly before," Val said. "How are you today, boy?"

She had practiced copying Edwina's writing for so many weeks now, it was very nearly perfect. The notepaper she produced from her inside jacket pocket was taken from Edwina's stationery cupboard the same night she had stolen the knife.

Remembering that disgusting meal made her smile; what was it Edwina had said to her? Something about how Richard always liked the way she cooked roast beef. Well God help him now, because he could well be in for more.

"What do you think of this Oscar?" she said reading from the paper.

I hope you will understand. I could not bear the thought of suffering or have you watch me do so. This is my choice, please forgive me. I just want to be with Richard again. I recently donated most of my savings to my favourite animal care charity. What's left in my account I want my friend Eileen Masters to have to look after my darling Oscar. I know you will love him.

Edwina

Val wiped the note on both sides with a tea towel and put it down on the kitchen table. "Not bad, eh boy?"

It only took a short time to unpack Edwina's small case and put all the things away in her room.

Oscar sat at the top of the stairs next to the bathroom door the whole time. Val gave him another final pat as she walked passed him and left, remembering to take the Purple Heather Resort pack on the hall table with her.

She got into her newly rented Jaguar and looked in the rear view mirror.

"Oh Walter, look. What have we done again?" she said.

As she drove away without looking back, she replaced her gold wristwatch, which she left in the car in case it got damaged or wet in Edwina's house. Its value to her was beyond words.

After she left the house, Oscar started to sniff and scratch at the bathroom door. Getting no response, he started to howl.

CHAPTER FIVE

Valerie or, as she was now, Veronica Stenning arrived in Auckland, New Zealand in early August.

She thought about seeing the whole summer through in England after the Jacobs project was concluded. It had been necessary to give the conveyancing company with whom she "worked" three weeks' notice on the pretence of going travelling. As with her previous occupations of necessity, being a conveyancer was simply a combination of research, behaving the part and having convincing documentation to back up her history.

By the end of those three weeks, she was done with Trowbridge and so bored that she actually decided to do some travelling and flew to Turkey. She spent a pleasant first week in Istanbul, seeing both ancient and modern sites of the marvellous city spanning two continents, as well as shopping in the Grand Bazaar for gold and fur and indulging in the abundance of the wonderfully aromatic food for which Turkey is renowned.

Then, on the following Monday, she took a one-hour domestic flight down to the southern airport of Dalaman and hired a car to drive herself to Kalkan, on the Mediterranean coast between Fethiye and Kas. She booked into a very nice hotel by the small but busy harbour and divided the next four blissful weeks between lying on the man-made shingle beach or by the hotel's pool, catching up on several books, seriously improving her tan and also completing vast amounts of research work on her laptop.

She found there was a high proportion of clinical depression in countries such as Australia and New Zealand where a great number of British moved to—ironically in search of a better life. Latest statistics showed rates were rising year on year and New Zealand had some of the biggest numbers of suicide linked to depression in the Western World. The opportunity of that adversity was not missed.

During the holiday, she briefly considered taking a year or so off, but her long-term goals were not fulfilled yet, and she was determined nothing was going to stand in her way. In the evenings she allowed her mind to wander as a way of giving herself something to do and as a distraction from the pestering advances of the local males, who saw her single status as an open invitation. She mused on how good it could be to have another friend to share times like these with, but her situation made it impossible.

She knew she was not a monster; by definition, they committed monstrous acts, and apart from Christopher, Mathews and Singleton, who all had debts to pay, her projects were assisting people who wanted to die she quantified and reasoned by a process of pure logic, even if her version of it was unlikely to pass anybody else's test of the term.

The Agency provided a service, like any other. The client may not receive the end result in the way they expected but their final expectation was always met.

It had started as a revenge mission after what that bastard Stephen Christopher did to her parents; she wanted him to suffer as they did. The months leading up to killing him, her first, were unbelievably hard and she almost gave up so many times. The planning in minute detail, learning to alter her appearance and especially taking on a false persona were physically and mentally draining. He had taken everything they worked so long for and made them take their own lives one night. That alone was enough to drive her forward then.

There were so many times she thought he had found her out, realised who she really was, but it was only her nerves and naïveté.

The rush she got from watching him literally exercise himself to death on the cycle machine (albeit at her engineered direction) was something she could not duplicate afterwards, and she found that she needed it like a junkie needs the next fix, which was why she invented The Agency and embarked on a whole new career.

What started as a revenge mission however, had long since taken on a life of its own, and now the truth of it was that she loved her life and all the excitement, danger and financial rewards it came with.

The selection of Sissy Mathews next was nearly as easy as Christopher; she was just as deserving, just as guilty as he was in her own way. At that time, Veronica Stenning's predecessors still needed such justification.

The others afterwards, less so, but she was enjoying it by then and most recently Edwina Jacobs; she had simply been for the money and the sport—to see how far she could take it.

As always, Veronica did serious and strenuous research about her next destination and her plans for what to do when she got there once she had made her mind up. She was meticulous in everything she did; in her line of work, there was no room for complacency. It was why she was so successful, and she had no intention of risking it all by being poorly prepared or badly executing tasks once they were planned.

Now that she was overseas and in a new country, Veronica had a whole new level of interesting research. Reverently each day, she worked on gaining knowledge about the whole country and especially Auckland, where she wanted to base herself. She was surprised to discover New Zealand and Britain were quite similar in size, but the population of New Zealand was barely four and a half million, a million of whom resided in Auckland. It wasn't the capital, that honour lay with Wellington at the southern tip of the North Island, but it was the hub of business and widely regarded as the country's first city. She found opportunities were plentiful for a woman with her qualifications; that is, whatever qualifications she decided to have when she entered the country. She also felt like a change of country meant she could safely afford to alter her *work practices* a little.

Experiences over the last decade gave her a broad palate of options to play with and she spent day after day checking out different cover job possibilities, lifestyles and all sorts of other necessary facts that might allow her to assimilate most effectively.

One of the more pleasant decisions she made was to keep the glamorous persona of Veronica. Valerie was *so* dull. The clothes, the hairstyle, the makeup (or lack of it) and the whole personality in general. She was certainly perfect for Edwina Jacobs, but God, a few more weeks of that and she could have been suicidal herself. Veronica and Valerie were polar opposites of each other and Veronica gladly disposed of Val like a veiled chameleon sheds its skin.

September hinted and teased at an end to winter in New Zealand. Her first weeks were predominantly rainy, but when the sun did come out and the sky was blue, she could not have wished to be in a better place. She loved the City of Sails: its feel, the people and the relaxed way of life that Aucklanders had. She wanted to be close to the middle of things and chose a high corner apartment of an apartment building in Vulcan Lane overlooking the downtown area and with a peek of the Waitemata Harbour from the balcony. The rental agent did a great job of selling it, and she had to agree having been there a short time. The fact it had secure parking and the view made it a glorious find. She rented it for cash and paid several months in advance.

Veronica settled in quickly and was soon fully immersed in further study to identify potential targets for The Agency. She talked to Walter often, updating him on her progress, taking comfort and sustenance from his encouragement; he would always find a way to be there if she needed him, even on the other side of the world.

It took three days over the course of her second week to hack the computer systems of The Depression Society of New Zealand and another advice and support group called Coping with Grief. Years of a social life consisting solely of night classes resulted in a high level of technical competence. Coupled with that were the benefits coming from training and absorbing information from a corrupt computer security analyst who used to work for Stephen Christopher, enabling him to illegally obtain information on clients, rivals and others who could serve his nefarious desires. The analyst now supplied her with false identity documents in return for her silence about his activities; she had been an insatiable student.

Veronica was not surprised to see how much information some people were prepared to divulge about themselves. *Halfway around the world and some things never change*, she thought one evening as she sat on her balcony, savouring a very good South Island sauvignon blanc and watching the yachts in the harbour. Her laptop was on the table by her side.

Over the course of the last week, through a careful selection process, she had compiled a short-list of one hundred and twenty names from the two websites. Tortured souls ripe for The Agency to offer an end to their suffering.

Setting up another safe and untraceable email and communications system wasn't a difficult task. Her intention now was to contact all the individuals directly by email and select one from the respondents. She hoped for six to ten replies as she made the final checks on the message just before sending it out into the ether.

This plan was new, but was still faithful to her tried and tested framework. As she went to hit the send button, she paused, raised her glass and made a small toast.

"To happy endings." She smiled and let the base of her glass touch the enter key and the short email disappeared from the screen.

CHAPTER SIX

Dan woke from the dream with a jolt, his heart jumping around in his chest like a jackhammer. The recurring nightmare meant he had soaked the sheets in sweat making them stick uncomfortably to his body. He lay for several moments trying to calm down, thinking, *It's not real.*

In his dream, he was in bed asleep but was woken by the sound coming from his parents' room. When he crept out into the hallway, the noise increased; his mother crying and pleading for mercy and his father angry, shouting. Dan opened their door and saw him kneeling over her on the bed, a raised arm gripping his shiny leather policeman's belt. Mother looked at him and smiled through her terror. "Go back to bed, John, go on, everything is alright." And he had closed the door and gone back to his room. The last thing he heard before he was startled properly awake was his father. "Laugh at me, I'll teach you to laugh at me." And then the crack of leather on flesh.

In his first book, committing his recurring dream to paper as the first chapter did, had been a "eureka" moment. It helped enough to keep his head from exploding at a time in his life where, on bad days, his whole future could have ended up being no more than the length of a sad movie.

The Depression Society of New Zealand website had been very useful in the last year or so. In that time, Dan visited it several times—after some bad days and, once or twice, even after a good one. He nearly didn't use it at all, as it required some personal information before allowing people to access the site, and so he had used a little poetic licence when completing the online form—including, for the first time in thirty years, using his given first name, John.

He had no intention of openly discussing his feelings again in a group or even with a personal counsellor; once was more than enough. But the site included self-help tests and other bits and pieces, which he was able to do in the security of his home. He joined in on several online forums, though, where he was able to speak in detail without divulging his identity or too much about his past and being careful not to give away so much that he might be identifiable as an ex-policeman or recent immigrant.

Whether he was clinically depressed, he still had no idea. Some days he would have said definitely and others definitely not. The one thing he knew for sure was that, having moved halfway around the world, the last thing he wanted was to get those old feelings back again. Those old feelings which haunted him for twenty years, off and on, and had made him seriously consider suicide a few times in England.

It had only been on a rare occasion in the three years since he had been in Auckland that his mind had wandered back to the subject of what his existence was all about. Usually this occurred when he was running or struggling for the next line in the book and also usually when the date corresponded with an anniversary of something shitty.

Unfortunately, there were more than a few shitty times to look back on in his life.

The most recent time he tapped into the Society was on another anniversary, the memory of which was as embedded as his father's brutality towards his mother. Not wanting to risk sleep again, he got up and put on fresh running gear, but then went to his study and sat in front of the computer for an hour before leaving the house.

Thankfully the running was going really well, and the day of the race was fast approaching. He had deliberately never gone the full forty-two kilometre marathon distance in training. Confident he was going to be able to complete it comfortably, he nevertheless wanted the race to be the first time for the full distance.

When he got home again he felt ready to write. The book's progress had been okay until this latest drought. He was now enjoying the process of writing as much as he disliked it with the first book, but even on the best days, he felt there was something missing. After the later, shorter run this Sunday morning, he tried to commit more productive time to the book before hunger caused him to take a break.

After baked beans on toast and coffee, he went back to the book again but couldn't get his train of thought back on track and decided on more caffeine instead. A reason to get away from the computer; it was always easy to convince himself that another fresh brew might stimulate the writer's block he was afflicted with. When he got back upstairs, he had drunk half already.

The little envelope icon was flashing surreptitiously in the top right corner of the screen. He opened the email to read the new message. He looked at the text, read it a second time and then read it again as the hairs on his neck and arms were telling him something was definitely wrong. Then for some reason he looked around the small room and under the computer workstation, as if he might find the reason there for the email's appearance.

If it was some sort of spam, then the meaning and intention were completely lost on him. If it was a joke email, then it didn't make a lot of sense either, and it definitely was not funny.

Obviously, he had not previously corresponded with the sender, so the only other reasonable conclusions were that it was just a random email from some bored soul with nothing better to do, or it was a virus or other computer nasty contained in an email.

With no evidence to the contrary, he deleted the message from his inbox, checked his firewalls and then ran an antivirus systems scan, for which he allowed fifteen minutes to complete and gave him the perfect excuse for an early return visit to the batch of fresh coffee.

As he stood at the sink putting water into the kettle, something in his head, a sliver of a memory, suddenly appeared.

He was transfixed. It was only when the sound and feel of the cool water rushing over his lower arm and hand alerted his senses to the overflowing jug that he was dragged back to the here and now. Putting the filled kettle down in the sink, he stared out of the kitchen window and into the distance.

There was something in that email which triggered the memory. He could not think why.

After a few frustrating moments, he emptied out half the kettle's contents and put it back in its cradle on the bench top.

When he got back to the computer, the scan was finished and he was pleased to see he was virus-free. He brought up the last page of the book again and as if by magic immediately thought of a next passage.

"Hallelujah," he said caustically.

A while later, very satisfied to see a page and a half of new text, he stopped to stretch his neck and purge the painful knot that had developed. Looking up to the ceiling, he remembered the earlier email again.

He tapped a few keys and went to the deleted message box.

It had the appearance of any run-of-the-mill email message. In the subject line was 'Depression NZ', which was not unfamiliar and had led him to open it in the first place.

The content of the message read:

Sad, lonely, depressed.
There is more than one way to solve the misery of anxiety and depression.

**Is it happiness you are searching for or just the
end of unhappiness?**

The answers could be a call away.

Tried and tested, safe and secure.

Contact The Agency for more details.

As he read it for a third time, something occurred to him and
he remembered an incident from his police past.

It took ten minutes to find the shoebox containing the remnants of his life in the police, held together with a thick elastic
band. He hadn't felt the need to do any more than put it in the
cupboard in the lounge when he moved in, and it had remained
there ever since, untouched and slowly becoming buried under
other stuff.

Once he had it, though, it did not take long to find the cutting
from the newspaper inside. It was L-shaped, due to the article's
placement on the page adjacent to an advertisement for ortho-
paedic shoes, as he recalled. Sitting cross-legged on the floor
he couldn't help but be drawn to the bold headline, "Detective
claims boss failed victim in robbery investigation," before re-
acquainting himself painfully with the cause of his departure
from the job.

**Garstone Detective Constable Daniel Calder has
spoken out about the lack of professionalism displayed by his senior supervisor Detective Chief
Inspector Jim Allen amid the collapse of the trial of Thomas and Brendan Edrich for the brutal
armed robbery of pensioner Frederick Bonner in
his own home on a summer's afternoon.**

**War veteran Mr. Bonner of Kipfield was attacked
in his two-bed chalet home in August last year
by two men who beat him unconscious and stole**

cash and valuables, including Mr. Bonner's Second World War medals and a silver frame containing a wedding photo of him and his late wife June, before leaving him for dead.

Detective Calder was clearly angry outside Garstone Crown Courts yesterday morning and told journalists that DCI Allen had failed to allow him to fully interview the Edrich brothers when they were in custody because "the time limit they could be held was going to expire and he wanted them charged. He didn't want to have to apply for an extension," Calder said.

He further claimed that important evidence had not been seized due to his boss' "lack of interest."

Senior officers at Garstone were unavailable for detailed comment later in the day.

Since then, police public relations head Superintendent Alison Adkins has said the police and the Prosecutions Service were disappointed at the Judge's decision to dismiss the jury and free the Edrichs.

An internal inquiry is likely to be set up to look into the matter.

Meanwhile Mr. Bonner, who now lives with his daughter in Garstone, will have to try and pick up the pieces of his shattered life knowing that the heartless thugs, whoever they are, that left him battered, bruised and blind in one eye are no nearer to paying for their crimes.

Reading the article again filled Dan with rage. His life felt like one bad experience after another. Most days he ignored the sadness but the anger was always there, simmering just below the surface.

He expected to see what had triggered the light to come on in his head relating to the rogue email, but there was nothing. That and reading the bullshit story again made it all the more aggravating. It wasn't factually incorrect but the spin on what he did say made it appear exactly how it did read: sensational. He read it again, but by the time he was finished was still none the wiser and even more frustrated.

"Fuck it!" he bellowed, swiping the shoebox across the room.

Taking a deep breath, he prepared to read it again. "Come on, detective," he growled at himself, "detect!"

After reading it out aloud twice more, the second time pacing the room, he gave up. That day had been his first back on duty at Garstone after his last disastrous undercover job and it had been a big mistake to think he could slip back into the normal work routine without there being some kind of fallout. However, he never imagined it could trigger the outburst at the courthouse. Leaving the cutting on the floor, he went back to the kitchen for yet more coffee, switching the radio on more by reflex than deliberate act.

The Beatles were into the last few bars of their 1966 number one 'Paperback Writer' and he involuntarily joined them to the end, singing angrily in his dreadfully broken baritone.

When the coffee was made, he went back to the computer to try to pick the book up where he had left off. He was halfway up the stairs and still humming the bits of the song he could remember when it all suddenly came to him.

He didn't know whether to carry on up or go back down. "Writer, you fucker. I wanna be a fuckin' paperback writer," he sang at the top of his voice. He dashed up the remaining steps and into the study. In his haste, he nearly spilled the mug of coffee all over the keyboard, setting it down too near the edge of the big blotter on the desk. He brought up the email message again and studied the text.

He then rushed down the stairs again and back into the lounge, where the newspaper cutting was still lying abandoned where he'd dropped it. He didn't need to pick it up. He could see the confirmation of what he knew and caused his alarm printed immediately under the headline. "Detective claims boss failed victim in robbery investigation. By Crime Correspondent Vikki Stenning."

He triumphantly went upstairs again with the cutting held in both hands. When he sat down in front of the computer he looked from the email on the screen to the cutting and back again.

The email had concluded with the various contact details for The Agency. The phone number was an 0800 number, the address was an Auckland PO Box and, finally, the contact email address was v.stenning@theagency.org.

CHAPTER SEVEN

In his excited state, Dan neglected to save the most recent lines that he had so struggled to commit to the page earlier, but he couldn't care less about that right now. It was a distant six hours ago in any case.

The cold coffee was the ultimate testament to the fact that Dan was completely in his element again. The subject was The Agency and, more particularly, Ms. Vikki Stenning.

As soon as he connected the email and the newspaper article, his instincts told him all he needed to suspect there was something amiss. After relentlessly going through page after page online and making notes, those instincts had borne fruit.

Now he knew there was something very wrong about The Agency and a number of V. Stennings, whoever they might be.

This was what Dan Calder did. This was what he was all about: collecting data, painting pictures in words, analysing them, corroborating and putting it all into order. If he ever had a hero, it was Sherlock Holmes. It made others laugh in the past, but one line from one of those old stories said it all as far as he was concerned: "When you eliminate the impossible, whatever remains, however improbable, must be the truth."

There it was—brilliantly simple and simply brilliant.

When he started checking out Vikki Stenning at the *Garstone Record*, nothing of too much consequence came up. She had been a reporter for the paper for just a few months when she wrote that article on him. Her earlier pieces were just the usual mix of mid-sized town journalism, and the ones after were of the same ilk. Nothing startling, nothing to suggest she was after more kudos, as you could sometimes detect in the stories of reporters who yearned to work for a bigger publication and become stars in their own right.

In fact, it was only another four months after the article that so screwed up his prospects of a longer, if not entirely happy, working relationship with that certain Chief Inspector that she left the newspaper altogether.

Initially, Dan went over every article she ever posted for the paper and drew a blank. Vikki Stenning's journalistic history at Garstone was, to put it mildly, bland and unimpressive. His next checks on the name showed the seven or eight months at the *Garstone Record* seemingly constituted the full extent of her reporting career. Furthermore, the journalist Vikki Stenning seemed to disappear completely afterwards, never to post another story for anyone else anywhere.

It was only after more failed attempts to find her that Dan realised he was trying too hard, or rather being too narrow in the search patterns he was using. He saw that the editor of the *Garstone Record* at the time Vikki was working at the paper had committed suicide. Not that she reported it, or that there was anything suspicious at the time. An overdose, the paper's lead writer said. That in itself was unfortunate, but not overly interesting.

The fact that Vikki left the newspaper just a week after her editor's passing was worthy of note, however. When he started searching for Vikki Stenning, along with the added search criteria of suicide or death, and then abbreviated "Vikki" to "V", he hit the proverbial mother lode, and the editor's death took on a very different complexion.

In 2002, Vanessa Stenning, a personal trainer, called an ambulance to the house of a wealthy London client who suffered a massive heart attack during a training session. The man died on the way to the hospital.

In 2005, Vivienne Stenning, a health-care worker for a private nursing home, found one of her elderly patients dead in the home's garden in Winchester.

Most recently, earlier this year Valerie Stenning, a conveyancer from Trowbridge in Wiltshire, spoke at the funeral of one of her friends, a certain Edwina Jacobs, who took her own life by cutting her wrists in the bath.

The local newspaper reported that Ms. Stenning brought Mrs. Jacobs' pet dog, Oscar to the funeral and then looked after it for a few days until a new home could be found with a local café owner.

At this time of day, there was no point in trying to make telephone calls to the UK, where it was still the middle of the previous night. Dan considered calling some old colleagues, but decided against it until he had collected some more information and thought what to do with it. Even without the required checking, he already suspected what the answers were likely to be and was sure that he was on to something big.

He could have stayed where he was and continued to work the information, but his years of experience told him to walk away from it now and let the accumulated knowledge percolate in his head for a while. That way, when he went back, he was more likely to be hungry for it and may also induce some new train of thought to follow.

The trouble was that knowing it and being able to do it were two very different things. For the first time in a long time, Dan was energised by the prospect of putting the pieces of a puzzle together, and it took every ounce of willpower for him not to go back to the study straight after turning the computer off.

His car had never been so clean. Washed, rinsed, dried and polished, it gleamed like a jewel in the late afternoon sunshine. It took a full two hours to complete the task and, while he put a lot of physical effort into it, his mind was exclusively focused on The Agency and Vikki, Vanessa, Vivienne and Valerie Stenning.

A few things were clear already. The various Stennings all seemed to be associated with death or suicide. The incidents of those deaths were spread out over a period of years. In the case of Vikki Stenning, she appeared not to have written another published article either before or after her term with the *Garstone Record*. The various reports he read were virtually all in local newspapers; only one of the incidents was ever reported in a national press publication or on the TV news, which meant that the minimal coverage was soon forgotten.

Obviously a lot more work was needed to confirm the facts as they were presenting themselves at that moment. It was still possible he had overlooked some evidence to further corroborate or cast doubt on his growing theories.

Personally, Dan could not remember much about the reporter whom he had foolishly spoken to on that fateful day when he walked out of the court. She was a woman average in appearance—average in everything, actually.

There was a big difference in searching for known facts about The Agency on the Internet and using The Agency as the criteria for an Internet search.

Dan found the latter immediately brought up over eighty million hits on subjects as diverse as Aborigines and airports to zebra and zombies and everything in between. It wasn't so much trying to find a needle in a haystack as trying to sift a mountain of pea-sized data bytes through a sieve with holes the size of footballs. Without examining everything individually, the chances of missing something relevant were almost one hundred percent. There had to be a better way.

Since The Agency was an open field, he reasoned that if V. Stenning was the conduit to The Agency then it was on V. Stenning he should concentrate his initial efforts. He could research his arse off on the computer and likely come up with some more in time, or he could just reply to the email and see where it led. Mentally cautioning himself against acting too hastily and thus compromising what he was doing, he decided on a little more intelligence gathering and then a reply, if it was still appropriate.

And so he worked; checking every female name beginning with V he could find with Stenning brought some more reward. He started with the names he already knew: Vikki, Vanessa, Vivienne and Valerie.

There were no personal trainers by the name of Vanessa Stenning listed anywhere in England, no phone numbers listed either, and the few newspaper reports about the death of an investment broker called Stephen Christopher were brief and lacking in any substantive detail.

He was able to identify the nursing home in the south of England where Vivienne Stenning worked at the time of the death of the elderly patient, and recorded the details to contact them.

There were four conveyancing businesses in Trowbridge but the name Stenning was not among the company names. Obviously there were other businesses, like law firms, which also offered conveyancing-type services, but he concentrated on the dedicated conveyancers offices first. Again he recorded all the contact details he could find.

As an extra line of inquiry regarding Valerie he also found ten cafés in the small market town of Melksham and took their telephone numbers, intending to try and identify the orphaned dog's new owner.

When he went back to check on Vikki he concentrated on the recorded details of the suicide of the editor. Mark Singleton had been with the *Garstone Record* for three years, the last two as editor, after working on several other local newspapers in the Midlands and north of England. One article written by him a year before he went to Garstone was a factual piece about his own experiences with addiction to painkillers and antidepressants several years before. He graphically described what led him to dependency for eighteen months before friends and family helped him get help for himself. He extolled the virtues of funded and voluntary groups who helped drug dependants and other addicts.

There was a photo accompanying the article; Singleton with his girlfriend, whom he met at an Addicts Anonymous meeting, and their two-month-old baby. Dan wondered why a recovering addict, with a new family and to all intents and purposes had everything to live for, could fall off the wagon and tragically die of an overdose.

As he printed off the whole piece and added it to the fifty or so other sheets of A4 he had amassed, he thought to himself, *maybe he didn't fall off—maybe he was pushed.*

By 8:00 p.m, his study was starting to resemble a compact version of one of the many major incident rooms he had worked in. He utilised a thin sheet of plastic-coated hardboard from the garage as a whiteboard and constructed a timeline along the bottom section.

Above were written other important details in a semi-permanent marker pen, and all around it were some of the printed information bytes he had gathered so far. A basket on his desk contained separate sheets of paper marked with prioritised objectives, one per sheet. Finally, a new lever arch folder that was currently empty stood up next to the monitor. This would house the daily records, so at any time he could easily access any information he needed.

It was going to be at least another hour before he could start making phone calls to England. Time enough for more coffee.

CHAPTER EIGHT

Veronica enjoyed a lazy Sunday. Taking the mid-morning ferry from downtown over to Waiheke Island in the Hauraki Gulf, she visited a winery and a nearby olive grove for a late lunch, before catching a bus back to Oneroa where she spent time looking through the shops and galleries along the small main street.

It was starting to get dark when she arrived back at the apartment. She opened a bottle of red bought on the island and settled down with a large glass and her laptop on the big sofa, an early Santana album turned down low on the CD player.

Immediately, she noticed there were two replies to her Agency email.

Earlier in the day, Neil Danes went to the refrigerator for the umpteenth time. Food had become his substitute for friends and family since his sister finally had enough of his up-one-day and down-the-next mood swings. He could still remember the last thing she said to him the night before she left: "I swear that one day I'll come home and find you on the living room floor dead. If not, I'll be the one who puts you there."

She became the focus for his life after their mother died. He transferred all of his feelings from one to the other, seemingly in an instant. Since then, she repeatedly told him to get a life of his own rather than try to constantly participate in hers.

Their parents split up when they, the twins, were seven, and their mother took care of them until she suddenly died when they were eighteen. God how he loved her, right up until the end.

Where their father was he did not know or care any more. From the time he walked out on them, they never saw or heard from him again, not even a birthday card from the useless prick.

Neil had not been out of his small house in upmarket Saint Peters Place for days, and both he and it were in a poor state of hygiene. He decided to go online and do more grocery shopping, seeing as he was out of cheese and mayonnaise; all the biscuits and chips were long gone too, as was everything in the freezer.

The one person he did talk to on anything like a regular basis was not working today. Toby at Coping with Grief was the only friend he had in the world.

The TV was on the same movie channel non-stop, all day every day; he didn't bother to turn it off when he went into the other room to turn the computer on.

He logged onto the supermarket website, bypassing the usual thousands of choices of grocery and homeware items, and went straight to the re-order menu as he had done on at least the last three such visits. The store kept all his credit card details, and within no time, his order was processed, and he was advised to expect the delivery before noon the following day.

As he was about to turn the computer off again, he noticed the new message icon flashing at the bottom of the screen. Reading it brought a smile to his face for the first time in ages.

"Shit yeah," he said, and hit the reply button.

CHAPTER NINE

Dan didn't get to bed until five the following morning, but it had been well worth it. All his telephone enquiries brought a rich harvest of information.

He said he was an estates and heirs investigator, which he hoped would spark people's interest and at the same time, prevent them from becoming too inquisitive about the real reasons for his call. Dan's feelings about having to be economical with the truth were more about his apprehension than anything. Investigating without being under the umbrella of 'the job' any more made it very different now.

From almost the first call, he got something useful from everyone he spoke to and finished with days' worth of material to deconstruct and analyse.

The Primrose Residential Care Home in Winchester confirmed that Vivienne Stenning worked there from the latter part of 2004 until June 2005. He knew from the newspaper report that the woman there had passed away in early May. The female administrator at the home also told him that Vivienne had been a quiet employee who took a particular shine to Mrs. Mathews, and she to her. Unfortunately, there were no forwarding details for Vivienne and no staff photograph they could send him.

The administrator refused to give him any details of Mrs. Mathews' family and only reluctantly agreed to see if there was a way she could find and get a message to them to contact Dan. When he asked if she could remember what Vivienne looked like, the reply resonated with him as if she had shouted it through a megaphone. "Oh, you know, sort of average really. She had light brown hair. To be honest, I can't really remember.

Isn't that funny, all that time and I can't seem to picture her at all now."

Heidi, the receptionist at the conveyancing company Clive Craddock and Partners in Trowbridge seemed totally disinterested as she answered the phone, and even more so when Dan explained he was calling about an employee called Valerie Stenning.

"Oh her, she's not here any more. She went off to see the world earlier this year."

"Thanks, yes, I knew that already. I was hoping to get some additional personal information, if it's not too much trouble," he said, deliberately placing extra emphasis on the word "personal."

He gauged Heidi exactly and she could not wait to assist him now. "Oh in that case, yes of course, I see. Can you tell me what it is you need and I'll try to help?"

"That is so good of you. I'm an estates investigator and I've been trying to track her down for some time now. What could be really useful is if you could tell me about anyone who may know how I can find her."

Heidi was completely hooked. "Has Valerie come into some money in a will or something?"

"I wish I could tell you but you know how it is with confidentiality." Dan let the sentence hang for a second and then, sensing Heidi's anguish, continued. "What I can say is there are some *very* important people who would like to speak to her *very* much. Maybe if the person who was able to help me find her …" he stopped.

Heidi's brain was already racing ahead and working at maximum. "Well, I can think of a couple of people. She kept to herself a lot even here in the office; she never came for a drink after work or anything like that. Mr. Craddock obviously. She might have told him where she was going and what she was going to do. I think also Mrs. Meredith as well down the road in

Melksham; although I only found out they were sort of friends when Valerie was in the paper with old Mrs. Jacobs' dog when she died."

Dan feigned ignorance. "What was that?"

"Well Ms. Stenning, Valerie, ended up looking after the old lady's dog when she died. Cut her wrists in the bath. Yuck, I couldn't do that, could you?"

Heidi was on a roll now and he just let her go on, waiting for the nuggets of useful detail he knew would come among the rest of the detritus she was bursting to share with him. After listening to some meaningless drivel, Heidi finally hit the jackpot. "She even took the dog to the funeral you know. My aunt's friend has got it now."

Dan was reaching for his pen before she finished the sentence. "You know where the dog is, could you tell me?"

Heidi sniffed, frustrated by Dan's ignorance. "I told you, Eileen Meredith, she owns the Penny Farthing Café in Melksham. The lady who died left her some money to look after it. My aunt says she loves the dog to bits, but her husband can't stand it and wants to get rid of it and keep the money."

Dan grinned. *She just saved me ten phone calls!*

"I don't suppose you have a photograph of Ms. Stenning there, do you?" he asked, wishing his good fortune could continue.

"No, sorry, I don't think so. Actually she was quite funny about having her picture taken."

Dan was not surprised and was about to ask for a verbal description when Heidi let out a little squeal.

"Hold on. I've got one on my phone. I took it when she wasn't watching one day just for a laugh. Do you want me to send it to you?"

Did he!? Dan could barely contain himself. "Again that is really very helpful. I'm sure my clients will be very grateful. Let me give you my number."

Heidi did not question the +64 New Zealand code and before he ended their conversation, he saw his mobile, which was set to vibrate, dancing on the desk in front of him.

"Looks like it's arrived, thank you." To keep up the pretence, he added, "Can I get your full details in case we need to contact you again or maybe thank you properly for your assistance?" Heidi didn't hesitate.

A few minutes later Dan was talking to a busy-sounding Mrs. Eileen Meredith. "I'm sorry, love, I can't talk right now, I'm rushed off my feet." He was able to get her home number before she hung up and promised to call her in the evening her time.

That was at ten to four and he was ready to call it a night then, until he had another idea to have a quick look at Stephen Christopher, the investment broker who died in 2002 when personal trainer Vanessa Stenning was present.

In no time, he had got his second wind.

Stephen Christopher was highly successful working as a broker and consultant. The hits on him ran into the hundreds, but the majority of them were concerned with his fall from grace, disparaging comments by dissatisfied clients and reports about his suspension and disbarring from the National Association of Licensed Insurers and Brokers.

Scanning the first dozen or so articles, Dan got a pretty clear and damning sense of who Christopher was: a scheming shit of the highest order. It did not appear that anyone mourned his passing. In fact, he thought as another load of pages printed off, *I bet there could have been a lot of people very pleased to see his demise and maybe one or two who wanted him dead.*

Before falling into bed happily exhausted, he set the alarm for the time to make a call to Eileen Meredith. He knew for the duration of this new focus there would be some respite from the threat of nightmares.

CHAPTER TEN

Over the next few days, Veronica hoped one or two more replies might arrive, but she was disappointed. She worked diligently each day researching and collating information, with subjects as diverse as statistics on methods of suicide in New Zealand to commercial premises available for short-term rent. The second of the two replies she did get the previous Sunday showed some promise, and it was probably that early indicator which had caused her to be a little too optimistic about the prospects of more miserable replies.

Her apartment block had a fully equipped gym in the basement which she made sure she used each morning from six thirty to eight.

When she got back from there on Thursday, she was hot and sweaty as usual after her workout. She took a long shower and proceeded to make a healthy breakfast, which she took out onto the balcony.

While exercising, her mind was occupied with Edwina Jacobs. She liked to re-examine a project after completing it, for a number of reasons. There were invariably things to learn, errors not to be repeated, lines that worked particularly well.

Jacobs was the best Agency subject yet for several reasons: she was by far the most successful in terms of falling for the planned death scenario, and she was different from the others, who required more manipulation to get them as far as the final situation. Christopher and Mathews died because they brought it on themselves. Most of the others had sought her out, but Jacobs really wanted to believe.

As she had worked hard on her quads, it occurred to her that the death experience was the key—Jacobs wanted to die in her preferred way more than the others, and for that reason alone, she was ready to believe much more than any of the others. Coupled with that was the way she found herself widowed, the way her husband had suffered.

In the years since Stephen Christopher met his deserving end and she started The Agency, Veronica's methods had evolved, as had her already extensive competency in computing. She was good, but knew things could be better, more professional. Her small network of contacts being able to supply additional identification documents and the like was still the biggest concern. If she could do everything herself, she would be much happier and feel even more secure.

She still felt sick to think of what she did to gain Christopher's trust initially, what she allowed him to do to her body for the sake of getting what she wanted and needed from him. Fortunately one useful thing the scumbag did was introduce her to some of his criminal associates, and now she had enough on all of them to be confident they were not going to do anything stupid—like get too greedy.

She realised the selection process, which she thought fairly careful and comprehensive already, could be better still. Increased depth researching the prospect's history, and investing more time in finding better reasons for a prospect wanting to believe, would ultimately make her work a lot easier when the final scenes played out.

The dog was an unexpected issue. When the undertaker called to say the bloody woman had *her number* to call in the event of an emergency and could she look after Oscar until better arrangements were possible, she had no option but to say yes. She made a new mental note: no pets.

After breakfast, when she returned to the two replies from earlier in the week, she considered employing some new tactics to see if her earlier thoughts were worthy of implementation. Reviewing the preliminary research material she gathered from various websites, it was glaringly obvious that one of them was much closer to the Edwina Jacobs model of a prospect than the other. She ran a comparison program and noticed with no small satisfaction that he had all of the required characteristics which made Jacobs more compliant—and also one or two others which could be very useful.

"Mr. Danes, I'm so very pleased to meet you." She smiled to herself with undisguised anticipation.

It was lunchtime when she took her next break from the computer. Neil Danes was looking every inch a suicide waiting to happen. His personal history was a procession of one disaster after another. Even his lottery win, years before, brought him nothing but despair. Veronica found his life history easily offered up, courtesy of the computer systems at some schools, doctors, hospitals and employment agencies, almost an autobiography. She listed some of the most significant points: born in 1980, twin sister, father deserted the family when they were six or seven; mother struggled to bring them up and then died in 1998. She thought, *a tough time at school; excelling only in the sciences, being bad at sport, a prime target for the bullies.*

At whatever age she checked, he had far more visits to the doctor than an average person for every physical ailment, in addition to anxiety and anger issues. He dropped out of university after less than a year to go back and live in the family home with his sister. He worked a raft of jobs from then, mainly with pharmaceutical companies until 2007, when he won four million dollars in the national lottery. In fact, he was one of a group of three from his work who won over twelve million in total. The photo she saw of the three of them celebrating their win showed him slightly detached from the other two, with his magnum of champagne held limply by his side, while the other two sprayed theirs into the air; even then his was a haunted look, and his comment of taking his sister on a tramping holiday as the first thing he wanted to do with his new wealth spoke volumes.

The more Veronica checked, the more suitable Neil Danes appeared to be, even when applying the new stricter profile requirements. The personal client details held on the Coping with Grief records were comprehensive, and the site's protection from the efforts of a talented hacker with the right motivation was very poor. Veronica gained access using a ghost protocol program she had used many times before which tricked the system into duplicating previous data inputs. Soon all Neil Danes' secrets and fears were at her fingertips.

He subscribed to the most expensive cable TV package available and seemed to watch movies constantly. He also rented DVDs online. From what she could tell, he hardly ever needed to leave the house; he even did his grocery shopping online.

Danes told Toby, his counsellor at Coping with Grief, about how he thought about death all the time, and it was only having his sister Tara close that made life bearable.

The money was a poisoned chalice; he bought them a nicer house only two streets away from their old one, which he did not sell and was now falling apart, periodically inhabited by vagrants and stray cats.

The last session with Toby—he could only talk to Toby—was a week ago, and he offered Toby the money to be available for another talk rather than go away as he intended to for a family visit to the Gold Coast in Australia.

Danes seemed almost too good to be true, Veronica reminded herself he had been virtually the first to respond; there may well be other better prospects that, for one reason or another, had not had the chance to reply yet. She decided to wait another week, continue to research him, and see what else happened. She was in no rush—the more time she spent in Auckland the more she was enjoying it, and with the summer fast approaching, life was good.

Later in the afternoon, she took her new scooter, camera and map-book for a drive around some of the places in Danes' life, past and present. Initially a scooter or car would have been out of the question, but Auckland was more undulating than she first imagined and the public transport system was lacking. The International Drivers Licence she used for ID only once before was impeccable, and it was more than sufficient to convince the hire shop staff. Having watched the roads for a few days, she chose the most common machine and immediately felt comfortable using it.

She went to the first family home and stopped on the street outside the unkempt garden; taking in what details she could while outwardly consulting the map-book as if she was lost. It once was a traditional New Zealand villa-style house. Nice in its day: white weatherboards under a corrugated-iron roof and a small verandah around at least two sides. She imagined Danes growing up there, experiencing the heartache of the family breakup and a likely miserable adolescence. She wondered which room was once his and whether there might still be remnants of that life for her to find and use.

If there was no chance of being discovered, she might have considered going in for a look around, but at this time, there was no need for such risk-taking.

Next on her sightseeing tour was the office of Coping with Grief, where she sat and watched the comings and goings from a coffee shop across the road from the main entrance. She pretended to read a magazine while watching with an expert eye.

Finally she went to Danes' local shopping mall, where his supermarket and video store were both located. Veronica was fastidious in her research; everywhere he mentioned to Toby must be checked, where possible.

On the way home, she started to make plans for the following day. Danes' sister Tara was the major figure in his life, and she needed to pay particular attention to her. She had Tara's address and other personal details already, and decided that, beginning tomorrow, she was to become the focus of her research for a few days at least.

The sky was a bright blue and the ocean looked very inviting as she drove her zippy machine back home along the waterfront. People were making the most of the day on the beaches of the many bays she passed. She saw herself being able to settle down somewhere like this one day.

When she got home, she uploaded the photos taken during the day onto the laptop and reviewed the information she had gathered. As she was reading, a new email arrived. When she read it, she was pleased to find another sad soul had made contact with The Agency.

Dan worked as many hours a day as Veronica had for the past week or more. His enquiring mind, eye for detail and relentless investigative nature paid massive dividends although his next phone bill would be a record breaker because of the number of calls back to Nick in England asking for favours, which tested their friendship to the limit.

"Are you going to tell me what this is all about?" Nick asked one evening.

"I thought you liked me getting you into things, especially when I left you in the dark."

"Don't remind me."

"I'll tell you when I'm certain okay? Until then I really appreciate your help."

Being sure he was on the right track about all his suspicions, he took another day to decide on how to proceed before finally sending a reply to Stenning's message.

The email to v.stenning@theagency.org was the fifth version he'd worked on. He was sure he'd only have one chance to make the right first impression. If he got it wrong, he would never hear from The Agency again. As he sat back looking at the blank screen, where the sent message was a moment before, all he could do was hope that it would make such an impression.

The amount of tireless evidence-gathering he accomplished was very impressive and the picture he built up was not complete, but it was good, very good.

His whiteboard, evidence book and job sheets were loaded with organised data, and the timeline was now a wall-length feature with more filled-in spaces than gaps.

From the moment he made the connection between V. Stenning and The Agency, the story had unravelled before his eyes, and each new line of inquiry led to a similar conclusion.

He was truly amazed no one else seemed to have made the discovery before him. As he mused that point over a cold beer one night, the answer was suddenly very simple: what reason was there for anybody to be looking? None.

He was now calling V. Stenning just "Stenning" because he knew all the different morphs were the same person. The fact that Stenning was using different first names each time she killed, all beginning with V, was a nice touch of distraction and deception. A new identity each time without having to worry about a new signature and identification documents could much more readily be recycled as and when required. Some might consider the multiple use of the Stenning name to be a security risk, but he knew better. If you were properly careful, repeated use of an identifier became natural, and being natural was the biggest factor in any deception.

Vanessa was the first to make an appearance in 2002. Before that time he could find no record of a personal trainer or fitness instructor with that name anywhere in the UK. Companies House in London had no record of any business registered with a person of that name and as far as he could tell there was never a telephone record for anyone of that name in London between the beginning of 2001 and the end of 2002. What little detail he could uncover about Vanessa was that she worked with and for

Stephen Christopher a couple of times each week for several months.

Christopher had a history of poor heart health due to his extravagant lifestyle, and one day during a session on a cycling machine, he suffered a severe heart attack that killed him before he could be rushed to the local hospital.

There was a post mortem, even though he had seen his own doctor regularly before. Dan could see there were some suspicious circumstances in the manner of his passing, but for some reason, there had been no formal inquiry. That was odd, certainly; if he had been the officer in the case, he would have insisted on it.

Afterwards Vanessa seemed to disappear off the face of the world. There were no records anywhere of any type. Thanks to Nick though, he knew she had no National Insurance or National Health number, she didn't pay tax or receive benefits, and she had no passport and was not known to the police. *Vanessa Stenning did not exist.*

In 2004, a residential care worker called Vivienne Stenning started working part-time at the Primrose Residential Care Home in Winchester. Vivienne had several excellent references, which were verified by the care home only by an exchange of letters. By the beginning of 2005, she had turned down a full-time position. She was a quiet and well liked member of staff, although she never socialised outside of work with colleagues. All of the residents liked her, but she had formed a particularly friendly relationship with an elderly lady, Sissy Mathews, who lived at the home since July 2004, just six weeks before Vivienne started her employment there.

When Sissy died one late spring morning, Vivienne found her and raised the alarm. It seemed Sissy Mathews simply passed away due to her old age. Her small and disinterested family took her back to the family estate to be buried with the rest of the Mathews ancestors.

Sissy, it seemed, was a very rich woman from a very rich family—old money that could be traced back to King James I, they said.

Vivienne stayed at the home only for another few weeks after Sissy died. She apparently took up a last-minute offer to go on some sort of expedition.

When Conrad Mathews contacted Dan to see what the hell he was doing asking questions at the home about his dead aunt, Dan managed to successfully placate him. He then talked expansively about the family and was at pains to say that dear old Aunt Sissy donated a large amount of cash to a charity for cats just before she died.

"Must have been losing it a bit at the end I suppose, I didn't even realise she liked cats," he confided.

Once again Vivienne Stenning left no trace of herself when she walked out of the care home for the last time. She had definitely not gone on an expedition, as there was no record of her leaving the country—not surprising, as there was no record of a passport either.

Unfortunately and all too coincidentally, there was a break-in two weeks later at the Primrose Residential Care Home; they suspected kids looking for petty cash or some prescription pills … If only they knew. A number of documents were also stolen, including several staff members' both current and former personal records. Vivienne's were among those taken.

The chronology next brought crime reporter Vikki Stenning into Dan's microscopic focus. Vikki Stenning, who in 2008, so successfully screwed his life up with just the tap of a few keyboard keys.

She arrived at the *Garstone Record* with no journalistic experience whatsoever; if a trawl of newspapers throughout the UK and a check with the Journalists Union membership for that name could be believed. She posted on average two articles a week for the duration of her tenure there and, as far as he could tell, the piece she did on him was the most explosive thing she wrote.

He studied every article attributed to her. It was mostly all crap, taking into account the fact Garstone was hardly a hotbed of criminal activity anyway and she didn't have much to work with, but her style was still fairly unspectacular. No wonder, when she left, there was little interest.

The paper's editor, Mark Singleton, seemingly took an overdose of prescription painkillers and left a suicide note in his office about four months after Vikki's article on Dan.

The more Dan read about Singleton, the less it appeared he was really suicidal—and he, more than most, knew what it took. More than once he reminded himself to stay objective, but he couldn't get away from it: Singleton had turned his life around. He had everything to live for and to look forward to. And Dan knew enough druggies, losers and no-hopers in his time to recognise a successful reformer when he saw one.

The most recent appearance of Ms V. Stenning was as Valerie, the conveyancer less than a year ago. This time she appeared to be a close friend of a suicide victim, and once again, she melted away soon after the death of another elderly lady.

There were similarities between Sissy Mathews and Edwina Jacobs: both were widows and both left money to animal charities immediately before their deaths. The strange thing was, while there were tangible links between them, the connection between Christopher and Singleton to each other or to the women was not apparent at all.

This detail caused Dan many sleepless nights and confused days. He knew there must be something, if he could only find it. The one thing he kept coming back to was motive. Money could clearly account for the two old women and possibly even Christopher, in that he was a wealthy man. But Singleton was not well off, so what reason was there for Stenning to want him dead?

When Dan reviewed all the information he had amassed after a week of solid work, he knew there were still holes in his evidence chain—parts he either missed, misinterpreted or not discovered yet. But he also knew, with absolute certainty, he was right.

The day before, again whilst filling the kettle, he had been struck by a moment of indecision which caused a feeling like panic. *This is all too bizarre, too coincidental to be real,* he thought, and was overcome by uncertainty. He went back to his study empty handed and stood in front of the whiteboard allowing his brain to draw invisible lines which connected one thread of evidence to another. It all fitted, but the nagging doubt remained. For the first time in his life, even Sherlock Holmes failed to calm his nerves. He went from the study to the kitchen and then decided to run.

The sea air helped immediately although it felt odd to be running in the afternoon. At the three kilometre mark, more of his usual surety had returned, and he started to think about justifying what he believed rather than doubting it. *How can such wild coincidences be true?* Another kilometre and all he could think of was it was just a logical conclusion based on the known facts. He looked down at the brass five kilometre plate embedded in the tarmac as he strode by. *The number five.* "Five," he said aloud. "Five, five." There was something in the number. He ran on repeating the number over and over again until he it came to him. *The number five, the number, numbers. It all adds up; it's just simple mathematics.* He turned back somewhere near the Tamaki Yacht Club, and once at home, went to the study again.

"It's all in the numbers," he said, now one hundred percent sure.

The world concept of six degrees of separation could be evidenced and had been shown to be a real thing; the idea of any one person being linked to anybody else by six steps. He thought of all the people he knew, or had met, and then imagined all the people those individuals would know or would have met in their lives, already it was tens if not hundreds of thousands. Six steps to link everybody, it was basic multiplication and common sense. Taking that principal and applying it to say, the near sixty million population of Britain rather than the whole world brought the odds down significantly, that was maybe only four degrees needed to link everybody.

"And what's the population in New Zealand? Four and a half million." He triumphed. "Three steps tops!" It wasn't too coincidental at all.

What there was so far all pointed to the same thing, and the unanswered questions that hung around him like a bad smell only added to his renewed conviction. This coincidence factor and all the circumstantial evidence in play brought to mind a well used police phrase that he gave a prominent position in marker pen at the top of the whiteboard: "If it looks like shit, smells like shit and when you step in it, it sticks like shit—IT'S SHIT!"

His most prized evidential item was the photo Heidi sent him of Valerie Stenning. It was still the only photo he had been able to find; even the *Garstone Record* told him Vikki Stenning declined the head and shoulders shot to accompany her reports, which every other journalist used.

The other noteworthy and astonishing thing about Stenning was that no one could remember or easily describe her, including him. Eileen Meredith at the Penny Farthing Café and Heidi herself gave the best descriptions of Valerie, but even their two accounts had marked differences. Dan studied the photo every day, sometimes for several minutes at a time, to try and commit every line on her face to memory. The photo was full length and taken from a distance of several metres, therefore the detail wasn't fantastic, but in the circumstances, he was very glad to have it at all. One day, if he ever got close enough to recognise her, he was desperate not to miss the opportunity to catch her.

His composite description would have made any self-respecting judge or juror laugh out loud. Stenning was a white female aged between twenty-five and fifty-five; she was between five feet five inches and five feet eleven inches tall and of slim, athletic or slightly stocky build for her height. Her eyes were either blue, green, grey or brown and her hair was any one of a dozen different styles and colours. She spoke with no distinct accent, and there were no obvious distinguishing marks, scars or tattoos. She was a chameleon.

It was reasonable to assume he was not the only recipient of the email. It seemed to be offering an alternative to living with depression, and knowing what he did now, Dan surmised The Agency was Stenning's vehicle to contact her potential and vulnerable murder victims.

She undoubtedly got to him via the Depression Society. Applying Holmes' rule, this was the only logical conclusion. She must have infiltrated the organisation and possibly hacked into the website and internal systems, so he must be one among possibly hundreds or thousands to get it in their incoming mail.

That eventually brought him to the moment when he needed to decide what to do next. He could report what he had found out so far to the police, either here in New Zealand or back in England, but he felt there was still too much he wanted to know for himself before he could entertain that idea.

There was also the probability that Stenning, like him, was now in New Zealand too. Could it be by design, or simply a fluke? This was another matter he wanted to know more about. And finally there was the most important reason. While he never let himself say it aloud or dwell on it for too long, it drove him onwards towards the truth: After her newspaper article about him, this was now deeply and irrevocably personal.

He watched the blank screen for several more moments, willing his email reply to convey the right message.

CHAPTER ELEVEN

Tara Danes was entertaining her best friend Shelley in her second-hand clothes shop in the heart of Ponsonby, one of Auckland's trendiest areas.

"See you arrive and I lose the ability to work. You are such a bad influence."

"Rubbish, you don't have any willpower, that's your problem." Shelley retorted.

"No, my problem is I love to get the clothes and things, but I can't stand being cooped up in here every day having to sell it. I wish there was another way."

Her brother Neil had set her up in the business with some of his lottery winnings and she enjoyed modest success from day one. It was never going to make her millions, but she was happy; she was able to work the times she wanted, for herself, with all the old fashions that she loved so dearly. She met lots of cool people, and as a result, made many friends. Though she and Neil were twins, her being the older by only thirty minutes, their personalities were polar opposites. Tara's effervescence in everything she did and the magnetic attraction she generated in others meant there had always been many male suitors, but her one and only serious relationship ended when her then fiancé decided the all-year sunshine and money to be earned in Australia was just too tempting. She had no desire to leave all her friends and the shop, although she sometimes felt like getting as far away as she could from Neil. The split was mostly amicable and because of her hectic and social life, she only really missed a full romantic aspect to make things complete. The one thing Tara did insist on was everybody she spent time with must be interesting in some way, and the more interesting a person was, the better.

Her shop was in a small arcade with seven others, all selling something different. There was no sense of competition among the shop owners; in fact they were more like a cooperative, sending customers to each other, minding each other's place when somebody went out for coffees or herbal teas, and standing in their doorways talking to each other when things were quiet.

"So why couldn't you make it over to ours the other night?" Shelley asked, broaching the real subject of her visit.

"Neil again as if you didn't know. Every time I think I've reached the end of my patience with him, something happens and I end up spending another miserable day or evening with him. And now I feel bad about talking like this."

"I do understand, but he might actually do a bit better if you were more severe with him sometimes rather than giving him the hard word one minute then buckling the next."

"Yes I know you're right, which is why you are the social worker, and I'm the shop girl."

"Unemployed social worker. Seriously Tara, next time let him get on with it. Anyway you missed a good night; Dan came back with Paul and we had Chinese and some laughs. Dan's got a great sense of humour when you get to know him."

"Is this the same guy who you told me last week has lived next door for months, and you still don't know anything about him?"

"I think it is going to be a karma thing; you've missed meeting each other up to now but when you do …"

Tara threw up her arms. "I could use some with what I'm going through with Neil; surely I deserve a bit of good karma soon. Look, I have to go out with Cathy next door in a few minutes, she says she has a business proposition for me; so can we continue this another time?"

"Sure, I'd better be going anyway. See you later."

After Shelley left, Tara closed the shop and brought a chai latte back with her from the café an hour later.

She was still blowing the heat off it when the 1960s bell above the door rang as a customer entered. She wiped her mouth on a napkin and turned to see a striking-looking young woman dressed in faded jeans, a Versace T-shirt and well worn, but quality cowboy boots coming in. The woman wandered around the rails of clothes with an ever widening smile. After a few minutes she approached the counter and enthused, "What a brilliant shop, you have some fabulous things."

Tara smiled back, sensing a sale. "Thanks—I love it. It's all original and it's all over fifteen years old; most is probably over twenty-five."

"I can see," the woman said, brushing her hand through her long, very blonde hair. "I'm so glad I found you."

Tara liked the woman straight away. "Are you looking for anything in particular? I love your boots, by the way."

"Thanks, they're from Texas, where I was a couple of years ago. I got into the whole cowboy thing while I was there. I wanted to wear the hat too today, but it's so nice to have the sun on my face."

"Well, have a look around and let me know if I can help. I'm Tara."

"Veronica," the woman said, still smiling warmly.

An hour later and Veronica was still in the shop. She and Tara were now chatting like best friends. She had tried on a dozen different things and set at least half of them on the counter to pay for when she was finished looking and trying on other garments.

Tara now knew Veronica had been in Auckland for less than two months. She was on a sort of working holiday as a freelance travel writer and decided to come to and stay in New Zealand for up to eighteen months.

They shared a love of old clothes and old music, particularly from the seventies, eighties and nineties, and compared concerts they went to and pop stars they fell in love with. Veronica was probably a year or two older than Tara, but it was difficult to tell.

When Veronica looked at her watch, Tara noted it was an unusually shaped gold one. Veronica moaned and laughed. "Oh my God, look at the time, I'm so late now. This is all *your* fault, you know, for having such a lovely place. Let me pay and get out of here, or I'll be in big trouble."

Tara giggled back. "I'll have to work it all out."

"Oh God, Tara, what am I like? Can I come back tomorrow to pick it all up if I leave you some cash now—or could you possibly deliver to my place off Quay Street?"

"Either. What is your preference?"

"Well if you could, I can wear the blue top tonight. Really, I'll pay for the delivery."

"Don't be silly, it's no problem, you've been my best customer all week so it's the least I can do. Just give me the address, and I'll bring it around when I finish. Will six thirty-ish be okay?"

"That's fine, come and stay for a wine too."

"Alright, I will. Have you got any Duran Duran?"

"We are going to be such good friends, I can tell," Veronica said, handing over a piece of paper from a notebook on which she had written her address. "Sorry I really have to go. You're a darling; see you later." With that she left in a blonde swirl of more laughs and exclamations about how late she was.

Tara was still laughing as she finished folding and packing Veronica's things into a paper carrier bag. She had spent six hundred dollars!

Even when Neil telephoned her just before closing time, he could do nothing to dampen her spirits. He was a little less morose than the day before, when she had put the phone down on him after repeatedly saying she could not take more time off just to go and sit in the house with him. "If you want to see me, get off your backside and come down here, we can go for coffee or something. It will do you good to get out once in a while." Needless to say, he did not come.

"I was going to, but in the end, a movie came on that I wanted to see," he said pitifully.

Tara could not bring herself to chastise him too heavily. "Well, next time then, and no excuses, okay."

"Okay," Neil replied with no conviction whatsoever.

"Look, it's hard enough running the shop without worrying about you all the time."

"Do you need more money?"

"No for God's sake, Neil don't you know me at all? Twins are supposed to be closer than other brothers and sisters. What I want from you is to know you are happy, that's all."

"Sorry."

"And stop saying sorry and feeling sorry for yourself all the time. I can't concentrate half the time."

As she ended the call, she wished she could have been a little gentler with her brother, but he seemed to make it impossible. She really did worry about him all the time, and it did affect her thinking and therefore her business.

It was almost 6:45 p.m. when she pressed Veronica's buzzer at the lobby entrance to the small apartment block.

"Hey is that you, Tara?" Veronica's voice came out of the metal box. "Come on up. Fourth floor."

"Lovely place, my God how lucky were you to find this? Awesome view too," Tara noted as she entered the open front door and looked through the hallway all the way down to the big feature windows.

The hallway led to a combined lounge and dining area with the kitchen to the left, spacious and open-plan. The windows, she could see now, were full length on two sides, so she could also see into the lower downtown area of the city. Not surprisingly, there were no obvious signs of personal items apart from a few books on the kitchen bench-top including a beautiful blue and gold edition with red Arabic style script.

Veronica was in the kitchen with a glass of red wine in one hand and a phone in the other. She motioned Tara towards the bottle and another glass and made a funny face, indicating the phone. "Tell Mummy I love her and you can always come here to see me. The planes do go in both directions, you know," she said and after pausing to listen, said, "I love you, Daddy, talk to you again soon. Bye."

Veronica dropped the phone on a chair. "The Koran," she said answering Tara's intrigue about the book. "I was brought up a very good Catholic girl, but I lost my absolute belief along the way; I'm still interested and like to read other books of faith too."

"It's lovely, where is it from?"

"I picked it up in Istanbul last year but haven't had the chance to read much of it yet. Anyway, enough of that, thanks so much for bringing this stuff over. Shall we go outside, it's still so nice. Sorry about that earlier."

"No worries, a balcony! This is heaven," Tara raved. "Lovely wine."

They sat on the balcony and examined all the clothes Veronica had bought again, swapping stories about similar garments they had worn in the past when they were originally the fashion of the day. Tara found they had so much in common and enjoyed her new acquaintance's company.

For Veronica, things could not have been working out better; Tara was at least relatively interesting, unlike her last best friend Edwina Jacobs, which made everything a lot less tedious. She balanced the conversation between her fictional life and Tara's real one, waiting patiently for the talk to get on to the subject of family. Eventually Tara asked, "Was that your dad on the phone when I came in?"

"Yes. He gives me a hard time about being away for so long. They should be used to it by now; I left home years ago."

"Nice, though, that they care and want to keep in touch."

"I suppose, but they do get a bit claustrophobic. Since my brother died, I get all the concern, and when I go away, they worry even more."

"I'm so sorry, Veronica," Tara began, before Veronica interjected with perfect timing.

"No, it's no problem. It was a long time ago, and I deal with it a lot better than they do. It was his own stupid fault; he got mixed up with bad people and bad drugs when he was young, and he wasn't a nice person in the end. Mummy and Daddy blame themselves though. What about your family?"

In light of Veronica's apparent tale of woe, Tara also opened up about her own sad family story. Veronica absorbed every detail of Tara's comments and logged particular points of interest in her bear-trap mind, particularly about the failed relationship of Tara's parents and the sudden death of her mother just when she was getting herself straight again and had a new boyfriend—the first since the former husband.

After Tara finished her potted version family history and Veronica had refilled both their glasses, she leaned back in her deckchair. "Jesus, what a pair we are. I wish Neil could start to get on with his life, you know. He just sits around all day."

"Perhaps he just needs more time than you, like my parents. It would be nice though if he had something good to occupy his time. What does he like to do?"

"Movies; all day and all night. He doesn't do sports or cars or boats; he used to like tramping, though. When we were younger, he always said he wanted to climb every mountain in New Zealand and do all the ranges and passes. But he doesn't even talk about that any more. I know how much he loved our mum, and

I know it sounds terrible to say, but I don't understand why he has never seemed to get over it properly."

"That is a shame," Veronica purred. "I'm so looking forward to doing all that sort of exploring while I'm here." With that seed also planted, she felt happy to move on to other things.

"Hey Tara, as I'm fairly new in Auckland, how do you feel about taking me on as your pet project? I know there's so much to see and do, but it will be much more fun to do it all with a friend. What do you say to some days out? I'll pay and you can be my personal guide. Come on, it will be such fun. Nights out too," she added, sounding excited.

The invitation was perfectly composed; Tara's thoughts turned to the exciting times ahead she and Veronica might share. "Okay yes, it will be *so* cool."

"I was going to a few bars in the Viaduct tonight. How about we both dress up and make a night of it? You can wear some of this stuff, or any of my other clothes if you want; we're about the same size," Veronica enthused.

Later, dressed and made up, Veronica and Tara left the apartment for the first of what Tara expected to be many nights out with her new friend.

"You look lovely Veronica. Is that Donna Karen?" she asked, touching the black silk dress.

"It is. You too—and by the way, just call me V. Veronica is such a mouthful after a few cocktails."

CHAPTER TWELVE

Veronica was up early the next day. She had a busy morning planned, even after their night out, which did not end when they got home after 1 a.m. They shared a small pot of coffee before Tara got a taxi home around two. After just enough sleep and her regular session in the gym, she now felt fully rested and energised again.

Neil Danes was due at his next counselling session at 9.30 a.m., and she wanted to be in position at the café in time to see him arrive. The first look was always important, as the body language signals were vital. She wanted to see how he appeared before they met and before he was able to see her.

She had a decaf latte in front of her when he approached from the western end of the road at 9:25 a.m. He was walking, which meant he had either walked all the way, or he had got the bus to a nearby stop. In the time he was in view before entering the Coping with Grief premises, she committed to memory his physical features and mannerisms.

Neil Danes was certainly his sister's brother in physical appearance anyway; obviously they were not identical, but the family similarities were striking: facial features, hair colouring and general build. He was an inch or so taller than Tara, but heavier by several kilos. He showed no sign of any real fitness and walked with nervous slouched steps. He was dressed in drab, ill-fitting clothes—khaki cargo pants, a knitted woollen sweater, an old green baseball cap and equally old tennis shoes.

He was, however, carrying an expensive-looking canvas computer satchel with the strap over his shoulder. The bag did not appear to contain a laptop, though, as it swayed and bounced lightly when he walked. Veronica wondered what was so important to him that he felt he had to bring it with him to the meeting with Toby.

His hands were buried deep in his trouser pockets and he constantly looked at the ground. As he pulled open the front door with his right hand, Veronica got the briefest glance at his wrist as the sweater arm rode up a little. Her trained eye recorded the detail instantly. It looked like a white gauze bandage fastened with a strip of medical tape.

An hour and a half later, when Neil sloped out of the building again, she was in position on the other side of the road to parallel his walk back in the direction he'd arrived from. The distance, pace and angle she allowed herself gave her the best view of him and also minimised her exposure to his field of vision.

He did indeed appear to have walked from home, as he passed two bus stops before she dropped back and let him go on his way.

She made her way back to the coffee shop and retrieved her scooter, which was still parked around the back. There was plenty of time to get home and do more on the computer before she had to meet Tara in the afternoon.

Neil carried on home. He did not notice Veronica, and even if he had, all he would have seen was a uniformed nurse with short black hair.

He and Toby had talked at length about the need for him to get out for more than just these visits. Towards the end of the session, Neil remarked, "Honestly, I'll try, but it's hard to get motivated."

"It will get easier, but you have to make a start. What have you done to your wrist?"

"I scalded it on a microwaved meal yesterday. Don't worry; I haven't done anything to myself again."

"I'm glad to hear it."

Neil watched as Toby made his usual notes to be transcribed onto computer later.

As he walked the familiar route towards home, Neil thought about going to the video store at the shopping mall, but by the time he got close, he had changed his mind.

He knew he was pathetic and even as he vowed internally to do better, the other side of him encouraged him to get home and close the door. As he walked along, focused on the pavement, tears welled up in his eyes and he didn't bother to try and wipe them away as they fell.

Dan went for a run first thing and then intended to do the weekly shop later in the morning. He planned deliberately to stay away from home as long as he could today and therefore to keep himself away from the study. He needed a break.

His recent work on Stenning and The Agency had become an obsession. He recognised the need for some time away, but it was also paradoxically so good to have something to concentrate his mind on again. The fact that what consumed him now was also so closely linked to his past and not just another investigation gave it even greater purpose. He had not felt so good about life in a long time—even if it all too vividly brought back the last days of his career and the Mapperley incident once more.

The running was going better than ever, too. His times were improving, and he knew having Stenning to think about was all part of it.

Before completing the essential grocery shop, he took time to stroll along Broadway in the busy Newmarket shopping district, looking in all the windows without paying full attention. He had not bothered to come to this part of town to shop for ages but today provided an ideal excuse to buy some new jeans and shoes and see Paul at the same time.

His next door neighbour and friend Paul was pleased and surprised to see him when Dan walked through the door. "Hey Dan," he greeted him, "At last! I thought you were never going to show your face in here."

"Hi mate. Well, I thought it was about time. Can you help me out?"

"Sure thing, what are you after?"

Dan was very satisfied when he was finished some time later. "This lot will probably double my wardrobe. You salesmen are all alike, I never intended getting half these things."

Paul's raised eyebrows spoke volumes. "That is one of the saddest things I've ever heard. I know I might be a sucker for all things clothing, but if that is true, we should have a full day out together sometime."

Dan grinned. "I'll do you a deal, if you can convince me of a reason I need anything else …"

Paul let him get no further. "Deal! In fact, we can discuss it at your place on Saturday; it's about time you invited us for a barbecue. I know you have one because I've seen it under the cover in your garden."

"I got it in a moment of madness; it seemed like the Kiwi thing to do. I haven't got a clue how it works."

"Awesome, I do. Saturday then?"

Dan held up his hands in defeat. "Okay, see you."

He went to the supermarket on the way home and filled his trolley with everything he needed, several things he wanted and one or two things he had no idea when he could ever use but just liked the labels.

Driving home, he wondered what Stenning was doing right now and how advanced her plans were for what she intended to do next. When he stopped at lights or in a line of traffic, he scoured the pavements on both sides, just in case she might happen to walk by. Although he had not actioned any of his conclusions yet, other than the email, he knew that phase was not too far away.

Once he got home and unloaded the car, he put some coffee on as he tried to find room in the kitchen cupboards for all the things he had bought. Halfway through, the doorbell rang and he heard Shelley calling. He met her at the still open door.

"Hi Dan. Paul tells me you're going to cook up a storm for us Saturday night."

"Hi, yeah. Well, I'm going to try anyway."

Shelley looked a bit sheepish. "I was wondering how you'd feel if I asked my girlfriend along to even up the numbers; you know the one who cancelled on us before."

Dan was taken aback and stood in silence; his look and the quiet making Shelley blush. The awkward moment lasted until she managed to say, "It was just a thought—we don't have to do anything." She looked very relieved when he smiled and touched her shoulder.

"No, it's okay, I mean it's fine, you just surprised me a bit, that's all."

"I'm sorry; I didn't mean to put you on the spot."

"No, really, it's alright. A nice thought, actually. If she wants to come, that's good with me. She's not a vegetarian though, is she?"

Shelley laughed. "No, a one hundred percent carnivore I assure you. She's really cool and fun too; I really think you will like each other."

She stayed for a cup of coffee and helped him cram the remaining items into drawers and cupboards. At one point, she looked at him quizzically. "Dan, truffle paste?" She held up the tube and joined in when he burst out laughing.

"Are you and Paul at the pub again tomorrow?"

"I think so, why?"

"Girls meeting at ours; I'm going to make sure she is fully prepared to meet you."

Neil was back in the sanctuary of his home. The television was on in the lounge, as was its smaller slave monitor in the kitchen, but he was watching neither.

Sitting at his old computer workstation, he carefully unpacked his laptop case which he reverently carried all the way to his meeting with Toby and back again, as usual. The three photo albums, each page stuffed with snapshots of his past, were as aged as the desk.

He selected the oldest one and opened it at the first page. The six by four prints were all slightly yellowed versions of what they had once been. The photos were taken by his and Tara's mother, back in the days when there was always something to smile about, and he had thought they would always be together. As he flicked through the pages of his childhood, he absent-mindedly picked at the bandage on his right wrist, which was feeling a bit tight.

Veronica had finally worked her way into Neil Danes' computer. The email she sent to him and all the other New Zealanders on her prospect list contained a highly sophisticated hidden Trojan program which activated when the recipient replied to her own email. She had encountered several problems with it in the recent past—mainly caused by improved antivirus technology people were using now—and it had taken a number of days and several attempts to iron these out, including a no holds barred call to a former IT associate whom she persuaded in no uncertain terms to find a solution or else. As Danes was the only prospect she was taking seriously at this time, she concentrated all her efforts on his computer, and this had resulted in the breakthrough.

She now owned a window into his heart and mind. If she had not been meeting Tara so soon, she could have taken some time to start work on the new information source straight away. As she closed down and quickly scanned the room to ensure there was no trace of The Agency or Neil Danes, she contemplated how long the project might take to complete. The speed at which she was able to work was mostly governed by the actions and reactions of the particular prospect, but she had become more efficient as she worked on successive projects in the last few years.

As a consummate professional, she was cold to the emotions and consequences of her murderous business in so far as the victims were concerned.

Danes was almost too good to be true. She knew already that just a small amount of well directed pressure and persuasion would see him departing this world quite easily—albeit not as he thought it was going to happen. The difficult part was going to be getting him to unwittingly pay her for the privilege. She believed the situation might develop very quickly, and she was determined to be fully prepared when it did.

Dan was also fully engrossed—with Stenning's current status. The more he thought and learned about her, the more he felt he was getting to know her and her modus operandi. She worked to a proven pattern. She repeated successful processes to suit the situation, and he intended that to be her ultimate undoing.

When he'd worked on major incident teams and other large-scale investigations in the past, where a number of similar crimes were committed by the same suspect, there were always evidential pointers to the offender. Criminals repeat what works for them, out of habit and also, importantly, because it increases their sense of being safe from detection. If you could deconstruct and decipher those areas, you could get one step ahead. As a detective, there were times when he wanted to follow his instincts, but procedures and codes of practice prevented it. He now discovered that the benefits from being 'freelance' included no longer having to be constricted by the rules of evidence, as the police were. He was able to pursue any line of inquiry in any way he wanted, and in doing so he had discovered a thrilling new level of artistic licence.

Stenning was a cold and calculating serial killer who took the minimum of risks. She preyed on fragile souls and, after discovering their weaknesses, used them as weapons. She was motivated by money, certainly, and maybe by other factors too that he did not yet understand. She was looking for her next victim in New Zealand and that victim was likely to be someone who was, or had been, in contact with the Depression Society.

It was all a good start, but he had improved the odds still further.

Using his new freedom of thought, Dan took a chance that if Stenning could access the Society's computer systems, she could also unlawfully hack into his own. It had taken days, but after he'd bought himself a new computer a week earlier and transferred all his files on to it using a different email identifier, and adding several new layers of anti-spyware, it now stood alone and secure from his home PC. What he left on his original machine was only what he felt safe letting her have access to, and what he wanted her to see and believe to be the true representation of his regular computer's use. He gave much thought to the chance of her recognising him in a picture, and whether or not to keep any, but that was unreasonable—he didn't know anyone who did not keep photos on their computer. He did his best, though, to keep only the ones where he looked the least possible like himself. His more casual and even unkempt civilian appearance hopefully being an asset.

The time and effort in selecting enough of the right photos especially, plus other saved documents, favourite sites, email addresses and emails was considerable to fabricate the sanitised version of himself that he wanted to be viewed and accepted by her. There was no reason to suspect she might do otherwise as she must believe, as usual, that she was the hunter and not the hunted.

He enjoyed the time and effort spent on creating a recent personal history for himself which was to act as bait and provoke a reaction from her.

Unless she had already deliberately targeted him—but this was unlikely, given his financial situation and her financial motivation. It appeared she had bizarrely made random contact with him and didn't know who he really was.

That very important point had crystallised in his mind days before, when he remembered who Vikki Stenning was, for when their paths had crossed in Garstone, she knew him only as Detective Dan Calder. It allowed him to begin formulating a plan in his head.

His email and all other identifiers were always the same, J.D. Calder—the one concession to his parents years ago when he dropped his given first name as changing official documents was too time consuming and difficult. It was reasonable to believe she would not have made the connection to him as Dan Calder. A major characteristic she repeatedly demonstrated was the lack of risks she took and to knowingly target him now was just too risky.

He had to be on her short list, if one existed, because he had now replied to the email, and she was surely only going after people who showed an interest in her mysterious Agency.

There were plenty of questions which filled his brain since he'd sent the email. What was the bitch doing now? Had his contact back been welcomed? When might she respond again? And was he to become the next intended victim?

He knew he could be walking a deadly tightrope; knew it and embraced it.

CHAPTER THIRTEEN

The following morning Veronica settled down after breakfast with her laptop to concentrate on Neil Danes once more.

The previous afternoon's meeting with Tara Danes had gone well for her. They met for coffee at a trendy café bar on Parnell Rise and spent the time ostensibly engaged in girl chat. Veronica was building and developing the impression of herself that she wanted Tara to know. A lot of the conversation was about family, and as the time had gone on, she asked the questions about Neil she needed to, even though she often knew the answers already.

Tara seemed happy and even relieved to have someone to talk to about her brother. He was depressed and difficult to deal with. She loved him and knew he completely doted on her, which only made the whole situation so much sadder, and she worried that he might do himself some real damage one day.

Veronica checked out Neil's last one hundred emails. There was an assortment of message types and styles, although there was little good news and cheer among any of them. She was quite surprised to see the number of people he was corresponding with; she expected to see only a few confidants, but there were at least thirty different people he sent messages to or received from. As she examined the first dozen or so in a bit more detail, she noticed names that were known to her already; they had been on the short list she sent The Agency email to. Her hacking ability didn't stretch as far as being able to isolate different individuals' correspondence with Neil, and so she set about trawling through one message after another to see if she could find a reason for so many regular contacts.

It didn't take too long to see that they were indeed all members of the Depression Society or Coping with Grief, who'd formed their own sort of self-help group. Neil had built one or two fragile friendships with a couple of them, and they met from time to time either in pairs or threes or fours at each other's homes. The messages all seemed to share certain traits; they were short, direct and contained no hint of joy.

Walter would like this stuff, she thought to herself as she expertly flicked between Neil's computer files and her own, copying useful information, adding notes and references and highlighting the most important pieces, which she could later frame a death scenario around. It was taxing work, requiring large measures of concentration and skill over a prolonged period.

When she stopped for a break, it was already well past lunchtime. She made herself a sandwich and poured a glass of sparkling water, which she took out onto the balcony. There seemed to be several plausible options available for the killing of Neil Danes. As she quietly ate her light meal, she considered the need for anything remotely elaborate at all. It would be no surprise to anyone if he were simply found dead in his bed, on the floor, hanging from a tree in the garden or even floating in one of the bays around Auckland one of these days.

For the first time in The Agency's existence, she decided to dispense with the time-consuming and complicated *perfect death*, and employ a much simpler strategy. The risks were minimal: get to know him a little, relieve him of a portion of his wealth and then put him out of his and everybody's misery with as little fuss as possible.

With the decision made, she felt content with her intended approach. She made a mental note to conduct more research into the depression help organisations in the area in the near future, as it seemed there was a potential for real success there. The important thing now, however, was to strengthen the bond of trust and friendship with Tara, and introduce herself to Neil as soon as practicable and appropriate. She thought his vulnerable state, coupled with the inside knowledge she had of him through his computer, was going to make her planning and execution straightforward; but even so, she warned herself against taking too much for granted.

Dan woke at midday and drowsily went downstairs to make the day's first pot of coffee. He had spent all night on the telephone and computer, talking to a few ex-work colleagues and acquaintances. One of the 'acquaintances' was in fact an old informant he handled and over whom he still exerted considerable leverage. It was 3:00 a.m. when he made the call; and if he had needed any more of an attention alert, the sound of the voice answering his call made his guts twist and the bile rise in his throat.

After the briefest of formalities, he recited what he wanted, then said to the weasel on the other end of the line, "I need you to find out as much as you can as fast as you can. You do this for me and we are quits; you'll never hear from me again, okay."

"It's a lot to do. I could lose my job if I get found out," Arthur Mountfield replied.

"Don't give me all that bollocks, Arty. You should have lost your bloody job and been a guest of Her Majesty long ago. So don't fuck about, alright? You're in just the right place to find out what I need to know about this Stenning woman. Just remember, it's not as if you've never done this sort of thing before. I'll call you again at this time in two, no, three days' time, and you'd better have what I need then."

Dan heard Mountfield's laboured breathing through the receiver and winced. He loathed Arthur Mountfield with a passion, and until all this Stenning stuff started, he had been very happy to believe there were no reasons in the world to ever see or speak to the obnoxious fuck again.

"Okay, alright Mr. Calder. I'll try and get what you need. Tell you what; it was a bloody shock to get a call from you all the way over in New Zealand. What's it like there? Lovely, I bet. Perhaps I can come for a holiday one day as I'm helping you out now."

"Arty, if I ever see you again once this is done, I will get myself a big new pickaxe and embed it so far up your arse that your little pervert friends will think you've got two Adam's apples. Don't you ever think we are friends, you're a piece of human waste who owes me, and now it's payback time, understand?"

"Yes Mr. Calder. I was only thinking."

"Well don't think, just fucking do what I say." Dan cut him off with a sneer and switched the phone off. He felt like he needed to shower with industrial-strength soap after talking with Mountfield.

Arthur Mountfield was the chief registrar at Garstone's Registry Office of Births, Deaths and Marriages, and he was also head of his local Masonic Order. In his time, he had worked in various areas of local government and had even been a county councillor. In his professional capacity, he was in a position to access the personal details of every person in the country, and through his many nefarious contacts, he could obtain a lot more information about most aspects of anyone's life.

He was also one of the most disgusting individuals Dan had ever met. A paedophile with a penchant for teenage boys and younger, he owned the biggest collection of pornographic photographs and videos of young males Dan had ever seen or been involved in seizing during his career, and it was to his everlasting shame that because of Mountfield's "friends in high places," he was not able to prosecute the bastard and put him behind bars for a very long time.

It turned his stomach every time he'd used him as an informant since then, but he was a great source of information.

It gave him some small pleasure, then and now, to think Mountfield must always have to live in the fear and expectation of a call from Dan demanding some piece of intelligence. With Mountfield, he didn't do polite requests—it was strictly a one-way thing, and Mountfield knew if he didn't do what Dan wanted, he might wake up one morning to find all the gruesome details of his depraved life in every newspaper and on every TV in the country, courtesy of a few select items and taped conversations which Dan unlawfully salvaged and kept from the wreckage of the defunct prosecution file.

To call Mountfield nine hours before was a big decision for Dan; it brought back more painful memories to the surface of his consciousness that he much preferred to keep buried. But he knew, if the chance he was taking paid off, he could get ten or twenty times as much intelligence in a few days as he could ever hope to get by himself in months.

He had to quickly change his call-back day from Saturday to Sunday when he remembered Saturday was the night Paul and Shelley were coming around for dinner.

The next few days he aimed to concentrate on reviewing what he knew so far, and when he called Arthur Mountfield back he hoped there was going to be a truckload of fresh intelligence for him. He wanted to be completely sure everything else so far was perfectly straight in his head and on paper.

He had the details of the various Stenning women, the names and some personal information about her victims and also a number of other individuals who were attached to the inquiry by chance or design. Dan decided before making the call to go for broke and included a lot more on his list than might have been safe or wise to obtain all at once, but time was against him.

Mountfield needed the toilet, but when he returned to his office, he closed the door. He had to write down the list of all the information Dan wanted, once the shock of getting a call from him in the first place wore off. He had hoped, with the detective's departure, he might not hear from him again; but within a couple of seconds, Dan had made it very clear that for this one last time, it was very much still business as usual. With a deep sigh he switched on his computer. It was going to be a long afternoon, and a late night.

Veronica had been so fully focused on Neil Danes up until that point that any new Agency message reply needed to be extremely compelling to take her attention so completely. Nevertheless she continued to stare at the screen reading and re-reading what was in front of her.

Next she went to her stored files and called up the list of names she had sent her original message to. Cross-referencing, she found the name she was looking for and went to the sub-file containing the information she had on that person. He was one of the curious ones whom she almost decided not to include on her message list at all. He appeared to correspond with the Depression Society via their website and online forums only, rather than have personal and direct contact, and he seemed to have a particular and very personal deep-rooted self-loathing.

John Calder of Auckland was clearly a man of significant mood swings. From the tone of his message in the few lines of his reply, she detected hopelessness, anger and despair all mixed up together. But there was something else about him too which she could not put her finger on.

She read the notes she'd made previously about him again. He was a dark person alright, or at least had dark places within him.

"John Calder, John Calder ..." She repeated the name several more times as if she could find the reason for the strange feeling she had in doing so ... Nothing.

She went into the bedroom, returning with a plug-in hard drive which she kept archived information on. The data on it was protected by three separate passwords and it took almost four minutes to get all her old files up on the laptop screen. She did a file search on the name, expecting it to come up straight away and was staggered when it did not. John Calder was not a name she had ever entered onto her computer. It made no sense.

Shelley's girls' evening consisted of her and Tara on the sofa drinking white wine, laughing a lot and discussing TV, fashion and men.

"Paul thinks he is the perfect twenty-first century man." Shelley giggled. "Bless him I haven't got the heart to tell him."

"Paul is lovely. You're only saying that because you've got him."

"No, no. He runs the shop, so he thinks he understands women's fashion, he loves his barbecue so he thinks he can cook like a Michelin chef, and he watches sport at the pub so he thinks he is Mr. Considerate. What he doesn't know is I sit here with his beer and watch the rugby when he is at the pub watching it."

They both burst into hysterical laughter again.

"So come on, tell me what you've been buying recently."

Tara took another sip. "Buying! I should be selling; you are no help at all. It's supposed to be a business not a warehouse."

"Sorry, I'm not business savvy, you know me."

"I keep promising myself I'll get better, but I love the shopping."

"What you need is a partner to let you do all that side of things, and they can control the business side."

"That's what Cathy next door keeps saying, she has the shoe place. She's keen for us to do something together as she doesn't like having to source all her stock."

"Well?" Shelley probed.

"Maybe one day. Anyway tell me more about this neighbour of yours; he's not like that last guy you set me up with is he?" They laughed again.

"Not me, that was all Paul's fault. No, Dan is different."

Tara sniggered. "You are not selling this very well Shel'. What does 'different' mean?"

"Different is good, he's sort of deep, you know, hidden layers. Think of him as an onion." This time they fell into each others arms; Shelley was crying with laughter.

It took some time before they were both calm enough to proceed.

"Seriously Tara, I really think he's a good man who's got a past. Paul really likes him too, and apart from his last selection for you, he is a very good judge of character."

"What sort of past?"

"We aren't too sure; he's never opened up enough to say. That could be your job."

Their conversation was cut short when Paul arrived home earlier than expected. He gave Shelley a peck on the cheek and repeated the act with Tara. "So wife, how was your interview today?"

Tara admonished herself. "Oh I forgot to ask, sorry, yes, how was it?"

"Who knows; they said they had a lot to interview for two positions. I should hear something in a week or so. What are you doing back so soon?"

"Dan has been working flat out for about two days and nights straight so he only wanted to have one drink," he explained.

"I have been telling Tara all about him. What do you think?"

Paul wandered across to the fridge in the kitchen. "I think the poor guy doesn't stand a chance. Hey Shelley, are we out of beer already?"

He could not understand why the girls found that so funny. When he took himself off to the other room to watch another game, Tara turned to Shelley again.

"Did they give you any clues in the interview?"

"Not really; they said I was clearly very qualified. I tried to actually play that down a bit; in the last three interviews I've had they all came back and said I was over-qualified for the role. It's as if they are afraid I might be able to do it too well; Paul said I should dumb down my CV. What do you think?"

"It's been a year almost; maybe he has a point. Would feel like a slap in the face though?"

"That's what I said. It's hard to stay upbeat sometimes."

They finished the bottle before Tara got a taxi home.

CHAPTER FOURTEEN

The water lapped against the large volcanic stones which formed an extra defence adjacent to the seawall. Its relaxing sound was a sure fire best-seller for insomniacs if someone recorded it. Dan was at his optimum pace, feeling comfortable within himself as he ran under the pale sky; he could almost feel the blood coursing through his veins. He was thinking about his breathing, trying to inhale through his nose and release the air slowly out through his mouth.

Today was as good a day as he could remember in a long time. The sense of well-being was brought about by the mosaic of his life's components fitting and moving in harmony with each other, for once. Perverse as it was, the course of his life had been dramatically altered, such was Stenning's impact. He needed the drama, and he had always known it, really—while he was in the job, and after he left. Coming to New Zealand was a dream come true, but it didn't fill that particular void.

The deadly game had moved on since yesterday, when he received another email from v.stenning@theagency.org giving him further details of the services offered. He had a new list of information targets, and at the top was discovering what the current V stood for. He rightly guessed she would not use a name she had used before, but when he did a search for female names beginning with the letter V, he was shocked and disappointed by their abundance.

The lack of contacts in his adopted country was also going to be an obstacle difficult to overcome—one of the main reasons for the phone calls back to Garstone two nights before. A number of old workmates he spoke to in the hope of being able to find a mutual acquaintance here, or someone who might be able to provide an introduction, had failed to produce anything good; he was all alone. He thought of going to the police and sharing what he knew with them, but dismissed the idea again like a jealous lover. He wasn't ready yet to liberate the cause of his well-being.

The updated plan was now not to respond to the most recently arrived email for several days, if at all. The dangerous game he was playing might move ahead if Arty Mountfield came through with what he needed, or if he was able to advance his investigation in another way over the next few days.

The Post Office box was his best option, or more appropriately the least risky. He could not take the chance of compromising himself by calling on the phone and have her recognise his voice, however remote the possibility. Having the box location gave him the opportunity to covertly stake it out—if he could just get a glimpse of her and maybe even surveil her. He decided to pay the Auckland City Post Office a visit sometime soon.

There was plenty to do when he got home. Paul and Shelley were coming over later and his house badly needed a clean. It was an ideal excuse to keep the study door closed for the day and try to have the whole day off. After getting showered and changed into some older clothes, he set about the house, moving from one area to another without ever really settling. Nevertheless after spending enough time to work up a sweat and more coffees, he was able to see an improvement. Impressed by his own will to also tidy up some of the small things, he took the three rugs from the living and dining areas outside and beat them senseless with his old tennis racquet before hanging them on the fence while he went inside again to wash the polished wooden floors.

By three, he was beginning to wilt, and he called it quits at around four. After taking a well earned rest, he went back to the kitchen and started on some of the preparations for the evening.

Cooking was not one of the skills Dan was endowed with, and it was with a degree of trepidation he viewed the fat steaks, vegetables and salad ingredients that came from the fridge.

Six-thirty arrived far too soon. He had managed to get showered and changed again and mixed a salad, which was back in the refrigerator awaiting the dressing. However the barbecue was still under wraps in the back garden, and he knew it could take some time for the charcoal to heat up. He bore a scar of combat with a cucumber on his left index finger, where he cut himself as he sliced it up. He grabbed a kitchen towel from the bench and went in search of a more suitable solution, already knowing he did not have a first-aid kit anywhere. The only thing he could find to bandage it was tissue paper from the bathroom secured with yellow electrical tape from his toolbox. It stubbornly refused to stop bleeding and the towel soon looked as if bloody murder had been committed close by; he didn't bother considering it may wash out, but threw it straight into the rubbish bin once the make-shift band-aid was in place.

When the doorbell rang he jumped. The balsamic vinegar, olive oil and dried herb dressing was still in need of further marinating according to the recipe instructions. "Fuck and shit," he said to himself as he went to the door and, taking a deep breath, put on his best smile and yanked it open. "Hi, right on time."

Paul and Shelley had come over to introduce themselves virtually as soon as Dan moved in. Good neighbours and friends as they were now, Dan struggled to reciprocate simply because it was not in his nature to. His appointments at the pub with Paul and occasional dinners at their house was the sum total of their social interaction. Many times, especially in the first few months, he sat at home with nothing much to do and thought about going over, but he never did. Even now he did not instigate their get-togethers and tonight was something of an event for all of them because of that. It was the story of his adult life—not a lot of friends, but not doing much at all to remedy it. He excused his inactivity by telling himself it was better that way; the fewer people there were close to him the less the chance of being hurt again.

"Hello neighbour." Paul smiled, holding out a bottle of wine in one hand and a six-pack of beers in the other.

"Hi," Shelley added. She had a large bowl covered with plastic wrap in both hands. "I come bearing dessert."

Dan opened the door wide so they could get past him and into the house. "Good to see you, guys, sorry I've been so crap at getting to grips with being more sociable here up until now. Make yourselves at home."

Paul dumped his drinks on the bench top and ripped open the packaging around the beers. "No worries, this will help," he said passing an open beer to Dan and waving one of his own at him in a casual toast. "You're one of us now."

"Cheers," Dan replied. "What can I get you, Shelley, wine, beer, soft drink?"

"Wine please. Paul's got red, but I'll have a white if you have any cold."

Paul looked sheepishly at her. "Sorry," he said.

They chatted as they drank until Dan said he had to fire up the barbecue.

"Need a hand?" Paul enquired.

Dan nodded. "Almost certainly. I hope you have a back-up plan just in case; I'm not sure salad and Shelley's dessert is what you imagined, if this all goes pear-shaped."

Shelley patted Paul on the shoulder. "It's okay; he's going to tell you what a top notch barbecue cook he is. Unfortunately, I have to concede that he is, but don't let his head get too big. I'll just text my friend—she should be along anytime."

"Lead me to it," Paul said as he and Dan headed outside.

Shelley had her cell phone in her hand already when she received a call.

"Hi, I was just going to text you … No, you're fine, the boys are only just about to start a fire, so don't worry." She laughed. "I think Dan's a bit nervous about the whole cooking thing."

As she gave parking instructions, she viewed the living room, taking in the few photos and mementos on display. There were a couple of framed pictures of Dan with an older woman who she guessed must be his mother; and another of him in a group of men she immediately took for policemen colleagues from his previous life. Other than that, the photos on display were landscapes or of Dan with a scruffy brown mongrel dog. Him appearing took her by surprise. "Oh Dan, I'm sorry I was just looking."

"I know, very bare still, isn't it?" he said. "Long story; I reckoned a fresh start was best, but I haven't quite got around to it yet."

Shelley hoped desperately she wasn't blushing. "Sorry, I was being nosy, I couldn't help myself. In all the time you've been here, I think I have only been inside a few times."

"It's a girl thing I understand, in fact, if you have any interior design ideas …? I just came in for some tinfoil; you carry on."

Shelley was saved by the knock on the front door. "That will be her. I'll get it," she said in explanation. "She's the design expert."

Dan retreated back to the garden where Paul had been stoking charcoal under the brick built-in barbecue. The heat was already intense and the smoke that billowed around them a while ago had mostly dispersed. Paul was inspecting the marinated steaks Dan had prepared earlier.

"Pretty damn good," he said as Dan started to probe the charcoal Paul had just finished piling up under the grill. Paul couldn't help but smile.

"Come on in, I've poured you a wine already," Shelley said to Tara. "I really hope you like Dan; he's a nice guy but a bit quiet, I told you I think he must have had some crap in his life before he came here. He really needs a female touch around the place, too."

"Enough already, you and your matchmaking. God, I've only just got through the door!"

"Sorry, here, drink. Come on, I'll introduce you."

Dan was aware Shelley and her friend were on their way out, and he was nervous. He was not good at meeting new people and didn't much like parties. "Dan, this is Tara," Shelley said emerging into the late sunshine. He looked up and smiled.

"Hi, nice to meet you," the athletic-looking young woman added, extending a small slender hand before Shelley could say any more.

He took it and they exchanged a polite shake. "Hello, yeah, you too. I hope you like surprises because I've got no idea how this is going to turn out."

"Not a barbecuer then?" Tara cheerfully queried.

"Not a cook of any description; New Zealand is full of firsts. Just as well Paul knows what he's doing."

"The secret is not to play with them once they're on," Paul said.

"What? Yes," Dan stuttered, answering as a reflex without understanding what Paul was saying.

"The meat, don't screw around, turning and prodding it. Wait until it's half done and turn it over, that's all."

"Right," Dan replied, as he focused again on the matter at hand.

Paul blew Tara a kiss as he slapped the first of the steaks down onto the hot grill, causing a noisy, satisfying hiss and a cloud of meaty smoke. Dan was at a loss as to what to say next.

He felt like his inability to function in social circumstances was accompanied by a big warning beacon to those around him, and it made it all the more difficult and embarrassing. After what seemed like an age he said, "How do you all know each other?"

Tara smiled. "Shelley and I have been friends since we were kids and our families lived in the same street. Even when they moved away when we were teenagers, we still kept in touch and all through our university days too. I've lived in Auckland all my life and these guys finally settled back here a few years ago. Now we see each other all the time."

"Except for the last month when she's been too busy with *new* friends to see us," Shelley said.

"I've got my own business, a little shop in Ponsonby. When I'm not in there working and trying to make some money, I'm looking for stuff to put in it."

Dan was much happier asking the questions and listening rather than having to answer them. "Oh right, what sort of shop is it?"

"Vintage clothes. My passion as well as my work. What do you do?"

"Long and boring story. Not a lot at the moment," Dan offered apologetically.

Paul interjected, brandishing a pair of tongs menacingly. "Come on, we don't that know much about you either. Let me get us another beer first and then you can tell us all." A minute later he was back with two beers and the wine bottle for the girls. "Save me going back," he said, putting it on the low wall next to Shelley and Tara.

"Okay, we are all ears," Tara said making herself comfortable on the wall.

Dan looked hopefully at the barbecue, then at Paul, but he was also obviously waiting for him to speak too. His chest tightened a little, he took a slow pull on his beer and then began.

"Well I first came to New Zealand in the early nineties and really fell for the place; you know, just felt at home here straight away and always wanted to come back. When I got the chance at early retirement, I jumped at it and here I am."

"And?" Paul asked.

"Well as you know I was in the police for a long time. Sorry—I was in the police for a long time." He looked at Tara and received a smiled acknowledgement. "Now I'm trying to find something useful to do here."

"Why not join the police?" Shelley said. "I've been thinking it might be something I could do if I can't find a job soon."

"Why not? I would recommend it to anyone. So far as I'm concerned, I did think about it, but I reckon it's time for a change." It wasn't quite a lie or the whole truth, somewhere between the two. He knew the events leading up to his departure from the force were sure to be brought up if he tried to join the New Zealand Police, and while he was certain he had done what was right at the time, he was also sure it would not come across that way. Much as he might have loved to continue his career here that part of his life was gone.

"My father was also a career cop," he continued. "We never got on and had nothing in common, apart from our first name, John, which I dropped in favour of my middle name when I was a teenager, an act of self-assertion that further alienated me from him. We also shared very little in common in our working lives; he reached senior officer status, Masonic handshakes, golf clubs and everything else that went with being one of the boys in that particular world. That definitely was not me; I worked hard, gained some respect of some of my peers and not much else."

"Did you know about his name?" Shelley asked Paul.

"No, don't interrupt woman. Let him go on," he joked. "Go on Dan."

"That's it I suppose. I'd been here several times before on holidays and it had a profound effect on me; it is honestly the only place I ever felt at home. The plan, from that first visit, was to retire here one day.

"Taking early retirement was a no-brainer when the time came to actually make the decision. There wasn't anything keeping me there anymore apart from work. Some of those who knew me might have said I was running away, though none of them were brave enough to say it to my face."

"Unfortunately the steaks are ready," Paul said, saving Dan from any further immediate disclosure and questioning. He got busy with the plates, salads and bread, feeling relief.

Dan caught the girls exchanging a glance, sharing a telepathic moment in which they held a full conversation about what Tara's initial thoughts on him were. He noticed Tara was non-committal and also Shelley's response: a pleased-with-herself acknowledgement of Tara's definite maybe.

Dinner was a success and Dan gratefully received the plaudits of his three guests. The meal and a few drinks continued into a very pleasant evening of conversation and conviviality. At ten Paul went next door and returned with a bottle of port, which they finished before the night ended.

Dan had not intended to pay particular attention to Tara but found himself unable not to. She possessed something familiar to which he was attracted to physically and drawn by emotionally. Although he welcomed the feeling, he was disturbed by it also in only the way he could be. At one point, he covertly observed her in the reflection of the French doors. She was quite tall, about five feet nine inches, with a good figure and shoulder-length, very dark brown hair. She had green eyes, clear skin and a slightly lopsided, honest smile. The tight top she was wearing clung to her perfectly shaped breasts, which he consciously had taken care to avoid staring at several times.

Each time the conversation got close to his past and current personal life again, he skilfully avoided letting too much out. Paul, Shelley and Tara were all interested in what he had to say but were sensitive enough not to push over-hard. There was enough to talk about in any event; another trait Dan liked about New Zealanders was that no one seemed too up themselves; they could discuss everything and anything without it getting too heavy, and the conversation swayed easily between a dozen different topics.

When Shelley offered to make coffee sometime after midnight, she and Paul took the empty bottles and drained glasses inside, leaving Dan alone with Tara.

"Great people," he observed as they watched them disappear from view.

"They really are. Good together, and good to their friends," she replied. "I'm surprised it took them so long to get you to throw a party. Paul's the type to invite himself in for the rugby—or any other sporting events, come to that."

"My fault, I'm sure. It's taken me a little while to find my feet here since I moved in six months ago and I am a bit slow to make new acquaintances anyway. I admit our rendezvous at the pub don't really constitute a full social life. Hopefully now we've broken the ice, I'll be able to get my arse into gear better from now on. Have you got work in the morning?"

"Sure have, but being the boss has its perks. Where I am, things don't get started until halfway through the morning most days. Just as well; I've had a few late nights recently. You'll have to come and have a look some time."

"I'd like to. My entire wardrobe is pretty much all that era anyway. Not especially your dream shopper although Paul did make a dent in my credit card the other day."

"You just need some more practice, that's all."

Dan found Tara easy to talk to. He liked the fact that she looked at him when she talked and the body language signals he studied and trusted were all open and good.

"I need to find some work and earn a bit of money first before I go off on any more wild spending sprees."

"Yes, you didn't go into detail earlier. What exactly does an ex-cop do?"

"This one wants to write a book, but realistically something investigative probably. Use my experience, maybe even in security."

"Write a book? How interesting, tell me more."

"Oh, a dream I've had for a long time. Wanting to do it and being able to do it are two completely different things though. More writer's block than writing recently."

Tara's eyes widened a fraction. "Oh, wow, you've started."

"Yes, a while ago."

"I don't think I have got the patience to sit down and write for hours and hours," she said honestly.

"I got used to being on my own with work sometimes and writing is one of the things I can do well so it isn't so hard unless, like I said, you have a blank sometimes, then it's just the most frustrating thing in the world. But what you do sounds interesting," he said in an obvious subject-changing way.

"It's what I do well, finding the clothes anyway; turning it into a profit is another matter. What I really need at the moment is someone to look at the business accounts without having the love for the clothes like me."

Whether it was the movement of her eyes he noticed, or the beer, wine and port, Dan did something he had not done for many years. He let his guard down a little.

"I'd be happy to take a look, I'm pretty good with accounts and I definitely have no interest in the clothes," he said without thinking and taking himself by complete surprise.

If Tara was taken aback it didn't show. "Yes, I'd really like that," she replied before he had a chance to get himself out of the hole he'd just dug. "What about a wine after I finish on Monday, or a coffee during the day?"

He was on the spot now, wishing he had not said it and also pleased he got a positive response from Tara. "Coffee during." He was sure it came across like a plea.

"Awesome, let me give you a card and you can come by anytime you like," Tara chirped, making it sound the most natural thing in the world. "Did you know Shelley has been going on at me for ages you and I to meet? I'm glad we did."

As she fished in her bag for a business card, Dan looked back into the house, hoping she could find it and hand it over before Paul and Shelley returned. When she found and passed over the small glossy card, he nervously smiled and put it in his shirt pocket without looking. "Just give me a call sometime before you come," Tara said.

"I will. Thanks." He quickly changed the subject as he heard Shelley approaching, but when he saw the two women exchange a smile, guessed he'd been busted.

An hour later, Dan was sat alone in his lounge, listening to a range of music selected by the multi-disc CD player. He had memorised Tara's contact details on the card she gave him, but still gazed at the image on the front of it. She seemed really nice—but then so were some of the others when they first met, which painfully reminded him of his vow to keep all his secrets to himself.

CHAPTER FIFTEEN

"What have you got for me?" Dan saw no reason for pleasant-ries after the initial hello.

"Mr. Calder. Right on time as usual," the weasel Arty Mount-field replied, trying to sound pleased to hear from the former detective again.

"I told you I was going to call now. Think of it as the last time you'll have to worry about me ever again, providing you've got what I need. So?"

"Well it took some doing, I can tell you," Mountfield began.

"I don't care if you had to sell your grandmother; come to think of it, you probably would without any worry at all if it was something you were after. So just get on with it."

"I'm a changed man, Mr. Calder."

Dan sighed disdainfully. "I said get on with it."

"Well you were right," Mountfield began. "Your Miss Sten-ning does not exist. There was once a Vanessa Jane Stenning, but she died within hours of her birth in 1976. From what I can see, a duplicate birth certificate was issued at the Windsor Registrars Office in 2001.

"After that there are no certificates issued anywhere around the country for Vivienne, Vikki and Valerie, and there are no National Insurance numbers or passports either."

"And?" Dan growled.

"There was no formal inquiry after the death of Stephen Christopher. He died on the way to hospital. I do have a copy of the death certificate and also the hospital record; it seems he had a weak heart for years and just overdid it. There is a note to say there were small rashes on the back of his hands where the hair from them was pulled out, but that was not explained."

"That doesn't make any sense. Why no post-mortem?"

"His position and money. It wouldn't be the first time embarrassments are concealed by people close to a deceased by making sure one did not take place," Mountfield explained.

Dan was writing as fast as he could. "What else about Christopher?"

"A very successful, but dishonest, investment broker. Ruined many investors and got away with it scot-free. There are reports of elderly investors especially getting completely wiped out financially and losing their homes. He was investigated, but nothing could be proved. He was struck off in 2000 by the association that regulates brokers for gross misconduct. There were even questions asked in Parliament, but it all came to nothing."

Mountfield's tone changed suddenly. "Now I did find out something quite interesting about Vikki Stenning."

"If it relates to me then I know already," Dan said dryly.

"Well yes, that too—but no, it's to do with Mark Singleton, the newspaper editor she worked for," Mountfield said. "I discovered a housing record which showed they were living together or at least were listed as joint tenants of a house in Garstone for a period of time in 2007 to 2008."

Dan silently punched the air in elation; until that point he could not connect Vikki Stenning to the dead editor in any way other than their working relationship. Mountfield continued without taking a breath. "I did get copies of all the documents so I can send them to you."

"So there's nothing else on Vanessa or Vivienne?"

"No, it's like they have never existed in any form."

Dan knew how simple it was for someone to drop off the grid if they wanted to. Ironically it was probably easier now than in the past. With the advent of the electronic age everything was captured on computers; if an individual was moderately careful, living a life without using computers and dealing only in cash, not credit cards and bank accounts, it would be very difficult to track them. If they put a bit more effort into it and didn't do things like buy their own house or car and kept a low profile, they could disappear altogether.

He was certain Stenning was a lot more than moderately careful.

"There is more, but I really don't want to go through everything on the phone. Can't I just send it? Please, Mr. Calder."

"In a minute. What about Valerie?"

"She's quite interesting. I pulled a few strings with a business acquaintance and found out some odd things about her."

"Spare me your self-congratulations, Arty."

"Sorry. Valerie gave her boss some story about her tax codes and National Insurance number being mixed up and got paid as a consultant by cheque each month rather than as a regular member of staff. Seems that soon after she left they found out the VAT number she provided for their accounts was false and she never banked a single cheque they gave her. More than twenty thousand pounds altogether."

Dan couldn't help thinking out aloud. "So she doesn't need the wages because she's making more than enough from the victims or has money coming in from elsewhere."

"Seems so and also maybe she is worried about being traced through the cheques?" Mountfield offered.

"Anything else Arty?"

"I've got pages and pages here."

"Okay then, email it all, but I still want you to send the all originals you have in the post." Dan's experiences told him there was always more to be found in original documents than any amount of detailed notes sent about them; however reluctant he was to give Mountfield his home address there was no alternative.

"But it will take me so long to scan and email them all," the weasel pleaded.

"Best you get started as soon as you can then, Arty. But remember, if I ever get so much as a suspicious caller trying to sell me encyclopedias, I will make it my life's mission to find and crucify you. Understand?"

Mountfield knew it was pointless arguing. He took Dan's details and meekly confirmed he would scan and email all the documents later in the day and then send the two hundred or so pages by express registered airmail.

In his closed office, Arthur Mountfield was sweating profusely. "So are we good then Mr. Calder?"

"Arty, if I never hear from you to the day I die, it will be too soon."

Mountfield was about to say something else, but the click of the phone on the other side of the world left him openmouthed and silent. Only when he replaced the receiver, did a few words come which were very unbecoming of a man in his professional position.

Dan couldn't stay still in his chair. He was up pacing the room; talking loudly to himself, rifling through his pages of information and feeling the rush of adrenaline prickle every nerve ending. He knew it could easily be hours before anything appeared on the computer, but he still clicked the send and receive button anyway and got nothing. He put some more clean paper in the printer and hit the send and receive button again.

"Here I come," he said. He could have been talking to Stenning or the coffee pot downstairs.

It was nearly four hours later when he finally got a positive reaction from the secure computer's inbox. The first email contained an attachment of twenty pages, the second another twenty and the third fifteen. During the night he received another nine messages from Arthur Mountfield. The final one being the only one which contained any message text at all and it simply read, "Last one, goodbye Mr. Calder."

He was caught between trying to read them one at a time as they appeared off the printer and looking for what might be the more interesting pages. After unsuccessfully trying both methods for a while, he gave up and just picked up a handful of pages from the pile he had amassed so far and read the top one first, then the next. The weasel had really outdone himself; there were copies of documents from his own office, Inland Revenue, various utilities companies, private businesses, county courts and even several police forces. If nothing else, it was a demonstration of the breadth of Arthur Mountfield's seedy influence, and it made him shiver a little.

Dan organised the new information according to date. The chain of evidence would have been similar if it was categorised by victim name or V. Stenning chronology, but it made better sense for his method of investigation this way. Some evidence, for example, relating to Vanessa only became clear when Valerie was active. It was his preferred way of interlinking them all, showing an evolving pattern of behaviour and, most important-ly, getting to know his adversary better.

He worked through the rest of the night, surfing a wave of caffeine and adrenaline that kept him as sharp as a razor. The early morning sun warmed the small room and kicked up a mus-ty smell, but he hardly noticed.

By 9:00 a.m. he had rewritten the timeline, and his evidence book was an impressive near-3 inches thick. He knew what she was doing; he knew how she was doing it; but he still couldn't be completely sure why.

With the help of Mountfield, he now even had samples of her handwriting. The fact she did not have passports for any of her clandestine identities meant one of three things: she was either not travelling overseas and therefore was not in New Zealand;

she was travelling illegally, crossing borders without a passport; or she was using another identity to travel legally.

The first he thought unlikely. She was targeting people in New Zealand and therefore it made sense for her to be here to be able to kill them. The second was possible but didn't fit with her careful approach to all things: the risk of capture trying to cross borders these days was too high for her to take the chance, especially as she must be feeling so secure about her anonymity.

That left the third option, which seemed the most practical, the most logical, the most obvious and the most likely. Dan looked at the one picture he had, the one Heidi had sent of Valerie Stenning.

"You used your real name, didn't you? Your own fucking passport."

At that moment of glowing certainty, another nugget of knowledge also cemented its place in his brain. She didn't take risks—she was too methodical and even overly cautious in the ways she went about protecting her Stenning identities, to the extent of not banking cheques in spite of her lust for money. Being that careful, there was no way she could have come to New Zealand and contacted him if she considered the possibility of who he was. The bitch didn't know. *She didn't know.*

Across town Veronica spent the previous day and much of the evening working equally diligently on the profile of Neil Danes. Even without one hundred percent certainty, her previous experience, coupled with the most intimate details lifted from his files and those of the Coping with Grief site, gave her more than enough to be confident.

He was as fragile as any of her more recent targets and, as such, needed careful handling to make the most of his vulnerability.

She was looking forward to a swift resolution in order to be able to move on again.

The name of John Calder popped into her head.

CHAPTER SIXTEEN

She had not been as excited to see someone for a long time. Even though Tara liked people and had many friends whom she shared great times with, she was fascinated to meet Dan Calder a few nights before. He was so multi-layered just like Shelley described, although she bet only a very few ever got to see below the surface.

He called an hour before to check it was still okay to drop by and arrived at the minute he said he would.

Tara smiled as he entered the shop. "Hello Dan. Good to see you. I hope you've brought your wallet because I haven't had a single customer in all day." She was wearing an orange gypsy skirt and a white shirt held closed by just the two middle buttons. He smiled back.

With no sleep after finally closing the study door at almost 10:00 a.m., he was very tired, but his body, fuelled by the excitement of the chase once again, did not need sleep to function at this point in time.

"Hi. No chance, I told you clothes were not my thing; so you're not busy then?"

"I wish. Just as well I'm the boss, otherwise I'd have to think about making me redundant the way things have been recently. Anyway, don't worry about that now; I was really glad you phoned before. How are you? What have you been up to?"

"Not too much. I had a late night last night doing some personal stuff. I sort of forgot about the time."

"Ooh, your book?"

"No, another project I've become interested in recently." He was tempted to add something like getting the old juices flowing, but let it go. "Shall I go and get coffee? Where's good nearby?"

"No, I'll come with you. I don't think it's going to affect business. Come on, my treat."

They sat outside a nearby café at one of the small tables, as traffic and pedestrians passed them by.

"Thanks again for the other night, I had a good time. I'm on a good run of meeting new friends lately."

"From what I've seen it's an easy place to meet people, although you've probably guessed that I'm not the world's best."

She didn't want to tell him that she thought it was kind of endearing and a little mysterious. "We are all on our own journey, I think. Are you here for good or will you be travelling again?"

"No, this is definitely home now. I don't want to live anywhere else, but I'll keep visiting and revisiting other places. The world's such an interesting place; it's just some of the people in it that occasionally screw it up."

"Oh, I've met a few of them in my time. What is it they say? Don't let the bastards grind you down."

Her words struck a familiar chord and the arrival of the coffee saved him from having to find a reply. "One of my vices," he said, taking a sip of double espresso.

"You've already seen mine. The shop—my God, if I could I'd carry on buying and never sell a thing," Tara replied, stirring her cup. "Well now, I am getting to find out a bit about you: policeman, coffee fiend, novice chef and author. What else is there to know?"

She wore the same lopsided and gentle smile he had seen a few nights before, and he noticed she also had a small number of freckles that highlighted her nose and cheeks. Despite her affability, he could not bring himself to open up. "No, that's it. Mine is the shortest autobiography you'll ever read." As he said the words they burned in his throat; some of the incidents he had experienced in his life so far could fill the thriller section of any library.

She knew that was untrue, but by the way he suddenly seemed fascinated by the bottom of his cup, she did not want to challenge him on it. It was also clear that the poor guy knew she knew, as well. "That's alright then, because I have a killer story."

When he looked up, she was holding her cup in both hands close to her mouth, concealing the lower half of her face from him, but her eyes showed warmth and understanding.

"I've got a twin brother. Our mum died a number of years ago. She brought us up on her own when our dad walked out. I'm an Auckland girl through and through; did a lot of swimming and surf life-saving when I was younger. I even represented New Zealand at under 18s. I've got a degree in art and design. I love to dance and I make the best chili you've ever tasted. Shall I go on?"

"Please. I like to know more about everybody than they know about me. Never know when I'll need the ammunition."

"Mm, I see—and will have to remember that." She smiled again. "Right; what else, Okay, I have a heap of really good friends like Shelley, and we tell each other everything. My house is a design nightmare at the moment because I have daubs of paint and bits of fabric stuck up everywhere but haven't done a single thing to update it since I moved in a year and a bit ago. It's old but so cute.

"I was engaged a few years ago but he decided he wanted something else and he's in Australia now. We keep in touch but only because I bother now and then to call him."

Tara paused for some coffee. She was hoping for something from Dan but not expecting it. He was watching her as if she was still talking and he was listening like a child having a story read to him. He shook his head belatedly when he realised Tara had stopped and forced an uneasy laugh. "Sorry, I didn't notice you had finished. That was a lot of information."

"Well, you asked. It's liberating; not having secrets is wonderful. What about you, do you have secrets?"

He was still watching her face, his cup floating somewhere below his chin. "I suppose that depends on your definition of a secret. I guess you would probably say I do."

"That's a practiced answer. Sorry if I'm prying, Dan, and I don't know you so I can't comment, but for me, sharing things, good and bad, works."

He continued to study her for a moment longer. All the body language was right, down to the virtually imperceptible movement of the eyebrows and her blinking pattern, her openness of posture and the skin colouration around her neck. She was hiding nothing; what she said was the truth as she saw it.

"I haven't been as lucky as you, but in my job I found it easier to be a bit guarded."

"Was it only the job that made you this way?"

His silence was answer enough for the time being.

"You are a bit of a strange one. Can I ask you a question?"

"Yes I am, and yes you can."

She laughed. Dan Calder was becoming more interesting by the minute. "Whatever it is you're getting over, how long have you been getting over it for?"

"A long time."

Tara nodded and pressed on. "For a while, when Mum died I thought I'd be unhappy forever. She was all my brother and I had ever known. I'm a lot better now, but he's still hurting; he's a mess, in actual fact. But you're not, you're—I don't know, you're different."

Dan looked at her long enough that some other people might become a little uncomfortable in the same situation. "You don't know a thing about me Tara. It's complicated."

"I can see that. Have you got anyone you can talk to?"

"Probably not anymore. Not here, that's for sure. No family in the UK either; I was an only child. The job was my life and my substitute family. That's what the police is, a family, dys-functional most of the time—but from what I've seen over the years, most families are." His words were bitter. "And it's not *it* by the way, it's *them*."

"Sorry, I don't understand."

He smiled again but there was no pleasure attached to it. "You said get over it, as if there was just one thing. I bet your brother has got more on his mind than just your mother. Take it from me; there is never only one thing."

If she was uncomfortable, it did not show. He looked again for the signs on her face, unconscious movements of her limbs or even some involuntary shifting of her weight, but there were none. She simply held his gaze, and he felt a resonance with her.

"You don't scare me, Dan."

"That's odd, because I scare the shit out of myself some-times. I'm a dangerous person to get to know; bad things hap-pen around me. Bad for me and bad for you if you stick around long enough."

"So are you worried more about what will happen if you get close to someone again? It's going to be pretty lonely for you if that is the case."

"Lonely is okay after a while. Lonely is safe."

"Wow, you *are* screwed up, aren't you? Tell you what, if I can tell you something about you that makes you feel good, will you let me cook my chili for us one night?"

He wanted to say no; wanted to tell her to mind her own busi-ness and wanted to crawl inside his coffee cup, because she was already too close.

"Tara, listen …"

"Tara listen smitchen," she said sweetly. "I see you, Dan; you can't hide your goodness and strength from me. I saw you checking me out in the window reflection the other night too. I see you now, looking for signals. Well here are a couple of signals for you: you weren't the only one doing the checking out; and you do not want to turn down my chili."

In a very rare reversal, he felt like he was the one under the microscope now.

They had another coffee before going back to the shop. The conversation did continue, although he didn't give much more away about his past, preferring to talk a little about his book project, the marathon, and her. When he went to reach for his wallet to pay she reached over and touched his hand. "No, my treat, remember. You can do next time."

As they crossed the road, he felt her arm brush against his. His first reflex was to extend an arm and place it in the small of her back in that old-fashioned way a gentleman assists a lady. His next reaction was to hold it there a fraction longer than absolutely necessary.

"Coming in?" she asked, unlocking the door.

"I'd better get going, I've got to go to the post office before they close. But why don't we meet again and I can look at your books?"

She looked up at him. "Well okay, if you're sure." She pushed open the door and went inside, leaving it open and him on the threshold.

He was tempted to follow her in but the doorway became a barrier he could not cross; instead he spoke from there. "Let's do coffee again, or your chili sounds great, and we can look at them then."

Tara turned to face him. "When?"

"My place again tomorrow; Shelley said you can do interior design as well."

"I'm out tomorrow, but I can do tonight, remember?"

"Tonight! Okay why not."

"It will be fun; I'll come over when I finish work here."

Veronica did not seem to mind when Tara phoned her to say she needed to blow her off for a man that evening. The fact was, she had more than enough to do to keep her busy and was at something of an impasse at the time anyway.

"Oh shame," she feigned and then giggled. "Well I hope he's worth it. Come to think of it, I could do with a man so ask him if he's got an eligible friend."

"I'll ask; sorry V, I will make it up to you. Soon, I promise. Wish me luck."

"You go get him girl. I'll call you for *all* the details tomorrow."

Veronica had been working on some of Neil Danes' recent emails and also trying to discover what was so important to him about the laptop bag he carried around on the rare times he left the house. So far she had drawn a frustrating blank.

Whatever it was must be important to him, and because of his unstable nature, she guessed it was probably more likely to be personal than anything else. There were no clues in his emails, which only gave more weight to her feeling it must be very personal indeed.

What she was certain of was that its importance could be used against him once she discovered the secret.

Tara's call temporarily broke her train of thought. Back on the oversize leather couch, she absent-mindedly scanned the room until her eyes came to rest on the framed photograph on top of the decorative table near to the balcony doors. The picture of her with her parents taken during on her university graduation day was one of only two mementos she took everywhere. The fictional stories as to its provenance she gave to various acquaintances over the years were too numerous to remember; she kept their sacred memory in the most private recess of her mind, visiting frequently, sometimes as a happy reminiscence and other times simply as fuel for the life she now lived.

They were so proud of her that day and she so grateful for all they had given her over the years. The happy photo and the memory were both perfect. They had driven up that morning to take her out for a special lunch and presented her with her precious watch.

"Dad wanted to get you a digital; I wanted a more traditional one. When we saw this with both we had to get it," her mother said.

Then all three of them went on to the graduation ceremony in the "Great Hall." As her name was announced and applause filled the room on her short walk to accept the scroll, she picked them out in the audience and blew kisses all the way back to her chair.

After the ceremony, they presented her with the keys to the little red MG, which was her first and most beloved car, even though it leaked like a sieve in the rain and only had two reasonably functional gears, one being reverse. It was the happiest day of her entire life.

At that moment, she knew without a shadow of a doubt what Neil Danes protected so reverently in the bag. Just as she would do anything to keep her photograph and her memory safe, so does he. *Even if that means carrying it around with you whenever you leave the sanctuary of your house,* she thought.

The volume and evident weight of the bag meant it was probably a collection or an album of some sort. Whatever the make-up, it was going to be the key to her success and his demise.

She decided to go back to the Danes' old family home the following day for a better look around. Since she discovered it was still in his name, it took on an increased importance, and she was sure there were more useful pieces of information there to discover.

"How was that?" Tara asked as Dan put his fork down on an empty plate.

"You were right, your chili is fantastic."

They had spent a comfortable evening together around his dining table, first while she cooked, and they talked then through the meal.

"I got the recipe while I was in Mexico a few years ago, have you ever been?"

"Not yet. I say that about everywhere I haven't visited. I really like travelling so maybe one day. Do you want to take a look at your books now?"

"Why don't we leave it for another time, this is too nice. Can you pour me another drink please?"

He went to the benchtop for the bottle while Tara looked around the sparsely decorated open plan area.

"How would you like to decorate in here?"

Dan returned and stood over her to pour the wine. "Nothing fancy, I like earthy colours and maybe some nice art."

He leaned forward to fill Tara's glass as he spoke and she turned to look at him causing their faces to become close. It seemed almost contrived, like in an old movie, and it took them both a second to realise they wanted to kiss; when they did it was slow.

"Mm, lovely. The wine as well." Tara said, breaking the silence which followed.

"Tara listen."

"Don't start with that again." She got up and wrapped her arms around his neck. "Does your bedroom need decorating too?"

Their lovemaking was as slow as the first kiss. Dan's recent celibacy was only part of the reason he felt apprehensive with Tara; she was for some reason special and he wanted her to know it. For her part, Dan's attraction was not just physical; she was fascinated by his apparent equal measure of strength and vulnerability.

Afterwards they lay in the dark talking. Tara was keen to learn more about him.

"So what do I need to know about you?"

"I've got to run early in the morning," he replied innocently.

Tara leant up on an elbow. "What! That's supposed to be the crappy line you use *in the morning.*"

"No, I mean, I literally have to go for a run in the morning, I'm doing the marathon, so I'm in training."

"You really do have to work on some of your relationship skills, Mr. Calder." Tara teased. "A girl could get the wrong idea very quickly."

"I bet you would not be surprised to know I've been told that before. Look at me as a work in progress."

"You wouldn't get me running twenty miles. Do you really enjoy it?"

"Twenty-six; to be honest it did take a while to get into it, but now I'm loving it," he said enthusiastically. "Even on bad days, it makes you feel good. A legal high. I only started because I didn't want to let myself go; no regular work, small circle of friends, et cetera. I'm doing between twenty and thirty ks every other day."

"Screw that. I know the race is coming up in a few weeks. Last year one of my friends did it but swore after she would never do anything like it again. Not exactly inspiring."

"I know what she means. I reckon that once it's over, I'll be either just the same or go the other way completely and want to do it all over again every month."

"Well I'll come and cheer you on; no wait a minute, it starts at stupid o'clock, doesn't it?"

"Yes six a.m. Why don't you cheer me at the end, hopefully between nine forty-five and ten?"

"That sounds more reasonable. Now about before. I meant I want to know about you."

"There's not a lot to say. I gave you the details on Saturday night."

"Now I know that's not true. You've got more facets than a diamond. Why don't you tell me a secret?"

"It wouldn't be a secret then would it."

"Come on, Dan. Let me know something about you that nobody else does."

He felt a twinge of panic, like being on a roller-coaster at the top of its ascent, waiting for it to rip downwards but not wanting it to at the same time.

"If I do tell you a secret, will you then let me off?"

"Okay, you tell me one thing, and then we can talk about whatever you want."

He considered a lame excuse about needing the toilet when he was suddenly overcome by a new feeling which took him by complete surprise. Instantly he weighed the alternatives of coasting through the rest of the night, or risk losing the certainty of more great sex and great company by actually giving her exactly what she asked for. It took the best part of a year before he told April any real detail about his formative years, and it was only after she left him that it struck home that she had never wanted to know. At the time, he was just grateful that was the case. *How stupid can one man be,* he later thought.

Decision made, Dan took a deep breath and began. "I never really wanted to be a policeman when I was young. It was just sort of expected because of my dad. He was a superintendent."

Tara stirred a little, and he sensed her surprise.

"Don't get me wrong, it was the best thing that ever happened to me in lots of ways. I found it was something I was good at, and I loved the job. I doubt if I could have enjoyed any other profession more, but I never got the chance to find out; the police was just preordained."

"Does it bother you now?"

"No, I don't think so. Aspects of the job are shit, you have to be tough enough to deal with it or it will deal with you. Of course, there are one or two regrets about some of the things that happened, particularly at the end when I left."

"Like what?"

Dan felt naked in more than the literal sense; it was more personal information given to another person about himself than he had managed in years. He wanted to say, "That's enough secrets for one day," but it came out as, "Are you sure you want to hear this?"

"Come on; don't turn it into a joke now. You were doing so well."

"Okay, but there is one thing you must know; don't push it. It won't work; all that will happen is I will get scared or stupid or both and whatever we have going will just end."

Before she could say, "You think we have something going?" he continued, ignoring her obvious need to make a comment.

"I've had three proper relationships in my life, and they all ended badly. Two of them were my fault. You wouldn't recognise me from the man I used to be. Believe it or not, I'm a much nicer person now. I try hard not to be how I used to, and it is hard work I can tell you. Sometimes I'm too honest for my own good, and that can be a bit scary for those on the receiving end. So be careful what you ask," he said, deliberately testing her tolerance and in doing so, giving her a chance to escape the situation if she wanted to.

Tara momentarily propped herself up on both elbows so she could look directly at him. "I told you before that I don't scare easily."

Dan was about to say something else generic and banal, but after a moment of further inner deliberation, his expression relaxed, causing Tara's eyes to narrow a little.

"Don't speak, just listen," he said with quiet authority.

She nodded.

He started in a little more than a whisper, Tara leaned in closer. "I grew up in a house where fear was the biggest part of every day. My mother and I were in constant fear of my dad. From the earliest times I can remember, he beat her and abused her.

"To everyone else, he was like Superman, universally loved and admired by family, friends and work colleagues, but to us he was a bloody monster, a beast. The nights I heard him hitting her in their room, I never did anything. I used to cover my head with the pillow and try to drown it out. The next day, the sure sign was how she always covered up the marks with clothes or heavy make-up on her face and neck. If I started to say something, she would look at me, make me stop and be quiet. I hated him for doing it, I hated her for tolerating it, and I hated myself most of all.

"She only carried on for so long, only managed to survive for so long because of me. She died when I was fifteen. Pneumonia—she wasn't strong enough to fight it, or didn't want to; and I couldn't blame her."

Tara remained as still as a corpse while Dan spoke. "I said to her all the time we should just leave, but she refused; he kept her under his thumb. She used to say that there was nobody to believe or help us and even used to make excuses for him. He controlled her like he was able to control his junior officers at work, he was never questioned.

"I joined the police as a cadet when I was just seventeen; the best thing about it at the time was I got to go away for three months training and then moved into a section-house to live with a bunch of other recruits. I never went home again.

"Right from the beginning there were comparisons, how I was expected to do this and that. Throughout the whole of my service, I was always referred to as Superintendent John Calder's son; even after he retired. We didn't often meet up, but he carried on the pretence of having a relationship and being the proud dad whose son was carrying on the tradition. He died a couple of years after retiring, heart attack. Ironic really as he was such a heartless bastard. The funeral was like a royal ceremony. I've never heard such a load of bullshit. I wanted to stand up and shout and tell them exactly what he was like and what he did to my mum.

"I used to dream, when she was still alive, but much more after she died, hear him beating her in their room. I'd go down the hallway and open the bedroom door; he was kneeling over her on the bed. When they heard me open the door, they both turn to look at me. She was always smiling, and he would have a face like thunder. Mum said, 'Go back to bed John, it's too late for you to be awake.' And I would. I'd just close the fuckin' door and go back along the hall to my room as her crying started again. It's all so real still."

Dan's voice crackled with dark power. "I could not help her, not once, in the dream nor in reality." He was looking into the far wall as if he could see right through it.

"In all that time growing up, he never once touched me. He used to shout and scream, but she took all the physical violence. We all knew she was taking my share too."

Tara shivered and Dan shifted to a more upright sitting position with his back against the headboard, Tara sat up cross-legged and pulled the blanket over her shoulders. He smiled briefly, touched her cheek and continued.

"I was with my last girlfriend for four years. We had a house and a dog. She now has both. I didn't see it coming, but should have. She told me I was too hard to live with, too much excess baggage and was incapable of loving like a normal person. That really pissed me off for a while until I realised it was the dog I really missed.

"I tried counselling for a few months, but I just couldn't do the whole talking thing. What it did make me see though was I am who I am. At the end of the day, you can only try to be the best version of yourself that you can be, but the fundamentals will always be the same." Dan relaxed still further as if a weight had been lifted. He slid down a little so he was face to face with Tara.

"There, I thought about just being the normal me and I almost did. Small talk, nothing really real, but then I just thought what the hell; you asked so why not let you have it all, both barrels. We've known each other for what, three days?"

She nodded again.

"Someone once told me to write down all my feelings as a way of releasing them. Since I started writing, it's come to mean so much more to me than that. I am secretive, I'm sure you have worked that out already, but I have also become even more brutally honest about some things too. It took me a long time to fall in love before, and yet I have some of those sensations with you already. I must be very hard to be in a relationship with, enough have tried, failed and told me so that I believe it's true. I may as well dump all this shit on you right now as drip-feed it to you for six months and then have you give me the elbow. If you can cope with it fine, if not I save myself another load of heartache down the line. You asked. This is me, take it or leave it."

Dan sat stunned by his own oratory, with a *where the hell did that come from and a what the hell have you done* voice pounding in his head. He tried to think if there was something else he could say to somehow make the last short period faintly sensible, but he had nothing.

He was about to get up and retrieve his strewn-about clothes when she placed her hand on his cheek as he had done to her before.

"Do you still have the bad dreams?"

"Sometimes. Too often."

"Have you forgiven them, both of them, for giving you the childhood you had?"

Dan was surprised by the "both" in her question and by the tone.

"Why should I have to forgive her for anything? It was all him, he killed her."

"Okay," she smiled, "but it does sound a little like you expected more from her, to help you and help herself."

He knew Tara was right. "I loved her, and I should have stopped him, done something. It's me that should have been begging for *her* forgiveness."

"Do you have to run in the morning? Have a day off," Tara asked gently.

"What? Why?"

"Because I want you to let me look after you, without the pressure of thinking you have to get up and go tomorrow. Just stay and see what happens."

Dan got up to fetch them some water, and when he returned they resumed their melded position and continued to talk until it started to become light again outside. Dan had told Tara more about his life one evening than he had said to anybody in a very long time, and yet the single most important factor remained unmentioned. He closed his eyes, hating himself.

Several minutes passed; he let her next question go unanswered and then felt her gently kiss him on the lips before hitching her leg up slightly higher over his and going to join him in apparent sleep.

Sleep was in fact still a distance away for Dan. Although he really opened up to Tara about his parents and so on, he did not come close to mentioning the subject of that night in Mapperley. He tried and failed to force those memories of what he could *and* could not remember from his thinking.

Tara may have believed he made a major communications breakthrough, but he knew he had just given her enough to satisfy her interest and cement a false position in her feelings.

He wasn't happy about it, but also he was not playing games with her; it was simply he was still unable to deal with what had happened, and his memory of the incident was so patchy he could not formulate it into a coherent account. He often wished he had not woken up the next morning in the dingy house.

Before closing his eyes again, he wondered what the morning with Tara held in store.

CHAPTER SEVENTEEN

When Dan woke up it was almost midday. Tara was gone and briefly before his waking consciousness returned, he thought the events of yesterday were all another vivid dream. He pulled on his jeans but failed to locate his shirt from the previous day. He grabbed another T-shirt and wandered down to the kitchen where Tara was working at the stove, dressed only in his missing shirt.

"Hi sleepy, are eggs okay?"

"Morning." He gave her a kiss and stole a grope of her exposed backside for himself.

"I didn't want to wake you," she said, looking pleased with the attention.

Dan glanced into the frying pan. "Actually to be honest, eggs aren't okay. I don't like them. I only have them hard boiled in sandwiches with mayo."

"And here I was thinking I knew all about you now. Not to worry, more for me, there's some cereal on the table," she said, pointing a spatula, "or there's fruit in the fridge and the bowl on the table. Coffee?"

"Definitely coffee, thanks. That was quite a night."

"It really was. I bet neither of us imagined this yesterday. How do you feel?"

Dan took his time to assemble a proper answer. "Lighter," he said and it was true to a point.

"Lighter?"

"Yes, like a weight's been lifted. I feel okay, I feel good." After a moment's pause he said, "And I feel like a run, it looks like a beautiful day."

Tara wrapped her arms around his waist and kissed his chin. "Lighter, that's nice. When I woke up and saw you, I liked the feeling I had too. By the way, thanks for sharing with me. It must have been hard for you; I love the fact that you trusted me enough to say all those things."

"I'm glad. You're not too bothered about all the stuff I unloaded on you? It wasn't exactly the usual first or second date kind of thing was it?"

"Bothered, definitely not, but it will take some digesting. Let's spend the day together."

"Okay," Dan replied with no feeling of guilt about a run free day, no thought about V. Stenning and other thoughts expertly put aside as usual.

Veronica got up early and scootered around to the Steele Street house where Neil and Tara Danes grew up.

She climbed in through a broken window which was invisible from the road and took her time taking in the layout of the three-bed house, committing as much detail as possible to her own memory and the tiny digital card in her compact camera.

She was in no doubt as to whose bedroom belonged to whom. Tara's room faced onto the garden, the inside door of the built-in wardrobe still bore a tatty magazine picture of the rock band Survivor, and she could even smell the faintest hint of lavender from a netting bag hanging on one of the clothes rails.

Neil's room had no window at all. A yellowing world map clung to a wall by a single remaining pin in the upper-left corner.

Unfulfilled dreams in an unfulfilled life.

The room was otherwise completely bare except for the sense of misery saturating and staining every surface.

Veronica realised he must have been unhappy for a long time, even before his mother died, and she wondered what other skeletons rattled around in the sad mind of Neil Danes. The carpet had been removed from the room altogether (it looked like it may have been used as the fuel for a fire in the lounge room hearth at one time). She scuffed across the dust-covered floorboards making a pattern with the toe of her shoe and was about to leave when something stopped her. Her toe caught on a board which was fractionally raised above all the others. When she bent down to examine it more closely, she noticed the nails were absent from the dark nail holes that once held it down firmly.

She removed the Gerber multi-tool from her jacket pocket and used the flat screwdriver attachment to lever between the loose board and its nearest neighbour to lift it up far enough to pull it out completely with her other hand.

It was dark underneath, and she opted to use the light of her cell phone to see into the void rather than blindly reach in. At first it looked like an empty space until the light picked out a thin silvery line which on closer inspection revealed itself to be a scratch mark on an old brown biscuit tin. As she lifted it out of the void, she could tell there was something inside as it slid across the inner surface when she tilted the box to get it free. It was dusty and had a little rust around the bottom edges where it sat on the cold surface below, but otherwise looked in good condition.

The lid held fast initially, and she needed to use the Gerber again to open it with a metallic pop. Inside, wrapped in clear plastic film and held with a piece of dirty string, was a rolled up exercise book. When she unwrapped and flattened out the book, a small brown pill bottle with a white snap-lock lid rolled out and slid onto the floor. Inside the bottle was a gold necklace with a small decorative locket attached. The sticky label had been crudely scratched off the bottle, leaving hardened traces of gum residue. When she held up the necklace and locket, its light weight, colour and general appearance told her all she needed to know about it being a cheap imitation. The book was a lined schoolbook just like the ones she remembered using when she was going through her junior and middle schools. On the front, written in childish joined up script, was the name 'Neil Danes 4B.'

The first few pages had been torn out, judging by the remnants still held in place by the central staples. The juvenile writing on the new first page was the same as on the cover.

dear mummy i love you and I promis to look after you always tara dont love you like i do and daddy dosnt love anybody

i have got you this becos its real gold and it has a picture of you and me in it and when i grow up i will still love you and look after you even when tara gos away

when can i come in your bed and sleep with you again like before and cuddell you like before please dont say no again i will be very quite i promis

love from neil xx

ps dont tel tara

On the next page was a reply.

Darling Neil. I love you too sweetheart very very much. Thank you for the lovely necklace and your lovely letter.

When you are older you will understand that you cannot come into my bed to sleep with me like before. I was asleep that time and I did not hear you come in. When grown ups sleep together and play bed time games together it is alright but only for grown ups.

When you are older you will find another girl to stay with and you can play those games with her.

Lots of love from Mummy. X

The next pages were filled with a series of dates and tiny Xs.
One kiss for every day from 18.03.89 until 02.08.98, when they
abruptly stopped mid-page. Veronica turned to the next one
and shuddered involuntarily.

In thick black printed letters of a much more mature writer
than Neil's first note, made with a marker pen or similar were
the words '*DIE BITCH*' and covering the rest of the page were
drawings of daggers, axes and swords all dripping with red
marker blood.

The rest of the pages were ominously blank until she found
a newspaper cutting stuck to the very last page. She needed to
hold it up to the light to clearly see the small piece as it had
faded badly. The National Enquirer of Tuesday 22 September
1998 read:

> **Marjorie Selma Danes. Much loved mother of
> Neil and Tara. Gone suddenly but now sleeping
> safely. We will be together again one day Mummy.**
>
> **Private Service 3.00 p.m. Monday 28 September
> at St. Marks Crematorium, Bays Road, Auckland.
> No flowers or charitable donations.**

It seemed as emotionless and cold as the departed Marjorie
was at that moment. Knowing Tara as she did already, she could
not imagine her as the author of the short piece. She looked at
the photos once more and the words from the newspaper took
on a darker meaning. 'We will be together again one day Mummy.' They could only have come from Neil.

Veronica took several photos of the book, death notice and
necklace. The inside of the locket revealed a black and white
photograph of a boy sitting on a woman's lap behind a piece of
cut plastic. It made her shudder again.

When she finished, she carefully replaced everything and collected a handful of dust from another room, which she skilfully scattered and placed to conceal any sign of her discovery.

Back at her apartment she threw all her clothes straight into the washer and took a long shower. Feeling only a little cleaner afterwards, she dressed, made herself a strong peppermint tea and then took her laptop through to the lounge.

Before powering it up, she took five minutes to try and put together the pieces of what she had found. Even to her, the facts as they presented themselves appeared incredible. She went through the photos on her camera twice, trying to find another explanation but also trying to contain her excitement and revulsion.

It took a little more electronic searching to find what she was looking for next. "Overdose," the Auckland hospital's database stated. She previously decided to try and hack the site two weeks before as a potential source of useful information about Neil, as he had been such a regular visitor in the past, especially as a child, but not thinking then she would ever be conducting this type of research.

Another valuable lesson Stephen Christopher had taught her was to know as much about things as you can. The computing night classes and acquired knowledge about the frailties of poorly funded databases, as all publicly owned institutions seemed to be, didn't make it easy but also far from impenetrable. She gained access using a viral-mole program perfected after she initially bought it from an associate in London nearly two years before.

Marjorie had taken a lethal amount of her prescribed Hydrocodone medication. Why was not clear. There was no suicide note and nothing other than a supposition by her doctor. It seemed from the hospital entry, she was taking the opiate-based painkiller for some time as prescribed by the doctor for severe headaches and neck pain.

She was dead upon arrival with a paramedic team who rushed her in from home after an emergency 111 call from her son. He was out with friends for the evening and came home to find his mother slumped in a chair. She never regained consciousness.

There was a further note on the information sheet from her GP. "He knew Marjorie was forgetful and also did not like to take tablets as they made her gag. She had previously been taking fifty milligram tablets and only recently started taking the much larger two hundred and fifty milligram tablets so she would not need to take so many at the same time. She may simply have forgotten." As she was seen by the doctor in the previous two weeks before her death, his opinion was seen as the most reliable. The post-mortem determined the cause of death was by overdose, the subsequent inquest delivered an open verdict as the reason could not be definitely ascribed to any single factor.

Veronica could hardly believe her eyes. Could it really have been so easy? Her trained mind in matters of the macabre visualised the scene unfolding over a decade ago.

Neil did not see himself his mother's son but as something altogether more twisted. Something happened when he sneaked into her bed one night as a young boy and from that moment, his sick view of the family set up was forever mutated. Did he just see himself taking the absent father's place, or could it possibly be he regarded himself as the new male lover in her life? Either way, it could not have turned out as he wanted. Tara would not have failed to mention something like that!

What she did say though was her mother had died soon after meeting a new man, the first one since their father walked out years before. It was as obvious as anything could be. After years of festering unrequited and very wrong feelings of love, the ultimate insult of another male presence tipped the balance of Neil's fragile hold on reality.

He even worked for pharmaceutical companies for God's sake!

Veronica was convinced he must have somehow been responsible for her overdose, maybe by substituting her Hydrocodone tablets for larger ones and the unfortunate Marjorie had taken enough to kill an elephant. The pill bottle she found under the floorboard probably contained the larger dose tablets to begin with, hence the obliterated label. To simply substitute them for the ones in his mother's usual bottle was easy.

These new revelations changed everything Veronica had planned or even contemplated before. Her new idea was devastatingly simple.

CHAPTER EIGHTEEN

Apart from the obvious fitness connotations, the greatest part of running was also the biggest failing. It gave Dan time to think.

He had never met anyone like Tara before: smart, sexy, funny, pretty wonderful all the way around, and as far as he could tell, completely genuine. She felt different to all the others, not that there were that many or his opinions on such personal things had necessarily proved right in the past. He could not help but compare her to April, who wounded him the most after they split by publicising what he shared with her in confidence while they were together. He still could not explain to himself the reason for such a detailed and heartfelt emotional release on their very first night together; it was such an alien experience. The closest he could find to an answer was it must have been a test, thinking back he did study Tara's responses as closely as he had watched any fraudster or thief in interview for tell-tale signs.

Therefore as much as he tried to find something wrong, a reason to throw up the barricades again or to hide away, he could not find a single thing to stop the feelings he had towards her. Above all, Tara oozed honesty; surely he could not be so wrong again.

The day before was one of the best he could remember in a very long time. They spent the whole day in each other's company. She said the right things at all the right times, offered advice and importantly chose the moments to say nothing at all. He talked with her at length and in more detail than he had ever spoken with anybody.

In return she gave something of herself to him too, and Dan felt like a bond was forming where none existed before with any previous girlfriend, even though he knew he was still cheating himself by denying the feelings that night in Mapperley still caused. By the end of the day, he could hardly bear to drag himself away from her, and she did not make it any easier with another attempted seduction which could have made Marta Hari blush.

More out of habit, he looked both ways as he crossed the intersection leading to the container port, and for a moment as his attention was on the road, he tried to make himself think of something else. Tried and failed.

In the afternoon, the planned visit to the post office but until then or at least until he finished his run there was just him, the present and the past.

At 3:00 p.m., he walked into the main foyer dressed in a suit and tie and carrying a handful of envelopes for posting; he blended into the throng of other Aucklanders and tourists all there for one of a hundred different reasons. Being natural here meant appearing to have a reason to be there.

He approached a teller at the long counter and made an enquiry about opening a PO Box of his own. "No, it's okay, I've got the form already," he said waving the application document he picked up at another post office on the way. "Whereabouts are the boxes?"

The helpful teller obliged. "We have two sections, against the wall over there," she said, pointing over his shoulder. "Or around that corner and along a corridor to where people can access boxes after hours at the back of the building," she said, pointing again.

"Is it okay to go and have a quick look before I decide?"

"By all means, sir. You can see any of us when you come back."

He was glad and not surprised to see Stenning's box number 1919 was at the back. The boxes in the front foyer obviously would not appeal to her. However, thinking ahead, it was going to be impossible to remain in the rear corridor where the boxes were stacked along one wall and conduct prolonged surveillance. There were simply not enough genuine reasons for anyone to spend more than a few minutes there at any one time, collecting or delivering letters and packages.

He grabbed a mail shot leaflet for office furniture from one of the rubbish bins and stuck it in the opening of box 1919 so it protruded out and then went through the glazed exit and into the large rear car park. He already had an idea of where to go, which might just afford him a view back through the glass. In a matter of highly trained seconds, he established two car park spaces which made the leaflet and the box visible enough for what he needed as well as performing an impromptu reconnoitre of his surroundings and a check for restricted parking signs in the car park; he didn't want to get clamped for being there an over long period of time. The fact he could be there for more than two whole days and may draw attention to it anyway, he couldn't do anything about.

He got the van rental company on the mobile just before they closed and made a booking for early the next morning. He wanted a good night's sleep but believed he was unlikely to get it. Before finally going home, he stopped at his local supermarket where he shopped for two to three days worth of isolation. Dry foods and chocolate; an abysmal diet in normal circumstances but experience dictated their necessity. To complement these rations, he just needed to prepare some cold water and strong, hot coffee in three big thermos flasks at home.

"Hello, my dear man. I missed you today," Tara said softly.

Dan was pleased to receive her call and was enveloped by

a warm glow at the sound of her voice. "Me too, how was your day?"

"Good."

"I nearly got myself run over this morning, concentrating on you instead of where I was going."

She laughed, and he imagined her smiling. "I told you it couldn't be good for you," she said.

"I'm going to be busy for between two and three days from tomorrow morning." He was genuinely sorry. "I've got some work that's going to take twenty-four seven attention."

Tara was silent for just too long, and Dan's stomach tied itself into a knot.

"Hey, please don't get upset or worried or anything. I'll have my mobile with me all the time, and I'll call you. It's nothing to worry about I promise," he said this time sounding desperate.

"Are you sure? I haven't scared you off, have I?"

"No, really no. Tell you what, why don't you come over to my house on Thursday, and I'll tell you what I've been up to the past month or so. I might even get finished earlier and we can do something before."

"Okay, I suppose."

The rest of the conversation was distinctly missing the edge of new romance and when he put the phone down, he wanted to call her straight back and tell her he could cancel everything. Instead, he went to put the kettle on.

The next morning, sleep deprived as he knew he would be by the thoughts of what lay ahead, breakfast consisted of a double dose of Imodium in the hope of limiting the need to have to take a crap. Dan collected the little utility van at 6:15 a.m. and drove into town. If for some reason, both of the preferred car park spaces were already taken, he was disciplined enough to abort the whole thing and try again tomorrow at an even earlier time.

Fortunately his number one space was empty, and he backed the van into it. Before turning the engine off, he jumped over the bench seat into the rear compartment and checked his angles and lines of vision through the tinted window.

"Good enough," he said to himself.

There was nobody about at that time, which was the best news of all, and so he deliberately and expertly arranged the front seat of the van as he wanted before climbing back into the rear and sticking up a sheet of black plastic from the back of the seat to the ceiling.

To complete the essential equipment for his enforced prison of up to two full days and nights, Dan had a small folding camp chair, digital camera, binoculars screwed into a mini tripod, a dictaphone, an extra fully charged battery for his mobile, a large aerosol can of domestic air freshener, a blank pad of A4 and several pens, a new pack of Blu-tac, a small LED light which could be attached to clothing, a change of clothes (tracksuit pants and top), a sleeping bag, the rest of the Imodium pack and his iPod.

Before settling into position, he used extra Blu-tac to secure more of the plastic over the inside of the rear windows too, and then cut a slit in each into which he could push through a camera or binoculars, thus making the best he could of his improvised covert observation post; not perfect, but hopefully adequate for this one-off use. Finally he put the binoculars up through the plastic sheet to the window, focused them in on box 1919 and then used three more blobs of Blu-tac to secure the tripod's feet to the metal floor of the van before positioning the chair.

It did not take long before he was ready. After another few minutes, he was remembering how tedious OP work had sometimes been in the past.

It was still too early to call or text Tara. It was way too early to think about cranking up the iPod or dipping into the supplies, even the coffee.

"Daniel, my boy, what the fuck are you doing this all over again for?" he whispered. At the same time, he could not help thinking about the chance of tasting that adrenaline rush one more time if things did go to plan.

Veronica had a sleepless night too. She didn't like the idea of diverting so radically from all her tried and trusted methods, but still, the opportunity her recent discoveries generated were tantalisingly attractive.

She worked through the night on half a dozen different scenarios, exploring the probable causes and effects of each, trying to plan for all eventualities and working out the wrinkles to make sure when she embarked on the "final play," it would be with complete confidence.

At 6:30 a.m. she went down to the gym and put herself through such a gruelling exercise session that when she was finished she was utterly exhausted. After a quick shower, she went back upstairs, crawled into bed and immediately fell into a deep sleep.

The telephone's ring was like a siren. She could have been asleep for a minute or for hours, and it took several moments for her to gather herself.

"Hello, this is Veronica."

"Hi V. Have I just woken you up?"

"Tara, hi. Um, yes, I had a bit of a late one. What time is it?"

"It's nearly ten. Sorry, I'll call back later."

"No, it's okay; I probably shouldn't sleep all morning anyway. How are you?"

"I'm good. Bored already and I've only been here in the shop for a little while. I thought as I bailed on you the other night, I should catch up. What have you been up to?"

"Working; I *must* get an article finished and so I've been holed up here for the last couple of days. What about you, are things working out with the new man?"

"I think so. Let's get together soon, and I can tell you all about him. He's got to go away for a day or two actually so I'm at a loose end."

"Oh, I see." Veronica laughed. "I've gone from new best friend to stop-gap for Mr. Wonderful in the space of a week. Well I'm not sure I have time in my busy schedule for *old* friends."

"Guilty as charged, have mercy on a poor love-struck girl," Tara pleaded.

"Love! Oh my God. What's he got, the money or the body?"

"Believe it or not, it's the personality," and after a short pause, "the body's not so shabby either. It's funny, I can't put my finger on one particular thing actually, but there is definitely something about him. He's a marathon runner," she added for no reason.

The last thing Veronica needed at the moment was Tara around mooning over some new man. After the initial period of having to get to know her, she was now getting bored with the predictable woman. Time was of the essence if she wanted to get this thing over and done with and move on.

"Sounds interesting, and I could do with an excuse to get out," she said lightly and then a little more resolutely. "No, you temptress, I have to get this story finished before I can go out to play again. Tell you what, give me a day or so to do what I have to do here and then we can have a day or two out somewhere. You tell me all about him then and make me green with envy."

"You haven't told me anything about your work yet, it must be so interesting?" Tara said sounding deflated.

"Sometimes, I love the travel, but writing is a bit lonely."

"Who is this story for?"

Veronica had planned answers for such questions and hoped they would satisfy inquisitive minds. "It's a new publication and all the writers are sworn to secrecy until the launch. I think they are going to have a big do in London or Frankfurt. Listen to me, I have probably breached my contract already."

"Don't worry, I won't tell." Tara laughed.

A customer came into the shop, bringing a quick end to their conversation. Relieved, Veronica set the alarm clock for noon and went back to sleep.

From about 8:30 a.m., there was steady stream of visitors to the wall of PO Boxes. Dan's positioning meant he could sit comfortably in the chair with his head up to the binoculars. It took some time to get used to the odd visual sensation and a longer while for his sixth sense of activity around box 1919 to kick in, allowing him a small degree of relaxation.

This extra ability was one of the reasons he had been such a successful OP operative too. It was an altogether different skill-set to that of a surveillance operative who followed targets around covertly as part of a team. He was one of the rare breed who could do both very well. Usually OPs were manned by two people, one to observe and the other to record the observations; after all, no matter how good any individual is, no one can write and watch simultaneously.

The mix of people attending to their boxes was unexpectedly varied. Business types and shop workers were supplemented by several altogether more shady characters—mostly seedy looking men of a certain age and questionable dress sense. Others included teenagers, elderly women, various members of clergy from at least four different faiths, and most surprising of all, several people he could only describe as vagrants.

Their presence was the antithesis of everything a PO Box stood for and for once he could not think of a single reason why it should be. Naturally he considered crime or dishonesty but that did not lead to coherent explanations. If he had still been in "the job," he would definitely have considered a longer investigation into the matter.

At noon, he drank his first coffee of the day and supplemented it with a muesli bar which he dipped into the drink to make it less of a chore. His eyes were unable to adjust to the simple task of opening the thermos and pouring the drink when he did and yet he still needed to re-focus them again when he went back to the binos seconds later.

It probably took twenty-five seconds altogether—having no view of box during that time was unfortunate, but unavoidable. There was no point in beating himself up about it; it was a scenario which was certain to be repeated over and over again in all likelihood before this tour of duty was finished.

He was pleased the presence of the van had not attracted any attention, so far as his limited view and the lack of conversation outside could tell, and just as happy the van was equipped with a small air vent in the roof which allowed some of the stale air to escape.

3:00 p.m., another coffee and a Mars Bar.

4:00 p.m., water.

4:30 p.m., a long satisfying piss into the juice bottle he brought for that sole purpose, remembering to make sure the lid was screwed back on tightly afterwards. During this light relief he remembered Tara. *How could I have forgotten!* he thought. The power of the work was as all-consuming as it ever was.

He pressed two buttons on his mobile without taking his eyes away. She picked up quickly. He had to say hello twice.

"You sound like you're calling from inside a cave."

"Good observations, you're not too far off the truth actually."

Tara was intrigued. "What *are* you doing?"

"A bit of secret squirrel stuff. Sitting and waiting for someone to turn up."

"Really! Where? Tell me who?"

"If only I knew. It's a bit of a long shot, may well be a complete waste of time, but that's the chance you take doing this."

"What's he done?"

Dan was tempted to tell her but decided against it in case she thought he was a complete lunatic. "Long story as well as a long shot. I'll tell you all about it Thursday. I just wanted to say hi."

"Can I come and play? It sounds much more exciting than sitting in the shop for the rest of the day."

"Sorry, I'm out of bounds now. One of the first rules is that once you're in situ; you don't have visitors or take yourself off for a walk if you get a bit bored. Must be why I was so good at it before; it's the ideal job for someone with no friends and no social life."

"Poor baby, when you put it that way, it doesn't sound so inviting. Are you really going to stay there for two whole days?"

"Yeah, it's all part of the fun. Not like the movies."

"You can say that again. If it's any consolation, you're the second person to have better things to do than see me today. Both of you new friends too, I must be losing my touch."

"Sorry about that. There's nothing wrong with your touch either. You have no idea how tempting the idea of it is right now."

"Why Mr. Calder, are you taking your eyes off the prize after all you've just said to me?"

He started to laugh but forced himself to stop. "No, that's a whole different prize Miss Danes. I better go before this gets out of hand."

"Be careful, call me again anytime."

"I will Tara, maybe tonight."

"Yes please, it's not like I'm doing anything now."

"Alright, see you." He clicked off before she said goodbye and regretted it instantly. Without thinking, he fumbled in the box by his feet for another Mars Bar.

By 8:00 p.m. there had been nothing more of interest at box 1919 than two junk mail deliveries by two different young men depositing identical leaflets into every box along the corridor. The lights had been on all day and showed no sign of having a turn-off time, which was a relief as it made the spotting of any movement easier to see after the sun went down.

When it was dark enough, he took down the plastic sheet so he could see out the tinted window without the need for the binoculars. The change in viewing restrictions made him a lot more comfortable for what was probably going to be a long night.

Though he felt no need to have to do any more than take another leak, when he finished, he swallowed another Imodium capsule anyway with another coffee. His old Thermoses still worked well and the strong caffeine fix was almost as hot as it was first thing.

The assortment of various artists' greatest hits, which had been playing randomly on the iPod for most of the day, did a little to break the monotony; however, by 9:00 p.m., Dan had enough of the music for one day, too. The peanuts and raisins which throughout the day had failed to find their target between packet and mouth, littered the floor around him, and even with the air-vent fully open, the little cell in which he was stuck remained hot and musty.

This was quintessential OP work. For many, it was intolerable and had broken more colleagues than he could count, but in a strange way, the longer it went on the more he enjoyed it. After years of extensive consideration, he came to the conclusion that the pleasure he gained in any positive result from an OP always seemed to magnify exactly in accordance with the length of time he spent doing it.

His record was almost five days, after which he emerged from a small bedroom in a fire-damaged house overlooking a warehouse used for drugs making, resembling a long term Middle East hostage. His eyes were ringed so red that he looked like a demonic circus clown, and he smelled so bad that the rest of his team point blank refused to drive him back to base in any of their cars. He had to take a very unpleasant trip back on a bus, during which he was almost lynched by other passengers so disgusted by his condition and appearance.

Tara sent a text at 11:30 p.m. "u not called r u ok xx"

"sorry busy lost track of time no probs call u in am x" he replied, happy to take his eyes off the window momentarily.

A few minutes later he got another. "miss u take care xx" When the options screen appeared, he pressed save.

Tuesday night became Wednesday morning and Dan started to wonder if two days was going to be enough. Whatever happened, he was not going to spend any longer than that here, but the more he thought about the chances of Stenning coming to check on her box in that time, the more he managed to convince himself that in her position, he might only bother once a week.

At just before two a.m., he was treated to a brief, but entertaining live sex show between a middle aged man and a much younger woman who parked their car on the opposite side of the otherwise empty car park. In the time they stayed, the woman assumed about five different positions on top of, under and head down into the man who incredibly managed to keep his seatbelt on the whole time. As in his working past, Dan could not help but judge their performance—he had been an unseen witness to similar encounters dozens of times. The life and times of a policeman at night were sometimes dull, sometimes repetitive, but you could never ever say you had seen it all.

He awarded them six out of ten for technical ability and seven for artistic impression.

The only other visitors for the remainder of the night were to be a cat and a hedgehog.

CHAPTER NINETEEN

With the treadmill belt whirring steadily beneath her feet, Veronica put the final touches on her intended plan early on Wednesday morning. It sounded right in her head and she could not find a flaw in the scenario she settled on.

She was experiencing a new sensation of excitement which had nothing to do with the exercise. The new Neil Danes project was virgin territory and the novelty of it was giving her the same rush she remembered from the early days of Christopher and Mathews.

Until now, she was sated with the familiarity of repeating her winning formula with each victim. The safety which came from taking as few risks as possible had not undermined the thrill of the chase and ultimately the kill; but now the chase was ascending to a new level and the thrill of it was not satisfied by the old methods.

She just needed a few more days of confirmatory research to be ready to go. This time next week she would have to think about where in the world to go next.

Tara kept her cell phone on the bedside table all night. She woke, disappointed her sleep had not been interrupted. Lying back, she punched in Dan's number and pushed her tangled hair away from her face.

Dan felt the phone vibrate in his shirt pocket and smiled. "Morning sleepyhead."

"Good morning to you. How was your night?"

"Uneventful, unless you like watching other people getting to have sex."

"Yuck! Sounds a bit pervy to me. You've only got yourself to blame for that."

"I know. I could do with a bacon sandwich or a run right at this moment. Either will be equally satisfying."

"So what does a policeman or ex-policeman on stake-out duty *do* all night?"

"Try to stay awake and alert is the main thing, and when you're out of practice like I am, that's a lot easier said than done." He ran through the events of the night, taking some pleasure in Tara's mewing at his description of the vehicular lovers. "Keeping the seatbelt on was a first for me though. Now that's what I call safe sex."

She laughed out loud. "Police humour. I've heard about it but never experienced it. You must have enjoyed some really fun times."

"Oh yeah, remind me to tell you a few stories one day. What are you up to today? Shop?"

"Yes. I'm going to have a moving around day. I get bored of looking at the same things in the same places every day, so I'll just move a few racks around to make it a bit different. I'm not sure if it has any affect on the customers, but at least it will pass some time."

"If nothing happens here today, I'll be leaving this time tomorrow. I'll need to return the van, get cleaned up and sleep, but I should be human again by the middle of the afternoon. Do you still feel like to coming over? Maybe when you finish work."

"You can come over to me in the morning, shower and sleep here."

"No, seriously, you don't want me in your house after a couple of days of this."

"Alright, how about I make something special to bring over for dinner?"

"That sounds like a perfect idea."

"Okay then, it'll give me something to do tonight. Will you call me later?"

"Definitely."

"Right, please make sure you take care."

"Don't worry, everything's fine, I'll call you later."

This time he waited for Tara to exchange goodbye twice before he hung up. The whole conversation had taken place with his eyes glued to the binoculars, but he quickly snatched a glance at the phone to check. There was still plenty of battery power indicated, so he put it back in his pocket.

Hearing her voice made him feel good. Involuntarily he let his mind wander away from the glass door and small metal box twenty or so yards away. He sometimes thought about the whole looking for love issue, whether or not it could happen again for him, or if he was too damaged to trust his feelings to another woman. April had taken his heart and stomped all over it. He was not the forgive-and-forget type and various other innocents suffered because of this inflexibility, which made the sensations he was feeling about Tara all the more inexplicable.

If he did tell her *everything* and that meant Mapperley, it could ruin a future he was not even sure they may have yet. But how could he tell her what he could not remember or be sure of himself?

Suddenly remembering where he was, Dan berated himself for his lapse in concentration; how long had it been? It didn't matter, too long was the answer. He decided on another coffee which he poured without looking away.

Veronica breezed through the rest of the morning doing nothing more strenuous than making green tea and toast and watching an old movie on TV.

At 12:45 p.m. and now casually dressed in jeans and a light sweater, she was ready to go out on the short collection run. She wandered downstairs onto the street and headed off on foot, in her handbag were the essentials for completing the task.

By 1:00 p.m. Dan had watched the array of PO Box holders come and go for thirty hours give or take a few minutes. The mundane nature of the exercise made it seem a lot longer. He learned nothing up to this point other than the amount of waste paper produced in Auckland was ridiculous. A lot of people opened their mail there, dumping the envelopes and unwanted correspondence rather than taking it away. Huge amounts of junk mail also went into the rubbish bins; most of it not even looked at. *The producers of this stuff should seriously do some sort of research to see if they were just wasting their time and money,* he thought.

Lunchtime seemed to be a busy time to collect from the boxes, and he had not been short of people to watch. Fat, thin, short, tall, young, old—but box 1919 remained untouched.

Reaching her destination, Veronica looked up and down the street deciding whether to approach from the front or the back. There were enough people in the area doing whatever people do during a weekday lunchtime for her not to obviously stand out, but she was far too good to take it, or anything else, for granted. She waited patiently, making sure there was not a policeman, ambulance or other unforeseen presence there attending an emergency or other unnatural visitor; only when she was satisfied, having walked around the stand-alone building noting all was well, did she finally decide on the main street entrance.

Despite being in an OP for prolonged periods of time, it was usually the case that it still surprised you when what you were waiting for actually happened. One of those oxymoronic things cops knew but could never explain.

Even though he was watching the box as he had been since the previous morning, the sight of a hand with a key reaching for the lock and opening 1919 made Dan jump.

He always tried to keep an open mind on these things, but he did really expect any visitor to come in through the car park where he was. This person had obviously walked through from the front of the post office and down the corridor.

It was a she, from the figure and the hair, he was sure of that.

In the next few seconds a number of things happened. Rehearsing in your mind helps, years of experience helps even more, but each time it comes to doing it for real, it hardly ever goes just as you planned.

Dan ripped down the plastic sheet from the window and grabbed his camera. He rattled off a number of shots with no idea if the pictures would come out properly through the tinted glass. He then sprayed himself from head to toe with air freshener and pulled on the spare tracksuit pants and hoodie over the clothes he was already wearing before spraying himself all over again.

During all this, he never took his eyes off the back of the female who was currently answering his prayers by dumping an array of junk mail into a wheelie bin—and by the look of things, not rushing for an exit.

"Come out this way, for fuck's sake, come on," he pleaded as he shovelled his feet into training shoes which were already very loosely laced for just this event.

With her back partly to him, Dan could not see everything she was doing with any degree of certainty, but he was sure she did have at least some mail from the box which had not gone straight into the waste bin.

He stood as best he could, hunching in the confines of the van, and tried to stretch his legs. They protested and he groaned with the discomfort.

"Fuck this, never again," he chided himself. Nevertheless he was ready.

As he sprayed himself for the third time, the woman turned and walked towards the rear exit and the car park. It was his first proper look at her. Five feet eight to ten, proportionate build for her height, short mid to dark brown hair with lighter highlights tied back, good tanned complexion, no glasses. She wore faded blue jeans, a loose-fitting, round-collared, long sleeved top and white casual flat shoes.

The face, he studied the face. Oval with good jaw and cheeks, eyes wider apart than normal but only very slightly, small nose, full lips and no make-up as far as he could tell.

"Like who? Like who?" he said more loudly than necessary. It was another of his golden rules regarding any good description; what does he, she, or it look like? Ask ten people to remember something red and you will get ten different shades; but tell them it's red like a London bus and you have instant consensus. She looked like Julie Andrews playing Maria in *The Sound of Music* but with slightly longer hair. There was no time to take another photo as she was already outside and almost out of his view. She was carrying a small handbag on a strap over her shoulder, no sign of the mail she just collected and importantly, no sign of car keys either.

Dan grabbed the sports holdall he brought all his things in and opened the back door of the van. Estimating her position from the speed and direction she took from the back door, he counted to five slowly and then got out.

The sun almost blinded him and he wished he had remembered to bring sunglasses or a baseball cap. He ached all over, but there was no time to do anything about it.

She was approaching the street with no sign yet of going left or right. Dan slung the holdall over his shoulder and moved off. He hoped the look of 'just come from the gym' was passable. One time in the past after a long stint in an OP, he was blown out within five minutes by a target he followed because of his smell. The air freshener trick worked a lot better than regular deodorants in these circumstances, but you could never fully mask the stink of stale human being, so the gym goer routine gave a reason for its presence.

He desperately hoped for her not to hop into a car and drive off up the road because it was likely he could not get back to the van in time to see where she went and initiate a follow. When she got to the street, she turned right and he temporarily lost her from sight as he made up the ground. She was still there, no hint of being in a rush and no signs of any anti-surveillance tactics. She crossed the road a bit further along and Dan paralleled her, continuing on the same side as before thirty metres behind, a good angle to observe and not be observed.

There were not too many other people around in the small side street, but he knew that was going to change when they reached the main road. As she got within twenty metres of the junction, he increased his pace and started to cross over, closing the gap. She turned left; when he did the same, he was no more than ten metres behind her.

Dan kept to the outside of the pavement, focused on her pony-tail and shoulder strap. Halfway up Queen Street, she passed through the main entrance of the Whitcoulls book store. He was not sure if there were any other exits. If he had been sure there were not, he may have considered waiting outside, but with the objectives he set himself and that uncertainty, he followed her in.

She was on the escalator heading up to the first floor. Non-fiction, Travel, History and Café, the sign hanging from the ceiling read. Dan waited until she was stepping off at the top, then got on himself and started to ascend. Before he got to the top, he checked his holdall—camera, dictaphone, thermos, paper and pens.

The woman was in the queue at the café, which consisted of the counter topped with the food and drinks displays and dispensers, and about twenty assorted tables and chairs spread out in an area about eight square metres.

There was a decision to make now. Of all the rules of surveillance, there was one more shiny and golden than all the others, which also happened to be the one which could not be taught; you either had it or you didn't. It separated the good from the great and had brought him borderline legendary status in his time in the police.

It was also his favourite lesson to teach at the training centres. "We have talked about behaving naturally in an unnatural environment, but the objective is to gather information and sometimes the only way to do that is to get close, very close. Close enough to hear a phone conversation in a crowded pub or see the number of a fake credit card placed on the counter to buy a Rolex.

"How we do that is by having the balls and the ability to be seen but not noticed."

By the time she was next in line to place her order, Dan was by her side, looking at the selection of paninis and muffins in a glass display cabinet. The holdall was on his left shoulder furthest away from her; concealed in his right hand was the dictaphone.

"Hi, what can I get you?" the girl behind the counter asked.

"Can I have a regular decaf latte and a choc-chip cookie please?" The first words he heard her speak.

"Sure, have here or takeaway?"

"Have here."

"That's six dollars fifty, please."

She already had her purse out of her bag. When she opened it Dan saw the tops of several plastic cards in the compartments designed for them. One was a BNZ bank card and another Fly-buys reward card. There was also a receipt from Hallensteins, a men's clothes shop chain, just visible sticking out from the cash compartment.

She took a ten-dollar note out and handed it over.

"Okay, take a seat and I'll bring it over."

"Thanks."

After receiving her change, she went to sit down on one of two armchairs with a small round table between them, in the middle of the seating area.

When she moved away, Dan ordered a large black coffee in a take-away cup. He put the dictaphone in the hood of his top before he left the counter and chose the seat behind the woman so they were back to back less than a metre apart.

Trying to assimilate information as it was coming in was never a good idea. If you were not concentrating on what was happening, you were more likely to miss the next thing and that could be the single piece of evidence which gets you the conviction.

She was reading a fashion magazine from one of the café's selection when he took his seat, her handbag was on the floor at her feet; closed.

He felt he had time to think.

Okay what do I have so far? She talks like a New Zealander; too much to hope I would recognise a British accent.

He racked his brain trying to remember what Vikki Stenning looked like and sounded like. He visualised Heidi's grainy photo of Valerie. Was it her, was he sat right next to her all these years later? Was he centimetres away from a cold-blooded murderer?

He could not remember, did not want to guess and tried not to hope.

His coffee arrived first. He took the pad of paper and a pen out of his bag and started to write the passage he still had memorised from years before. For obvious reasons he did not want to write anything related to what he was doing in case she turned around and saw, and he did not want to sit doing nothing which might also draw unwanted attention. It also gave him the opportunity to record anything really important if it did happen.

His old friend Nick used to do crossword puzzles in circumstances like these. He could doodle round the edges of the page, fill in answers and sit for ages ostensibly thinking without having to write or do too much else, but still be ready to make evidential notes if required. Every good operative had one and sometimes more, a favourite, a default or fall-back with which they felt comfortable in the most uncomfortable times and places.

There were no mirrors or reflective surfaces he could utilise to watch as well as listen but that was okay, he knew what to do if the need arose to get a view.

The woman's order arrived with a short apology for the delay. "That's alright, thanks," she said. Dan hoped the dictaphone would pick up her voice from inside his hood as it had in the past.

He could feel and sense her move and heard the sound of her handbag being placed on her lap, and then the zip of an opening. He picked up his coffee and went over to the counter where the condiments were arranged in chrome cubes. While he selected two sachets of raw sugar and slowly poured the contents into his cup, he saw the woman remove envelopes from her bag and then another larger one which was folded in half to fit. As he walked back towards his seat stirring his cup, she opened up the larger envelope and put the other smaller ones inside. It was done too quickly for him to possibly see what names and addresses were written on them before they disappeared from view.

By the time he was back at his seat, she still had the large envelope on her lap. Picking up his own bag for a spurious reason gave him the precious time he needed to look over her shoulder before sitting back down in his chair.

White, A4, already stamped and writing on it; a name and address, frustratingly it was partly obscured by her left hand.

When he sat, he turned over the top leaf of his pad and wrote what he had seen before flipping back to his poem.

orner
tment 6
an Lane
uckland

Another ten minutes passed, she drank her coffee, ate her cookie and continued to read her magazine in that time. Dan slowly continued to compose his poem until it filled the page. At this point, he decided to pre-empt her next move, take a chance on missing something by getting a step ahead for the next part of the game.

He got up and moved away so as to be ready for her when she left and not be a person who followed her in and then followed her out when she departed.

When she appeared on the downward escalator and left the shop, Dan was outside; ahead and waiting, it used to be called.

She set off in a continuance of the direction from before, leisurely taking her time to look in a few shop windows as she went. He was certain this was no attempt to use the reflections in the glass because her angles were all wrong to look back in the direction she came from.

The crowded street offered protection, and he was able to remain within ten metres, constantly looking ahead of her to see what hazards to 'the follow' she may be approaching. What he didn't notice was the red, white and grey mail-box cemented into the pavement until it was too late. By the time he realised what was happening, she had taken the large envelope out of her bag and pushed it into the narrow slit.

It was an opportunity missed to get another look at the name and address.

Angry with himself, Dan resolved not to screw-up again.

One hundred metres further on, the woman approached the Britomart train terminus at the bottom of Queen Street, which he knew incorporated several entrances and exits. As well as the two platforms below the entrance level, the large stone building was surrounded by bus stops and also several taxi ranks which gave her numerous options and him a potential problem.

After spending time close to her in the café, Dan was now conscious of burning himself without a change of some description, and so by the time she entered the terminus building, he had settled on a plan of action.

The instant she was inside and out of sight, he pulled off his hoodie complete with dictaphone which was still running, removed his trackpants as fast as he could and stuffed them into the holdall. Strange looks from some passers-by could not be helped; he was being driven by the risk against reward balance.

Dan scanned the terminus lobby after entering through the same doors she did; she was still walking towards the platforms but stopped to look at one of the small shop cubicles as he spotted her.

He ran across to the ticket office. It was always quicker to buy from a person rather than try to work out the self-serve machines and running in a train station was a normal activity.

Watching the woman, he said to the middle aged man behind the security grilled counter, "One day travel-pass for the whole city please?" It was the one sentence you could say in any place in the whole English speaking world with a train system and be universally understood. He paid in cash and was on the move again before the woman finished her browsing. There was one more thing to do before he was ready to travel.

It took three rubbish bins before he found what he was looking for. The plastic carrier bag he recovered from it had an empty sushi meal in the bottom which he did not bother to remove before he rammed his holdall as far into it as he could.

Since getting to the terminus, he changed his appearance and managed to conceal the holdall as well as obtaining a ticket that allowed him unlimited travel. He was really enjoying the afternoon now.

The woman took her time going down the wide staircase to the platforms; she seemed not to have a care in the world. She walked across to platform two, looked up at a large digital display, then checked her gold watch before sitting on one of the metal bench seats dividing the platforms.

Dan went to platform one and waited.

With the arrival of the next train imminent, there was an automatic announcement over the tannoy which caused the woman to check her watch again. A good sign he thought. Sure enough the next train to arrive at platform two caused her to pick up her handbag and stand.

When she was aboard, Dan went to the door behind where she got on. The seats behind where he could see her sitting were already occupied. As there was little chance of being able to overhear anything from the next nearest seat available, he took another one at the rear of the carriage where he had a clear view and put his new carrier bag on the floor; settling for observation with minimum risk of compromise.

The train moved off promptly, another announcement gave the final destination as Onehunga via Newmarket, Remuera, Greenlane, Ellerslie, Penrose and Te Papa.

Newmarket, Remuera and Greenlane stations came and went without incident but as the train pulled into Ellerslie the woman got up with several other passengers and headed for the door. Dan waited again until she was walking away before he got off.

She walked the short distance out of the station and through the underpass below the motorway into the small suburb of Ellerslie. She seemed to be walking with purpose, sure of where she was going.

Dan paralleled again.

Courtland Street was a short and quiet residential road. Older style houses on both sides of a tarmac and concrete patchwork strip. Cars were parked on the street as well as in driveways, giving him a modicum of cover.

The woman stopped at the gate of number twenty-six and checked her watch again. Seemingly satisfied with the time, she walked up the path and knocked on the front door. After a moment, it opened but Dan could not see who the occupant was. The woman said something to the occupant and went inside, closing the door behind her. The time was 3:08 p.m.

Dan's options were very limited. He didn't have any props he could use to give him a reason to remain in the street for any length of time. There was no cover affording a view of the house and there were still several hours of daylight remaining.

Rather than take any unnecessary risks, he double checked the house number and headed back to the train station. On the way, he called Tara.

"Good news. I've got finished early, and I'll be home by six."

"Want to come over?" she asked. "I'll be home by six thirty."

"Shall I bring wine?"

"Mm, good idea. Has today been worthwhile? You sound happy, like a little boy."

"It's been good; tell you all about it later when I'm clean."

"Alright then, see you Dan."

"Bye."

It had been a good day, a very good day. He was already mentally reviewing the information as he reached the station.

The woman could have fit his memory and the descriptions he had of Stenning. If she was, the use of a New Zealand accent was a very accomplished touch.

What did trouble him were two things: First, the re-posting of the envelopes she collected from the post office box. Very clever as a method of concealing a final destination, but was it really necessary? Even to the most careful criminal that was caution to the 'nth degree but conversely Stenning had not become as successful as she was without taking the utmost care.

Secondly, the BNZ bank card and the Flybuys card. Valerie Stenning had not banked thousands of pounds worth of cheques; she avoided banks; so why have a bank account here? Similarly the Flybuys reward card used to acquire points with purchases made no sense other than to build an identity and blend in.

He would have to do a lot more work on the information gathered so far before he could be sure one way or another.

Veronica had a successful afternoon too. In the end she decided it made no difference if she went in the front way or the back way to the old Danes house, so she walked in through the open front gate, which hung like a broken limb on one remaining hinge.

Possession of Neil Danes' hidden secrets was now essential; after quickly checking there were no other trespassers in the house she went straight to the bedroom to retrieve the book, pill bottle and necklace.

She was back in her apartment in less than an hour.

CHAPTER TWENTY

"You look like the cat that got the cream," Tara said after a long kiss with Dan at her front door.

"Meow." He grinned.

"I want to know everything. Pour us a glass of wine and you can start while I finish cooking. We are having confit duck."

"Are you sure?" he was not used to his working life being of such interest to a non-police person.

"You are kidding? The more I find out about you the more interesting it gets; plus it is a bit of a turn on," she confessed.

Dan needed a few minutes to relax back into a normal environment. "Tell you what. I want to hear about your day first while I sit here, then I'll tell you."

"Okay, well the shop wasn't too bad today. I'm not sure if I mentioned it before but the girl in the next door shoe shop is pretty keen for us to do something together so we had a director's meeting."

"A what?"

"Alright we went out for lunch to discuss it." She giggled. "I think it could be good, she likes the shop side of things and I like the shopping. What do you think?"

"Sounds like a match made in heaven."

"We need to sit down and hammer out some details but it could be good, great in fact. Right enough about me; please tell me everything."

Veronica waited until 8:00 p.m. before making the call. She did not need a script; she was sure to command his full attention.

Neil Danes picked up after several rings, dragging himself from the chair in front of the TV. "Hello," he said quietly, nervousness already present.

"Hello Neil."

"Who is this?"

"That really is not important," the voice in his ear said. He wasn't sure if it was male or female.

He tried and failed to sound authoritative. "If you don't tell me, I'm going to hang up."

"Go and look at your emails, I'll call you back in five minutes. You will answer before the phone rings twice, or the next ring you hear will be the police at your doorbell."

The phone went dead.

He stared at the handset for a moment, processing what had just happened. He was scared, did not know why, but knew he was right to be. His computer was in the next room.

When the phone rang exactly five minutes later, he picked it up before the first ring ended.

"It seems we have an understanding already, Neil. That's very good," the voice said.

"What do you want?" said Danes in a terrified whisper.

"I want you to listen very carefully and do exactly what I tell you to do. Is that clear Neil?"

"Yes," he replied after a short pause. He appeared beaten already.

His newest email was from v.stenning@theagency.org. He remembered the previous exchange he had with the address; this latest email was only sent about twenty minutes before the first phone call.

In the subject box it read, "Open the attachment Neil." There was no text in the message box.

When he did open the attachment, the screen was filled with a series of photos he recognised instantly. He whimpered and almost pissed himself.

"Did you watch your mother die, Neil, or did you really go out with your friends?"

"Please. Oh Jesus, please." He was like the little boy inside the locket; it was one of the pictures filling his screen taken from several angles, as were the book and the medicine bottle.

"I think you were probably there Neil, watching, maybe even touching. Out with friends? I doubt that very much."

He started to cry.

"Stop that now," the voice snapped. "Neil, you killed your mother and now you are going to pay for it. To be exact, you are going to pay me some of your lottery winnings for what you did to her and then do you know what you are going to do?"

"What?" he sniffled.

"Nothing, Neil. After you pay me you are going to do absolutely nothing other than live the rest of your miserable life with the knowledge that if you ever say a word to anyone, I will let the police know how you poisoned her with Hydrocodone and what you did to her in her bed that night when you were a little boy."

"Oh, Jesus."

"No Neil, not even Jesus is going to help you, nor Tara or your friends at Coping with Grief."

He started crying again like a wounded dog.

"Do we still have an understanding, Neil?"

His reply was barely audible. "What choice do I have? I'll have to see how much there is in the bank."

Veronica smiled. "You have three point seven two million dollars. That's three million, seven hundred and twenty thousand dollars and some change in your ASB Gold account. With interest, that will have gone up by another thousand by the morning."

"But ..." was all Danes could manage.

"I am not the type of person to play games; I thought even you might have seen that by now. Are you ready for me to tell you what to do?"

"Like I said, what other choice is there?"

"Quite. Get a pen and write down what I say." When he came back on the line, she continued. "The following is a bank account number and references. At eleven p.m. tonight, you will go online and conduct an international transfer of two million, three hundred thousand dollars to that number. Do you understand?"

"No," he replied. "Why don't you just take it all?"

"I can't transfer it because I cannot access your password, not yet anyway, and I see no reason to have to wait any longer. If I left you with nothing, it wouldn't take long for you to get yourself in so much trouble, people would start to ask questions. This way you will still have plenty to keep you in your squalid little way of life. Now write this down: BIC Code BNRSRYKY, Account 801 354 5684, Beneficiary account name W.S., Beneficiary account number 440 045773504 02." Veronica repeated the numbers a second time, and then got Danes to repeat them back to her.

"Now listen very carefully, Neil, because the next part is extremely important and you really do not want to get it wrong."

"I'm listening." Even as he said it, he wished he was not.

"If you deviate from my instructions in any way, it will have the severest of consequences for you and for your darling Tara. Am I making myself clear Neil?"

"No, I promise," he begged. "Don't hurt her, not her."

"Well that will be entirely up to you. Tonight at eleven p.m. exactly, not a minute before or after. Use the clock on your computer, I will be watching too. You will not use your computer again after completing the transfer until this time tomorrow. You will not make or answer any other phone calls until this time tomorrow. You will not speak to another person until this time tomorrow, and of course I don't need to remind you, if you ever say a word about our little discussion and agreement ..."

"What if I can't transfer that amount in one go?" Danes interrupted.

"Do you really imagine I have left that to chance?" Veronica snapped.

His silence was her reply.

She mellowed. "Now Neil, as we have no secrets between us, tell me, just how did your mother get to overdose?"

Neil gagged and held back the sick which threatened to overwhelm him. "What! You cannot be serious?" It was the only moment in the time they had been talking that he showed any strength whatsoever. Unfortunately for him, Veronica was stronger.

"Answer me Neil, or Tara will suffer more pain than you can imagine," she hissed.

"Alright, alright; I was able to get the maximum strength Hydrocodone from the lab where I was working. One thousand milligrams are used for pharmaceutical testing and also have industrial uses. The week before I replaced her new tablets with the old fifty milligram ones and of course after a few days she was in a lot of pain as she was taking less than a quarter of what she needed; I put the thousand milligram ones in when she asked if she should take more. She thought they were the two fifty's, she took eight of them in a few hours."

"I'm impressed Neil, I've always found that simple is often the best approach too; very well, go back to your movie and make sure you don't fall asleep and miss your appointment." She clicked off the phone again, leaving Neil Danes clinging to a disconnected handset for the second time that evening.

Dan was telling Tara about the day he'd had. He saw no reason not to share what he was doing with her, and she was genuinely interested. Another benefit was while talking freely about this, he could avoid divulging more personal details which he was still unable to bring himself to open up to her about.

"So you knew or at least hoped she could turn up, and you were going to follow her?"

"Hoped for sure, you can never really tell what's going to happen."

"You should be telling Shelley this as well. I think she would make a good cop. It must be really exciting."

"Today was good because I *did* get to follow her too. Normally the person in the OP has to stay where they are and miss out on the fun part while others do the following. Can you imagine thirty hours of zip happening and then nothing to show for it at the end? That's a very usual situation; it's just days like today make all the others worthwhile."

"So what happened then?" Tara asked.

"We went for a walk and an afternoon coffee."

Tara smiled and shook her head. "What?"

"She collected the mail and went to Whitcoulls in Queen Street, the café upstairs; she went in and had a latte and a chocolate biscuit. All she did while she was there was read a magazine, but then she did do something a bit odd."

"Ooh. Tell me."

"She took the letters from the post office box and put them in another bigger envelope which she posted in another mailbox when she left. What do you make of that?"

"What did she do that for? Oh I get it, post it on to yourself at another address, the home address; that way you're the only person who knows where you live. How do some people think of these things?"

"Hey, there is no limit to how devious some people can be," Dan assured her. "I got to see in her purse as well. A BNZ card, a Flybuys card and a Hallensteins receipt ..." he let the sentence hang.

Tara thought but obviously drew a blank. "So?"

"Think about it, dangerous female criminal with murder on her mind in Auckland; likely to be moving on very soon after completing her task. If it was you what reason is there for you to be buying clothes in a menswear shop or bother to get yourself a Flybuys card?"

"What if she needs to get some men's things to help with her plan?" Tara asked.

"Possible, I grant you. Perhaps it's because I know her a bit, you know, how she thinks. It just doesn't sound quite right to me. And the Flybuys card, it's all just too much."

"Okay, what happened next?"

"She took the train from Britomart to Ellerslie, Courtland Street. When she knocked the door, someone answered and she went in. I couldn't safely hang around so that's when I decided to stop; and then I called you."

"You still haven't told me how all this started."

"It's a long story. I actually met her briefly once before when I worked in Garstone. She was pretending to be a newspaper reporter—no, she *was* a newspaper reporter for the purposes of killing someone for money. A freak coincidence here a month ago, and she appears again. Now I'm trying to find her."

"Then what?" said Tara, with rising excitement in her voice. Dan noted the open question; when drawing more and more information out of any suspect, it was a valuable trait to have.

"I've been thinking about that a lot recently. I started all this because I was feeling pretty depressed before I discovered she was in Auckland—that was before I met you—and I needed something, a sense of purpose maybe, I don't know; call it pathetic male syndrome. The last week with you has changed all that, I feel good with you, unbelievable in fact. But I still have to stop her."

Tara put her wine glass down and came to him, wrapping her arms around his neck.

Dan's face was serious. "So I'm going to the police tomorrow. With the information I have, they should be able to locate her somehow, and they'll be able to liaise with the police in England too. Then I'll be able to concentrate on what's important to me now."

Veronica's opinions of Neil Danes placed him somewhere below single-cell pond scum. He was a snivelling waste of oxygen and did not have a redeeming feature save that of caring for his sister.

Unfortunately for Veronica, he was about to prove her wrong about that matter.

It was just after 9:30 p.m., an hour and a half until he was due to make the money transfer. When he finally put the phone down after the voice terminated the call, his first act was to be violently sick on the kitchen floor. His mind spun uncontrollably. It felt like a horrendous dream, but the vision on his computer screen still displaying the graphic evidence convinced him otherwise.

He was sure the owner of the voice would not leave him alone, even if he did send the money. He didn't care about the money anyway, he never had.

He continued to blubber, slowly regaining some control, and as he did, he came to a decision.

It was too late to call Toby, and he could not possibly tell Tara. Neil went to his bedroom and picked up his computer satchel with the photo albums inside. Although it was cool outside, he did not think to put a jacket on as he left the house.

His walk took him along residential streets, which then gave way to a mixture of shops and offices. He was oblivious to everything and everybody around him; the chill wind brought his flesh out in goose bumps, yet he was sweating profusely too, and the combination made him shiver and shake like an alcoholic. His mother was dead, Tara would never understand; by the time he reached the Newton Gully Bridge, he had no coherent thoughts or feelings left in his entire body. The loud hum of traffic all around and below was no more than a background whisper, which was being overwhelmed by a pounding in his head he just wanted to stop and any cost.

Without pausing, he climbed up and over the security barrier, made awkward with the satchel dangling by his side before straightening up on the top. In one seamless movement, he wiped the snot from his nose with the back of a hand, clutched his precious satchel tight and took his last step into the air a hundred metres above the southern motorway. When his last journey was over, Neil was spread across the hard shoulder and first lane of the northern carriageway with dozens of old photographs fluttering around his crushed body, but at least the pounding in his head had ceased.

Tara rolled off the top of Dan and wiped some sweaty hair away from her face. "Did you really mean it when you said you loved me a little bit already the other day? How does that even work?"

"Of course. Feelings are the strangest things, they can make you do things you shouldn't and stop you from doing others that you should. They can make good people turn bad and vice versa. I'm an expert in criminals' thoughts and feelings, but it has also made me very aware of my own.

"I felt something that first night. I decided some time ago that I can't be a bullshitter; I mean I prefer to tell people exactly what I think rather than keep quiet or dress it up in a fancy way that won't offend. What's the point of that if you are offended? I have to say though it's not a universally approved method, and I have managed to piss a serious number of people off in my time."

"I'm not surprised. So diplomacy and tact are not in your vocabulary then?"

"Sorry, no."

"I love you a bit too." She grinned.

"How does it feel to say it to someone you hardly know?"

"Liberating and real." She kissed his chest and laid her face against it.

The landline phone rang in the living room. "Be right back," she said.

Dan watched her naked body pad into the other room. He propped up a pillow and sat up with his back against the headboard. He could hear her talking but not what she was saying.

When Tara reappeared in the doorway, she was clutching the phone against her chest.

"That was the police. It's my brother."

CHAPTER TWENTY-ONE

Veronica watched the screen as 11:00 p.m. approached. Her latest screen sharing application, which she took delivery of after the Jacobs project, meant her computer was linked in to Neil Danes' so she could piggyback his activity, to make sure he logged into the bank's website on time.

10:59 became 11:00 in the bottom right of the screen. 11:00 became 11:01 then 11:02; Danes' computer remained in hibernation mode.

She was furious, he had disobeyed her instructions. Veronica was used to things going as she planned them.

When he did not answer the phone, she considered maybe everything was somehow okay, and he was now following her orders not to answer, but when she double checked the computer again and found it still the same state, her fury made a little room inside for apprehension. She telephoned his number again. It rang unanswered until she hung up.

Something was wrong.

Tara and Dan arrived at the city hospital with many more questions than answers. The uniformed receptionist made three calls before she was able to tell them, "Take a seat; somebody will be through to see you as soon as they can, it won't be long."

"What do you think it can be?" Tara asked again as she did several times in the car.

Dan had no better idea but knew it was far more likely to be bad news than good. "Who knows, but it might be an idea to at least brace yourself for what it may be," was the most diplomatic response he could muster.

A policewoman arrived at the reception desk and looked over towards them when the receptionist indicated. She tried to smile, but it was a vain attempt.

"Miss Danes, Tara Danes?"

"Yes," Tara replied.

"I'm Constable Julie Lambert. Do you have a brother called Neil?"

"We are twins."

"Tara, I'm so sorry, but it appears Neil committed suicide earlier this evening. He was brought into the hospital a little while ago, but there was nothing anybody could do."

Dan remembered being in this position many times, delivering bad news to friends and relatives of a deceased. Tara's reaction could be anything.

She was quiet, no immediate tears, no questions or baleful looks. She sat with both hands clasped in her lap, eyes on the floor.

"Can you tell us what happened?" Dan asked.

"There were a couple of witnesses who saw him on top of Newton Gully Bridge. It looks like he jumped. Tara, can you tell me if he has been upset recently; or if you think he may have wanted to hurt himself?"

Tara looked up with a wistful smile. "Neil's been unhappy his whole adult life."

"So this isn't altogether a surprise?"

Her mouth quivered at the corners. "No."

"You obviously have very good reason to believe it is him, but is there any chance it isn't?" Dan asked.

"Sorry, no, he had his wallet in his jeans pocket, driver's licence and some other things including a photo which looks like you and him as teenagers with an older lady."

"Our mother," Tara said. "I've got the same photo in my wallet."

"I'll need to get an identification from you; do you feel up to it now?" the officer asked.

The mortuary was like being inside a giant igloo, white and cold. Even the large tiles on the wall looked like big blocks of frozen snow. Neil's body lay under a green cotton sheet on a steel stretcher that had been wheeled into the middle of the room.

When Tara was ready the attendant pulled back the sheet. A large crack in his skull gave his whole head a gruesome appearance and a distorted, comical hairstyle.

"Can you confirm this is your brother Neil?" Julie Lambert asked.

"I hope you're happy now," Tara replied to her brother's lifeless body. "At least you are safe."

Dan stood at Tara's shoulder. His concerns were only for her; after all, he never met Neil, but he could not help looking down inquisitively at the cold figure on the stretcher. He was surprised at the family resemblance, even though he was fully aware of them being twins. Seeing one alive and one dead together was a first for him.

Neil's upper body and face were covered once more, and they were led from the room into another ante-room with comfortable chairs and a table, where Tara answered more of the officer's questions.

As they were leaving some time later, Dan said, "They'll have to do a post mortem because of the way he died. I expect you will have two to three days to make some arrangements. We can do it together if you want."

Tara smiled wanly but said nothing. She was quiet all the way home—which was fine with Dan; anything she wanted to do would be okay.

Once inside the house and they were seated in the lounge, Dan asked, "I'm here for you, but if you prefer I go, you only have to say."

Tara looked exhausted. "I always used to say to him that if he didn't try to help himself something like this could happen. We might be twins, but we are so different."

Dan did not point out her use of the present tense. "Don't try and think what your feelings should be, if you want to be sad or angry or whatever; just do it. Do you want coffee, alcohol, anything?"

"No, just stay with me please."

"Sure, as long as you want. Forever if you want."

Over the next few hours, she talked in small chunks. Childhood memories, arguments they had, concerns she held about Neil's mental state, regrets she had not done more.

She fell asleep, finally, in Dan's embrace on the lounge sofa. He remained awake, deep in thought, in case she woke and needed him.

For the rest of the night, Veronica's rage and mounting concern prevented her from thinking about sleep.

She called Danes' landline one more time and also checked the computer once more at 3:00 a.m., even though she knew what the result was going to be.

She tried to imagine what he had done. Called the police? No, impossible. Contacted Tara? Maybe, but she just could not make herself believe it. Contacted somebody else? Again, maybe, but she could not think who or how. Her last possibility made the most sense. Nothing, he was still there in his lonely house crying his eyes out and too paralysed by fear to function.

When she convinced herself that whatever he had done, she was still in a strong, safe position, she relaxed a little and decided to wait until the morning to make contact again. It seemed he required an extra incentive, and she had just the thing in mind.

CHAPTER TWENTY-TWO

Dawn and reality arrived together for Tara. She woke with the first rays of the sun coming through the window, still wrapped in Dan's arms and instantly remembered why they were there and what happened the night before.

She was engulfed in sadness again and started to cry silent tears.

Dan felt the drops like acid on his arm and just squeezed her a fraction tighter, an assurance he was there was all he could offer. He had not slept.

When she was able, Tara said, "I need a shower. Do you want anything? We didn't even eat last night."

"I'll make us some breakfast, you take your time," he replied, allowing her the room to get up.

When she came back, coffee and toast were waiting. "What am I supposed to do today?"

"I'll call the police; the officer gave me her card last night. They will be able to tell us what the latest is. You should probably think about an undertaker, you can do all you need to with phone calls."

"Can you help?"

"Absolutely."

He called the police station first at 9:00 a.m. A post mortem had been ordered because of the nature of Neil's death. It would probably be held later in the day or the following day at the latest. Dan wrote down the police reference number.

Cousens Funeral Directors happened to have the ad in the Yellow Pages that caught Tara's attention when they turned to the appropriate page. A sombre but professional-sounding man took all the necessary details from Dan and assured them he would call as soon as permission was granted to release the body from the mortuary. They also made a preliminary time and date for a cremation; the undertakers confirmed they were able to take care of everything.

When they sat down again on the sofa, Tara looked bewildered. "Is it all as simple as that?"

"I know what you mean. It's as if you expect a more complicated process because it's a death."

"Right. It feels like we aren't taking it seriously."

Dan gave her a moment and then said, "There is one more thing; lawyers. I'm not sure if you and Neil have a family lawyer or wills and that sort of thing, but if you do you should call them."

"He does; did," she corrected herself. "Because of his money, he had a lawyer to take care of a trust and a few other things."

"Money?"

"He won Lotto a few years ago. Fat lot of good it did him though."

"Sorry, I wasn't being nosy, I just didn't realise. Makes it even more sad, doesn't it?"

"So do I call the lawyer and tell him what's happened?"

"Yeah, like the undertakers. A phone call and they will pretty much do everything else."

Tara sighed. "I should do that. Do you think you can do something for me?"

"Just say the word."

"I really don't want to go over to his house, but I think someone should. Could you?"

In the car travelling towards Neil's house, Dan could understand why Tara had little interest in her dead brother's home. There were no pets or concerns like that, but after she mentioned it they came up with a list of things to do which he was happy to attend to.

The front door was closed but not locked, even as he walked up the path towards it he noticed the lights were on in the rooms facing the front garden. There was no reason to suspect anyone else would be inside, but he could not help feel a little anxious.

"Darling, it's me. It's been days." Veronica put a lot of thought into her action plan and decided on a call to Tara first.

"Hi V. Sorry it's been …" Tara broke off unable to find suitable words.

Veronica bristled with anticipation. Tara hadn't screamed abuse or slammed the phone down. Her brother could not have spoken to her but something must have happened.

"Tara, what's the matter? You sound terrible."

"Oh V, it's Neil. He … he killed himself."

Veronica could hardly believe her ears. The contemptible bastard! "Oh my God, Tara; I'm so sorry darling. I'm coming over right now."

"You don't have to, but thanks that's so sweet of you."

"No really, I'm not going to leave you on your own at a time like this."

Tara sighed. "No, Dan's here. He has been fantastic, but if you want to come over for a coffee or something, it'll be lovely to see you. I'm actually okay, I think. I can't imagine what Neil must have been thinking, but he has been so screwed up for so long."

"What happened? Shit, sorry I didn't mean to be, um …" Veronica waited for the explanation.

"That's okay. Well, you know, I told you the issues he's had ever since we were young. I suppose he finally found it all too much. I probably will never understand, to be honest."

Veronica was smouldering inside. She had been robbed by Tara's brother.

"Did you have any reason to think this might happen?"

"No, we haven't spoken for a week or so. I've been trying to think of what might have happened, but I really have no idea."

Veronica still needed to know more and continued with her concerned friend routine.

"What are you going to do? Lots of arrangements I suppose. Is there anything I can do? You know you only have to say."

"Thanks. Dan seems to have it all under control. He's sorted the undertaker and I'm going to call Neil's lawyer in a while."

"Is Dan who I missed out on you for the other night?"

"Yes. V, he's so wonderful. I think you'll really like him. He's from England, too."

"He sounds incredible. When do I get all the interesting details?"

"He'll be back in a while. I couldn't face going over to Neil's, so he's gone over to sort some stuff out, turn off the power and so on. Just as well he thought of it, I would never have; must be his police background; you know, think of stuff we never do."

Veronica felt a lump grow in her throat and drop like an anchor into her stomach. Although she had just received the barest of information, her instincts were crackling like wildfire. She managed to spit out a laugh. "Oh policeman; now I understand. I can't resist a man in uniform either."

"Ex policeman. He was a detective before he came to New Zealand, somewhere called Garstone."

"I can't say I've heard of it." Veronica's heart almost burst from her chest and sweat appeared on her face and forehead like a sudden storm shower. Panic overtook caution; she needed to ask another question but could not find an innocent way. "What's his last name?" she asked before she could stop herself.

"Calder. Why don't you come over and you can both meet properly?" Tara answered distractedly.

Veronica contemplated finishing the call. A big part of her was saying *get away now*.

"V? Veronica, did you hear me?" Tara was still speaking.

"Sorry I was miles away, what was that?"

"I said Dan will be back when he's finished at Neil's, but he has to go back to his house later on as he is working on something about a woman he followed from the Central Post Office yesterday. I'm so glad you called; it's nice to talk about something else. Perhaps you could stay after he has to go later?"

Veronica felt the ground give way under her feet; she staggered backwards as her knees buckled. This could not be true. She slowly sat, fumbling with her spare hand for the arm of the sofa. "Yeah, okay sure."

"Are you alright? You have gone all quiet and strange now," Tara said.

"I'm just thinking how I can get over to your place. My scooter's broken," she lied in a growing panic. "Tell you what, I'll call you back when I'm about to leave. I'll talk to you again soon." Veronica clicked off and sat back in stunned silence.

On any other day Tara might have wondered why Veronica went from being her normal self to something less like that so quickly and for no obvious reason. Instead she had no such thoughts. She steeled herself to make the call to the lawyer's office.

Dan's first thoughts were that he wished he brought rubber gloves to Tara's brother's house. He smelled it before his other senses confirmed the dank and dirty state of the place. If a house could be depressed, this one was, just like its recently departed owner.

The sounds from a TV in the main living room were the only noises present and when he turned it off the hush that enveloped the whole house was very unnerving.

He started at the top and worked down. Not paying any particular attention to the details of each room, he made sure all the electrical items were unplugged, windows closed and locked and lights turned off. In the kitchen, he emptied the contents of the fridge and freezer into bags along with all the foodstuffs from the small pantry. He unplugged the fridge, disconnected the gas main, closed the water stop-valve and finally switched off the electricity at the fuse box too. Outside, he put all the bags of food into the rubbish bin and placed the bin on the pavement for collection. There was no shed or garage to check.

Before he locked up, he decided to walk through one final time just to be doubly sure all was secure and because he did not want to have to come back again any time soon. Everything was fine. But as he walked into hallway from the lounge to leave something caught his eye: a small green light. At first he thought he had made a mistake; he had turned the electricity off, so how could there be any sort of light?

Neil's computer was in hibernation mode when Dan came in, and the blank screen did not give him any pause for thought. Overnight it had fully charged the battery, but because it remained plugged into the mains power, the battery light was off. He went to close the laptop lid, but when he moved it, it went from hibernation to a live state automatically, and the screen burst into bright colour. Even if he did not mean to, his eye was drawn to the pictures on the screen. At first they made no sense at all, and then when he did take in what he was actually looking at, it made only slightly more sense until he noticed the email address. He stared, slowly, comprehension arranging itself into order. "Oh—my—fucking—God," he said aloud.

PART TWO

THE HUNTED

"I am who I am ... and I am not ashamed of that ...
even though I should be."

— *Unknown*

CHAPTER TWENTY-THREE

The front door opened and banged shut. "Hello? Dan is that you?" Tara called. When he burst in to the room, he looked deathly pale. "Is everything alright; was there something wrong at Neil's?"

Dan had raced back from Neil's house with a hundred thoughts playing out a battle in his head. None of it made sense and yet at the same time *it all did.* He parked the VW on the driveway and carried the laptop inside; still on, still displaying the pictures of a book, a necklace and a medicine bottle on the screen. He put it down carefully on the hall table with Tara's assortment of keys and unopened mail before he went through to the lounge.

"Tara, come and sit down. We need to talk."

"You're scaring me. What is it?"

"Shit, wait!" he exclaimed and disappeared into the hall again. He found a power socket in the wall and plugged the laptop lead into it immediately turning off the little green light.

Tara felt her shredded nerves could not take much more. "For heaven's sake, what's going on?" she croaked.

Dan grabbed her by the arm and led her to the sofa. "I did find something. It changes everything; I think Neil might not have killed himself."

"What are you talking about? There were witnesses who saw him. Why on earth could you think that?"

At that moment, he wished with all his heart that the gift of diplomacy would suddenly be his, but it was not to be. "Tara. I found a message and some photos on his computer."

"Oh no, what? A suicide note."

"No, sweetheart, it was an email; photos were attached to it."

"I don't understand."

"It was from the woman I've been trying to find; maybe the one I was following yesterday. The killer from England."

He saw she was looking at him, watching his lips move and yet knew she could not fathom the meaning. For Dan, it took an agonising wait to see something like understanding or at least an acknowledgement surface in her. She then visibly crumpled, like a giant vacuum was sucking the air out of her.

"Noooo." It began as a small sound somewhere in the depths of her being, but by the time it manifested in her mouth, it was the sound of utter despair.

Tara submitted to the completeness of pain and misery; of losing her twin whom she shared every moment of her life with since conception. She wailed uncontrollably. All Dan could do was hold her, try to whisper comfort into her ear, all the time knowing it was wholly useless.

What made it a hundred times worse were the other thoughts he had in his head dating back to his childhood. He held her trembling body with fervent desperation; he held her like he held his own mother the night she died and something died inside him this time too.

Veronica was angry and bitter by what Neil Danes had done. It was some time before she started to more coolly reassess her current position and see if there was a way to salvage something from the wreckage of the situation.

As Vanessa, she had been driven by revenge for the deaths of her parents. Stephen Christopher *had* to pay the price and that price was his life for theirs. The money was only a welcome and useful extra when she first conceived the idea and planned it out. Later it became an additional pleasure taking the other thing he valued most above all else too. She had not really thought at the time that acquiring money would later become a driving force in her other subsequent incarnations.

If she had still been that Vanessa now she may well have cut her losses and prepared to disappear, but Vanessa was long gone. The others also came and went too and with each new persona, she grew further away from what Vanessa was born for.

She was Veronica now and her perspectives were dramatically different.

She had been cheated by Neil Danes; the pathetic creature cared less about his excuse for a life than she bargained for.

She told him the truth about not being in a position to access his Internet banking yet. It was unlikely she could ever be able to access it at all now. He was dead; therefore any activity on his accounts would raise concern, undoubtedly followed by suspicion as to why. Most of the other things she said to him were just necessary garnish, basically true, but largely rhetorical.

As Veronica, she became consumed by it. One of the threats she dangled in front of Neil came back into her mind. *If you deviate from my instructions in any way, it will have the severest of consequences for you and for your darling Tara.*

Now it seemed there was a certain poetry in being true to her word and an irony in going back to Vanessa's first concerns. She could not help but feel he had somehow won, and she was the loser. The thought disgusted her.

Tara's crying was another painful experience in Dan's life; her tears soaked into his shirt, but by the time she was able to speak, his shirt was practically dry again.

"I need to understand everything. Will you show me, Dan?"

"Are you sure? Maybe I should just go to the police now."

"We *will* do that together, but not until you have explained it all to me first."

He could feel the resolve returning to her and arguing was pointless. She was going to experience more pain, but perhaps it was better to have it all now than drag it out.

"Okay, but it's going to hurt. I can't make it sound any other way than how it is. Are you sure?"

When she nodded, he went to fetch Neil's laptop from the hall.

They sat together on the sofa, and he balanced the laptop on his knees. "You will have a better idea of what some of this means than me," he said. "What I noticed was the email address. It's from her, I know, because I got one as well." Tara went from staring at the pictures to him briefly and back again; she did not speak.

"This is the way she contacts her targets," he regretted using the term immediately, but it was out there now so he continued. "She operates a bogus organisation called The Agency, offering a cure for depression; no that's wrong, not a cure. An alternative. Did Neil deal with the Depression Society, do you know?"

Without taking her eyes off the screen, Tara replied. "Coping with Grief; same sort of thing. He had a counsellor or a mentor called Tony or Toby."

"I'm sure that will be how she found him. Tara, are you okay with this? It's some pretty crazy stuff."

She placed a hand on his arm and managed a weak smile. "Yes, keep going."

"Stenning is the name she's used to contact the various people in the past. Always the same but with a different first name. That's how I remembered her from my days at Garstone police; she went by the name of Vikki Stenning then, but she has used Valerie, Vivienne and Vanessa too."

A moment of something flashed in Tara's eyes, but it was gone as quickly as it appeared.

"You sure you're okay?"

"Yes, go on."

"Obviously all the names are fake. I still don't know her real identity, but I think I'm on the right track. I do have a photo of her taken a few years ago, but it's not good enough to identify her. The woman I followed yesterday could be her, but something tells me she's not. I'll have to show you all the info I've put together at my house, so you can get the full picture. Talking of pictures, what do you make of these?"

Tara took a deep breath. Using her index finger, she pointed at some of the different shots on the screen. "That's a picture of Neil and Mum. I guess we must have been about seven or eight. Can't say that I remember seeing it anywhere or remember it being taken. It's not one I have or Neil had out at home.

"This one is one of his old schoolbooks. We were both in class 4B in the juniors one year, at that time we were put in the same classes a lot. I think I've got a couple of my old ones somewhere, they were always this colour.

"I'm guessing this one must be the inside of the book, the red line of the margin and the grey lines are the same. I don't understand the messages, that's Neil's writing and that was Mum's. I don't know what the dates mean at all."

"The way he's written the first message; sleeping in her room again. Does that make any sense to you?"

Tara stiffened. "No, it just sounds creepy. I don't really want to think about what that does mean. Do you think ... no, I can't even say it."

Dan stopped her; it was pretty obvious to him what the suggestion was. He changed the subject. "How old were you in 1989 and 1998?"

"Um, nine and eighteen."

"Do the first or last dates mean anything to you at all?" Although Dan was fishing, he knew he was at least in the right pond.

"Mum died in '98."

"The eighteenth of March 1989?"

Tara looked blankly at him. "No, nothing."

"What about August the second, 1998?"

"No, she didn't die until September. I can't believe he would have written a little kiss down every day for nearly ten years."

"I'm sorry Tara, but what bothers me is why he then stopped and wrote that. Are you sure nothing else happened around then?"

"She did start seeing Mike only a few weeks before. I remember being so sad after all that time of being on her own; she died so soon after meeting him. He was a nice guy; a little bit older, had a taxi company."

"Can you remember how Neil was about it?" Dan asked.

"Not really; why? Oh God no!" she exclaimed. "You don't think he had anything to do with what happened to Mum?"

"I have no idea, Tara. I'm sorry, but to me it does seem odd that he could be writing kisses to her everyday for years and years and then suddenly stop around the time she meets a new man. And then what he wrote and drew straight after."

She was desperate for a logical reason. "We don't know he wrote it straight after, it's just on the next page."

Dan conceded that point. The last date of 02.08.98 was half-way up the page. The rest of it was bare and the "DIE BITCH" and knives appeared on the next. It was possible he could have done that at any time before.

It might have been possible, but Dan knew it was *not* what happened. He chose to move on. "The pills bottle, have you seen it before?"

Tara seemed only to have a tentative grasp on things now, and Dan felt her anxiety. He knew very well how easily she could lose that grip at any moment.

"She was on tablets for years for her bad back. I can't remember if she had pill bottles like that; probably, they are all pretty generic aren't they?" Another point Dan had to concede.

"Is it okay to look at his other emails and documents?"

"I don't think we have a choice now," she replied.

The contents of Neil's email account made for depressing reading. Not one single item to raise a smile or any *normal* conversation pieces. Everything was connected to how miserable he was; emails between him and other Coping with Grief clients, messages from the video store or the supermarket confirming purchases only served to confirm his loneliness.

The original message from Stenning was gone, but Neil's reply to "The Agency" was also there. Dan and Tara read it together.

Hello. When my mother died I thought I would die as well. She was the loveliest person in the world. I have tried to move on, but most of the time, I can't even think straight.

I go to counselling and talk about my feelings. It's bullshit really.

I have money and a sister who I know cares about me, and I do love her, but really all I want is my mother back again.

Your message says you can offer a way out, my mother is not coming back, so maybe getting out is the best I can do.

Please can you give me some more information about what you do and what you think you could do for me.

Neil Danes.

Tara was crying again before she was halfway through. By the time she was finished, she was a complete mess once more.

Dan kept his immediate feelings to himself. Pity, annoyance and embarrassment Tara had read what he did and how she must be feeling about her loser brother. He also felt unadulterated rage towards V. Stenning.

"How could his life have been that bad?" Tara pleaded.

"I wish I could answer you. But you cannot possibly think you had anything to do with it or you are at all to blame."

"You only have to read all this to realise Neil did. Anyway, what did I do to help? Nothing."

"Hey, that's not true. You could not have known any of this. Did he ever talk to you about how much he missed your mother, or what his feelings were towards her were? If not, you would never have thought of those sorts of things on your own."

"Dan, he's saying he wanted to sleep with her. Nine years old! It's unbelievable, it's all unbelievable."

"Right, it *is* unbelievable, that's my whole point. Please try not to blame yourself. I know it's human nature, and probably more so because you are twins, but none of it has anything to do with you."

"I'm sorry, but some people are ..." He talked himself into a corner and was struggling for a way out. Tara rescued him.

"Fucking crazy," she said.

He managed to get her to eat a little, and they had more coffee. Talking was minimal; any other subjects were hopelessly inadequate in the circumstances and always led back to Neil.

Tara changed her clothes; she felt like the ones she had on before were now a week old.

"Feel better?" Dan asked as she emerged from her room.

"Much. Can you take me over to your house now so we can look at what you have on this Stenning bitch?"

Tara did look better; she had even put a little makeup on.

"Are you sure you want to do it now?"

"Yes. What Neil's life and death ends up being about is already determined. I'm sure we don't know what all the facts are yet, and I have got a horrible feeling I'm not going to like them when we do, but there is still another issue. There's a killer somewhere out there, and she has to be caught."

He opened the study door and flipped on the light switch by reaching around from the opening. Dan then stood back so Tara could go in first. She hesitated before entering and then stepped into what was soon to become her worst nightmare.

Across the walls were printouts and photocopies of letters, emails, newspaper cuttings and all manner of other documents. She instantly recognised some as birth and death certificates as well as some tax forms and other official-looking articles.

Spread along the length of one wall was a timeline of dates and incidents on a long board with maker pen lines jagging off in various directions to hand-written notes on three different-coloured A5 sheets.

There were two computers, a home PC and a laptop plus a laser printer and a scanner, copier, fax combo machine all connected to each other with a plethora of multicoloured cables. The desk was groaning under the weight of pages and pages of copies and print-outs, as well as several lever arch files, books and enough spare pens, pencils and stationery to open a shop.

"Here let me show you," Dan said. He started with the timeline board. "This is where I think it all began. Stephen Christopher; he was some big-shot investment broker in London. At some point in time, he employed a personal trainer called Vanessa Stenning. She reported him as dying without warning during an exercise session in 2002. It turns out that Vanessa Stenning was a fake; whoever this woman really is took the name from a baby who died within hours of her birth years before."

Even at this early stage of telling Tara what he knew, she was already in a state of disbelief. She was trembling and her red-rimmed eyes only confirmed her lack of full understanding "This is like a room from a movie or TV show—what do they call it? The incident room."

"Well a smaller version, maybe, but yes I suppose so. It seemed logical for me to set it up like this, it's how I've always worked on major police inquiries.

"I still don't know why Vanessa wanted Christopher dead. The money is the obvious reason, but I reckon there has to more to it than that."

Tara nodded. "That policeman's sixth sense?"

"I think so. Anyway after he dies, Vanessa disappears as if she *really* has never existed.

"In 2005, Vivienne Stenning is a part-time nurse at an old people's home in Winchester which is fifty miles south of London. In the time she works there, an old lady called Mathews also dies. Now I know what you're going to say, old people die in homes all the time. True, but this one turns out to be a very wealthy one who has a love of animals."

"What?"

"When she dies, according to her relatives, she leaves a big bucket of cash to an animal charity. You need to remember that okay. Anyway, hey-presto as soon as she dies, Vivienne leaves soon after saying she is off to travel the world, but like Vanessa, that's all nonsense too. Any questions so far?"

Tara looked. "Dozens probably, but keep going."

"Okay, 2008. Vikki Stenning, local crime journalist for the *Garstone Record* newspaper. I'm still struggling with this one. She and the paper's editor, a man called Singleton, must have known each other in the past or something; they had a rental house in both their names during the time she was working there."

"But if she isn't Vikki, because there is no real Vikki, how could he have known her from before?" Tara interrupted.

"Exactly, I know, that's what I mean about struggling with her. It's at this time I met her." Dan took a deep breath. "I was working on a case that went to trial. Two nasty, violent brothers, who beat up and robbed an old man. The case was thrown out of court for technical reasons because my boss at the time fucked things up through laziness and incompetence. Outside the court as I was leaving, reporter Vikki asks me the right question at the wrong time; wrong for me that is. I blow my top and tell her what a prick my boss was and the next day I'm headline news. Soon after that, to make matters worse, I get hauled in front of a disciplinary board and get given an official police bollocking." He smiled apologetically at Tara. "One thing led very quickly to another and soon I'm out of the job with a chip the size of a railway sleeper on my shoulder, looking for a way out of everything else too.

"Over three years later and I'm standing in a wardrobe telling you the weirdest story either of us has ever heard."

"I don't know what to say."

"Don't worry, because now it's going to get weirder still. Mark Singleton, the editor commits suicide, and guess what?"

"Vikki disappears," Tara said, shaking her head in disbelief.

"Bingo! Right, next we have Valerie Stenning. She comes to work for a conveyancer in a little town called Trowbridge last year. She's working as a consultant and gets paid every month by personal cheque. She works there for several months and never once banks a cheque. Only after she leaves does the company realise her tax numbers and so on are bogus. Shortly before she left, another woman who she became friends with dies, suicide in the bath allegedly leaving another bucket of money to another animal charity."

"Dan, how can all this be true? I mean, I'm sure it is, but how has nobody else realised what's happening?"

"Would you believe it is all too simple. The way I discovered what I did was by pure chance. All these dead people; but logical explanations for all the deaths. No one is going to take notice of what appear to be isolated unconnected incidents, and the police can't investigate anything if it's never reported to them in the first place.

"Okay, bringing us up to date—and sorry honey, but this is where it becomes personal. Stenning arrives somehow in Auckland; I don't know when, probably in the last few months. She must have used her own real identity to get into New Zealand though, of that I am sure. She discovers potential victims through the Depression Society and Coping with Grief. That's how she knew about Neil and me."

"You said that earlier. What do you mean, you as well?"

"I corresponded with the Depression Society for a while. I have been pretty miserable at times here and in England. I'm sorry, I should have told you. I can only think she must have hacked the websites and got information which she used to make contact. Neil obviously got an email and replied to it."

"But there were people who saw him jump off the bridge. You don't think that was her, do you?"

"No, I don't think so; but look—she sent these pictures to him. Somehow she got the book and the locket and the medicine bottle, God knows how, but she had or has them and sent the pictures to Neil."

"Oh shit. As blackmail!" Tara said, banging her fist down on the desk.

"Well, it has to be possible. Maybe Neil told her about his money in other emails."

Tara was staggered at what they were embroiled involved in.

"Where's the photo you have of her?" she asked.

Dan went to one of the files on the desk and quickly found the print. The details of the picture taken by Heidi at the conveyancers were already ingrained in his mind, and so he did not pay much attention to it or Tara as she examined it closely.

"This is all too far fetched Dan. It's just impossible."

"There was a time when I thought so too," he acknowledged. "It took me a while to understand coincidences operate differently in different places. You know this six degrees of separation people talk about?"

"Yes. So?"

Dan explained how he shared her doubts early on in the investigation and how he resolved them. "So in the end, some coincidences are just not very coincidental; in a small country like New Zealand, they can be inevitable."

Tara gasped. "I don't know what's more scary; this crazy story or the fact you can unravel it."

Dan picked up the A4 pad he had with him during the surveillance at the post office the desk. His poem was on the top sheet and he started to read it without thinking. After a moment, he remembered Tara and looked to check on her. "You okay?"

"Fine. It's funny, she looks familiar to me."

He knew that was impossible. It was Valerie in the photo. Valerie Stenning, the conveyancer from Trowbridge. Dan put it down to a combination of all that happened in the last day.

"Do you fancy a coffee? I could use another one."

"Sure, but I'd like to see the rest of this later," she replied still looking at the photo.

Dan went downstairs to put the kettle on leaving Tara in the study. He had been in the kitchen a long enough for the water to boil when he was aware of Tara coming into the room.

"Shall I make it strong?" he said without looking up.

"What's this?" Her voice was pinched, and he knew something was wrong.

"What?" he asked, spinning around.

She was holding his A4 pad. She looked like she had just seen a ghost, and the pad trembled in her hand. "Oh it's just a poem I write when I'm on surveillance sometimes," he said, coming around to her.

Her trembling hand flipped the page back over. "No, this?" she said, turning it back to reveal the part address he gleaned from the big envelope the woman in the Whitcoulls café had taken from her bag.

"It's all I could see from the woman in Whitcoulls yesterday, when she put the mail from the post office box in the bigger envelope. Her hand was covering the rest. Do you remember? I told you about it?"

"It says Apartment 6, 29 Vulcan Lane," Tara said slowly, her eyes boring into Dan's.

"How do you know that, Tara?" He was not questioning her knowledge: more than twenty years of policing told him when somebody was providing accurate information.

"I said she looked familiar. Dan, I never forget a figure. I can tell a thirty-four small from a thirty-two medium at twenty metres or size six from size seven shoes. The picture upstairs—I knew I'd seen her before."

"Okay."

Tara leant on the bench top for support. "My new girlfriend I've talked about, her name is Veronica. I took some clothes around to her apartment the first day I met her. I've been there a few times since. It's number 6, 29 Vulcan Lane. Dan, it's her in the picture. I know it is."

Dan was like a deer caught in headlights. He tried to move or speak but nothing worked. Tara seemed not to have blinked since she entered the room. When she finally did, it broke the spell.

"Tara, honey, do you know what her last name is or anything else about her?"

"I was just thinking that coming down the stairs; she's never mentioned her last name. She's a travel book writer, has only been in Auckland for a couple of months I think. Oh my God, Dan, I've been in her house. She killed my brother."

It was true; undeniably, unbelievably true. He struggled for what to say or do next.

"What else? You have to tell me everything Tara."

She grimaced. "She called me this morning while you were out at Neil's. I told her about Neil, and she did seem a bit odd. She's coming around to my house later!"

"Okay you're here so you don't have to worry about that. We can call the police from here."

"No, you don't understand." She sounded tortured. "I wasn't thinking. She asked about Neil and I told her. But I told her about you too; that you were in the Garstone police, that you had followed the woman from the post office yesterday. Oh fuck, Dan, I even told her your full name."

Tara started to cry. Dan was rooted to the spot again.

"What have I done? It's all my fault," she managed between sobs.

"Hey, none of it is your fault."

"Dan, I've told her about Neil's depression, I've told her about his Lotto win. I have told her everything she needed to know. She's played me all the way, and I have fallen for it every step of the way. What are we going to do?"

"The only thing we can do. We have to contact the police, *now*."

Tara watched helplessly as Dan punched in the numbers on Julie Lambert's card and waited for his call to be answered. She heard a voice on the other end, but Dan did not speak.

"Dan?"

He ended the call and put the phone on the bench.

"Dan?" Tara said again.

"It's too crazy. I can't just call to report a serial killer like reporting a lost dog." He looked at her. "Do you trust me?"

"Of course."

"We now know about amazing coincidences too; what about luck?"

"After today, I'm prepared to believe anything," she said.

"Come with me then and pray for some good luck."

In the living room, he emptied out the cupboard where he stored the box containing the Vikki Stenning newspaper article. Under it, almost at the bottom of the rest of the junk was another box.

When he opened it, Tara saw a bunch of photos, some in protective or decorative covers. They all appeared similar. Three or four rows of men and women arranged like a sports team for the official team photo with the appropriate names and ranks printed at the bottom of each.

"What are they?"

Dan carried them all over to the table. "All the courses I went on as a trainer, they always took a photo of the people taking part. Can you get Neil's computer?"

"I don't understand," she said.

"Go onto the New Zealand Police website and then to the online monthly newsletter archive page. See if you can find a photo or anything to do with the recruitment campaign they ran in 2003. In that year, a load of British police were recruited by the New Zealand Police to bolster numbers in and around Auckland. I remember it happening, it caused quite a lot of interest in England at the time."

"So? What's that got to do with us now?"

Dan tried to sound hopeful rather than desperate. "If any of them came over, I might've met them in the past. It's the longest shot ever, but if there is a chance, it will be a lot easier to try and make us sound remotely credible."

"On any other day, I would probably say you were out of your mind," Tara said. "But not today." She kissed him on the cheek and powered up Neil's laptop.

It did not take long before they were feeling despondent once more. There had been nothing on the police website and their idea to see if there were any photos taken by one of the two national papers also resulted in failure.

Tara looked through Dan's photos. In most he sat in the front row with the other trainers and the students in the rows behind. "Do you think we should just call anyway? Maybe even take some of your stuff from upstairs with us to the station."

"Yes, that's probably the best idea."

She touched his arm. "It's nice that you kept these, there must be some good memories here."

"And that the names are all there to put to the faces to," he said.

"That's it," exclaimed Tara. "The names."

Dan looked perplexed.

"Some detective you are my sweet; start with all the names, one at a time."

Dan didn't get it until she tapped in the first name he gave her. She was back on the website of the *National Enquirer*.

"Alan Soames," Dan said. She typed the name out and added police in the search bar and hit enter. The results of the search were not what they wanted, but Dan was in awe any way.

"You're a genius," he told her.

"Thank you. Next?" Tara replied.

They went through name after name, photo after photo, once or twice thinking they struck gold only to have their hopes dashed.

Until she searched for Harry Spiller. Detective Sergeant Harry Spiller of the Kent Constabulary, Course 4/12 Level 1 Surveillance. June to August 2000.

The *National Enquirer* resulted in four hits. Detective Senior Sergeant Harry Spiller as he was now, based in the Avondale police division in western Auckland. The articles related to a current investigation in 2006 and a court case he was involved in. The latest one was less than a year old.

It was 4:30 p.m. Dan spoke on the phone, Tara so close she could hear the other end too.

When Dan asked to speak to Harry Spiller, he was put through without a word of enquiry.

"Spiller." The voice sounded as English as HP Sauce.

"Hi there, is that ex D.S. Spiller of the Kent Police?" Dan asked, expecting to achieve some immediate interest.

"And who am I talking to?" Spiller replied cautiously.

"Serg, this is Dan Calder speaking," Dan said, desperate for the abbreviated term to have a positive effect. "I'm really hoping you may remember me from a surveillance course we were both on in 2000. I was one of the in-car trainers. I'm only guessing, but I think you were in Chris Gilkes' car."

The pause that followed had Dan and Tara grasping each other's hands like teenagers.

"Dan Calder, Dan Calder then Dan Calder! Bugger me; what the hell are you calling me for from the other side of the bloody world?"

They both heaved a massive sigh of relief but maintained their hold.

"Harry, you have got no idea how good it is to talk to you. I'm in Auckland, mate, and I need some help."

Spiller was old school in the best possible way. He was a devoted family man apart from one ill-judged affair a few years before which he was constantly trying to make up for. He grew up on council housing estates where he learned more about crime and criminals than he ever did at Police College in his late teens. All his English police service was in inner city areas, and he knew how lucky he was to now be in the relatively harmonious environment of Auckland. The only thing he loved as much as his family was policing and the people he worked with. He sounded as if he'd just lost a ten-dollar note and found a fifty to hear Dan's voice.

"Dan Calder. I can't bloody believe it. Do you know I have still got your sign up here in my office? 'You are only limited by your imagination' Do you remember that one?"

"I sure do Harry."

"I tell my blokes all the time. Cunning bastards out there, we have to be more cunning."

"Harry, I really need to see you ASAP."

"Trouble, Dan?"

"A shit load."

"I don't have to rush home."

"I know Avondale; I can be there in thirty minutes."

"Tea or coffee?"

"Thanks Harry, and by the way, that sign: you are going to need all the imagination you have."

Harry Spiller had added a few kilos around the waist but otherwise looked just like the photo.

"I still can't believe it," he said.

"I've been here for three years now Harry. Just the best place to live isn't it?"

"My wife found it a struggle for the first few months, but when we saw the weather back in England in our first winter here, their summer, she soon changed her mind. The kids love it too. What's your story?"

Dan and Tara were in Spiller's first floor office. The initial introductions and reintroductions over, they had not yet broached the subject which brought them there.

"I left the job in 2008; came out here after that. I'm still trying to find work that suits, but in the meantime I've got a house to finish renovating, a book to finish writing and a pension that just about covers the monthly bills."

"Didn't you think to join here?"

"I did, but I'm not sure my heart would have been fully in it. I miss it every day though."

Tara recognised the need for the polite conversation but found it difficult to sit still; the knowledge inside her was threatening to boil over. Dan and Harry continued to exchange war stories before they finally leant back in their chairs in perfect synchronisation, and Harry said, "So to business." They both looked at Tara.

"My brother Neil committed suicide last night; he jumped off Newton Gully Bridge."

"I'm sorry," Harry said, sounding like he meant it.

Tara went on. "He was a sad soul. He'd been depressed for years and years, since our mother died when we were eighteen; we're twins. I didn't realise what a state he was in, and it's only been today that we have found out some other things which make the whole situation much worse.

"Neil was a Lotto winner a few years ago, we think there is a woman here in Auckland who was trying to blackmail him, and he took this option out."

Harry was not taking notes; he did not need to.

Dan began to explain further. "That's not the half of it Harry. We believe the blackmailer is also a serial killer from England. I've been doing some of my own investigations for a while. I'm certain; I've got all the information you'll need, just one or two things to complete the puzzle."

Tara expected at least some scepticism on Harry's part, if not downright disbelief. Instead he crossed his arms across his chest and looked at them both. "How long will it take to get me up to speed with all the details, Dan?"

"Three hours, maybe four. Just tell me what you need."

"What's your critical index?"

"Identification, locating the bitch or at least restricting her movements and then finding a way to do the business."

For some reason, Tara found the two men engaged in police jargon comforting.

"Right, understood. All this stuff you have, can you transfer it here?"

"Yes, you will understand its composition, not sure about your colleagues though."

"It's alright I've got them pretty well trained now, some are good, and they are all enthusiastic."

"Is this something you can simply take on? Do you need to talk to someone first?"

Harry smiled. "Yes, my guv'nor at Auckland Central. Don't worry though, we're fishing buddies. They have got a couple of biggish jobs on the go at the moment so he'll be keen to help me to help you. Now Tara, you've met her, spent time with her?"

"Yes."

"You can help us now by making up a digital picture of her. A picture's worth a thousand words."

She looked at Dan who gave her a reassuring smile. "Okay," she said.

Harry made a call which quickly resulted in a knock on the door. The police artist took Tara off to the ID suite.

When they were alone in the office, Harry came around the desk to sit in the chair that Tara had just vacated. "So tell me," he said. "What have I just got myself into?"

Dan rubbed his hand across his forehead to the back of his head. "If you can get her before she disappears again, it's going to make your career."

Harry grinned. "Okay my friend; let me have it."

She could not believe her misfortune and also her failure to put the pieces together before now.

Veronica was now trying to learn all she could about John Daniel Calder. The police detective she first met in 2009 as Vikki Stenning had unbelievably reappeared in her life on the other side of the world years later.

At first she thought it could not be a coincidence and somehow an international co-operation between the British and New Zealand police was closing in on her. That had given way to the slow realisation of the truth. By some freakish twist of fate, their lives and paths now crossed again, and he knew more about her than she did him. Until now, it was all there in her research notes for the article she wrote about him.

John Daniel Calder aka Detective Daniel Calder of Garstone police station, born 26th of June 1963 in Nottingham. Only son of John Calder senior and Claudia Calder nee Pooley. Followed in his father's footsteps into the police in 1984, served in the county police until he resigned in 2008.

She could remember every detail of her single meeting with him, even without the aid of her external hard drive to remind her, but nonetheless, she had read her Vikki notes and the copy of the *Garstone Record* article three times.

Detective Constable Daniel Calder has spoken out about the lack of professionalism displayed by his senior supervisor Detective Chief Inspector Jim Allen amid the collapse of the trial of Thomas and Brendan Edrich ... etc. etc.

Now plain Mr. J. D. Calder, resident in the Eastern Bays area of Auckland; alone and trying to come to terms with the ghosts of his past. Sometime correspondent with the Depression Society of New Zealand but unable to share all his troubles—which meant there must be some darker secrets to reveal. All this came from the computer; but Veronica knew there was more if she could find it.

As fated luck designed it, the fabled six degrees law of separation had done a somersault and Calder had very recently found new female companionship in one Tara Danes, twin sister of the recently departed Neil Danes, *who still owes me 2.3 million dollars. You could not possibly make this up.*

Veronica believed there was still a lot more to learn before the end of this day, and some of those dark secrets Calder travelled halfway around the world to try and escape could soon be in her grasp.

After so much time in the ID suite with Tara, the police artist, Sina Eaton, could not drag the process out any longer. The instructions from Spiller had been clear: "Don't come back until

I call." But when Tara repeated for the fourth time that the digital image in front of them was "perfect," she made an executive decision, and they were now in the police canteen drinking coffee.

"You must be in a state of complete shock; thank goodness for your boyfriend," she said after Tara gave her a run down of what happened.

"I'm trying not to think too much about any of it at the moment," Tara replied, sipping from her chunky white mug. "I'm not sure I could cope if I understood it all; he told me recently that he loved being in the police but parts of it were shit. He should have substituted shit for fertiliser."

Sina frowned. "What do you mean?"

"Same stuff isn't it. But when you fertilise something with enough of it you get a bigger, better, stronger end product."

Sina's beeping pager instantly stopped their giggling.

Harry listened intently to Dan. He absorbed all the information, even managing to commit various dates and times to memory.

By the time he was finished, Dan was pretty tired.

"Why leave it for so long before contacting us?" Harry asked.

"Honestly, because I'm a stubborn arsehole." There was no point in trying to portray it as something it was not.

"We've all been there before."

"Yes, but I made a career out of it."

Harry smiled. "That's not how I remember you from the course. You wouldn't know, but before it started, I was trying everything I could to get out of it. The thought of three weeks driving around the country; jumping in and out of a car to follow a fake suspect. I wasn't happy, I can tell you. It turned out to be one of the best courses I ever did. I learned a hell of a lot, most of it from you. Gilksey told us every day if we do nothing else, take on board what you did and said in your lessons."

"Stop it; you'll make me blush."

"I told you, still got the sign," Harry said, pointing to the legend above his desk.

"Do you think you can get her?"

"It probably depends more on her than us at the moment. She's still at least a step or two ahead; she could melt away without a problem if she wants. What do you think she'll do?"

Dan's face looked as hard as stone. "She's got unfinished business here, she will want to finish it," he said coldly.

When Tara came back in, Harry explained what he was going to arrange for the following day and tried to reassure her he aimed to bring Veronica Stenning to justice one way or another. She and Dan still had a lot to do before morning. On the way back to his house, she showed him a copy of the image Sina produced. Veronica did not look like his vague recollection of Vikki.

"Well, I can definitely say it's not the woman I followed from the post office," he said, silently confirming to himself the face did not match any other from those saved on his camera during his observations stint either.

Tara asked, "Would you have recognised her if you'd met at my house or in the street?"

"I'm not sure, maybe."

"Let's hope you get to find out soon."

CHAPTER TWENTY-FOUR

It took a lot of persuading to make Tara promise to stay at his house, not go to work, not even to go outside. They spent much of the night awake and talking, still amazed by the incredible circumstances which now enveloped them.

Neil was gone, along with at least one terrible secret. Whatever the feelings he had for their mother at the time of her death, and what they resulted in, would never be fully known now. Likewise the other exposed secret; that of Neil aged nine remained unexplained fully.

Veronica had injected herself into Tara's life like a slow acting poison. Her existence was an orchestrated sham; Tara was so completely taken in by the vivacious, blonde travel writer whose sole intention was to get to Neil. Much as Dan tried, she was overwhelmed by feelings of guilt.

She sat in his study chair looking around the bare room. Yesterday began with sadness tinged with relief and hope; it ended with shock and desolation. Dan was going to be away all day; Neil once said there was a big difference between feeling lonely and feeling alone. She now knew exactly what he meant. With nothing else to do, she picked up the phone.

"Hi Cathy, it's me."

"Oh Tara, how are you? I'm so sorry for your news."

"Thanks, it still hasn't sunk in yet. I need a favour, if possible."

"Anything, of course."

"Can you look after the shop for me; it might be a day or two or maybe even a bit longer?"

"That's what partners are for. I have got everything I need here already so don't worry about a thing. Sue is here with me so it will be no problem, honestly."

"You are a life saver," Tara immediately regretted her terminology and Cathy was quiet on the other end. "Can I call you in a day or two?"

"Whenever you are ready. Just take your time and look after yourself," Cathy re-assured her.

She called Shelley next, and they both cried on the phone together for several minutes, managing a conversation between the sobs.

"You must not blame yourself though. Promise me," Shelley implored.

"I'll try, but you know how it is."

"I do sweetie. And don't keep your feelings locked up inside either; you can call me or come round any time or I can come to you."

"I'm glad you are a social worker Shel' even if you are an out of work one." They managed a little laugh, which Tara strangled with feelings of guilt.

"Actually, not any more. I got a call back last evening; they offered me the senior's post."

"Oh Shelley, that's great."

"Thanks, it seemed a bit inappropriate to tell you before."

"You are such a darling." Tara started crying again. "I'm going back to bed for a couple of hours, why don't you come over this afternoon?"

"Okay I will. Try and sleep. I'll see you later." Shelley clicked off.

Tara tried sleeping but lay awake with her head spinning for an hour before she gave up and went for a bath.

There was a buzz in the room. Despite the time still being quite early, the formula of mixing a policeman's interest and expectancy always resulted in what Dan could feel now. He and Harry spent the last couple of hours setting up the incident room and going over some of the points he failed to mention the day before, clarifying and confirming. What once covered the walls of Dan's study now partly filled two walls of the ground floor conference room at Avondale Police Station. Harry called for attention. "Right, sit."

The four plainclothes and two uniformed officers all took a seat at the centre table, Dan and Harry took the other two.

"Morning all," Harry began. "We are going to have a few more early mornings as well before this is finished; late nights too," he added.

The faces around the table were a mixture of wondering, pleasure and determination. For Dan, it was just like old times.

"This is Detective Dan Calder. Do you all remember the day we did that video surveillance and log keeping lesson?" There was a murmur of remembrance around the table. "This is the guy that wrote the book and taught it to me. Phil," he said, looking at one of the plain clothes, "the sign above my desk, *that's* Dan Calder."

Phil looked at Dan and extended a hand. "Good to meet you; Phil Brown."

"A pleasure, I should also say ex-detective."

One of the other plain clothes officers asked, "The boss once said that you went into a pub as a deaf priest and played pool with your target, is that right?" Dan recounted the tale at Harry's insistence, drawing a mixed response of incredulity and wonder.

After the story, Harry spoke mostly uninterrupted covering more details of the case.

When they broke for a well-earned coffee, Dan pulled Harry over to one side. "Do you really want me to be this involved? I'm wondering what your guys will make of it."

"It's different here. I mean here in New Zealand," Harry replied. "It took a while for me to integrate and become accepted, but at the end of the day, it's about how you perform. I've got their respect now; they are a good bunch in general here. I wouldn't ask if I didn't think you or they might have a problem, besides you're not one of them; you're a consultant to the police, just another of my resources." He grinned.

"Well, if you want rid of me at any time, I'll understand."

"Let's just concentrate on finding this mad bitch for now."

"Fair enough."

Harry got them all back around the table and started allocating duties. He and Dan came up with a list of individual tasks; each one specific to a single matter. Dan's role was to be the conduit through which all the information flowed in both directions. He would prepare the tasks, examine the results, re-task follow up inquiries and assimilate the evidence for Harry's incident file, called the "Evidence Book," which was be the cornerstone of the whole investigation. Obviously he could not get involved in the duties of a police officer per se.

As a non-police officer, he considered the concerns of the others. It was a fact of police life that anybody who was not in the family was automatically viewed with curiosity at best and absolute derision at worst, no matter how qualified they were. He could recall many lectures and seminars he had been on in the past where the fact an expert speaker was not in the job made his contribution less worthy than that of the newest recruit with no experience at all.

By chance, there were three different Phils in the assembly of six who formed Harry's major incident team. Phil Brown, detective, was teamed with Phil Larson, uniform. Phil ("Call me Philip") Te Tuke, detective, was paired up with Glen Johannsen, uniform. Jerome Brett, detective, was matched with Kiri Ieremia, detective.

The detectives were as many as Harry's divisional commander was prepared to allocate from his office complement of fifteen. Phil Larson and Glen Johannsen were seconded from their patrol duties as they had experience on major incidents and because it was invariably useful to have a uniformed presence there at certain situations.

Phils B and L were tasked with researching the woman Dan followed from the post office. Philip T and Glen were asked to compile the reports necessary to obtain search warrants regarding the PO Box and the Vulcan Lane apartment. Jerome and Kiri began inquiries of the Customs and Immigration Departments in order to try and identify Stenning's initial appearance into the country and therefore hopefully her true identity.

Dan and Harry started working separately on other areas of the investigation. Dan especially had little else to do until the others started reporting back to him. Harry went to work on composing a report to be sent to police forces in England requesting information and assistance. They considered a media release but decided against one at this early stage. Depending on results in the first forty-eight hours, they agreed to reassess again then.

All this and it was barely 9:00 a.m.

When Tara woke, she made herself some scrambled eggs and ate them standing up at the kitchen bench. She was still at a complete loss as to what to do. She wanted to call Dan, but his last words before leaving were that he would call as soon as he was able because the morning was sure to be very busy.

She should call the undertakers, bank and the lawyers again to see if there was any new news or to see if there was anything else she should be doing, but the thought of any one of those conversations did not give her any pleasure.

As she was running out of excuses not to pick up the phone, Dan called. He told her about his morning so far and that he was likely to be home after 6:00 p.m. When she said how empty she was feeling, she was grateful that he tried to say the right things.

"Just try and take it easy, you don't *have* to do anything. At least give yourself a day or so before thinking about being normal again. It probably won't feel any better until after the funeral." Although none of it was quite correct even as he heard the words himself, it was the best he could do.

Candice Drysdale left home with time to spare in order to stop off at the shop on the corner of Courtland and Main in Ellerslie to buy some chewing gum and a magazine before the bus came. The bus was on time and she exchanged a greeting with the driver whom she recognised; it was a regular journey for them both.

A young man, complete with greasy fringe covering his eyes under an even dirtier baseball cap, who ran up the street and jumped on just before the bus moved off, sloped to the back of the bus in that manner adolescents across the world have in common, like they're the victims of a personalised global conspiracy. Candice did not take any notice of him, she was already engrossed in the glossy headlines when he passed her seat; but he was very quick to notice the name tag she wore on her shirt: "Broadway Fitness. Candice. Reception."

Veronica had eventually settled on her priorities. Tara Danes said Dan Calder was working on some investigation. The thought it could be a coincidence was absurd. Calder also contacted her by email in response to her Agency email and had come into Tara's life soon after she did herself. The few things she knew about his and Tara's new friendship led Veronica to believe he was not also just using her to further his own agenda.

Weeks before, Candice Drysdale answered the ad Veronica placed on the customer's notice board of her local supermarket. It was money for jam really; twice a week, collect mail from a Post Office box in the city and repost it to another Auckland inner city address. She called the phone number supplied on the postcard and spoke to Lesley Horner, the name on the card, to confirm the details. There was no more to it than that. She would be paid fifty dollars per week; the cash left in an envelope in the Post Office box. It took her a week to work out that Lesley Horner must be mailing the cash there herself. They never met and other than Lesley Horner's bland voice, she could not describe her in the least.

What she never realised was the ever vigilant Veronica checked her out in detail and chose her specifically because of the way she looked; like the sister she never had and always wanted and a potential ignorant aid to assist her.

Candice worked part-time at a leisure centre complex. Her husband earned decent money and she just wanted something to keep her from getting bored. Free use of the facilities meant she could work and socialise at the same place with a minimum of cost to her. Today the two other girls with her on reception duty meant a fairly leisurely shift was in store at the leisure centre.

Veronica studied the back of Candice's head through her lank fringe as the bus rolled along. When Candice started to prepare herself for her stop, Veronica did too. They got out on Broadway. Candice walked purposefully the few hundred metres to the centre, oblivious of the sullen teenager a short distance behind.

Veronica waited before going inside making the final mental preparations so she was completely ready to act as soon as it was necessary. Candice was sat behind the main reception desk with two other women, similar age, similar appearance, like they came out of one big receptionist box. They were more interested in each other than the comings and goings on the other side of the long counter that divided their domain from the rest of the world.

Veronica located a public seating area where she could sit and watch unobtrusively. She had the requisite teenager's headphones and the latest copy of an indie music magazine. She was set for a long wait if necessary.

Candice Drysdale was the safest of the options available to her at that time and Veronica decided that a little safe information gathering first may consolidate her position. If Calder followed her from the Post Office, it was likely he had not made contact yet. That had to be his next move, and she needed to know what he did.

The Phils arrived at lunchtime. A morning in the office was all it took for them to identify the residents of 26 Courtland Street. Photo identification was confirmed comparing Dan's hastily taken OP photos against the driver's licence picture of Candice Robyn Drysdale. All manner of other police checks confirmed Drysdale had no criminal record, not so much as a caution or a parking ticket. To be doubly sure of themselves and to be as well armed as they could be, they also ran similar checks on her husband. The last time either of them were out of the country was in 2009 when they went to Fiji together for two weeks.

The appearance of the two police officers, one in uniform, brought Veronica to a state of immediate alertness. She needed to be sure they were there to see Drysdale rather than just asking for assistance at reception on another unrelated matter. When she saw Candice pale, then blush accompanied by a nod, she swiftly went into action.

By the time she got to the reception, the plainclothes policeman was obviously still going through his introduction spiel. "So there's nothing to worry about Mrs. Drysdale, we are investigating a matter that you may have some information about which can help us."

Her two companions were so fixated on what was happening to Candice, they both failed to notice, let alone pay any attention to the scruffy youth who waited patiently to ask about joining the Centre, all the time taking in every word that was being said.

"I don't understand," Candice stuttered.

"We are trying to find out as much as we can about a woman called Veronica, last name probably Stenning. We think you may be collecting her mail from a post office box at the Queen Street Post Shop," Phil Brown said.

Knowledge flashed across Candice's face. "That's right, how did you know that? But the name's not what you said; it's Lesley Horner. Oh my God, I'm not doing anything wrong am I?"

One of the other receptionists noticed Veronica and looked at him dubiously. "Can I help you?"

"Is this the form to join?" Veronica said, not missing a beat.

"It is, you need to complete it and either leave it here with us or you can take it away and send it in."

"Gotta pen?"

The last thing the receptionist wanted to do was hand the surly youth in front of her her own pen. She rooted around in a drawer and produced another, all the time trying to keep up with what was happening with Candice.

Veronica started to complete the application form.

"We need to ask you some questions. Is there somewhere we can go?" Phil Larson asked.

"Of course, come through," Candice said, lifting a hinged section of the counter. "We can talk in the back."

It was a close run thing as to who was more disappointed, Veronica or the two other receptionists, Andrea and Corrine, according to their name tags. The two officers followed Candice out of the public reception area. Once they were out of sight and hearing distance, Candice's work-mates could hardly contain themselves. They were about to launch into a full scale verbal autopsy of what Candice must be involved in when they both noticed Veronica again.

"How are you doing with that?"—glancing at the name on the application form—"Mr. Terry?" Corrine asked acidly.

Veronica grunted a monosyllabic reply, which made them both look at each other in disgust. "Maybe you'd prefer to finish it at home and bring it back next time you are passing. You can keep the pen," Andrea said.

Without a further word, Veronica dragged the application form off the counter and headed for the door. Unlike Candice, she was not out of earshot before Andrea started laughing towards Corrine. "Ooh, yuck!" then without taking a breath, "What do you make of that with Candice? Do you think they'll take her away?"

Veronica looked about outside. The unmarked police car stuck out like a beacon; two aerials on the roof, supposedly concealed red and blue lights behind the radiator grille and parked in a disabled bay as close as they could get to the entrance. She hoped something visible inside might give a clue as to which police station they were from. That could be very useful.

Her first cursory glance failed to assist; there was an open map-book and a police uniform jacket on the back seat but nothing else obvious on display. Her next move was forced on her by the surprise early return of the two policemen.

"Are you waiting for something?" Phil Larson said.

"You're not supposed to park here," Veronica sneered. "Unless *you're* disabled," she added with as much teenage sarcasm as she could muster.

"Very funny," Phil Brown replied.

"I should complain, just 'cos you're police."

"Do you want to make an official complaint?"

"Maybe," she said, deliberately sounding slightly less confident.

"Be my guest young man, you can call my Commander at Avondale or even the Commissioner in Wellington. I'm sure he'll be really pleased to hear from you."

When the Phils got back into their car and drove away, Veronica wandered happily back towards the bus stop. "Avondale, thanks for that." It had been a good morning's work.

Recent events had necessitated an urgent change of address and identity. She left the apartment the day before making as sure as she could she removed everything. Hotels and motels were numerous, and it did not take her long to find something small but comfortable. When she got back to the hotel, she showered and changed. After a snack, she headed out again; this time as Abbey Turner the nurse, the same disguise as on the morning she first saw Neil Danes. The cab she hopped into moved into the flow of traffic before she gave her destination to the driver.

"Avondale please, the Macabi Hospice near to the police station."

Tara was relieved to have made the calls to Cousens, the undertakers and to Neil's lawyer, Edward Cheam.

Mr. Cousens quietly explained the process and arranged to come around to Dan's the next afternoon when she could decide on a casket and one or two of the other arrangements. She could tell he was not surprised at the prospect of a very low profile funeral service.

Edward Cheam did his best to ingratiate himself with what he obviously considered charm but came across as sycophantic preening. Thankfully Neil's affairs were in excellent order, and his will was revised within the last calendar year. Tara made an appointment to go into Cheam's office the following week.

It only really occurred to her during the call that the lawyer's behaviour must have been due to the terms of the will, that she was going to be the beneficiary of Neil's unhappy millions. It was going to take a while to fully absorb all the consequences of her brother's death.

When the policeman mentioned the name Veronica Stenning, she knew that her use for Veronica's persona and all other future Stenning women for that matter were at an end once and for all. All the names beginning with V were tributes to her dead parents and she felt a sense of betrayal doing away with them now. Stenning too had become a part of her; originally a calculated risk to assist with utilising expensive forged identification, it had been a long time since she ever thought of using another surname. If that's who they were looking for then, difficult as it was, the logical conclusion was for her to be someone else. She had her own passport, but while the current situation existed, that was impracticable, particularly as she had entered New Zealand under her real name a few months ago. Fortunately, she always planned for every scenario.

As Nurse Abbey Turner, Veronica felt a little more secure again. Now she had a little more information, her next priority was to find somewhere else to rent in order to properly plan ahead; but first things first.

The lunch bar opposite the police station public entrance and car park was ideally placed for her purposes. With a weary, "I'm glad that shift is over," to the middle-aged woman behind the counter, followed by, "I'm waiting for my car to be fixed. Is it okay to sit and wait?" she ordered a latte and sandwich combo to eat in and took a seat looking out. She used her time productively, always aware of movements across the road while reading and reviewing information recently downloaded from her hard drive onto her Dell.

The Phils updated Dan upon their return. The evidence Candice Drysdale had to give was limited. Dan was not in the least disappointed; however, the small details were his forte, in all their forms: witnessed first-hand, discovered in documents or revealed in any other manner, the small things were the mortar that held the brickwork of an investigation together.

As the Phils went off to properly document their morning's exploits, he made notes on their tasking sheet and updated the daily incident file.

Stenning had made herself practically invisible; she accomplished the task of receiving posted mail from potential targets without disclosing her location. Even the third party, Drysdale, could not identify her. The name Lesley Horner was new to him although he bet it would also turn up in at least three English post offices and PO Boxes. The Vulcan Lane address became the next big priority. He caught himself relishing knocking down that door and realised simultaneously, he could not actually join in at that police-only party.

When he next looked at his watch, it was already after five. Harry came out of his office as Dan was preparing to leave. "What's this—part-timer?"

"Consultant's hours," Dan reminded him. "I might even bill you for my travel time too. No, I want to get home for Tara. I'm having all this fun again, but she's still lost a brother and has had her world come crashing around her ears in the last few days."

"Too true, anything more I need to know?"

"No, you're all up to date. Can we get the warrants sworn tomorrow, do you think?"

"That's the plan. We'll do the apartment first; it might have been nice to get in there already."

"I know, but the rules have to be followed, same shit, different country. See you tomorrow."

"Yeah, night Dan."

Abbey Turner's eyes shot up and honed in on the figure in the dark green Volkswagen Passat emerging from the car park. Her recently refreshed memory of a day outside Garstone Courthouse in 2008 played back like a re-run of a once-loved movie in her mind's eye, and she compared it to what she was looking at now.

The two profiles merged into one person, the same person. Detective Constable Daniel Calder, J. D. Calder, Dan Calder: all one and the same. She copied down the registration number of his car before collecting her things together and taking a cab back to the city.

The hotel room was small but comfortable. Abbey Turner, as she was now, was comfortable too with her temporary new look and identity. She settled back on the bed with her laptop on her knees. The New Zealand Transport Agency's online vehicle registration database was a bargain at thirty dollars per search. Soon she was poring over the details of the four owners of a green Volkswagen Passat. The only one that held any interest for her was the current owner, John Daniel Calder of 11 Beach View Parade, St. Heliers, Auckland.

Google Maps allowed her to get her first view of Calder's home both aerially and from front on. After a little more work, she also found the real estate agent's original listing for the property, which supplied her with more written and photographic information of the inside and outside of the two bed house.

At first she had been disturbed to see Calder leaving Avondale Police Station. It wasn't an unexpected development, but it did represent a new dynamic. She never seriously thought of herself as a target up until that second. Once the feeling reached its crest, she was able to quickly content herself with the knowledge she was still several steps ahead of her opposition.

Not only that, but also there was no fear inside her. She was genuinely surprised during the taxi ride back to the hotel; having seen Calder and recognising the fact she was being actively investigated by him and the police, her feelings only intensified. The unfinished business she had with him and Tara Danes was unaffected. She was better prepared, more dedicated to her task and unconstrained by regulations. She was not going to back down; she would not fail.

If the two police officers she came across the day before at the leisure centre were representative of what she was up against, there was little she needed to concern herself with. Calder himself though was altogether different; he was intuitive and smart, and now he also had the use of police systems.

The rental agency she used for the Vulcan Lane apartment was no longer an option, but there were plenty of others to choose from. She scanned through the websites of several, making a short list of other apartments and small houses within a five kilometre radius of St. Heliers. She wanted and needed to be close. Over the rest of the day and early evening, she submitted a dozen enquiries for properties to a number of different agents.

Next she trawled the Internet for everything else she could find about Calder. In truth, there was not too much to discover. A few articles regarding his police career; he was badly beaten once by a group of drunken men, commended in another for disarming a man with a Samurai sword and also praised early in his career assisting a woman to give birth in the middle of a supermarket.

Somewhat more interesting was the fact he was the son of another much more prominent policeman. The hits on Calder Sr. ran into many dozens. Abbey had a feeling this connection ought to be analysed a little more before she laid it to one side. She allowed herself to dismiss a concern about Calder once before; it was an error she would not repeat again.

Superintendent John Francis Calder seemed to covet the attention. He appeared across the spectrum of public meetings and social events all over the police division he was in charge of, up to and after retirement, and then even more until he died two years later. Southleigh was a major residential, light industrial and retail town and area to the south of Nottingham.

Working backwards chronologically, he had been in charge of the division for ten years before retirement. Prior to that he regularly moved up the promotion chain, always as a uniformed officer within the Nottinghamshire area.

There were several references to him being a senior figure in the local Masonic scene, photos of him handing over cheques at charitable functions and also a mention as a hole sponsor for an annual golf tournament. This entry also listed his wife, Claudia, as part of the presentation group.

When Abbey searched Claudia Calder, she found two separate newspaper obituaries. One from her husband and another from her son. She studied the words of each.

Claudia Calder. Died after a short illness on 6 February 1978. Service and cremation at Nottingham Central Crematorium Monday 11 February. Goodnight sweetheart. John.

Claudia Calder nee Pooley. Beloved mother and best friend. Finally able to rest. Passed away in her sleep on February 6 after a short illness. Missed already by her family and friends. Celebration service at Nottingham Central Crematorium Monday 11 February.

Immediately, several things occurred to her. First and foremost, there were two! Why did the Calder men do that? She had not had much experience in her life of writing obituaries, just the one, in fact, for both her parents. It could simply be an innocent desire for a last personal message to a wife and a mother, but that didn't ring true for some reason. The words talked volumes to her as well.

The first one was obviously from John Calder senior. The last three words conveyed emotion but for them the short text was dry and cold.

The second from Dan Calder was all emotion from beginning to end. However one or two words still stood out:

"Beloved mother." "Finally able to rest." "Missed already."

Why say she could rest finally now? Rest from what? The other thing that then drew her eye again was the name 'Calder nee Pooley'. He wanted to identify her as not just the wife of his father, but someone separate, different.

These revelations made her think. She went back to the father again and looked for his obituary notices. There were two for him also, one from a grateful police organisation for his years of dedicated service indicating a formal funeral service in his honour, and another from his friends and associates within the local Masonic order. There was nothing from his son. Abbey quickly stored what she needed and then went back to her hard drive again for something else she stored on it not so long ago.

Dan Calder supplied the bare minimum of information to the Depression Society in order to gain access to the website forums and was economical with the truth on several of the introduction pages to say the least. She was not so interested in that as the subject matter of some of the forums he participated in.

Bullying, The Future, Dreams, Forgiving, Parental Pressures, Sibling Rivalries and Death and Loss. She devoured every word.

When she came across Calder's details while she was initially searching that site and Coping with Grief's, she saw enough in his profile to shortlist him. His emailed response to her original email was probably contrived though, and she was wary of placing any importance on it now.

Reading his forum comments again with a more informed eye, she drew some fresh conclusions. He suffered from depression in his life, pain, upset and distress. Now she believed there were other things too: conflict, failure to meet expectations, disappointment.

She felt a stirring inside; the dark places of Calder's past were starting to illuminate. She could sense his weaknesses for the first time—and with it, sensed her own strength rising again.

Tara made stir-fry for dinner describing it as, "Power food for your running but good for me as well." She was enjoying being in his home and kitchen.

"Does that mean no fish and chips or meat pies for me anymore?"

"Yes, Mr. Pom, you are in my country now and we eat healthy here."

Dan waited for her to tell him about the boring day she spent before filling her in on all the details of his. She was understandably desperate for as much information as he could give.

They tried to be normal too. Discussing his running programme and her shop was a welcome respite. The accounts for the shop were fairly simple to understand.

"You just have too much stuff," Dan said very un-diplomatically.

"I need to keep a good variety. It has to be exciting and interesting."

"Okay, but it has to be what's exciting and interesting to the customer, not you. You have to agree you have far too much in there, you have a shop-full in the stock room."

"So are you saying just buy less?"

"Why not have a sale to get things out the door? A big sale where you can get back what you paid, give your balance sheet a boost and then re-assess."

"I suppose I could."

"Make it an event; say an evening rather than usual shop hours."

Tara liked the sound of that, and soon she was shooting ideas of her own which got her even more excited and amorous as a result. Despite the intensity of their circumstances, they were still very much in the first throes of the relationship and it didn't take long before the lure of the bedroom became too hard to resist.

Dan prepared his running gear for the morning and put it outside the bedroom door so as not to disturb Tara. He then set the alarm for 5:45 a.m. guaranteeing she would be.

For the first time in nearly a week, they slept reasonably soundly. Dan woke momentarily twice during the night but was reassured to see her at peace both times.

The next morning Tara groaned when the alarm woke them both. "Please tell me it's just this one marathon you're going to do."

"Sorry honey," Dan replied stepping out of bed.

"That's honey, sweetheart and darling you've called me in the last few days."

"Too much too soon?"

"No I like it. I'll be here when you get back."

"I won't be too long, duty calls."

"You're loving being back in a police station again, aren't you? Don't worry, I am happy to see you happy. Go on, run. I'm going back to sleep."

By the time he had gone three ks, he could tell today's effort was going to be a struggle; fortunately, there was no shortage of subject matter to take his mind off it. He drove himself onwards into the stiff offshore breeze.

Not quite as early to rise as Dan Calder, Abbey Turner was still up and out of her room by 8:00 a.m. She had an early appointment at a hair and beauty salon. By late morning, the all-new Abbey stepped out feeling very good and looking satisfyingly different.

The tanning session gave her skin a natural golden glow, at least two shades darker than she was the day before. It was complemented by the shortest hair style she had worn for many years, copied from a magazine picture of a European royal and one she had seen in Auckland recently. The colouring was new too: light chestnut brown with honey ash blonde 102 highlights. Along with a bag full of new make-up toners and foundations, the shape of her face now appeared to be less round and more oval. The shading of the make-up also made her nose seem a little smaller.

She stopped to get some passport photos taken at a mall on the way back to the hotel and hurriedly got changed, ready for her first appointment to view a modern second floor unit in Kohimarama, the next bay along from St. Heliers.

At 11:00 a.m. Dan left Tara at home again. Mr. Cousens' appointment was not until 4:30 p.m, and so she had another day of nervous tedium ahead. He promised to be back well in time for the undertaker's visit before heading out of the door with a "Make yourself at home," over his shoulder.

Once she was alone again, Tara decided to take him at his word. The photos they studied of Dan's old courses were still on the coffee table in the living room; she collected them up and went to put them back in the cupboard from where he retrieved them a few days earlier. One thing led to another and before long she was conducting her own investigation of Dan's house, peering into every other cupboard and drawer. It was more inquisitiveness than deliberate effort to discover Dan's hidden secrets.

What she found made her feel hollow. It was almost devoid of history.

The search warrant for Vulcan Lane took longer than anticipated to obtain. Harry was like a bulldog in a pen waiting for Philip

Te Tuke and Glen Johannsen to return from the West Auckland Court, pacing around the incident room and stopping here and there to look carefully at whatever nearest document or photo was attached to the wall.

"About friggin' time," he bellowed at the two unfortunate men as they stomped through the double swing doors into the room.

"Sorry boss," Te Tuke offered. "Magistrate wanted to know every detail before he agreed to sign it off."

"Have you checked it? I don't want it ballsed up because we've spelled the street name wrong."

"No it's fine, we both checked," Johannsen added, supporting his partner.

The whole team was assembled. Harry conducted a short briefing, and they left in a state of high excitement, leaving Dan at his corner desk chewing on the end of his pencil. Harry nodded as he swept out of the room, but otherwise Dan was ignored. If frustration could be bottled, he could have filled several barrels.

There was a good chance they would not be back before 4:00 p.m. and he promised to be home in time for Mr. Cousens. "Priorities, priorities," he thought and got back to work.

CHAPTER TWENTY-FIVE

Mr. Cousens' pleasantness shone through as abundantly in person as it did over the phone. Dan got home late but only by a minute or two. "Sorry, traffic on the motorway," he said to Tara, kissing her cheek before shaking the man's hand.

The meeting was conducted with quiet efficiency. Tara selected a simple oak casket with brass handles; while he said nothing, Dan was amazed at the cost of even the most basic coffin and the *essential* costs for a car to transport it, personnel, cremation and the other associated services.

The service date and time was confirmed. Tara re-iterated that the chances of any more than five or six people attending were slim. Mr. Cousens made the appropriate comments, shook their hands again and left.

They went to bed at 10:00 p.m. Neither were tired yet; both felt the need for skin to skin contact.

"So how was your day?" Tara asked.

"Good and bad. I'm sorry again I was late home."

"You weren't really, don't worry. What happened today?"

"Harry and the rest of the team went to execute the search warrant at the apartment this afternoon."

"And?" she said tensing against him.

"I don't know, I had to leave before they got back. I thought Harry might phone me, but he didn't."

"You could have stayed."

"To be honest, I thought about it, but I realised I wanted to come home more. It's not my job any more; I'm just a resource as he put it. I was pissed off when they all ran out this afternoon, but what can I do."

"Thank you for coming back."

"I wouldn't have in the past. I suppose you can call that progress. Dan Calder's growing up."

She breathed heavily, warming his chest. "I looked through the house today."

Dan tilted his head to look at her, she was looking back apologetically. "And?" His voice was non-committal.

"It was a sort of an accident. You said to make myself at home and I started by just wanting to put your old pictures away but before I knew it I was ..."

"Being a girl," he said softly. "It's okay; there isn't anything here that I want to be a secret from you," and instantly remembered otherwise. "Did you find anything interesting?"

Tara relaxed again. "God, you're wonderful," she said. "What was interesting was there was so little of your life anywhere. Hardly any photos, although your dog is the most adorable I've ever seen. But seriously, have you really got such a small amount of personal stuff?"

"Is it that hard to think I have either lost out in the possessions lottery at the end of relationships, or don't want to keep bad memories around?"

"It is for me."

"You have to remember that I'm just a man. I've known who the real strongest sex is for years. There was an old actress who once said she was a good housekeeper, divorced three times and kept the house every time."

Tara giggled. "Funny and true. Seriously though. I was quite sad to think there is so much you must want to forget. What about the good times?"

"The truth is I don't recall too many of them. I told you before what it was like to grow up in our house, nobody laughed when we were all together. My mother died a scared and probably scarred woman; believe me, it was no fun after she was gone

either. He was so bitter; like she had robbed him of more time
to abuse her.

"After I finally got out, I was so anti-relationship it took five
years before I even wanted to get involved with a female. My
first girlfriend only wanted to get married and have babies, not
necessarily in that order. She saw the pound signs attached to
getting involved with a policeman, security with which to breed.
I was lucky to get out of that one with my salary and parental
status intact."

"And you never found the right woman after that, one to settle down and be happy with?"

"I came close once. I thought we were happy, turned out it
was only me and only because I didn't know she was screwing
half the doctors in the hospital where she worked. You saw
the pictures of my dog, he was like our child. I wanted to keep
him when I split from her. She said she wanted him too. No
contest."

"So was it really a fresh start coming to New Zealand?"

"It was meant to be, yes."

"You don't sound convinced."

"What I found is fresh starts necessitate leaving the past behind. I didn't or couldn't. The dreams and the bad days; they
came with me."

Tara pulled herself even closer to him. "And now all this.
Christ, Dan, I'm so sorry."

"I'll let you into another secret," he said. "Since this thing
with Stenning started I've felt the best I have for some time,
and I don't really know if I should be sick with myself about it.
How's that for screwed up?"

Tara did not reply, and for a while, they lay quietly together
intertwining fingers and caressing each other's bodies.

Dan spoke next. "There is one more thing."

"Oh yes and what's that?"

"It happened today and I can honestly say it's a first." Tara waited for him to continue. "You mentioned it earlier, and it made me think. I came home today when there was something to keep me at Avondale."

"Yes."

"Tara, I've never done that before, *ever*. The job was always the most important thing, much more so than any woman waiting for me."

"Oh, my darling man."

And with that, the talking was finished for the night.

After making love, Dan went to the study door to extinguish the light and looked in to where his first manuscript rested on a shelf with other books and papers. He looked at it for a long moment, thinking about chapter fourteen which was locked away from view in a case in the other bedroom before switching off the light and closing the door. He was glad Tara seemed not to notice the pause and ask why, or he would have had to lie again and he did not want to lie to her.

The next morning they ate breakfast together before Dan went off to Avondale.

He found the entire team already working in various sections of the room when he entered; most looked like they had been there for some time already. He was greeted almost as a second thought by Phil Brown and Kiri Ieremia.

Dan was grateful not to be completely ignored. "How did it go yesterday?"

"Crap," Brown stated flatly. "No sign of her and the apartment was cleared out. I don't think she'll be going back any time soon."

Dan was disappointed but not shocked. "It's alright, we are getting closer, and she's obviously on the run now; a much better position than this time a week ago. Where's the search log?"

"The boss has got it," Kiri replied.

The search logbook was open on Harry's desk. "Morning Dan; you're wanting this I imagine?"

"Yes. Morning, Harry."

"Not a lot to go on, but take a look and let us know what you think."

Dan took the book back to his desk, grabbing a coffee on the way from a small machine which arrived in the room overnight. He resisted the temptation to open it before he was fully settled and had all he wanted around him so he could give it his undivided attention. All he needed comprised of a fresh pad of A4, a pencil and the phone on divert.

He felt a slight tingle run through him as he turned the cover back. The log was written by Phil Larson. The method of completion was for one room at a time to be searched by several officers; whatever item was to be logged, either noted and left or noted and seized would be brought to Larson who remained in one place to record the details of each item, the person finding, the location of the find, and a reference number of the find.

The rooms searched were, in order; hallway, kitchen, living room, bedroom one, bedroom two and bathroom. Phil Brown was right, there was not a lot of interest from any of the rooms; a few pieces of miscellaneous paper in the form of shop receipts and a movie ticket stub from the rubbish bin in the kitchen formed the sum total of finds from all rooms except from bedroom one. The finds from the bedroom looked innocuous enough too, on first examination; empty Band-Aid box, a copy of the previous Sunday's *National Enquirer* newspaper, a CD of *Louis Armstrong's Greatest Hits* without the case and a blue disposable pen with 'NZ Wheels 09 311 14141' printed on it.

Dan wrote on his pad all the thoughts stirred up by the listed items. He propped the pad up against the phone and leaned back in his chair, examining what he had written. He took all the time he needed to be sure he covered everything and was satisfied, he then took his pad again and made several additions. Soon he was back in Harry's office.

"We need to have a look at the newspaper," he said without explanation.

Harry's eyes twinkled. "We did. Nothing in it."

"Trust me, we do." Dan smiled. "And are we checking NZ Wheels to see who they are and what they do? And has someone checked the CD?"

"The CD is just that, played it myself last night. I think Kiri's checking the pen, we are fairly sure they rent and sell motorcycles, got several branches."

"Okay. I need the newspaper and also a light-table."

"What the hell is a light-table? I can tell you right now there is not one in this police station."

Dan laughed. "No problem; get me as many Maglites as you can find and a sheet of glass or clear plastic."

It took a while to gather enough of the standard issue torches for his purposes and assemble the impromptu table. When it was ready, Dan and Harry along with Kiri, Phil Brown and Philip Te Tuke stood around it atop Dan's desk. Twelve police issue torches, turned on and stood facing upwards like soldiers inside a cardboard box filled with polystyrene beans to prevent them from falling over. The sheet of square glass laid across the torches like a tabletop had been borrowed from somewhere unknown to Dan with the torch lights shining through.

"Go on, I give up," Harry said clearly speaking for the others too.

"I can't take credit for this. An old Scenes of Crime friend of mine showed me this trick years ago. Where's the paper?" Dan said.

When it was handed over Dan separated all the sheets out, took the first one and placed it on his ad-hoc light-table. "You'd be surprised at the number of people who have to lean on something when they write," he explained. "Sometimes when you do, you leave an imprint ... like this one," he added triumphantly.

They were all following his pointed finger.

Showing up clearly in white on the edge of the open front page were the words 'Wed 4' and 'chestnut/ h a b 102.' The result of ballpoint pen pressure on the paper.

"You are kidding me!" Phil Brown enthused. "What does it mean?"

Dan couldn't help but smile. "No idea, maybe nothing at all, but that's not the point. There might be something on one of the other pages *and* we've got a handwriting sample now. We need to do them all."

"I've never seen it before," Harry said putting a hand on Dan's shoulder.

"A proper light-table would be useful, quicker and easier."

Harry was ahead of him already. "Phil, call admin. Get one and someone from Scenes of Crime to come and get evidential photos."

At 12:30 p.m., Harry had a casual lunchtime debriefing session, for which he supplied two plates of assorted pies and sandwiches to facilitate the feeling he wanted.

Dan could detect a different air about the group, and it didn't take long to realise why. The light-table was fast becoming stuff of legend. Phil Brown was going over the episode for at least the fifth time that morning, this time with Jerome and Glen even though both had heard the story already from some other team member.

"You should think about joining NZ Police," Philip Te Tuke said.

"I think my days of all that are finished, despite this," Dan replied.

"Don't you miss it though?"

"Every day."

"So?"

"Long story, several long stories actually. No, it's definitely time to find something else to do."

Everybody was listening now. Glen Johannsen joined the conversation. "The boss said you did surveillance for years. What was that like?"

"The best time of my career. It's what I did best too, I sort of had a knack for it, loved the whole scenario of being covert. The downsides of being such an unsocial job didn't really affect me. Then I got into training and found a whole other world which I enjoyed just as much."

"How long were you in the job for altogether?" Philip asked.

"Almost twenty-six years."

"Why not see your thirty out? That's a fair bit of pension to give away," said Harry.

"If I went into all that we'd end up here with Stenning again. Three years, twelve thousand miles and I'm right back where I was." The quiet around the table meant he needed to change the subject quickly.

"What happened with the pen, Kiri?"

Having deflected the attention away from himself, he listened with the others as Ieremia described a possible good avenue of further investigation.

"NZ Wheels rent and sell small motorbikes and scooters. Fortunately each branch gives out these pens only with their own number on so it was easy to find this one came from the Parnell outlet. Two of the sales staff are fifty-fifty sure that a Vespa was leased to a woman matching our artist's impression picture. We should get copies of all the paperwork by the end of today."

This was very good news indeed; if they could identify a scooter being used by Stenning, they became a lot closer to finding her. Kiri confirmed no similar vehicle was in the area of the Vulcan Lane residents parking area when they conducted the warrant enquiry, and she had asked for a uniform patrol car to visit the area again to double check the current status.

Harry went on to update everybody on what else was happening in other areas of the investigation as they all ate. By 1:15 p.m., they were finished.

Dan had been back at his desk for five minutes when Phil Brown wandered over. He asked a superfluous question for which Dan had no answer. As he went to go back, he said, "We're all glad to have you here."

Dan nodded his thanks. When he left the big room for home later in the afternoon; acknowledging a full house of goodbyes, it was with a completely different feel to the one he entered that morning.

Dan went to Avondale on Friday morning too. Neil Danes' funeral was set for 3:30 p.m. and up until the night before, he had not considered doing anything but being close to Tara for the whole of Friday and probably the weekend.

Harry had a policy of an end of week wash-up and wanted Dan there; when he called on Thursday evening, Dan felt he could not decline. It was an important part of Harry's role as a supervisor for as long as he could remember and any such meeting without Dan would have been unthinkable to him.

Harry gave an overview of the ongoing investigation without going into specifics. He was generally pleased with progress. There was no news from England yet. Each member of the team took turns in then going over what they had done during the course of the previous five days.

The Phils followed up on their meeting with Candice Drysdale by obtaining a full witness statement from her. Phil Larson then covered the search warrant execution at the Vulcan Lane apartment which led to another animated discussion involving the light-table findings.

The phone number of a property lettings agency was easily the most exciting find. At first, everyone thought they had lucked upon a short-cut to Stenning's new home, but it came to naught because she appeared not to have called. Nevertheless they were primed to contact the police urgently if any woman named Stenning or Horner or with the first initial V made an enquiry. Copies of the available photos and descriptions were also left in the office to assist.

Philip Te Tuke stated inquiries regarding the Post Office box resulted in nothing positive, so far. Jerome Brett and Kiri Ieremia reported first that liaison with Customs and Immigration was ongoing. They made the initial applications for information to be released and Jerome had an appointment early the next week to visit both offices at Auckland International Airport.

Kiri confirmed the known information about NZ Wheels. Veronica Stenning of Vulcan Lane had indeed rented a Vespa for a six-month term. She paid cash in advance for all the rental and insurance fees. The machine was a black 125cc EFI model. It had a tan-coloured seat and twin visor mounted mirrors. The registration plate number was CMT 5590.

An alarm was placed on the scooter in case it was seen or stopped by any police officer anywhere in the country. If it was boarded on one of the ferries which travelled between the country's North and South Islands, its presence would be automatically red flagged.

Dan then briefly outlined the priority tasks for the next few working days. Budget constraints meant only one person was allowed to work on Saturday and Sunday. Whether it was by volunteering or an order from Harry, Phil Larson was going to do the Saturday shift and Jerome the Sunday.

Dan was home again by midday. He told Tara what he could as they shared a sandwich and then they got ready to go to the crematorium. Harry was going to represent the police as head of the investigation which the unfortunate Neil became embroiled.

Dan also said Philip Te Tuke was going to be there in order to speak to other people in attendance and obtain relevant details in case they may have anything to say to shed more light on Neil's hermit-like existence.

Dan did not add that he wanted someone else from the team there as well just in case Stenning decided to make a secretive appearance. It was highly unlikely, but not impossible, to believe she might want to see the result of her handiwork and the more eyes and hands, the better.

It was a desolate affair. The weather was the perfect accompaniment: overcast grey drizzle and cold enough to penetrate their outer layers. The only other people in the chapel other than the staff and those they expected were a couple in their mid-twenties who sat in the middle of an otherwise vacant pew towards the back of the room. Tara and Dan went to thank them for coming and to see who they were.

"Toby McCallister," the male said and then introduced his girlfriend Hinemoa. "I'm really sorry for your loss. I hope you don't mind us coming."

Tara recognised the name straight away and Dan a moment later. "No, not at all. I think you were probably his only friend," she said. "He talked about you as much as anything else. Thanks for what you did for him."

"I wish we could have done more," Toby said. "If there is anything I can do for you?"

Dan hoped there was. "I work with the police investigating what happened to Neil and also some other matters which we believe are related. Are we able to come to see you at your office sometime? There are some questions."

"I thought it was suicide."

"It was, but there are complications."

Toby gave him a card and Dan promised to call over the next few days.

The service lasted twenty-five minutes and Dan got the impression the celebrant did her best work to get it as far as that.

Tara had no desire to speak and requested no hymns as the thought of just a handful of people singing into an otherwise empty room was just too miserable a prospect. Instead there were two of Neil's favourite songs played over the chapel's audio system before his casket was mechanically shifted backwards and a blue velvet curtain closed.

The rain fell a little harder when they made their way outside. All Tara wanted to do was go home. Harry and Philip walked her and Dan back to their car. They were still standing in the empty car park watching when Tara had a final look back before Dan turned right onto the main road.

The last thing Abbey wanted was to go to Neil Danes' funeral service. That Friday afternoon she spent unpacking her suitcases and making herself at home in her new rental unit in Kohimarama. Payment in cash for a six-month tenure had secured a swift move in.

Well prepared as ever, she considered the police were looking for a "her" and utilised another persona, William Terry, to complete the rental agreement at the agent's office for him and his partner Abbey Turner. As far as the staff were concerned, Abbey was following him up to Auckland in a day or two. Later she went for a walk along the beach for some fresh air. The walk from Kohi to St. Heliers was so pleasant, she nearly allowed the temptation of going as far as Beach View Parade to get the better of her, but in the end, stopped at a bakery to buy some fresh bread before returning home. There was work to do.

Due to recent events, she had destroyed any reference there was to Veronica Stenning, including all identification and supporting documents. Even the computerised data on her laptop and external hard drive was deleted. Stenning was as dead as her victims.

She had also been waiting on a reply from the regular associate who supplied her with forged documentation, and there were also several questions which needed answering regarding her travel plans in the not too distant future.

She entered New Zealand using her real passport; there was no reason to do otherwise and due to the difficulty in obtaining the counterfeit documents required to defeat modern security methods, it was by far the safest. Unsure as to how much the police and Calder knew, she felt trapped in the country for the time being. If things had gone to plan, she could have departed as she arrived but the risks were far too great.

The Abbey Turner identity was currently sufficient for her needs, and she felt very safe that Calder and the police were completely unaware of her existence. But she could not discount they might somehow discover it sooner or later; therefore she required a new exit strategy. As always, she had one in mind already.

She was pleased to see the email reply she was waiting for when she powered up her laptop again. The message answered her queries. There were five attachments which she copied on to a flash-drive to print off another time. All she needed now was the passport to go with them. She checked the bus route planner for a trip from Kohimarama to Ellerslie on Mondays and Tuesdays. She wasn't sure what days Candice Drysdale worked, but it would not be difficult to find out.

CHAPTER TWENTY-SIX

Dan was glad the weekend was over. A new week hopefully meant the beginning of a whole new start for Tara, and she could look forward to getting back to her shop and on with her life. She still had to go and see the lawyer about Neil's will, where no doubt she would be told that what money he had was going to become hers. He hoped it may give her pause to think about what she wanted to do with the shop long term, but the way she pined about being away from it for the few days made him believe it wasn't something she was ready to give up.

With less than four weeks until the marathon, Dan's training regime was starting to wind down. The months of one hundred k weeks were gone and the new routine of a twenty k every second day for the next week to ten days and then maybe just a couple of fives or tens between then and race day was all that was needed to keep the muscles in top condition.

As he ran, thoughts of the investigation crowded into the forefront of his mind. The woman who existed as Veronica Stenning must have jettisoned all links to that persona by now, and most likely Lesley Horner too. He knew she would have alternatives ready.

The major pluses were few but important as a new range of pressures started to build around her. They had the details of the scooter, and as it had not been located up to now, she may still be using it unaware it was known to the police.

Secondly, they had the best possible up-to-date physical description of her.

Last but most importantly, he was still certain she used her own real passport to enter New Zealand, and therefore, probably planned to use it when she left. She might be concerned about how much the police knew and could be worried about trying to leave. He hoped she was feeling stuck here.

He splashed through a lone puddle, causing him to look down. His latest pair of Brooks were just over a month old and felt good on, comfortable and dependable. Over the years, good friends had been very few and far between in his life; almost entirely of his own making. He used to wish lots of things could have been different, but where he was now, in a place that he loved with a woman he had come to feel so strongly about in the most extraordinary of circumstances, he was grateful. He was never quite able to believe in fate, despite the periodic relief it might have brought him; but today he could no better explain how and why he was where he was; the coincidences, freakish events and downright unbelievable twists beggared all rational explanation. One thing was certain however, if there were such things as past and future lives, he was sure he must have been an absolute shit in a previous existence, or he was going to have a great time the next turn around.

Increasing the length of his stride, he quickened the return journey home where Tara was waiting for him. With each footfall, his resolve to find this woman, whatever her name was now, grew stronger. For Tara, and for himself.

Dan was mostly correct. What he failed to realise and could not know was Abbey Turner had no intention of leaving New Zealand yet.

If she had been gazing out of her living room window overlooking the sea-front at that moment, she might just have been able to see the back of Dan Calder before he disappeared around the bend from Kohi to St. Heliers.

In fact, it was another three hours before Abbey woke up. She was surprised to have slept for so long but was glad to have done so; she felt refreshed for another day on her computer. As she no longer had the gym to go to in the mornings, she went through an abbreviated exercise routine in her living room, then she focused on discovering everything else there was to know about Dan Calder.

By lunchtime, she was beginning to think there might not be any more. Calder's secrets remained obscured. His career did not produce many headlines and the police electronic systems were inaccessible. All that remained was the information he had on his own computer, which she was previously able to hijack when he answered her email from The Agency, but something about it continued to stir her curiosity.

To a casual observer, it looked like a not too frequent computer user's home machine. Emails, documents, photos, etc. were all there, but it seemed to her like they were *put* there rather than organically grown over time like any normal store of data. She examined the dates of various entries and found nothing to alert her otherwise.

The oldest photos were of him as a young man, nothing from his childhood and also nothing recent; the lists of emails in the various in, out and deleted boxes were all dry like stale bread. Even the bookmarked favourite sites he visited on the Internet looked like those of a bored and boring man. She read it again and ran a comparison program of her own design to identify similarities between him and some of her previous victims.

The program immediately returned dramatically mixed results, which in itself was cause for concern; it had never done so before.

She knew one thing about Dan Calder for sure; he was not bored or boring—and so she could not resolve what she was looking at. At that moment, she realised what had been staring her in the face and making her uneasy.

It all seemed put there because it was.

He must have known she could access his computer; he deliberately placed each email, and every photo. That also explained why only those photos which looked less like the Garstone detective she remembered were in that file. Not only that, but he had been able to make sure the dates of each message and entry appeared genuine and that was something even she could not do.

He knew about her before she knew about him!

She hated to admit it, but Dan Calder was a man not to be underestimated. In fact, he was as good at what he did as she was at what she did. Abbey decided that she must only rely on what she knew to be true where he was concerned and deal with him accordingly from now on.

She started back at the beginning with a fresh perspective. It appeared he was going to be running in the upcoming Auckland Marathon. The regular update emails from the event's organisers were the usual mix of hype, information and advertising. She also found the electronic copy of his application, acceptance and entry fee confirmation. It was very unlikely he could have manufactured this for her viewing. It gave her an idea.

There was an air of excitement in the room that hit him as soon as Dan pushed through the doors. At the cremation the day before he told Harry he would be a little late in today; a perk of being a consultant and not tied to regular police duties.

"What?" he said to Jerome, stopping him scurrying across the room.

"The boss is on the phone to England; he's been in his office for ages."

Dan got himself a coffee and went to his desk; like the rest of the team, he tried to get down to some work, but his neck was on a pivot, and he spent more time looking at Harry's closed door than on what was in front of him. It was another fifteen minutes before their torment ended when Harry emerged from his office.

"Morning, Dan. Everyone please grab a seat and let's get down to it." Nobody needed to be asked twice.

Harry required that any developments over the weekend be explained and discussed first; there were none of real consequence. Jerome thought the scooter may have been found in an Auckland car park, but it turned out to be a false alarm. A black Vespa EFI minus its registration plate, abandoned in a corner looked good until a chassis number check showed it to be unrelated.

"Anything else before we get on?" Harry asked.

Silence.

"Okay then. I've had a call back from the UK. I sent a request for information last week regarding our girl and Dan's evidence going back to 2002 on Vanessa Stenning. Due to his work already, we have probably got most if not all we are going to get on Vanessa, Vikki, Vivienne and Valerie so I asked them to start with our victims.

"So far only the very first one, Stephen Christopher, has produced anything useful. On top of what Dan obtained, the London Metropolitan Police have been able to add a few things to the story.

"Christopher was subject to a class action lawsuit by a group of clients he'd screwed out of many hundreds of thousands of pounds. That class action was headed by two particular clients, one old lady and another couple. The prosecution didn't ever get to court because the old lady changed her mind without warning and settled with Christopher. She got paid out and made a statement which could have cast sufficient doubt on the other couples' claim that the lawyers gave up. They were basically shafted, not once but twice."

"Shit, how unlucky can you get?" Phil Brown stated in typically blunt police fashion.

"The old couple, you can say that again, they were the ones who committed suicide. Dan, did you ever get their names?"

"Yes, Mallinder, I think it was, Norman and Irene. I didn't know about the other old lady though."

"Iris," Harry corrected him. "Norman and Iris. The other woman was Cecilia Mathews."

The team around the table looked at each other. It was good new information was coming in but no one thought what their leader had said so far was particularly interesting. Except for Dan.

"Mathews?"

A small smile was playing on Harry's lips. "Yes."

"Cecilia Mathews—as in, short for Sissy Mathews, our second victim?"

"Yes," Harry said again.

As he and Dan sat looking at each other across the round table, the rest of the team were in uproar. Dan and Harry waited for the noise and excitement to calm before Harry continued. Dan just sat back in his chair keeping his steady look on the big detective; he could tell there was still more to come.

"Alright, that's enough," Harry eventually said to restore order. "That obviously got someone over there thinking and they went back to look at it in more detail. The Mallinder couple lost everything they had; even their house was going to be repossessed. The night before the bailiffs were due they went to the garage and connected a hose to the car exhaust. The bailiffs found them holding hands in the back seat the next morning."

Philip Te Tuke said, "And Christopher got his just desserts sometime later. There must have been a long queue of unhappy investors lining up after what he did."

"That's a lot of suspects, too," Kiri added, verbalising what everyone was thinking.

"I thought so too until I got these," Harry said turning over two sheets of paper he brought from his office. "Norman and Iris Mallinder's death certificates."

Phil Brown snatched them up and looked at them before handing them to Phil Larson, who was to his left. "Suicide, carbon-monoxide poisoning? Yes, so what?"

Larson was as bemused, as was Jerome who looked at them next. Dan was ready to leap across the table but Kiri saw what the others missed and saved him the trouble.

"You are fucking kidding me!" she blurted out, shattering the perception Dan had of her up to that point. "Their middle names: Norman Victor and Iris Virginia."

"Exactly," Harry said.

Bedlam enveloped the room again and this time Dan could not stop himself from taking a full part.

That Christopher was linked to the Mallinders was not news, but the nature of the connection itself was a huge discovery. Dan attempted to compute the ramifications and at the same time tried to take on board Mr. and Mrs. Mallinder shared a middle name initial.

V. It was barely believable.

Harry and Dan sat in his office. The revelations of the morning were finally sinking in.

"No such thing as coincidence in our game," Harry said.

"Only limited by your imagination," replied Dan.

"What do you think then?"

Dan had been thinking of nothing else. He got up and started to pace the room. "Someone related to the old couple or with a strong connection to them. It has to be."

"To honour their memories with the V," Harry added, watching him go back and forth.

"Yes, got to be. When do you expect to hear from them again?"

"You know what it's like, plus the time difference. When have you known a major incident investigation ever to be straightforward?"

Dan laughed. "But we always live in hope."

"Always. In the meantime, there are other tasks to be completed. What have you got for them today?"

Dan returned to his seat and ran through the list of jobs to be done, enquiries unresolved from the previous week and new ones that had come in.

"You should really think about coming back; you know, joining, you have got so much to offer. It pisses me off to think that all your talent is going to waste," Harry said after a while, almost as a thought to himself.

Dan leaned back, pushing the front legs of the chair off the ground. "Sometimes I can't think of anything I'd rather do either, but I took early retirement because I had a problem with authority and I could not stand arseholes. I don't want to go through all that again."

Harry looked at him curiously. "I spoke with a DCI Allen from your old station."

"The chief arsehole in person," Dan said.

"He wasn't very complimentary about you either. Told me you couldn't follow rules."

"He might be right about that. What did you make of him?"

Harry looked up and pointed to the sign above his desk. "He's got no imagination."

"Yes, but he has got the rank; checkmate."

Harry seemed to take umbrage at Dan's comment. "Bull crap! He's got the rank because he passed a few exams and talked his way through a few promotion boards. The fact he might be a complete idiot is beside the point. If you cared so much about things being done right, you should have got promoted yourself so that you were in a position to make them right. Don't moan about others' incompetence if you aren't prepared to do something about it.

"And one more thing, don't try that 'I wanted to stay a DC because they do the real work' on me; that's a cop-out."

Dan was taken so far aback he could have been outside in the car park. "I ..."

"Yes, yes. I, I, I." Harry cut in. "I used to think like you, and I know I was wrong."

He mellowed as quickly as he sparked up a moment before. "You could have been a superstar, you should have been one of the new breed of modern policemen to take the job to the next level and to deliver a service to the public they deserve. It's your loss and theirs. And now you're here with another chance and still you can't see it."

The two men sat in silence on opposite sides of his desk. Harry looked tired, like a boxer in his corner between rounds. Dan looked slightly ashamed: the truth hurt.

"What is it you really want, Dan?"

"I don't know."

"So how will you know when you have a chance to grasp it?" Dan had no idea.

"Look, it's not my business, but it just seems to me that all this is like home for you," Harry said finally.

"I have been having these conversations with myself every day for as long as I can remember. I'm a bit of a mess truth be told. I won't bore you with any of the details; you'll have to take my word for it."

"Listen Dan, how long have we known each other for? Two weeks," Harry said, answering his own question. "You're a born natural whereas I'm a worker, but I do get there in the end. Even I can see enough already to know there are some skeletons in your cupboards, but who in our line of work doesn't have a few. If you don't, you've not been working hard enough.

"The thing is it's never going to be perfect. I came here for the quality of life for us and the kids; for the most part, it has been a dream but it still isn't perfect."

"So what are you getting at?" Dan asked while thinking about his own cupboard full of skeletons.

Harry looked at him ruefully. "For a genius, you're not too clever sometimes. It's enough, that's what I'm getting at. If we found perfect, how long would it stay perfect for, before there was something else we wanted? Appreciate what you have and perfect isn't all it's cracked up to be all of a sudden. Take it from one who knows."

Dan looked at Harry with something akin to brotherly concern. "One of your skeletons?"

"Yes. I nearly lost it all a few years ago; with my wife and family, I mean. I got carried away with a younger female colleague looking for perfect and thinking it must be something I didn't have already. I'm lucky that some friends sorted me out in time and thank God they did."

"Enough. That's an interesting concept."

"It's also pretty good in reality too. You should try it."

"Thanks, maybe I will."

Dan went for coffee for them both, when he returned they got back to the matter in hand. The new information was going to start leading them in a slightly different direction.

Stenning was now known to be a serial killer who at least began her murderous career on a mission; what they didn't know yet was whether she was still on the same mission or had embarked upon a new, more sinister one.

Dan knew there must be a lot of the answers in the evidence they had in their possession already; hidden in the details, waiting to be discovered. It was the nature of this type of inquiry that data came in which seemed innocuous at the time until another piece of information suddenly brought it to life. That was the good news, the bad was it would take him an age to go through it all again.

"I can maybe free up one of the guys to help. But we're getting a bit behind on the tasking and re-tasking. If we're not careful we will have to stop altogether just so we can catch up. That is not a scenario I want to get into," Harry offered.

"Thanks, any additional help is good."

"I'd like to throw people at it, but we've only got the eight of us who have sufficient knowledge of the case and not enough time. That's less manpower than you had in one of your classes when you were teaching."

Dan was about to get up and leave when Harry's words took on an interesting meaning. The more he considered the idea the more desperate it seemed. He had never done anything like it before. There probably wasn't enough time, it probably wouldn't work and Harry was going to probably think he was mad. And yet he found himself talking. "Harry, can I ask you something?"

Harry looked but did not speak. Dan took the plunge. "How do you feel about a training day tomorrow, for everyone, including you?"

"Have you forgotten what we *just* said?"

"I may well be crazy, but let me explain."

When Harry strode into the main room calling for everyone's attention ten minutes later, Dan was behind him. "Change of plans for tomorrow; I want you all here by eight."

Dan worked all night long getting only a little sleep just before sunrise. Tara stayed up as long as she could, but in the end she went to bed alone for the first time since she had been staying at Dan's. When he told her what his plan was, she agreed with him; he probably was mad.

The incident room looked more like a classroom when the team arrived the next morning. Seven desks each with a single chair, telephones piled up in a vacant corner, new pads of A4 and pens in their place. Dan also closed the window blinds cutting out most of the daylight and put a lamp on each desk to compensate.

"I was supposed to be going to the airport today," Jerome said. "I'm not complaining, but shouldn't we be doing this another time?"

Dan held up his hands in submission. "You're right and I'm sure the rest of you are all thinking the same. We are a bit behind, and I want to see if we can catch up a bit with a lesson I used to run but on a much grander scale.

"Do you remember the log keeping exercise Harry did with you a while back?" There was a group acknowledgement. "We're going to do the same thing but with all the evidence we have." Blank expressions all around. "Let me explain. I used to love going to court to give evidence, it was like theatre. What's the best evidence?"

"First hand," Phil Brown answered.

"Right. 'I was there, and this is what happened.' Second, maybe a video from a CCTV or something like that, and then a written record, someone's statement read out." There was a general agreement, and Dan sensed he was starting to carry them with him.

"Remember that phrase 'a picture paints a thousand words'? Well I found with surveillance, a word picture can do that job for you too and my way of log-keeping seemed to be very effective with painting word pictures.

"How many people do you need to complete a logbook in an OP?"

"Two, one to watch and one to write," Philip replied.

"Yes, you can't watch and write simultaneously," Phil Larson added.

Dan smiled and nodded enthusiastically. "I see Harry did a good job teaching the lesson. That's right, and both have to have complete confidence in the other to do their bit.

"Okay, I'm going to be the watcher, and you are all going to be my writers. I'm going to start at the beginning with the Mallinders, Sissy Mathews and Stephen Christopher and we're going to go through the whole lot. I'll be making those word pictures for you and you're going to create logs we can make into a combined document at the end. Basically we're going to have your seven individual views of the same ongoing job. I know you'll pick out all the details between you."

By now he had the enthused attention of the whole team. "Trust me like I trust you. Listen and let your skills and abilities interpret what I say into what you want to write. It's going to be a long slog, and I want to try and do as much as we can before taking a break to keep us all in the moment.

"Questions?"

There was no reply from anyone. Harry was the first to pick up his pen.

Dan checked his watch and turned off the main room lights; the individual desk lamps transforming each desk into its own private space suspended in the gloom. There were a few dubious looks between the assembly as Dan got himself ready.

When he began talking, he deliberately kept his voice a little low so as to make the team have to strain to hear each word.

"It's England in the spring of 1999. Norman and Iris Mallinder have joined forces with Cecilia Mathews. They have become unwitting victims of an investment broker called Stephen Christopher. Norman Mallinder is sitting at the kitchen table with his head in his hands. His wife Iris is pacing the room. She can't bring herself to sit still."

Before anyone knew it, they only had ears for his voice. Dan continued speaking, reaching a comfortable tone and pace he could maintain forever if necessary; just like running a marathon; referring constantly to the notes he stayed up all night refining. Bullet points highlighted, dates and times, places and descriptions, he was relentless in describing every aspect of one linked incident to the next.

Introducing what things sounded like and smelled like as well as the more usual description of visual only, he filled out scenes bringing them to life once again there in the incident room. Occasionally he paused just long enough to look up at his *students* but not so long as to break the flow of what he and they were doing. Everyone was writing continually, sometimes frowning, sometimes smiling, all the time concentrating. It was one of the most wonderful things he had ever been a part of.

When he described Valerie Stenning's dealings with Edwina Jacobs, he included details of Jacobs' little collie-cross dog to add greater depth. Dan liked to use ancillary facts in statements and logs because it focused attention and aided visualisation. As he spoke, Oscar could have been in the room with each of them lying at their feet.

When he next looked at his watch, he had been talking for three hours and not one member of his team had made a sound the whole time. He continued without any reduction in the pace or precision of his word pictures as the team soaked up every single word like a cluster of sponges.

As he spoke, he noticed details in what he was saying that related back to other evidential points he failed to put together himself before. This was exactly what he was expecting. By the way the team were responding to his unique training day, he knew that when it came to compiling the final written piece from all of their individual logs, his aim of squeezing every last drop out of the information would rise to the surface. After another mammoth effort, he finally paused again.

"What's the matter?" asked Kiri.

"Have you looked at the clock?" Harry said by way of a reply. When they all saw the time, no one could believe it.

"Don't look at what you've done so far and try not to talk about it either," said Dan. He was concerned about being able to re-capture what just happened in the room, but he was exhausted and needed to take a break.

The level of concentration required to speak as he had done for four hours straight was astonishing; he invoked the descriptive power of all five senses as he never was able to before. Nothing he was involved in before could compare with the level of sheer descriptive drama he exerted at that moment. It was like combining every OP he'd ever worked and running them all at once.

"That was really something," Jerome said above the general buzz of excited conversation. "How the hell are you able to do that?"

"It's like being there when it's happening," Phil Larson added.

Dan needed the toilet, and he needed a coffee. "Paint the picture, all you have to do is paint the picture."

Harry interrupted, unable to contain himself. "I remember now; in your lesson that was the other big one-liner quote. I'd forgotten that one. Hey, but even so, in your lesson back then it was nothing like this."

"I reckon I would have been in the funny farm within a week if I tried and do that every log-keeping lesson."

Dan excused himself from the group to take his bathroom break. As he left his request for them not to talk about it was being completely ignored, Harry being the chief miscreant.

Dan's fears they might not be able to continue where they left off were soon proved unfounded. If anything, it was he who had the most trouble in getting back into the zone.

Taking up again at the point where he found the email from Stenning at Neil Danes' house, he took more time than was absolutely necessary setting the scene again to reach the same tone and pace of delivery.

"Coming down the stairs after double checking the rooms on the first floor, Dan Calder is already thinking about getting out of the house and not wanting to come back again. The stillness of the house feels like a heavy weight on his shoulders and there is a smell of stale air because the windows have been closed for so long, and Neil Danes has not been there to move around and make it circulate. At the foot of the stairs, there is something not quite right; initially he senses it rather than sees it, and then he makes the connection. The electricity to the house is off, and yet there's a light on; it's only a small green light, but it should *not* be there. It's coming from a laptop computer in the lounge; he hadn't taken any notice of it before because the screen was blank, and there were no lights to suggest it might be active.

"Calder approaches it slowly; carefully looking around the room as he does in case there are other changes. The green LED is the battery light, the computer was on all the time, but it had dropped into hibernation mode. He decides to take it with him and is surprised when he picks it up that it's warm to his touch because the rest of the house feels so cold. He is even more surprised when the screen explodes into life revealing a series of photos on a white background, emphasising its brightness."

Dan looked up again; his team of writers were entranced.

When he stopped next, this time for good, the sun was low in the sky on the other side of the covered windows. He felt like he did not have a single word left inside his entire body.

The thought of now going through a long logbook debrief process and document construct was too painful to contemplate, although it had been in his over-ambitious plan the day before. If he'd known this was how he was going to be at the end, the idea would never have entered his head.

Harry and the rest of the team, prompted by the sudden halt, shook themselves out of their stupor and began chattering like school kids in the playground.

Phil Brown was waving his make-shift logbook like he had just finished translating the texts from the Ten Commandments for the very first time. As a group, there was a sense of wonder at what they had just been a part of.

If Dan was exhausted almost to the point of collapse, they were the complete opposite. Save for a few sore hands and fingers, which were being stretched and massaged to work out the cramps, they were already in full and very loud flow. Galvanised into action suddenly and feeling a need to make up for the day spent in constant quiet, they were in a frenzy of animated discussion. Comparing and agreeing on some of the evidential diamonds they had uncovered or exclaiming amazement that one picked up on something another missed.

They were all so busy with each other that nobody noticed Dan semi-slumped in his chair, leaning back as far as he could with his legs stretched out in front of him, eyes closed and smiling contentedly.

Kiri glanced across and went over. "Are you alright Dan?"

"A bit tired, to tell the truth. Can you put the lights back on?"

The return of the harsh office lighting brought with it a return to reality for everybody. Lunch had come and gone unnoticed; time had stood still, but now it seemed like it was rushing to try and catch up again.

Harry was experienced to know that any attempt to get back to "normal" work would be futile. Instead he ordered his troops to pack up for the day. "But I want everyone back in by eight thirty in the morning, okay?"

Kiri and Phil Larson put the desks back in their proper positions and then followed the rest of the team over to where Dan was still sat, taking their thanks for the day and eulogising over how they found it.

When they all left, rather than go off to their homes as instructed, they went to the sports bar at the end of the street where many station staff routinely went to unwind after their shifts. A significant amount of beer was consumed over the course of the evening as they discussed and pulled apart the events of the day and to find an appropriate explanation for what sort of freak of nature Dan Calder was.

Thirty minutes after being left alone, Dan and Harry remained in the incident room and Dan had yet to make any attempt to leave his seat. In that time, Harry got them both coffee from the machine and collected the team's logbooks, scanning through a couple of them to compare with what he wrote in his.

Holding the handful of paper up to Dan's face Harry said, "Now that was some training day. It's going to take another big one tomorrow to go through it all."

"I think it went well," Dan replied.

"Very."

"Don't ask me to do it again any time soon though. I feel like I could sleep for a week."

"Tomorrow morning then?" Harry grinned.

"Yeah, I'll be here."

CHAPTER TWENTY-SEVEN

Abbey wanted to go to Ellerslie on Monday, but after calling the Broadway Fitness Centre, she knew Candice Drysdale was not working until the following day.

Instead she spent Monday completing the support documentation for Abbey Turner. She took the flash-drive with the recently received email attachments to a large shopping mall and used two different shops to print off the birth certificate, airline e-ticket and itinerary, nursing certificates and ID tag blank.

While she was there, she also went to a hardware store for some do-it-yourself materials and a small laminating machine, then clothes shopping to suit an English nurse on a working holiday. Later at home, she made up and laminated the tag using one of her new passport photos. The finished article was more than adequate for her requirements.

On Tuesday morning, she waited near the bus stop in Ellerslie to see Drysdale go off to work. She phoned the house hoping to get no reply. On the third ring, a male picked up. "Hello."

"Hi, is Candice there please?"

"Sorry, no, you have just missed her, can I take a message?"

"No that's alright I'll call her at work in a while. Thanks."

"Okay, bye."

It appeared she needed to wait a little longer at least. When a man with a briefcase finally emerged from the house and went to a car parked on the street, she had had time to down a takeaway coffee.

The man hung his suit jacket on a hook above the rear passenger window and placed his briefcase on the back seat before driving off towards the motorway. Abbey phoned the house again; no reply. She hung up on the voicemail.

The house was a double-fronted weatherboard construction, very similar to thousands of others all over Auckland and the rest of the country. Attractive, if a little old-fashioned in style for her taste, it seemed to have been renovated to a high standard and many of the original features remained, including the front door and windows; she hoped the back proved to be the same.

There was a side gate which led around to the back of the house and a two metre high fence all around, enough to offer her decent protection from the neighbours. The back door was a lot newer than the front and therefore not best suited, so her attention shifted to the nearest window. It was original and in equally good condition to those at the front. Its sash design she was sure slid up and down effortlessly, probably on new ropes and refurbished weights. It was locked from the inside with a polished brass fitting, operated simply by a thumb or finger moving it from one side to another.

Fortunately she was stood beneath a decorative pergola which, along with the garden fence, assured her she could not be seen. It was important that her break-in go unnoticed; especially by the Drysdales.

She took the small battery powered drill she picked up the day before at the hardware store from her pocket and drilled a tiny hole through the window frame close to the brass fitting. She then pushed a short length of stiff wire through the hole and bent it on her side so it curled around towards the lock as it went through the hole. She was close on the first attempt but just missed the pivot point. On her next try, the brass slide gave easily under the pressure of the wire.

Once inside, she carefully picked up the small amount of sawdust and repaired the hole in the window with a white flexible filler so as to make it virtually impossible to notice.

She found herself in a dining room decorated in modern styles that contrasted but did not clash with the older tenor of the house. When it came to home decoration, Candice Drysdale was not completely without intelligence, she thought.

Abbey started searching methodically. She wanted to be out as soon as possible and didn't want to have to search twice if she failed to find what she was looking for. She went through the dining room and then the adjoining kitchen; even though she did not expect to locate the item there, it may save time in doubling back between rooms. The living room proved unsuccessful too.

There were three bedrooms and a family bathroom upstairs. She was drawn to the smallest bedroom first; it also held a desk and a large cupboard as well as a made-up single bed. On top of the cupboard were two big suitcases; she felt she had reached her destination. The cupboard was full of spare household linen and towels and for a moment, she thought she might be wrong, but then she saw the bedside table included a drawer. It was open by a fraction and a piece of paper was protruding through the small opening. She opened the drawer and saw a number of used chequebooks, opened letters in their envelopes, a car registration document and what she was looking for: two New Zealand passports.

The passports of Alex and Candice Drysdale were not well used; a few stamps from Australia and one from Fiji in 2009, although it seemed Alex also travelled to Europe several years before. Each supplied the other's details as the emergency contact person. Once she gleaned all she could from Alex Drysdale's, she put it back in the drawer and closed it, being sure to leave it open enough for the stray piece of paper to stick through once more.

With Candice's safely pocketed, Abbey was quickly out of the house again. She had no choice but to leave the dining room window closed but unlocked. It was more than likely the Drysdales would not even notice, and if they did, only blame each other for not locking it.

She controlled the temptation to examine Candice's passport photo until she was all the way back home to see if her visit to the beauty salon nearly a week before achieved what she wanted. When she did compare it standing up to the bathroom mirror, the results pleased her. The shading around her nose needed a little more refining, but if necessary she could always claim a little cosmetic surgery. "Oh just my woman's vanity Mr. Airport Immigration Officer." She was equally pleased that nurse Abbey Turner was completely unknown to Calder and the police, and when the time came, she as Candice Drysdale could jet out of New Zealand unhindered.

Now there was a marathon to plan for.

Dan arrived at Avondale and was at his desk before 8:30 a.m., but was still the last to arrive by some margin.

Everyone greeted him like a favourite relative and stood around chatting about the previous day and other aspects of his police career until 9:00 a.m., when they all moved to the big table.

Harry redistributed the logbooks and once everybody was settled, they looked as one at Dan.

"We need a volunteer to write the debrief document for us all today."

Unsurprisingly they all wanted to have the chance to go back through their own logs as part of the debrief session, but after a short, uncomfortable pause, Phil Brown reluctantly offered his services. He was the senior member after Harry and in the long run, the other junior members would benefit a lot more than he from going over their own logs.

"Thanks Phil," Dan said, passing a fresh pad of A4 across the table to him in exchange for his logbook. "Okay I'll use Phil's and I'll be the narrator." He went on to explain the rules for the debrief and confirmed everyone was ready to go before he started, reading verbatim from Phil's logbook.

"Norman V. Mallinder and Iris V. Mallinder." He looked up. "An obvious possible link to our suspect?" Everybody agreed and Phil made his first notation on the pristine sheet in front of him.

Dan continued and the others followed. "Invested with Stephen Christopher in 1997 and through his fraudulent management of the monies invested, lost everything two years later. At around that time, as a result of the same fraud, Cecilia Mathews invests and loses a large sum."

Jerome interjected with some detail of his own that Phil had not recorded. "How did they come to get involved with Christopher in the first place? Also, is this the only Mallinder/Mathews association?" There was an interested murmur around the table and Phil's pen flew across the page again.

Dan continued reading and prompting, the others all contributing as the flow of information grew from a trickle to a stream and before long, a full-on flood.

As time progressed, they were adding more layers of detail to the known facts, expanding the picture and filling in gaps in the timeline they didn't even realise were there. As questions were asked, answers followed, new ideas were floated and they tacked this way and that through the information like a racing yacht searching for the best wind direction.

When Dan reached the point where Christopher died, Kiri had an observation in her log.

"The heart attack on the exercise bike; his feet were in clipped on pedals, but if Stenning is there next to him, *trying to kill him,* wouldn't he have tried to fight her off? *Fight for his life?*"

"I got that too," Phil Larson agreed. "No marks, scars or abnormalities noted on the body except for the appearance of a rash where hairs were pulled from the backs of both hands. That doesn't sound like defensive wounds."

Philip Te Tuke supplied the answer. "It's what you get if your hands were taped to the handlebars though and the tape was removed later."

Dan could not contain his delight. "Brilliant. Now we're really talking."

Phil Brown had been writing as fast as he could almost continuously. Without meaning to he said, "I don't believe this."

"What is it?" Harry asked.

Apologetically Phil replied, "Sorry no it's nothing, just talking to myself. For God's sake, just keep going."

Dan understood very well what Phil was alluding to, but it took another three hours before the full extent was revealed.

"And that's it." Dan said, closing Phil's logbook. The debrief concluded as he expected with every ounce of intelligence scoured clean, resulting in a mass of new information and evidence.

The timeline of Stenning's activities could be improved two or three fold. Answers for questions they didn't know they had, new questions and lines of enquiry, other ideas for forwarding the investigation and suggestions for improving their performance were now all contained on the pages of Phil's debrief document.

Despite one or two protestations, Harry insisted on a short break before they continued. He and Dan retreated to his office with coffee and the debrief document.

"I've been on maybe twenty major incidents in my time but I've never been involved in anything like this," Harry said sitting down. "Is this all a National Crime Squad thing?"

"I tried to introduce something very similar in my own force first and then at the national centre, but never got very far with any of it. I think because I was a bit unconventional."

"And had a hard time following the rules?"

Harry caught Dan off guard a little. "Yeah, maybe."

The coffee did its job of reviving them after the heavy morning, and for the next few minutes, they discussed some of the documents' contents. Dan thought Harry's interest in his past had waned.

"There's a barrel load of excellent stuff in here," Harry said tapping the document on his desk. "I could really have used these tactical aids before. It's a real shame it wasn't available."

"I'm glad to see how it has been working so far."

"Don't you get frustrated that because you couldn't be more reasonable, maybe one of the best investigative initiatives I've ever seen has gone to waste?"

Dan's obvious discomfort and loss of words again meant Harry knew he had got his measure.

"There's no point in dwelling on the past; after all, that was the reason we both came out here, Harry," he said in an attempt to salvage some wounded pride.

"You are dead right there. I think the trouble is you brought a lot of yours with you and it's still dragging you down. Something to think about if you really want to make a go of things here."

"Come on let's get back to it," Dan said, ending the conversation.

Phil's debrief document was a list of new tasks, answers to existing ones, extended information strings and a mass of evidential material to more thoroughly examine.

The first part of that process was another team meeting to go through it all and quickly identify any immediate priorities. After that, the long job of analysing everything else in order to properly categorise, assess, reassess and see where to allocate new tasks.

The result of the last two days' effort was to have caught up with and got ahead of the whole investigation. With some expected updated information due from England at any time, Dan felt he was getting closer and closer to Stenning.

Tara decided she was not going to be able to get on unless she started to do things for herself again and the first thing was to get the meeting with Neil's lawyer over and done with.

"Please come through, Miss Danes," said Edward Cheam, holding his office door open. He was dressed and appeared years older than his actual age, which she estimated at somewhere between thirty and forty. His office was purely functional, three walls made up as bookcases containing collections of legal volumes. His desk was as big as a dining table.

"I'm so sorry for your loss and for the fact we have to meet in these circumstances."

Tara's impression of the man on the phone had not been good, but she got the distinct impression now that he was far happier in the company of his books than he was talking to clients. His title of Estates Manager for the practice did not leave much latitude for interaction. She found herself mellowing towards him.

"Thank you, Mr. Cheam. I imagine it can't be the easiest job in the world to have to talk to the relatives; at least it's only me today rather than a big group of arguing family members."

He was clearly not used to such understanding. "Well, maybe, sometimes. Shall we get down to the reading of the will?"

Neil operated two bank accounts, one a term deposit with a higher level of interest and another regular everyday current account. It appeared he transferred a regular sum into the current account every six months from the term deposit and lived on that. There were no other savings, bonds or shares. His house was owned outright and their mother's old house was also solely owned by him.

"The terms of your late brother's will are very clear and very simple. It all passes to you, Miss Danes. I cannot see any reason to believe there will be a delay of any kind. If you wish, I can take the details of your own legal representative and your bank, and you can leave it all to us. I should think the matters can be concluded within ten working days."

"That really is very good of you," Tara said. "I don't have a lawyer of my own; can I ask you to do it, or is that not allowed?"

"No, of course, I am more than happy to assist you. I can send a letter later today to confirm our acting on your behalf and also let you know our fees."

"Thanks, I appreciate it."

When she left, Tara went into the first bar she passed and ordered a large white wine. She had lost her brother and gained several million dollars as well as two properties. It was all light years away from how she remembered growing up once her father was gone; the three of them were really happy then. Poor but happy.

When her glass arrived, she raised it and wished Neil a final farewell. "God bless, darling," she said and took a large sip. Then she put the glass back on the table and left.

When Dan got home, he was so tired he could have gone straight to bed, but he was also famished. Tara was sitting in the lounge on his big leather sofa gazing into space and did not notice he was there until he walked in front of her.

"Hey," she said quietly.

"Are you okay?" he said, sitting next to her.

"Yes, just been thinking about lots of things. How was your day?"

"I'm fine. What sort of things? You sound a bit strange. Has something happened?"

"I went to the lawyer's today, about Neil's will."

"You should have said; I could have come with you."

"No, I wanted to go alone. He was nice." Dan was not sure if Tara meant the lawyer or her brother; she was still speaking in little more than a whisper.

"He said all Neil's affairs were in order, and I was the only beneficiary. He's going to do all the paperwork, and it should all be over in less than two weeks. I can't believe that's it, it's such a waste of a life."

He put his arm around her shoulder. "I don't think we'll ever know what was going on in Neil's head."

"Or his heart," Tara interrupted.

"No, or his heart. If you believe in that sort of thing, you can only hope that he has found some peace now though."

Tara looked into Dan's eyes. "I don't."

She gazed into space, oblivious to everything around her, but then she spoke again, more clearly as if she was trying to wake herself from a dream. "Have you eaten? Let's go out; you can tell me about your day."

"Sure whatever you like. You choose and I'll drive."

The little Italian she selected in St. Heliers was walking distance from home. In the warmth and comfort of the restaurant, Dan ordered a bottle of Chianti and looked through the menu while Tara predominantly stared at the floor and the exposed brick walls. When it came, the red wine helped them both feel more at ease.

Dan thought about saying a few words and maybe toasting Neil but decided against it. Instead he went through the events of the day while they waited for their meals to arrive, and Tara chewed on a long bread stick.

"It sounds like you're getting closer to catching her. Are you?"

"Closer to knowing who she really is and definitely closer to having all the evidence to lock her away. But knowing all that and actually catching her are very different. She's very skilled at keeping her identity hidden, and also changing it as often as she wants so she can keep herself hidden."

"And you think she's still in the country?"

"I'd say so."

"If it was me, I'd want to get as far away as possible as quick as I could."

"From what we can tell, she doesn't think like us. She's got no feelings. If we believe she killed the broker Stephen Christopher and the old Mathews lady because she wanted revenge for the deaths of the Mallinder couple then that's one thing. But that doesn't explain the other two. I still cannot see what the connection to the first two may be."

"So she has another motive? The money." Tara said, suggesting an answer for her own question.

"For Neil and Edwina Jacobs definitely yes; but that still doesn't explain Mark Singleton. And that is what is really bugging me. I can't help but feel that I'm missing something that does link them all, and I'm a bit worried I might be on the wrong track altogether."

"Maybe you are over thinking it."

"How do you mean?"

"Well as a man, you try to find solutions to problems. As a woman, I think about what led up to the problem in the first place. Men are logical; women are all about the feelings."

"Go on."

"Okay, if I was her, revenge is a really strong reason to start with Christopher and probably Mathews too, she backed out of the lawsuit leaving the Mallinders completely helpless. The money doesn't even come into the equation. Remember the phrase about a woman scorned?

"If I found a big pay day was also an unexpected extra, it still would not be enough motivation to want to kill again."

"What would be then?"

Tara twisted her fork around in her pasta. "If I liked it."

Dan shivered as the thought of what Tara said sank in. If Stenning was killing for the thrill, then of course no amount of investigation could find a link which did not exist.

Tara was still randomly shovelling her food around the plate. "There is another thing."

Dan had not taken his eyes off her. "I thought there might be."

"The broker was 2002, then 2005 Cecilia Mathews, Singleton in 2009 and Mrs. Jacobs earlier this year. If it was me and I liked doing something as extreme as killing people so much to do it again," she hesitated and Dan held his breath, "I would not be waiting two, three, or more years, money or not."

She looked up from her badly mangled meal. Dan's eyes were now like saucers. "It takes a woman to understand how another woman thinks."

"It never even occurred to me. I was so set on what I'd discovered, I didn't stop to think there could be more. It also explains why I have so many exes," he continued. "I've never understood any woman I have known up until now, so why should I think I know this one! Please feel free to put me right on anything else that occurs to you. I'm obviously in need of the female perspective."

Tara smiled for the first time all evening. "My darling man, I always make allowances for the weaker of the species."

Dan put his cutlery down and reached over for her hand. "In that case, you might be able to understand something that's been on my mind. You said that men are the logical ones and women are all about the feelings?"

She smiled. "Of course."

"I am definitely Mr. Logic when it comes to looking at problems and trying to solve them as you well know, but I have an issue in dealing differently with feelings as opposed to experiences."

Tara shifted. "I'm sorry, I don't understand,"

"I can talk about my feelings, in fact I am really good at understanding them, especially in more recent years because they are real to me, you know, tangible."

"But experiences are the same, I mean you're having an experience, it doesn't get any more real than that," she queried.

"Okay, but stay with me a while on this. In my time, there have been one or two," he took a deep breath "five or six more like, experiences which I cannot get my head around. Things which have happened that I cannot explain or worse cannot remember, and it's those I have trouble explaining and coming to terms with, and it's those which have damaged me. I think it is them which are at the root of whatever it is that is wrong with me."

"There is nothing wrong with you. What sort of things?"

"Sorry Tara, I can't talk about them if I don't understand them, I just can't."

"But ..."

Dan tensed. "Don't but. Don't ask or try and work it out on my behalf either. I'm trying to be totally honest with you; after what you've been through, I owe you that much at least. It's just there are limits to what I can do. Remember what I told you, all I can do is be the best version of me I can, and that is not perfect by any means."

After that Tara seemed to relax quite a bit more and ate some of her dinner. They finished the bottle and ordered an espresso too, before walking home in a much better frame of mind.

In bed, they wrapped themselves up with each other, enjoying the mutual warmth. "I didn't finish telling you about what happened at the lawyer's office this morning, did I?"

"Was it alright?"

"Neil won Lotto in 2007. He bought his house and Mum's and set me up in the shop. Four years on, I don't think he spent much more of it."

"That is a shame. Obviously I didn't know him, but it is sad he could not enjoy it a bit more." Up until then Dan had not really thought about what the sum of Neil's wealth might amount to.

He was tempted to ask the question, but Tara saved him the trouble.

"Three point eight million, give or take."

Dan stayed calm and quiet, although he could just have easily screamed *Wow!*

"I'd swap it all and my shop to have him back again."

"I know."

"It feels wrong to have his money, very wrong to use it and try to do something good with it when he didn't."

"I've never had real money either, so I can't help I'm afraid. There's no rush to do anything is there? So maybe just give yourself some time."

CHAPTER TWENTY-EIGHT

News from England arrived the following morning. Phil Brown was in Harry's office depositing the team's time sheets from the previous week when the direct dial line rang. He picked it up instinctively and stiffened when the person on the other end identified himself.

"Good evening, or should I say morning for you. This is Colin Palmer, NCIS in London. Is Mr. Spiller there please?"

"No, he's not in yet. I'm Detective Sergeant Phil Brown, next in line."

"I have some information for you regarding a request sent recently. It says here to call first and then confirm by email."

"Let me grab a pen. Okay, go ahead."

"Norman and Iris Mallinder had a daughter called Katrina, no middle name, and one or two surviving extended family members. I won't give you all the details I have here because I think you'll be more interested in the daughter.

"Born in May 1974, she went to Sheffield University, was studying media and drama. She graduated in 1997, two years before the parents died. The interesting thing about that is at the time her media studies course director was a Mark Singleton; we have done the checking, and he *is* one of your other deceaseds. That being the case, he will be one of our deceaseds quite soon I'd say."

"Je-sus!" Phil exclaimed.

"If you like that, you're going to love the next part," Palmer continued dryly.

"Go."

"Katrina Mallinder; very interesting recent history. She hasn't worked for several years according to the taxation office records. She left the UK for Istanbul, Turkey via Heathrow Airport in June this year and has not returned. Immigration confirm at the beginning of August, she departed Istanbul for destination … Auckland. She entered New Zealand on the tenth."

Phil was ecstatic. "You're a star Colin."

"I'd say she's your girl," said Palmer.

"Incredible if she isn't," Phil agreed.

"In light of what you guys have discovered, a new investigation is going to be launched here at NCIS into the deaths of the four individuals where Stenning, or Mallinder rather, has been present. Someone senior to me from here will be in touch with Mr. Spiller in the next day or so I expect. Will you let him know?"

Phil waited impatiently until his boss arrived and he was able to disgorge the news they had all been waiting for. Harry printed off the information Colin emailed and was even more pleased upon reading it: the text included Katrina Mallinder's life history as discovered so far and other supporting documentation attachments such as birth certificate, driver's licence, passport, tax and national health records.

At the morning briefing, there was a lot to discuss.

A significant amount of progress on a number of outstanding tasks had been achieved as a result of the work done in the last two days. This latest input from London was valuable for more than just identifying Katrina Mallinder.

They had to be sure she was in fact the correct suspect; until it was beyond doubt, some tasks would be kept on file but could be placed at the bottom of the pile, giving Dan and Harry some breathing room.

Comparing the new photos of Katrina Mallinder with those descriptions already in the inquiry system showed how expert she was in the art of disguise and demonstrated how vigilant they needed to remain. Facially, the driver's licence and university photos of the eighteen- to twenty-year-old were very different to the passport photo and also the image Tara produced with the police artist. Looking at them all, Dan had some cautionary words for his colleagues.

"I would not have recognised any of these as the Vikki Stenning I remember, so she could be looking a lot different again today."

"I'd put money on it," Harry added.

"I think it could be worth a media release if we are certain about her," Philip Te Tuke said. "Really make her realise how close we are getting. I don't think she will give herself up, but getting the public onside as well will make it all the more difficult for her."

Phil Brown agreed. "Good idea. What do you reckon boss? I'd like her to be the one who's sweating for a change."

"I agree. I'll talk to the Superintendent and the Press Office and see what we can do."

Harry set the team a revised priority list with the emphasis on locating Katrina Mallinder. He still held personal reservations she may already have escaped the country, despite Dan's thinking. But if she was still in New Zealand, then it was more important than ever they close the net around her before she could execute a getaway.

Abbey Turner had other things on her mind. Her exit strategy was in place thanks to the recent acquisition of Candice Drysdale's passport. She now also possessed all the supporting documentation required in the event of a questioning airport official and everything was safely locked away in her travel bag.

Far more pressing was her need to commit to memory the route of the upcoming Auckland marathon. The route map showed the race was in two distinct parts on either side of the harbour bridge; starting in Devonport on the northern side, the first twenty kilometres ended with the runners crossing the bridge onto the city side for the one day of the year when it was closed to traffic. The second half was all along the waterfront to St. Heliers where they turned around and ran a return to the city and the finish.

It seemed very appropriate; because they ruined her sport with Neil Danes, she wanted to spoil Calder's sport, literally.

At that moment, Tara emerged from Dan's house and walked without purpose towards the sea-front. She wandered along thinking of nothing in particular and especially not about the tall youth with the black fringe and black baseball cap covering his eyes who was loitering on the sea-wall.

Abbey liked the disguise. An addition of a hairpiece was all she needed, in combination with the right posture and attitude. An added bonus was that the less she cared for the oversized hoodie and old black jeans, the better it suited the impression she wanted to convey.

She watched Tara all the way along to the short stretch of shops without moving, noting her enter the St. Heliers branch of the Country and Coastal Bank. She was not bothered by the several minute wait that followed. By the time Tara did emerge, Abbey had repositioned herself closer, in a bus shelter on the opposite side of the road. She now saw Tara as someone other than a tool to serve her requirements as she was with Neil Danes; to that end, she felt a need to acquaint herself with her afresh.

Tara's next visit was to a cancer charity shop; Abbey rightly surmised it was a habit she got into over the years of not being able to pass up an opportunity to look for retro clothes and shoes although she could tell Tara's heart was not in it.

Abbey watched Tara's slow, unhappy walk with keen interest.

Jerome Brett had been working on putting more of the Katrina Mallinder story into recognisable order. She was the only child of Norman and Iris, who had her fairly late. Her parents owned and operated a small carpet cleaning and restoration business and struggled for their entire lives to scratch out a living and provide for themselves and Katrina. There were one or two uncles, aunts and cousins on her mother's side, but the contact with them was always poor at best.

Life was never easy. Iris Mallinder suffered from arthritis, which meant she was in almost constant pain. Norman was one of those people who seemed to have more than his fair share of luck; unfortunately for them all, it was usually bad. From losing more contracts for work than he ever won, to picking the wettest weeks for their summer holidays. The Mallinder family were devoted to each other, which was just as well, because outside of their group, there was not a lot of love for the family from anywhere else.

Jerome tried to imagine how Katrina would view the world through her formative years and concluded she might have struggled to be a happy girl. Life could be unkind, and to people who were naturally quiet too, and accepting of their situation, it could be much more so.

Norman and Iris went without to make sure Katrina did not, and she would have been acutely aware of those sacrifices. Young Katrina was a shy, studious girl with few friends in a small village in the south east of England. From all the early school photographs, she looked to be plain, emphasised by a done-at-home haircut which did not change from the age of six to sixteen.

When she went off to university at nineteen, it was the first time she spent more than a few days away from her protective parents. She chose dual degree courses in drama and media studies; in all her previous school reports, the one constant was her love of books and stories. However she was always on the periphery. During school plays, she was encouraged by some teachers to take a more active role, but she never did more than behind-the-scenes activities.

An obvious change took place in the first year of her university life, and she became a lively member of the campus theatre and literature clubs. At an end of term performance of *Children of a Lesser God*, she played Lydia. By the end of the second year, she had become a lead in several productions, and her drama course director noted in a report that she exhibited a natural ability to immerse herself in both male and female roles. The reason for the sudden change in Katrina was not explained anywhere in the information so far as Jerome could see.

Mark Singleton was her media studies course leader. In her first year, his written reports on her stated she was progressing satisfactorily but offered no other relevant detail. When Jerome examined the terms of the house lease the two of them shared, it clearly showed they took on the small house halfway through her second year. There were no details on who made the monthly rent and utilities payments. Katrina obtained part-time work in the Student Union bar and in a dry cleaners shop in town. It looked like financial support from home was limited.

Jerome was pleased with his results by the time he finished just after lunch. He believed he now had a pretty good idea of how Katrina Mallinder's personality may have developed and been influenced. There were also some questions left hanging about what caused the change in her during the early university terms and the extent of her connection with Mark Singleton.

Glen Johannsen and Philip Te Tuke spent the morning preparing a list of property rental agencies to contact. The prospect of being able to locate a current address for Mallinder could mean an early arrest.

They now had the names Lesley Horner and Katrina Mallinder to go with Stenning and also three or four different descriptions to compliment the most recently received information. The list of agents in Auckland alone was well over two hundred; it was not going to be a quick job. When they told Phil Brown the size of the task, he called Kiri in to help with the phone calls.

Harry spent a big part of the morning in discussions with the commander of the Auckland City Police Area. This was now ranking as one of the most significant police investigations in the last twenty years because of its international links and the number of victims. More manpower, greater resources and handling the release of information to the public were all covered before a call to police headquarters in Wellington was made so the Deputy Commissioner could be appraised.

Later Harry put in a call to the incident room to let his second in command, Phil Brown, know he was going to be out for most of the day. "This thing has grown legs all of a sudden now. I'm going to see a press officer next to be prepped; they're talking of a category one release in time for all the evening newscasts. Can you talk to Dan and make sure you get back to me if anything we need to include comes in before about four p.m."

"Will do. It's alright at the moment, everyone is busy, and it's going to be like a telethon in here for the rest of the day."

"Okay well, good luck. Remember, keep in touch."

Dan was deep in thought. The rush of new information was certainly welcome, but they needed to make the most of it. The temptation to go mad with it, forgetting there was already a lot of established evidence, was always there, but the trick was to interweave the existing with the new and that was what had been occupying his mind.

"That was Harry," Phil Brown said breaking his concentration. "He's going to be the main feature on the news tonight."

"Rather him than me."

"Yes, it's not my idea of fun either; done it a couple of times and hated it."

"I was lucky; covert duties meant one or two benefits. Do you know how far he's going to go?"

"No, and I don't think he does yet either. More likely to be someone from Wellington making those decisions. Have you got anything else he should know about?"

"No, I've just been sitting here wondering about it all."

"Wondering what?"

"I was talking with Tara last night; she suggested there might be more victims. She thought that Mallinder was killing because she enjoyed it, and if that was the case, she wouldn't wait so long between them."

Phil did not like what he was hearing. "How is that possible? You've got her Stenning history covered."

"I know and that is exactly what's bothering me. I'm sure we have identified all the victims, but I can't fault Tara's thinking either. I'm thinking about asking Harry if we can ask NCIS to widen the scope of their investigation."

"Can I ask you something?" said Phil. "What's the point? I mean at the moment. It's not going to help us find her; she's going to get a life plus sentence. Shouldn't we just be concentrating on what we have? And finding her here?"

"True, true. She did also say I was over thinking. Still I can't shake the feeling that I'm missing something though."

Harry felt uncomfortable about the interview, which in the circumstances was as good as he could have hoped for. The one saving grace was it was going to be recorded, not a live statement and questions session, and he was mighty glad of that.

"Are we ready?" the prissy police media relations girl called above the cacophony of noise in the main conference room of Auckland City Headquarters.

Harry adjusted his tie and cleared his throat; he seemed to be the only one to take any notice. He was sitting between the area chief and a man in a suit he had never met before and was not introduced to beforehand; they were all behind a long table covered with a dark blue cloth in front of a large NZ police logo on the wall. At one end of the table sat two small covered easels.

In front of them stood about two dozen assorted TV, radio and print media reporters and cameramen, milling around, far more interested in themselves than Detective Senior Sergeant Harry Spiller.

"Ready everybody," Miss Prissy announced again over the loud hum of the reporters. For a moment, there was no change in their behaviour, then they suddenly starburst like a highly trained SWAT team, taking up positions that instantly formed three ranks of eight or nine.

Before Harry knew it, the Superintendent was speaking. "Ladies and gentlemen; Auckland Police have been conducting a joint investigation with the National Crime and Intelligence Service in London since earlier this year." Harry knew the tenor of the introduction was going to be as discussed and agreed upon nearly two hours before. The Superintendent continued his generic introduction piece and then brought a halt to his part so Harry could take his turn.

"I am the detective in charge of the local investigating team," he began. "The joint inquiry has been seeking to identify a British woman, suspected of being involved in a series of suspicious deaths in England since 2002.

"We have reason to believe this woman entered New Zealand earlier this year, and now we are seeking your help and the help of the New Zealand public to locate her current whereabouts.

"We believe she has used several different identities since arriving in the country. She arrived in Auckland as Katrina Mallinder. Since then she has gone by the names of Veronica

Stenning and Lesley Horner to our knowledge, but we do not discount the chance there may also be other names.

"This is the most current description we have." As he said this, the man in the suit to his side removed the covers from the easels to reveal a large copy of Veronica Stenning's image as described by Tara and an enlargement of Katrina Mallinder's passport photo. TV cameras focused in and still cameras clicked.

"The picture nearest me is a very good representation of the most recent description we have. This woman was using the name Veronica Stenning in the last two to three weeks. The other photo is taken from a passport in the name of Katrina Mallinder.

"If anyone thinks they recognise the woman from either of these images, we ask them to contact the incident room here in Auckland or even their local police station. There is an 0800 number which has been set up, and it will be monitored twenty-four seven from the end of this interview. That number is 0800 989 121.

"If anybody thinks they know where this woman is now, please do not approach her but contact the police."

Several questions and answers followed before the media were finally satisfied and scurried away to put their own spin on it. Harry endured it as best he could not wanting to appear as uncomfortable as he felt.

The entire team worked through, waiting for their leader's return, which came at 5:30 p.m. He was accompanied by the Superintendent and two other uniformed constables. Harry explained a little about what he had been doing and how it might affect them all. They all gathered around a TV at 6:00 p.m. when the national news was broadcast while the two new uniforms set up a desk with a phone console for the 0800 calls.

Dan phoned Tara so she could watch at home.

Abbey was watching the TV news as well. The headline story involved the latest housing figures and how it may affect job creation over the next twelve months. She listened, rather than pay close attention to the story as she finished preparing some fried noodles in the kitchen.

The second story started with the male newsreader saying, "Auckland police have today launched an appeal in the hope of locating a British woman here in New Zealand who is wanted in the UK regarding a series of suspicious deaths there since 2002. The woman, Katrina Mallinder, arrived in Auckland in early August this year."

Abbey saw two pictures of herself looking back at her from the screen as the newsreader continued. She was drawn into the living room and found herself standing directly in front of the TV as she struggled to take in what was being said. She missed a sizeable chunk of the next narrative because she could not coordinate her senses.

The story ended with a middle-aged detective asking for the help of the public and repeating an 0800 phone number. Abbey stared at the screen long after the next news item came and went into an advertisement break.

She managed to get sufficient grip of herself to switch to another channel where another national news programme was also running; but there was nothing about her in its next section before the next advertisement break, she had probably missed it. She turned the TV off and went back to the kitchen where she found a bottle of brandy. She was shaking and needed both hands to pour the alcohol. She downed it and immediately poured another, taking it to the dining table, where she sat try-ing to absorb and understand.

Soon the calming effects of the brandy started to set in. The shock of seeing herself and hearing herself being spoken about was a whole new experience, one that at first provoked an over-whelming feeling of panic, soon dissipating into determined indignation. The second shot took a lot longer to drink than the first one as she re-calculated her position and considered the likely outcomes.

She was no longer a secret, her life was now exposed and she was being hunted. The feeling was so alien as to be overwhelming—until she thought hard about what they, the police actually said.

They were looking for her, but they were looking for Katrina and Lesley and Veronica. Veronica meant all of her Stenning lives undoubtedly; Katrina clearly meant they knew why; and Lesley meant their knowledge was current up to a week ago.

There remained the question of what they had not revealed in the TV story, how much more they knew than was made public. It made sense they must include the best evidence possible to assist the public in locating her *now*. If what they said was the best they had, it gave her some comfort.

She was Abbey Turner now, but she also had Terry and Drysdale. Abbey Turner was a first timer so unless they were able to trace her back to her friend in England who created her documented identity, they could not possibly know about her. To add to the feeling of safety, there was no photographic history of Abbey other than the photos she took herself only a few days before.

Therefore, they could not know about Abbey.

Similarly she had obtained enough to become Candice Drysdale very recently. The police certainly knew Drysdale was associated to her by way of the PO Box, but could they possibly think or know she had the capacity to *be* her? Not impossible, with Dan Calder involved, but unlikely.

That left Terry. How much did they know about *them?* The name of Terry was not mentioned and therefore it was unquantifiable at the moment.

The first priority was to dispose of everything else which connected her to Katrina and Lesley. After the other day, all the

Stennings were history already. The easiest and best way was to simply get rid of everything; that meant the computer, the other hard drive and even things like her wardrobe of clothes older than one week when she became Abbey Turner.

As she stood at the sink, the process of shedding the past so completely saddened her. She smashed the computer into pieces and divided the pieces into three piles, inflicting a similar fate on the hard drive.

Watching Tara Danes earlier in the day gave her an idea about all her clothes and shoes. She cut all the labels out of every item and set them alight in a large frying pan until they turned into a stinking black mass, then poured cold water onto it to solidify it on the bottom of the pan.

The next morning, two elderly ladies of the Kohimarama SPCA charity shop were happy to accept the suitcase of good quality clothes. "Thank you. Oh and the case too, that's lovely."

When she got home again, Abbey went to the garage, still contemplating not using the scooter, which could be identifiable now as she rented it under the name of Veronica. Deciding speed was of the essence and it too needed to be disposed of, she instead smeared some mud over the number plate, fastened her three packages to the carry rack behind the seat and set off.

First for dumping were the frying pan and one part of the computer pieces which she put in a half-filled skip outside a house under renovation in Glendowie, a few kilometres from home.

Next, the second lot of computer debris went into the sea in the next bay along and finally the third and last lot went into the bottom of a council rubbish bin in Meadowbank ten minutes in the opposite direction.

Abbey needed to get rid of the scooter before she went home and the answer to that problem came accidentally as she made her way towards the Meadowbank train station.

A small track leading down to the Orakei Basin was wide enough to free-wheel down and then walk it the last few metres. She was pleased to see the expanse of water at the bottom of the track and knew this would be a far better resting place for the machine than the station car park as she initially intended.

The scooter disappeared into the murky water and with it all remaining evidence to each of her pasts. Almost all anyway, there were two things she could never part with.

Dan ran his idea past Harry of suggesting to the NCIS that there may be more to discover than had been revealed, as they sat in his office after everyone else was gone for the night. It was becoming a nightly tradition.

"It's no longer in our hands. All well above my pay grade and I can see we will be the last to know what's deemed appropriate from now on. I'll pass on the message anyway."

"That figures," Dan said despondently.

"Look, don't worry about it; we can only do what we can do. Have you got any further today?"

"Not really. I'm going to take some stuff home to work on tonight if that's okay."

Tara had left a note for Dan when he got home. He was disappointed she'd gone back to her house and that she wanted a night or two on her own.

When he called, she reassured him there were no hidden meanings. "It'll do us both good but don't worry; I won't be able to stay away for long."

"Call me if you need anything."

"I will. Remember to sleep. This is not an excuse to stay up working all night." And with that she was gone.

He made some pasta and added a jar of sauce. Taking the bowl through to the lounge, he picked up the folder of notes and photos off the table as he passed. Even with all the evidence they assembled, he could not get the thought out of his head that there was an important piece missing.

As he ate, he flicked through the sheaf of papers and tried to think back to how far he had gotten in his own private investigation before he and Tara first went to Harry. They identified Stenning as the killer, as being in Auckland, and having targeted Neil. Next he imagined what he intended to do next if they had not reported it to the police and he was left to rely on his own resources.

Candice Drysdale and the apartment at Vulcan Lane were the first things which came to mind. That day he followed Drysdale, and Tara was able to identify the address. Later the death of Neil led to them to where they were now.

"Okay, Drysdale," he said to himself as he set about reviewing what was known about her. Going over the documentary evidence it looked like there was nothing missing. She was simply used for one purpose and never actually met Mallinder. She was interviewed at length, supplied a statement and had been extremely co-operative.

After three coffees, he was sure Candice Drysdale was a dead end.

He was even less hopeful of turning up something new on the apartment as the team executed the search warrant and all the seized items were examined with a fine tooth comb several times. The copies of the handwriting impressions lifted from the newspaper were in the file along with the rest of the notes associated with the search of the apartment.

The phone number of the property rental place led Harry to order a search of every agent in Auckland, which Johannsen, Ieremia and Te Tuke were now undertaking. There was nothing else which seemed to be relevant or could be investigated further. They had spoken to neighbours, workmen and visitors and even checked the council's CCTV for the areas surrounding Vulcan Lane without success. There was nobody else to talk to.

He looked at the clock and thought about calling Tara again.
"Tara!"

Tara had been inside the apartment when Veronica Stenning was living there. She saw it before it was stripped bare.

"Hi. I'm sorry to call this late."

"That's okay I was just trying to write something up for Cathy and I about making our shops a joint venture. I suppose you're working?" she replied.

"Can I ask you something?"

"Sure."

"When you were in her apartment, can you remember much about it? Sorry to have to ask you to go over it all again."

"It's alright. It's not as if I can think of much else at the moment anyway. The first time was when I dropped off the clothes she bought from my shop … I still can't believe it was all a part of her plan to get to Neil."

"Well now we know so much more about her, it's not so surprising that she did lots of homework." Dan wanted to ask direct questions to get to what he was most interested in, but the whole situation was still incredibly raw and painful for Tara to wrap her head around. "If it hadn't been Neil, it would have been someone else."

"I know."

"What I really want to know is how much of the inside and the things in it you remember."

"Not a lot; that is, I don't remember much *and* there was not a lot in it to remember anyway. It was pretty sparsely decorated; it was a rental."

"I thought you might say that. It's personal things I was thinking of."

"She had a laptop, a white one, maybe a Dell, but I can't be sure. I saw it on the table or a chair. There were other clothes and shoes in her bedroom wardrobe. I saw all her clothes. She had quite a few CDs, mostly stuff from our teens and some a lot older."

"Okay Tara. Anything else?" He could not think of how what she said so far was any use, but he still wanted to encourage her.

"No I don't think so."

"How do you feel about coming down to the incident room in the morning and playing a little game with me?"

"Mr. Calder! That hardly sounds very professional. But it sounds fun, you like me to wear anything special?"

"Mm, tempting. Perhaps we can hold that thought. I'd like to see if I can help you remember a bit more. An interview technique I used to use."

She laughed. "Oh, shame."

"Ten o'clock?"

"Okay, I'll drive myself in. Are you running in the morning?"

"Yes, last few weeks now. Try and get some sleep too. See you in the morning."

"Is this going to be another Dan Calder special?" Harry asked the following morning.

"Harry, all my interviewing and statement taking is hardly rocket science. There is no real secret to any of it."

"Yes and my wife tells me all the time how easy it is to make my favourite meatloaf, but I've never been able. Easy when you know how."

"Alright, point taken. I need someone there to record details because hopefully we can get enough for a statement and that should be taken by a sworn officer."

"Agreed, who do you prefer?"

"Kiri or Philip are probably best suited."

"Okay, whatever you want. Would it be okay to tape the interview? I'm thinking of future training aids not just evidential requirements."

"Okay with me, but I'll check with Tara."

When Tara arrived, Dan showed her around the room and updated her on the investigation. Harry came over to check on her too and introduced her to the other team members.

After she was made to feel as comfortable as anybody could be in a room full of evidence about a dead loved one, Dan took her through to the interview room where Philip was waiting. The video camera was already running; Dan had secured Tara's permission to be filmed, but did not want to make a big deal of it, hence the early commencement. Harry was in his office with Phil Brown to watch and listen to the interview on a linked monitor.

She brought in her small CD player and a selection of CDs Dan requested, but not explained the reason for, the previous evening. When they were ready, Dan told her what he was going to do.

"I'm going to get you to take yourself back to that day you went into Veronica's apartment and then see if we can do a type of virtual reality tour. The secret of being able to remember back like this is to use all your senses; that's why I got you to bring the music in."

In Harry's office, Phil Brown said, "Have you ever seen something like this?"

Harry looked at his deputy and shook his head.

"Can you put on a CD that most reminds you of that day but keep the volume low. Then just relax and get comfortable." Tara did as he asked and as a song unknown to Dan began, he turned the volume down another notch from where she set it.

"Okay, just start to listen to the song and think about it playing in the apartment when you first got there. Imagine it's playing as you walk in the door." Tara was smiling as the song played; she looked a bit self-conscious.

"Don't worry about me or Philip; sing along if you want. Anything you want at all." He could see her foot tapping on the floor.

"Okay. Close your eyes, but keep listening to the music." He gave her some more time to get used to being blind. "That's good Tara; right now think about any other noises in the background, has she got the air-conditioning on, are there any sounds from outside?"

Dan watched Tara as the song finished and another started. He waited for the intro to finish and the first lyric to be sung then said, "So she opens the door and you walk inside; what can you feel? Think about the floor is it wood or tile or carpet? Then think about what you can smell. Is she cooking, are there fresh flowers?"

He could see Tara thinking even with her eyes closed. Philip was focused in on Dan.

Tara nodded, it could have been the music, but then she said, "The door was already open. I called hello and she called back."

"Great, that is great. Okay, think about the music, think about the other sounds, think about the smells and what you can feel." Dan gave Tara more time, he looked at Philip and they exchanged a quiet smile. Philip had to concentrate on his part of this process, but he seemed so taken by Dan's scene setting he could easily have forgotten to write down what Tara said.

"It's carpet on the floor, it smells new. She's talking, but not to me." Tara said.

Dan pointed at Philip's page and he started to write. Dan was very pleased to hear Tara talking in the present tense. *It smells new. Perfect*, he thought.

"What do you see? Keep listening to the music; keep thinking about those other things."

Tara was tapping fingers on the table now too as another song began. "She's on the phone to her dad. She has a wine, and I get one off the counter."

Dan needed her to keep going, to immerse herself in the memory of that moment. Whether she could do it on her own or had to be guided, he could not tell yet. "Listen to the music, but look around the apartment; tell me about the colours and the furnishings, what does the wine taste like, tell me all about it."

Tara's eyes were still closed, at first tightly, now relaxed. He could tell she was almost there.

"All cream and white. The sofa has lots of cushions in all different shades of brown. The wine is good. There is a big mirror on one wall and there is a palm in a ceramic pot which is made to look like bamboo. Her computer is on a chair in the far corner; I didn't see it at first because it's white like the chair; it is a Dell, it says so on the lid."

"That's perfect Tara, keep looking."

"Some books, on the kitchen counter a small pile of books including a blue and gold Koran; she said she got it in Istanbul."

Istanbul, Dan thought, *she came from Turkey to New Zealand.*

As if she were watching a video, Tara continued, describing the open plan space that made up the lounge, dining and kitchen areas. None of it was particularly relevant to what Dan needed, but it at least continued her right mindset.

Then she said, "We go out onto the balcony. We are talking about old pop groups we used to like. There's a small table by the door leading out to the balcony. There's something on it."

Dan looked at Philip; he appeared to be holding his breath as he was writing.

"It's a photo in a silver frame."

"Look at the photo Tara, look at it really carefully."

"Nice frame, antique by the look of it. There are three people in it and they are really happy. There's a little red car as well. The two older people, a man and a woman, are looking inwards to a younger woman who's stood between them. She's holding up something shiny."

Philip stopped and stared at Tara. Dan was looking at her, but he had his right hand up towards him with a finger extended. Philip got the message.

"What is it?" Tara queried herself and tilted her head to get a better view of the photo in her mind's eye. "What is … it's a gold bracelet, no, it's a watch, a gold watch. She's holding it up to the camera."

"Describe her, describe them all Tara."

"She's in her twenties, taller than the man and woman, she's got the same mousy hair as the older woman, and the man's got short darker hair and glasses, metal framed glasses. The car is long and low, not a big car. She looks so happy. The watch face is square but with the four corners cut off. It looks funny though."

"What's funny about it? Look really carefully, you can get as close as you like."

As the CD came to an end and stopped, it had been forty minutes already, Tara stirred as if the sound of it finishing might break the spell. Dan interpreted her thoughts, assessed the situation, decided on a course of action and began speaking again all within the blink of an eye. "Keep focused Tara; keep looking at the photo, at the watch. Listen to the sounds in the apartment, keep thinking about the smell and the taste of the wine, feel the sun on you as you sit on the balcony."

"What's so funny about the watch, Tara?"

Her fingers continued to tap the table and her foot the floor. "I don't know, it's just funny. It's got small hands, straight lines of delicate gold, not arrows or anything like that but the hands aren't in the middle, they are at the bottom of the face. The numbers are straight lines too, not actual numerals.

"There's something at the top of the face above where the twelve marker line is. It's a different colour to the rest of the face. The face is black and this thing is light grey." She tilted her head back the other way, straining to see what she could not. Three seconds passed, four, five. "Numbers, it's numbers, real numbers."

"Good girl. What else can you see from the balcony inside the lounge?"

"Not much, the TV is on the wall, there's a fruit bowl on the kitchen counter with bananas in it and some of he CDs are on the counter too."

Not long after Tara had identified three of the CDs Dan felt he had got as much as he was going to.

Harry and Phil Brown had been writing as well as Philip in Harry's office. Phil could not help himself, it was no reflection on Philip at all but he could not just sit still during Dan's interview. Harry also tried drawing his version of the watch Tara described.

"That was unreal," Tara exclaimed. "I would never have believed I could remember so much. Was any of it useful do you think?"

"Are you kidding, that was brilliant, you were brilliant!" Philip said, unable to contain himself.

"You really were," Dan agreed. "We need for you to make a statement now; Philip will do that with you. Draw pictures too: a plan of the apartment, the photo frame, photo and the watch. I'll be the tea-boy, what do you feel like?"

"I actually remember the watch now; she was wearing it the day we met in my shop."

Once he took their order for refreshments, Dan left them to start the formal statement and returned to the incident room where Harry and Phil Brown were waiting for him.

"What do you think?" Dan asked as they corralled him by the coffee machine.

"Could be really useful. You obviously think the photo and the watch are important," Harry said.

"I do, but what about you?"

Phil was keen to add his say. "A photo of her and her parents, it has to be. The description of their hair and his glasses matches them. They died when she was twenty-five. It could be that this is her one remaining contact with them."

"I reckon that's right. The watch too; she's holding it up to the camera so it's new. Maybe a present from them," Harry said.

Dan felt like he knew her a little better. "Not just that, but a really important gift from her parents who struggled every day just to live let alone to buy her presents. That's why she's kept the photo; it's probably her fondest memory. She has kept the watch too." He then became more serious. "Harry, I know what we said about getting London to do more but we have to find out if anyone from 2002 until she left this June remembers the computer, photo or the watch. They could be vital in putting her at certain places at certain times. Also it may help people like property agents here, if they have them to identify her by, especially if she's changed her appearance again."

Abbey decided to cycle the route. The mountain bike she bought to replace her scooter had hydraulic suspension and power assisted brakes; the seat was ergonomically designed for maximum comfort over a multitude of conditions. Things had definitely moved on since her second-hand childhood bikes.

Victoria Park marked the finish line, and around there, a temporary stand was erected each year to seat several thousand spectators. Today it was still a busy intersection of three streets controlled by traffic lights. She examined the pictures printed off the Internet from the last two years' races as a guide, but she did not discount the possibility of some changes, even though they appeared identical from one year to the next.

She rode down through Viaduct Marina and passed the "Big Boat"—KZ-1, the racing yacht which competed in the famed America's Cup for New Zealand in 1988 and now stood for all time as a monument to the feat at the main entrance. She took Quay Street, an arrow-straight line out of the city towards the Eastern Bays for two kilometres before the road started snaking in and out as it followed the contours of the coastline all the way to St. Heliers Bay. It was another beautiful day; the water out to her left as far as the eye could see was emerald green; in the near distance, Rangitoto Island and further away Waiheke Island looked like brochure pictures. She could see why people loved it here.

The second half of the marathon would as usual, follow the route she was now on, emerging from the Viaduct and go all the way down to St Heliers before returning back to the city centre. On the day, the roads were closed and the runners would have the freedom to use the tarmac while spectators lined the pavements. She tried to imagine how big the concentration of both may be, how much cover and protection she may be afforded by runners and onlookers alike at different places. She also thought about where Tara Danes might wish to stand or sit in order to watch; somewhere giving her the chance to cheer on her boyfriend.

She continued out through Okahu Bay where more boats and yachts were moored, bobbing around in the water as if balanced on submerged springs, and the Pohutakawa trees overhung the pavements. She pulled off the road and stretched out on the grass leading to the sand and the sea. With her eyes closed and the sound of the traffic a lulling complement to the lap of the gentle waves, she let the warm spring sun penetrate her skin. She had been constantly on the move for nearly ten years; in that time, grown from weak and distraught to strong and driven.

At twenty-six, she was deeply upset when her first love so completely betrayed her, and she had not looked at another man since. She was so angry then, that all the confidence she developed, all the good times she had at university, seemed to disappear, leaving a hollow feeling where nothing existed except a festering poison. Then her mother and father passed away in the most desperate of circumstances; also betrayed like she was, robbed of a chance at comfort in their old age, everything they worked for was ground into the dirt again beneath the boot of a world which did not give them one single chance in their whole lives.

Now in her mid-thirties, she still could not forget or move on fully from the past, from what happened to her parents. If she tried to be a better daughter, more successful during their time alive, they may be enjoying retirement and she might not have had the life she did now.

She managed to purge some of the sense of guilt, but most of the emptiness remained. She was on her own by necessity and made up for the void of caring and being cared for with the intoxication and addiction of murder, for lavish financial reward and for the satisfaction of being the one in control.

As Stenning, she made a considerable fortune from the clients of The Agency. As Walter Terry, she satisfied the need for the excitement and the thrill of power in taking another life. Both those lives were going to have to come to an end soon. She wondered if she may regret their passing, but thinking about how it was all soon to end, she was overcome with a sense of relief and finality. Dan Calder and Tara Danes had brought it upon themselves; her dealing with them also put the perfect full-stop to her career. She could move on.

The one small misgiving she did have was it would not be Veronica Stenning to have the last say.

This task called for Walter to complete and put to rest all her memories. Let the survivor take them on instead of her. The one she would leave behind could carry the misery, guilt and hurt. She liked the symmetry.

Dan made Harry get Sina Eaton in again to make up a drawing of the photo frame, photo and watch, as Tara's artistic skills were inadequate for the job. They went off to the ID Suite together as Philip brought the finished statement into Harry's office.

"I'll get back to helping Phil and Kiri with the property agents. Thanks Dan, that was quite an experience. Another one!"

"No problem, you did a good job. Perhaps you can try it for yourself some other time if the need arises."

"I'd like to give it a go. She was really back there in the apartment, wasn't she? I could even feel it." Philip took his leave to spread the news among the others.

The results of Tara and Sina's second session were good. The photo frame looked like it came from the 1930s and Phil Brown offered to do the donkey work of trying to find something close to the drawing on the Internet, leaving Dan and Harry alone once more.

The drawing of the photo merely served to add weight to the belief it was a Mallinder family portrait taken around age twenty-four or five. The watch, however, was the most interesting picture. Tara and Sina produced a full-size image. The bracelet or strap was two centimetres wide; it looked like a flexible flat mesh of golden yellow wire, tightly knit into a herringbone pattern. If there was a clasp, it was not visible, consistent with how Tara described it in her statement.

The face was wider than the strap; a square gold case surrounded it with the corners cut away to make the finished shape octagonal but with elongated sides, top and bottom. There was no bezel present—Tara could not remember if there was one. The face itself was another black square. The hands and number markers were the same flattened gold, only made different by the length of the hands. The number markers were a quarter of an inch long and positioned in a circle at the lower half of the face. Above it was a small rectangle coloured several shades lighter than the rest of the face. Inside the rectangle were small angular numbers.

When they looked it, it was obvious what it was. A watch with a traditional mechanism at the bottom and a digital display above.

"That's it," Dan said.

"That's what?"

"That's what is going to give her away."

Harry looked sceptical. "How do you mean?"

"I'm not sure yet my friend. I wish I did. I'll bet you if the NCIS checks with witnesses in England, the watch will be remembered. They gave it to her on the day that photo was taken; it represents everything they ever did for her. Find it and you find her."

CHAPTER TWENTY-NINE

The next ten days were a tough slog. While the team continued their hard work, new breakthroughs failed to materialise, and all the phone calls and database searches got them no closer to their objectives.

The free-phone number received dozens of calls in the first forty-eight hours before slowly tapering off. There were many reported sightings from all over the country; fortunately however, not too much time and effort was wasted following up most of them. The only ones which proved to be reliable were from a bar in the Viaduct and another scooter hire shop in the city which Veronica visited before she went to NZ Wheels. Dan and Harry believed Mallinder's time had been spent entirely in and around the Auckland area.

The only result of consequence was being able to establish a date for the photo. London also answered another question by trawling the Driver Vehicle Licensing Authority computers to check on all cars owned by Katrina Mallinder. A red MGB GT was indeed registered to her in the week she graduated from university in May 1998, placing her age at almost twenty-four when the photo was taken.

Having telephoned three hundred different property rental offices without success, Harry made an executive decision to give up with phone calls and start again with personal visits. He was given an extra two detectives to assist in getting through the mammoth task. Each day, he sent out a total of six officers, each armed with photocopied images of Valerie and Veronica Stenning, Katrina Mallinder, the Vespa, the Dell laptop and the watch. By the end of day six of this new initiative, the original three hundred plus another hundred enquiries had been conducted with no positive result. Every female who rented a property in the last three months was checked, regardless of age, ethnicity and physical description.

Dan and Tara spent as many nights apart as they did together. She went back to work, and he fell into a regular routine of working at Avondale and more at home.

During his early morning runs, he tried his best to concentrate and forget about Katrina Mallinder, but it never worked. He had read every word there was written about her right back to her childhood in an attempt to get inside her head and predict her intentions.

Most nights, the work he took home served more as a frustration than an incentive; the pages seemed to mock him.

Dan woke with a familiar, terrified start. The nightmare of his father taking to his mother on their bed with his shiny black belt again. She, urging him back to his own room with the same sad smile, and him, now a full grown man in boy's pyjamas apologising, closing the door and walking away as the belt came flashing down.

He was sweating profusely, and even though he was instantly wide awake, he could still hear the sound of thick leather, snapping like a whip. Over the years in the dream, he aged while everything else was the same, something that made the dream only more real and debilitating.

Tara appeared not to have been disturbed at all and lay motionless under most of the duvet, which had found its way over to her side.

Dan got up and put on his trackpants and top. The green light from the oven clock provided just sufficient illumination to the kitchen to supplement his subconscious memory, and he moved around the immediate area without bumping knees, toes or elbows. He took a banana and a glass of milk through the lounge and into the conservatory where he creakily sat in one of the wicker chairs. Alone in the dark, he remembered back to Powton Road, Mapperley and to poor Zoe. She could not have been older than sixteen or seventeen, although her eyes belonged to a much older woman who had seen things nobody should. When he arrived at the squalid house, there were at least eight people crammed into the tiny bedsit, mostly sat around on the floor or leaning against walls as if the place may fall down if they moved.

He was involved in a hundred test-purchase operations like this one in the past; following up on information about a building being used for the sale and use of drugs. Number 22 Powton Road was typical: filthy, insect-infested and reeking of cannabis although a dozen far more dangerous and illegal substances were within arm's reach.

What led him to accept her offer of a drink, he still could not fathom after all these years. Zoe looked like her life depended on him sharing the can of cheap cider with her before the occupant and supplier was willing to hand over a small wrap of heroin in exchange for Dan's three dirty ten-pound notes. It was against all the rules of the job, against all his training and against his better judgement.

The next thing he remembered was being woken up by the unmistakable stench of human vomit.

"Hey, are you okay? I woke up and you were gone."

Dan jumped. He was so lost in thought he did not notice Tara approaching. She was wrapped in a blanket from a chair in the bedroom.

"Dan, what's the matter?"

He needed to think quickly. April had repeatedly asked him to go and see a professional about his dreams—"It's no big deal these days," she said, "and if you can find out what's causing them, you might be able to get rid of them once and for all. I don't want you acting crazy forever."

"Crazy! Thanks for that April; I *know* what's causing them, don't I! My bastard father used to beat the shit out of my mum." He never mentioned Mapperley to her, and she always attributed Dan's problems to his childhood. At this time, he could not bring himself to tell Tara the whole truth either; about which ghastly experience was currently torturing him, although he accidentally hinted at it on their first coffee date when he told her there was never just one thing which explained an individual's troubles. It was better for them both she think like April.

"I didn't hear you. Sorry, did I wake you up?"

"Only by not being there. Have you had another bad dream?"

"Yes, well, you know, the same one," he admitted, and for once that part was true.

"Have you ever thought about talking to someone about it?"

Here we go again, he thought, but bit his tongue.

"I mean, did you talk to your exes, friends? You don't have to pay to see some shrink; just someone who's prepared to listen. You can talk to me anytime," she said.

Dan felt embarrassed and a little ashamed about what he almost blurted out. "Thanks."

"I might not be able to help, but I'd rather share it with you than you watch you suffer on your own," Tara said, settling onto his lap and wrapping the blanket around them both.

He shivered a little. "It's not so much the dream as it is the memory. I can still remember her making excuses for him all the time. How he didn't mean it, or there was an accident. I always hoped she might say enough is enough, one day; but it never happened. Why do you think she put up with it?"

"For you."

It was the answer he was most afraid of. "That's what I've always thought too. It makes it so much worse; like it was my fault."

"You must know it wasn't. She loved you and probably thought she was protecting you and doing the best thing for you."

"Since Neil died, have you found yourself feeling guilty? It's the same sort of thing, isn't it? Logic comes a poor second to emotion most of the time."

When they went back to bed, Tara slept. Dan could not; he was unable to rid himself of the thoughts about lying to Tara, and the reasons why.

Abbey was not sleeping either. As a light drizzle began to fall, she listened with interest after the initial surprise of seeing Calder in his kitchen at that time wore off. She wanted to get a look at the various entry and exit points to the house and was in the back garden when Dan came downstairs. Dressed in black, staying calm and still outside when he came to sit down in the conservatory, she heard fairly well the discussion between him and Tara. Ignoring the rain, she then waited after they disappeared from view; there was no reason to abandon her reconnaissance of the property. From what she could see, there were a number of ways to gain access if and when the need arose.

As she listened, her thoughts also travelled back in time to when she was a victim of other people's actions—before she made the decision to take control of her destiny, inexorably and drastically altering it along with some others'.

Ever since she made the decision to make Stephen Christopher pay the maximum penalty for his offences, her subsequent victims had all been subject to similar levels of scrutiny. In his case, she took a long time and got very close to him; so close that in order to complete the gruesome task, she *had* to become another person, or she would never have been able to go through with it. The result was Vanessa, who was tough enough to do everything that needed to be done; so tough and so dead inside to all but her purpose. During the days and nights she spent with the pig, when he used her for a lot more personal activities than simply training and exercise, she was using him too. It was the only thing that kept her going.

Christopher's private life was immeasurably different from his public one, where he portrayed himself as a shrewd, successful and honourable businessman with a passion for horses, fast cars, good food and expensive French wine.

In private he was cruelty personified; his wealth enabled him to secretly indulge other passions for bare knuckle boxing, sadistic sex and substance abuse. These concealed aspects of his life brought him into close contact with the shadowy darkness of locally disorganised crime and the far more dangerous and organised world of the new East European mafia. Vanessa managed to exist in both his lives for as long as she needed to learn and gain his trust and acceptance; although there was hardly a day that passed when she was not terrified. Eventually she worked out how to finally rid herself and the rest of the world of him in an appropriate way. When the day came, it could not have gone better—or given her more satisfaction.

He was pumped up on chemicals and a recent sickening liaison with a teenage girl; Vanessa had little trouble convincing him to do as she asked. He even laughed as she taped his hands to the handlebar grips in expectation of what he believed was to come.

Another syringe, another rush inside his head, as she set the top-of-the-range training bike to maximum. He pedalled his way to a deserved early grave, unable to stop himself or the excruciating chest pains, he begged for mercy and then his heart exploded.

The fallout from her time with Stephen Christopher took months for Katrina Mallinder to get over. It could have destroyed her emotionally, but instead it transformed her and gave her insight into her true potential. When she was able to properly analyse it all, Katrina decided there were parts of her and parts of Vanessa which could exist together. The whole Vanessa was a different animal, she had been through so much and been damaged so much by it, no amount of time could repair. The subsequent Stenning women were refined evolutions.

As the lust for the act of killing developed, Katrina knew Stenning was not the answer. She was cultured and clever, an artist who should not be tainted by the stain of wantonness. Walter emerged as the solution; he was suitably different with none of the additional artistic complications Stenning had to deal with; he was just a machine, a vehicle for fulfilling a need.

Katrina remembered how he was created. All the Stenning women's first names began with V after her parents' middle names. The engraved inscription on the back of her watch was an entwined pattern of all their initials, which made no sense to anyone except them. The two Vs close together more resembled a W and the name Walter popped into her head one day as she was looking at it and reminiscing.

A male name? she thought. *Perfect.*

In Dan Calder's back garden, she was Abbey Turner in appearance, but she was thinking like Stenning and Walter Terry. She completed the task at hand, making a mental note of the visible layout of the ground floor, also the gardens and the boundary fences. She saw no sign of an alarm.

She checked the locks on the back door and also the front one on the way out; noting they were modern, the same Kinglok make and model, probably installed during renovations in the recent past. It was a well known brand, and she could pick up the same thing at any number of hardware stores; the fact she knew was further testament to her tenacious research and made the job of obtaining suitable keys much easier. As she left, she made sure to avoid leaving footprints on the path by stepping lightly over the grass.

When she got home, she wrote down some of the salient points before she went to bed; but like Dan Calder, she found sleep hard to come by.

While Dan was running the following morning, feeling tired after his broken night's sleep, Abbey was eating breakfast at a café in Mission Bay. The Kinglok range of door locks was good; the model on Dan Calder's front and back doors was the Sentry 2000. Her new laptop informed her that Kinglok prided itself on one of the largest number of key configurations for each model of lock.

After her light, healthy meal, Abbey visited four different DIY superstores to collect a respectable thirty-two different door locks of the sixty that Kinglok professed to have. The staff at each were all corporately pleasant and very helpful; though she earned one or two scornful looks when she asked to open the packaging of every lock. She explained it was to check the numbered identifiers to guarantee no repeats of key variations and for once she was telling the truth. She hoped one of them would fit either the front or back door of Calder's house. The odds were on her side.

She was only questioned once and happily explained that she wanted different keys for all the bedroom doors of her new house she was renting to students, so they couldn't get into another tenant's room with their own key.

Her backpack was weighing her down as she cycled towards home from the last store. It was an expensive exercise, but well worth it.

The day began much the same as any other. When Dan got in, only Harry and Glen Johannsen were there.

"Morning, Dan, how is it?" Johannsen asked.

"Hi. Where is everyone?"

"Just out catching up on some of the outstanding tasks, there isn't anything special going on. You want a coffee?"

Harry opened his office door and called Dan in. "I've got some news—*not* good news," he said when the door was closed behind them again.

"Oh?"

"I've been instructed to tell you your services are no longer required. I tried to argue with them, but the way it's going with the liaison between here, Wellington and London. I am becoming a much smaller cog in the machine." Harry really was genuinely sorry.

"You're kidding me. You can't, *they* can't."

"Dan, I am as pissed off as you."

"I guarantee you are nowhere near as pissed off as I am!" Dan snapped. "You said it; I'm just another resource."

"If it was down to me, of course I'd want to keep you on the team, I've told them I think it's a big mistake; but they want a more traditional approach."

Dan was bitterly disappointed, but unfortunately it manifested itself as temperamental. "This is bullshit, Harry, complete bullshit," he spat as he stamped out of the office.

Harry sat back in his chair and slowly shook his head. If Dan had been one of his staff who just spoke to him and then walked out like that, he might have torn him a new hole in his backside. He had seen and worked with all types, but only come across the damaged natural genius type once or twice before. He felt a brotherly concern for Dan, but at that moment, Dan was behaving like a petulant teenager, taking every comment as a criticism.

When Harry wearily made his way out into the main room, Dan was clearing up things at his desk. At Dan's shoulder he said, "It's not personal."

"Yes, it is. It's personal to me!"

Harry's brotherly concern cracked and he spun Dan around by the shoulder so they were nose to nose. "And that's the problem, you stubborn bastard. The guys who are making these decisions are all at Auckland HQ or down in Wellington. They don't know you from a bar of soap. So tell me how it's personal to them.

"When you learn to be as smart and professional with the easy parts of the job as you are with the hard, you'll think a lot differently and be a lot happier. It's a job, you've been employed to do a job, and you have done it. They have jobs too, to make decisions about the other people who work for them. You decided a long time ago that you did not want to do what they do, remember?"

He mellowed a little. "If you can't separate yourself from the Neil and Tara Danes association during work time, then you are not the man I think you are. So go home, work out your bill and send it to me for payment. If I were you I'd also be thinking about some sort of report and letter to the Auckland City commander, offering your services in future training and consultative capacities."

Dan spoke without thinking. "And be treated like this again? You have to be joking."

The comment sparked Harry up once more. "Treated like what? The organisation received a complaint from you regarding a suspicious death. Your previous experience gave you the skills to gather a large amount of evidence, which we could also have gathered eventually. You were given the opportunity to use your skills as a paid employee of the police to assist the investigation *you* asked us to conduct. You have been given preferential treatment and been paid for it! We acknowledge and thank you for your assistance, which has been welcomed, and we hope you may be able to offer us the benefit of it again sometime. But don't you dare talk to me about how much we owe you, and just remember who you are talking to." Harry had not taken a step back during the heated exchange. If anything, he seemed to have grown slightly in stature. Dan's intimidation and embarrassment was clear.

Glen Johannsen stared at them from the other side of the room, unable to take his eyes off the confrontation.

"Harry, I'm sorry. I didn't mean to take it out on you."

The big detective would not be placated by Dan's uncomfortable apology.

"Take what out on me? What the hell have you really got to be upset with anybody about?"

Dan had no answer. "Well, I am sorry. I'll finish packing up and leave you to it."

"What is it with you Dan? Why do you think everybody is out to get you?"

He stopped next to his desk. His father had been dead for nearly ten years. *Good riddance to bad rubbish*, Dan thought, although no one apart from his mother ever seemed to agree with him on that score. But thanks to *him*, she died many years before; bullied to an early grave, robbing Dan of the one parent who genuinely loved and cared for him.

When James Allen, his last supervisor had shit on him once too often for doing the right thing, he was hung out to dry. The events in Mapperley which eventually led to that day were still a constant shadow hanging over him. He miserably took the official bollocking and fine of two weeks' wages, but after a sleepless night, he thought, *screw this*, and less than a month later he was just plain Mr. Calder. Six months after that he touched down in Auckland to start afresh.

It was not meant to be like this.

"It's only paranoia if it's not true," he said under his breath as he yanked the desk drawer open.

"Well, this is a nice surprise," Tara said as Dan walked into the shop.

"Hello, have you got time for a coffee?"

They sat at the same table they did on that first day. Dan told her about his morning at Avondale, sparing no detail. The drive home was a painful journey because the truth of his situation jabbed him in the ribs all the way. "I am such a dumb arse. Harry has had my number from the beginning; he got it all completely right, he got me completely right."

"I'm really sorry for you. You've probably not been that happy for ages," said Tara, reaching out for his hand.

"I was, but for all the wrong reasons."

"Tell me?"

"It's been about me, hasn't it? Right from the beginning. When I noticed her name on the email, how bored, frustrated, however you want to put it I was, that gave me something to get interested in again and gave me the sense of purpose I'd been missing.

"Your brother died because of this woman. Others died before him—and all I could think of was how I could get the old buzz back again.

"I told him I was sorry for getting angry, and he tore another strip off me."

"Oh poor you; I bet you're not used to being told off."

"I have had my fair quota, but not like this. The trouble is he's right about everything. I can't think of any time in the whole of my career where someone as close to the case as I am to this has been able to become involved. It's fed my need on any number of different levels. Harry balling me out has made me realise I owe you an apology, too."

"No, you don't. God knows what might have happened if you hadn't got the email and started working things out. Neil could have been the first of even more, and we might not have got together like we have."

"At this moment, it feels like I have wasted all my working life," Dan said. "When I was in Garstone, I was constantly banging heads with my bosses. I'm starting to wonder now if I was wrong all the time; because Harry certainly is not. He's the first man to be that honest too. I feel so stupid."

"Hey, come on; there's no need to be so hard on yourself. We have all had reality checks at some point in our lives. I'm sure Harry is seriously sorry as well. You should call him and talk to him."

"And say what? I tried, sorry. I think it might be better to wait a while at least. You didn't hear him or see the look on his face."

At the end of the working day, Glen Johannsen was telling his colleagues about that same look and the preceding conversation in the sports bar, when Harry came in and went to get himself a beer. He did not see the others sitting around two tables in the far corner.

Phil Brown noticed their boss and called him over. The slightly uncomfortable silence accompanying his joining them made Harry smile and sigh. "I suppose you know all about what's happened with Dan?"

"I'm sorry, I couldn't really miss it this morning," Johannsen said.

"Don't worry about it. Have you given them all the details?"

"It was hard not to hear what you said. I've said it's a good idea not to get on your bad side."

Harry's laugh broke the tension. "Yes, think of it as another training lesson. Seriously, though, I was and am disappointed to lose him, I think it's a mistake, but like I told him and I'm telling you, there are decisions being made now which are made at the highest levels. We may not like some of them, but we do our jobs and they do theirs. Okay?"

There was general agreement all around. "What happens to Dan now?" asked Jerome.

"I hope when he calms down he will see it for what it is. I told him to put forward some sort of proposal to the police regarding training. What do you all think of going on a course delivered by him?"

"After what we've seen him do, I'd want to go in a heartbeat. All that log stuff was fantastic," said Phil Larson.

"And the light table, that was unreal," agreed Kiri.

"I would recommend Dan to everybody," Harry said. "Let's hope he thinks about it."

Dan was having trouble looking at anything reasonably at that moment. After the coffee with Tara, he took himself home in a solemn mood and drifted around the house aimlessly. By mid afternoon, he was feeling no better. He put on a load of washing and then another immediately afterwards.

As he absent-mindedly strung the first load of clean washing on the clothes line, allowing it to turn freely in the breeze, he tried to work out how best to demonstrate his remorse for how he behaved at Avondale earlier in the day.

He was not good at apologies at the best of times. During his youth, he witnessed his mother constantly apologising and making excuses. He too said sorry to his father a thousand times when he did not mean it ever. Sorry for not being good enough, sorry for not living up to expectations, sorry for witnessing what he did to her. Sorry, sorry, sorry!

He used up all his sorrys a very long time ago.

He wasn't sure how long he was standing there with the washing line going around and around in front of him. Long enough for his sleeve to become damp from the wet sock in his hand.

What a complete fuck up you have made of things, he thought to himself. *Will you ever learn?*

He finished with the washing and started to go inside again when he noticed something. To the side of the conservatory nearest the path that led to the front of the house was a thin strip of lawn—well, poorly maintained grass—that got little sunlight and trapped moisture when it rained. The result was a sometimes sticky patch with a few tufts of green, where he never had cause to go in the usual course of events. He was not concerned by the poor state of his garden, but by the partial footprint he could see.

He went back indoors and emerged again with his camera, an old towel, a white plastic ruler, a shoebox and a carrier bag. In the garden shed, he found a short length of corrugated metal, which he hosed off to clean as best he could and then wiped dry with the towel.

He carefully stuck the metal sheet into the ground where it butted against the path so no more rain could wash onto the mud where the footprint was. Next he laid the ruler down on the ground close to the footprint and took several photos from different angles until he was satisfied he had captured every possible detail. He put his camera aside and studied the print by lying down to get his head directly over the top of it.

It was not quite a full print; the end of the heel section was missing because of some scraggy grass that managed to survive there. It was a much smaller foot than his own size nine and significantly narrower too. There was a faintly discernible pattern on the sole section, which consisted of about fifteen diagonal lines from upper left to lower right and a series of concentric oval shapes near to the heel end.

When he got up again, he put the shoebox in the bag to weatherproof it and then gently placed it over the print. He was about to go inside again when he stopped and removed the box again. The print was from the right foot; it was also facing outwards from the conservatory, which meant the person who left it there was stood with their back almost up against the wall. For a moment he could not think of any possible reason for it to be there; then he could think of one, inwardly thanking Sherlock Holmes for providing the reason.

He called Tara first and briefly explained what he found. "I need you to come and have a look please."

"Okay I'm not sure what use I can be."

"Your expert opinion," he replied cryptically.

Tara looked quizzically at the plastic-covered shoebox until Dan explained why it was there. When he lifted it off, the print was just as he left it. "Do you remember when you told me you could spot the difference between a thirty-two and a thirty-four at a distance? Well, you also said you could tell the difference between a size six and a size seven shoe. So what can you tell me about this one?"

Tara looked at him hard. "Seriously?"

"Very."

A minute later and they were both lying down as Dan had done earlier. "It's a woman, which I suppose you knew already," she said.

"Guessed, not knew," Dan replied.

"It's a five and a half, unusual pattern, maybe European, which means it's probably from a good make. It's a casual shoe, not a formal one."

When they got up Dan gave her a kiss. "There I told you: expert opinion."

"My pleasure," she said, clearly very pleased with herself. Then they turned to look at Harry, who had been watching them both. Tara called him as soon as she got off the phone with Dan and they arrived together. At that point Dan experienced further embarrassment and apologised again. Harry offered his hand and the subsequent shake cemented their even keel status once more.

Harry peered down at the muddy imprint and sniffed. "Are you sure Tara?"

"Harry Spiller! Are you questioning my fashion expertise?" She laughed.

He chuckled back. "Not if you are going to get as emotional as Dan."

They all remained stood over the mysterious footprint, each waiting for one of the others to speak. Tara broke first. "Well what does it mean?"

"Maybe nothing," said Dan.

"But neither of us thinks that," Harry said, finishing Dan's thoughts if not his words. "What size are you?"

"Four," Tara said.

Dan looked at her. "The only other woman I can recall being anywhere near here is Shelley at the barbecue. But I don't remember her standing here, especially not with her back to the wall."

"She's an eight," Tara said with certainty.

"What do you remember of Veronica Stenning's feet?" asked Harry hopefully.

"I knew you were going to ask that. The first time we met she was wearing some fantastic cowboy boots under flared jeans. They had long pointed toes though so I'd be lying if I said they were a definite size. After that I don't remember much about what shoes she wore at all."

"An educated guess?"

"Bigger than me."

When Dan and Harry looked down, she went on, "I'm not wrong."

Harry nodded. "That's good enough for me. I'll get a Scenes of Crime unit down to shoot some more photos and take a plaster cast. I'll also get them to run a check on shoe sole patterns we have on our database as well."

"Get them to start with European," Tara directed him.

"You two are perfectly matched," he replied and then much more seriously added, "In the meantime, what are we going to do about this?"

Dan forced himself to discuss the mystery of the footprint. But it was the older man who first noticed Tara; she was pale and close to tears. Harry's altered expression had the desired effect on Dan, and he went to her.

"It's alright. We'll make sure nothing happens to you," he said, thinking reassurance was best.

"It is not alright; you and Harry are experienced in all this stuff. It's not a game of cat and mouse to me, I'm really scared. This bitch as good as killed my brother, she has history of killing several other poor men and women, she knows where I live and work, she's not been scared off and now she has found out where you live. Why should I be anything other than terrified?"

"No, you are absolutely right. See, there I go again; doing just what I was talking about before. Come and sit down, let me explain properly."

They all went inside and sat at the kitchen bench. Dan asked Harry to start, hoping Tara might see it as the policeman taking control rather than him.

"Look Tara, the first thing is we don't *know* it is her. We probably just got a bit caught up with it all there for a while. I'm sorry. It was not a very clever thing for us to do."

"So what other explanation is there?"

"Well, I haven't got an answer for that one yet. There could be another reason, but to be honest, I am not big on coincidences."

"Do you think it's her?"

"I can't think of another reason. What's important now is to make sure we do all we can to take the right precautions until we catch her."

"Dan?" she said, looking for the reassurance he tried to offer earlier.

"Harry's right. Let the police do what they must. That may mean some more time away from work for you and away from home for us both. I'll stay with you and won't get involved with the investigation any more.

"I think it must be her as well, as to why she has been here, I can only think of one or two reasons."

"She's not going away, is she?"

"No, honey, I don't think so. But we are."

"What?"

"Let's get out of Auckland for a while. You could ask Cathy to look after the shop as another sort of dry run for when you join up proper."

"I could, I know she would not mind."

"Okay, that's decided; we can leave in the morning."

Before they got off topic altogether, there was another obvious point Tara wanted to make to them both. "Why do you think you can catch her when nobody else has?"

Dan looked as if he was going to answer, but did not. Tara could not help but say what she was thinking. "What if she's better than you Dan?"

CHAPTER THIRTY

The feeling of excitement was starting to return to Abbey. Her good fortune in overhearing Dan Calder and Tara Danes' late night conversation had given her scope for research and also a degree of imagination.

She found herself feeling altogether closer to Calder now that she had a better understanding of some of his personal issues. What she heard him say made a good fit with the previously unexplained double obituary for his mother and the lack of any for his father. It also explained the contact he made with the Depression Society.

She needed to focus in order to plan effectively, and that was difficult with the rising excitement levels. The solution to her dilemma was the same as it often had been, and the reason why she had been in the bedroom for so long getting ready. As each layer was applied, she also reacquired Walter Terry's personality, so when the last of the actor's putty around the nose and false teeth were in place and his spectacles were adjusted, *he* was already cursing; this time at the local council who positioned a street lamp directly outside the bedroom window.

Walter left the unit at 10:00 p.m. He walked as quickly as his years and the inflammation in both knee joints allowed; however, the cane he carried was more for looks than apparent functionality for the time being. He was in his early sixties, some guessed in the past, which was fine by him, as Katrina intended mid-sixties when she created him.

He was dressed in a smart but casual combination of beige trousers and a blue blazer with a wool coat over the top; it served many purposes other than keeping out the cold. The clothes came from the charity shop in Kohimarama and needed hardly any alteration to make them fit.

He selected the bus stop with the worst street lighting in case an early opportunity presented itself, and sat down on the plastic bench seat. There was no sign of anyone else in the street, let alone another passenger, before the bus arrived on time. He paid in small change with a gloved hand and took a seat towards the back. There was only one other passenger on board at that time, a lady of similar age to him and in no way a candidate for him tonight.

Although Walter still had a good head of greying dark brown hair, he kept his brown tweed hat on, and his steel framed glasses carried enough tint to make describing him a challenge if anybody happened to try.

The only other passengers to get on before the city centre destination were a young couple, again not suitable.

When he got off, the driver offered to help him, but Walter declined, grateful that decency and manners still existed in some parts. He made his way up to Aotea Square, where fast food outlets, little cafés and bars seemed to occupy a large percentage of the available space.

Looking in from the outside it appeared that Pizza Palizza was winning the war for customers on this particular evening, and so he went in and joined one of the three identical queues of pulsating humanity moving towards the greasy chrome counter. The throb of conversation surrounded him, a few single people who all seemed to be older than forty, couples who looked like they just came from the movie theatre opposite and the younger customers especially feeling the need to shout over everybody else. It was enough to make anyone mad. It made Walter very mad indeed, that people could not simply wait politely without having to disturb everybody around them.

He was incensed by the apathy, rudeness and lack of proper behaviour of the world in general and the people he came into contact with in particular. Someone ought to teach them a lesson. Someone like him.

And he had done. With corrupted justification implanted in his brain, he taught more lessons to more people than he could now remember. However, Katrina remembered each and every one and how they satisfied her needs, which in turn allowed her to concentrate on other matters.

Walter placed his order when he reached the counter and waited for the loathsome youth to deliver his small thin crust vegetarian and drink. When he did, Walter observed how he slid the tray across the counter towards him rather than place it down properly. This, accompanied with a sly grin, infuriated him, and he nearly said something, but the queue behind was getting increasingly restless. He took his tray to an uncomfortable moulded seat and glared at the youth, who paid no attention at all.

You need to be taught a good lesson, he thought.

His meal was disgusting, every bite an insult. As he looked around the restaurant, he was amazed at the poor standards of behaviour. People who talked while they ate, people who chewed like camels with their mouths wide open, others grabbing and reaching over. The list of offences was endless; they could all do with a sharp reminder as far as he was concerned.

He could not finish his food and left the remains on the table when he got up. The relative quiet of the street outside was a relief, and with a final sour look, he walked away. He guessed it was a normal weekday evening in the middle of the city; some smaller shops with carousels and plastic tables outside remained open; mostly they seemed to be catering to foreign tourists on limited budgets. Other department stores and mainstream shops were closed but lit up like Christmas trees so passers-by could be tempted to come back another time.

A pair of intoxicated women in their late twenties tottered out of a bar in front of him, dresses too short and heels too high.

They were asking for trouble. As they giggled their way down the street in front of him, a group of men coming the other way leered at them like zoo animals. Walter shook his head at the display. When they passed each other, the women giggled louder and the men leered harder; they exchanged lurid suggestions until the men noticed another group of three slightly younger women further up the road and their attention was re-directed.

Walter carried on, his head down but his eyes raised, his cane tapping the ground. When he reached the intersection of Queen and Quay streets, he decided on rail rather than road for his next journey. He was content to make several journeys tonight, if necessary.

He tapped his cane into Britomart's main concourse, noting the bright lights everywhere which turned night into day and bought a ticket at the machine, which was anything but customer-friendly; then he took the escalator down to the platforms. The first train to depart was destined for Pakuranga and South Auckland; he got on and sat in the middle of an otherwise empty carriage. As the doors started to close, another passenger stuck an arm through the doors from the outside, and they automatically opened again.

When the train moved off, Walter was already checking the inside pockets of his coat.

She was in her late teens, although with so much makeup on, it was difficult to tell these days. She had wires going from the inside of her open jacket up to her head where they disappeared into her ears, and he could hear the faint sound of what passed for music. She wore the same uniform shirt he saw earlier on that evening behind the chrome counter at Pizza Palizza. Walter's mouth formed a hateful sneer.

The girl paid no attention to the old man; she was just glad to have made the train and not got stuck waiting for the next one. In her bag were two books, one for pleasure and one for study.

She got out *The First Farmers: A History of the Late Bronze Age*, and opened it at the page she last marked.

Before she settled into the book, she took a miniature bottle of perfume from her bag and sprayed a little on herself to try and mask some of the horrible restaurant smell. She hated working there, but it was relatively good money and the hours suited; she couldn't wait to finish next month and do some real work at the museum where she was recently accepted for a post in the much admired research department.

Walter watched with growing distaste. Not only was she another one of those revolting bunch who saw it as a chore rather than proper work to serve decent paying customers, she obviously also liked to tart herself up to make degenerate young men want to paw and pant after her.

As if that was not bad enough she seemed to be reading some violence-provoking trash; he could not read the title, but there were swords or knives or something like that on the front cover.

"What is wrong with some people today?" he muttered to himself.

The train was approaching the Panmure station when he got up from his seat. As he did, he extracted the concealed blade from inside his cane and held it close to his side.

"You're no better than a common whore," he spewed as he stopped next to the girl.

She removed her earphones. "Sorry," she said. "I didn't hear you, is everything alright? Do you need some help?"

"Whore, I said. You should learn how to behave."

She was so shocked that she did not know what to say and was rooted to the spot. The old man leant forwards and she thought he might spit.

The blade entered her chest, cutting one of her earphone cables. Walter pushed hard at the sign of first resistance until it was buried up to the decorative handle. A crimson flower blossomed and grew on the fabric of her shirt.

The girl looked down, total incomprehension on her face. She started to speak, but the blood now flooding into her perforated lung choked and muffled her words.

Walter wasn't sure, but it sounded like, "Mummy."

He pulled the blade out quickly and plunged it into the girl's chest again. This time she groaned and tilted sideways. He left it there until the train came to a stop and then pulled it out again. He had just enough time to wipe both sides of the blade on the girl's jacket to remove most of the blood and then slid it back into the body of his stick; he got off before the doors closed.

As the train moved off, the girl slumped fully over on her seat as her book started to become saturated with blood. Regardless of where she was going before, death was her new destination now.

Walter calmly walked out of the station tapping his cane on the ground as he went. Despite his bad knees, he had to walk all the way home; bus and taxi drivers were potential witnesses who might be able to place a fare at or near a scene at a particular time, even if they could only vaguely describe an old man with a walking stick.

Harry started by updating the team of some new events that were going to affect them all.

"There was a particularly vicious attack last night. A uni student on her way back home from work in the city around 1eleven forty-five p.m., stabbed twice. Auckland Central has determined this is a top priority and they are taking back all the extra staff we've had recently plus one more detective. First thing we have to decide is who from here is going over to join them. Sorry guys, I have to ask for a volunteer, or I'll have to decide who goes."

"Do you know how long it will be for?" Philip Te Tuke asked.

"At least two weeks I'd say, but who knows."

"I live over that way, so if no one else wants to, I'll go."

"Thanks Philip. Any other takers?"

Soon Te Tuke was on his way over to the city leaving two empty chairs around the table.

"Okay, we have had some new developments of our own," Harry said. "There's evidence to suggest Mallinder has been at Dan's house sometime in the last few days. It's not confirmed, and I'm not sure we will be able to say with one hundred percent certainty it was her until we actually find her, but I'm convinced."

Phil Brown spoke up. "Is Dan alright?"

"Pretty angry, but he's fine. Tara Danes is not so good. I think she is just about hanging on to her senses at the moment. I've suggested they go away for a while and see if we can get this concluded for them both.

"London is very interested. They are going to launch formal murder investigations and will be seeking extradition as soon as we lock her up."

"Good for us," Phil Brown said. "No prosecution file or trial."

"Unless the bosses want to pursue the computer fraud and blackmail of Neil Danes. I won't be pushing for that I can tell you."

He spent time next explaining the details of the footprint and asked Kiri to liaise with the Scenes of Crime Department regarding the print pattern. Jerome volunteered to do the work on trying to establish what size Mallinder's feet were.

"What are Dan and Tara going to do?" Phil Larson asked.

"Tara wants to go to Africa or South America or anywhere a long way away until it's all over. Dan, as you can imagine, is not keen on that idea," Harry replied. "He was saying something about being back for the marathon at the end of the month when I left them yesterday."

"Whatever they decide, Dan will let us know. In the meantime, let's concentrate on doing everything we can to get the right result for him and for Tara especially."

All modes of transportation around the country were being monitored where it was possible, to trace and identify passengers. Glen Johannsen did a good job of coordinating a communication chain with private bus services, train and airline companies, so every ticket office had up-to-date names and descriptions of Mallinder. He also set up a way of relaying details back to the police.

Phil Larson was monitoring the banks and credit card companies, but they all knew from her history, it was unlikely to produce anything useful. He completed the tedious task without complaint; the others were very glad it wasn't them.

The Vespa was recovered from the waters of the Orakei Basin several days before after a kayaker spotted an oily spot on the surface where some of the sump contents leaked out from the machine. By the time it was salvaged and examined, there was no usable forensic evidence to assist the inquiry.

The next day Dan and Tara drove into Ponsonby to speak to Cathy before heading down to Wellington.

"This is so good of you, thanks again," Tara said.

"It's absolutely fine. This must be Dan?"

Dan could now see exactly why they were contemplating a partnership; Tara's friend was in her mid-thirties and clearly had a bubbly character based on her choice of colourful clothing and rainbow-streaked hair. She was also walking with the aid of an aluminium frame. He could see her lower right leg appeared wasted and guessed she may have suffered from polio in her earlier life.

Tara apologised and made the introductions. "We'll be gone a few days at least, but we were talking last night about us making our arrangement a bit more formal. It seems like a brilliant idea to me, so I wanted to see if you're still sure."

Cathy was. "Are you kidding? Leave the shops to me and you can do all the running around trying to source new stock. I can't think of anything better. If you are sure now, I can get something written up, or we could both do that and choose the best or even make up something from them both."

"That's a good idea," Dan said. "You could do that while we're away."

Tara was pleased and relieved. "Okay then partner, let's do it."

She was in a much more relaxed mood as they set off, and they talked about how the shops might best operate all the way to Taupo where they decided to break the long journey to the capital with an overnight stay in a bed and breakfast overlooking the lake.

They next day, they made it to Wellington in time for the 2:00 p.m. ferry across the Cook Strait to Picton. They were in the Abel Tasman National Park by nine. Tara insisted on paying; while Dan could not argue with her ability to do so, he still felt uncomfortable allowing her. Their private lodge in Totara Bay was picture-perfect, and Tara had pre-ordered a fully stocked kitchen so they need do no more than unpack and open a bottle of local Pinot Noir when they arrived.

As they sat out on the deck looking up at a star-filled sky, she finally felt like she could relax. "It's not so bad getting away is it?"

"No it's beautiful; I have never been to this part of the country before. I can't wait to do some walking and maybe a bit of kayaking, if you want to. Thanks for bringing me."

"It is lovely, wait until you see it in daylight. It's been years since I was here, and we stayed in a backpackers then. This is a real step up."

"It must have cost a bomb; I'd really like you to let me help pay."

"We've been over that darling, so forget it. I'm happy to be able to do something nice with it for both of us. You're going to have to get used to it."

The main bedroom suite was as superbly appointed as the rest of the lodge. They shared a shower after the wine and fell into bed around midnight.

When Dan woke up, Tara was at the bedroom window looking out onto a vista of blue sea, white sand and almost clear skies. "Wow, you were so right, it's amazing," he said.

"Morning; coffee's on," Tara replied coming over and sitting on the end of the bed. "How did you sleep?"

"Good."

"It's the first time since Neil died I have woken up and not immediately felt sad. I nearly forgot what that was like."

Dan smiled. "Time does make a difference; I'm sure when all this is over and done with, you'll be able to remember the good times without all the bad stuff being there too."

"What about you. Can you take your own advice?"

"I don't know about that, I hope so. After what you and Harry have said recently, I might not be able to do it on my own."

"Mr. Calder, you are the dearest sweetest man. I wish there was more I could do to help."

"Believe me, you are helping all the time."

After breakfast, they went for a walk along the beach and then up into the bush. They talked about any subject that popped into their heads, held hands, took photos and the time to breathe in the fresh air.

"This was the best idea to come here," Dan said as they were making their leisurely way back along the dirt track to the beach.

"Thanks for agreeing. I know you preferred to stay in Auckland."

"That might have been true yesterday, but not now."

"What do you really think will happen? Will she make a mistake? Can Harry catch her, or do you think she might even just decide to disappear forever?"

"The truth is nobody knows the answer yet, not even her. She is obviously very disturbed, although she can appear to be normal as well. I guess she has considered leaving New Zealand and decided not to, but has an escape planned out which she could implement at a moment's notice.

"If we catch her, sorry, if the police catch her, it will be because she takes one risk too many or does make a mistake. I just don't see them locating her unless it's by accident."

"I can't begin to understand what people like that think like."

"I'm glad to hear it. She's crazy, Tara; even before her parents' death, she must have had severe problems."

"So where does that leave us?"

"I'm the one she's directing her feelings towards." He tried to make it sound as far away from scary as he could, for Tara's benefit. "She is very focused on her targets, we know that from all the time she spends planning. So when we go back, I'll talk to Harry about it and try and sort something out." He read her thoughts and tried to head her off. "I can't hide forever; I have to go back sometime, and you already agreed about my marathon run. I won't be taking chances on my safety, that's why I'll talk to Harry."

Tara was not persuaded. "Now it sounds like *you* are the crazy one, wanting to go back knowing she is after you."

They reached the beach again and went down to the water which lapped in no more than gentle ripples around their bare feet. "Don't worry; having you to think about and care for means I'm not going to do anything which is going to stop me from being able to do just that. Besides, we don't have to be back for over a week, and a lot can happen in that time. So please don't worry about it now."

Tara stopped. "Have you thought anymore about what you told me regarding what to do with the things you don't understand?"

"All the time. Maybe I never will be able to resolve them all. Harry told me he learned the hard way that sometimes you can't have everything you want and that you can find less than perfect is enough. If I never do fully understand, I hope that what I'm left with is enough."

"And if it's not? I don't want us to end up like you did with April."

He took her hand again, and they walked the rest of the way back in silence.

Abbey spent two days watching the houses of Calder and Danes and also went to Tara's shop three times. In that time, there was no sign of either of them, or Dan Calder's Volkswagen. She did not want to be out too late and risk drawing any unwanted attention, so she limited herself to just one night-time visit to both houses. It seemed they were not at either of the premises. Still, she was not going to take any chances, which was why she had been watching from a bench seat, pretending to read a book and listen to her iPod for the last hour on the third morning. Dan ran during the mornings, but there was no sign of him today. Tara worked to suit and so no conclusions could be drawn from her non-appearance, although her car was there.

Abbey had a pocket full of keys ready to be tried in the Calder back door, and all day to wait if necessary. The iPod almost guaranteed nobody stopping to talk to her, and she was content to sit for at least another hour *not* reading before she needed to think about repositioning.

Harry got off the phone to Dan with a second apology for waking him up. "You must have fallen straight into a very pleasant routine. I'll call you later next time."

"No problem," Dan replied. "We've only been here a few days, and it feels like a million miles and a million years away. I have to say it is good; Tara's so much better too. Talk soon, bye."

"Harry checking up on us? He's a good guy for a Pom, just like you," said Tara as Dan put his phone away again in the bedside drawer.

"He says hi. Just called to say there was no news and to say you were right about the shoe size."

"Has he found out the make yet from the pattern on the sole?"

"Not yet. It's less likely to be on their database if it is an expensive European brand like you think.

"I'm going to go for a run; you've got my routine all out of sync since we've been here but I have to keep it up for just another week or so." He got out of bed and padded to the bathroom to throw some water on his face.

As he looked at his face in the mirror he called, "You do make it very hard to leave."

Tara pulled herself up to a sitting position. "I'm glad I'm doing my job. Will you keep running after the race?"

"Probably for the exercise," he said coming back into the bedroom. "I'll see you in a while." He kissed her on the lips and headed for the door.

While he was gone, Tara put in another call to Shelley. "Reporting in for my daily chat," she said by way of a hello.

"Hi, Tara. How are you?"

"We're okay; more to the point, how are you, is it tomorrow you start the new job?"

"It is. I can't wait."

"Good luck, I'm sure they will love you. Can I ask you something, in your professional capacity I mean?" Tara asked.

Shelley became serious. "Of course, is everything okay?"

"Yes, it's just Dan. I've learned so much about him in such a short space of time, but I really think he needs someone else to talk to. Do you remember when you told me he had hidden layers? Well you were so right, you would be amazed."

"Does he know you're asking me this?"

"No. I'm not sure how he would react to be honest."

"It's really for him to want to talk first; maybe you could suggest it, but he has to want to. Think about how best to introduce the subject, and we can talk about it again when you get back; I take it you don't want me to say anything to Paul?"

They spent five more minutes gossiping by the end of which Tara was laughing again properly for the first time in quite a while.

"It sounds like Dan and Tara are having a good time. They were still in bed when I called," Harry said to Phil Brown who was sat in his boss's office.

"I'd be tempted not to come back at all. I love it down there," Phil said. "Anyway I'm afraid the only thing to report today is what we were expecting. Tara was spot on about the shoe. Kiri had the idea of getting that guy Colin Palmer at NCIS to run it for us as a favour; it's a Spanish make called Los Campas. They aren't available here or Australia. Good quality and expensive, that particular pattern appears on two different styles from 2008 until present. Colin's going to email me the link to the company website so we can see what the shoes look like."

"Good work. I told Dan we hadn't got the answer to that yet, so he'll be pleased when I call him next. Perhaps Tara will recognise seeing them on Mallinder when she sees them."

Abbey was, in fact, wearing her favourite Los Campas sand-shoes at that moment; they were stylish, comfortable to walk in, and she could wear them with a number of different outfits, including the faded denim she was dressed in today. The other big bonus with them was she could wear heel blocks inside which made her taller by up to five centimetres.

Most of the details were decided already in so far as how the final act would play out. A Stenning was not practicable as she was known and probably expected to make an appearance, as would a female of any description. Therefore it fell upon Walter Terry to finish the job.

That was more than okay. Walter's executions stayed in the mind with far more meaning. His senses were always so heightened that at the moment of death, she could not just see and hear it, but she could really feel, taste and smell it too.

In order for her to have the upper hand and the feeling of control of the situation *and* to make Calder suffer properly, it was necessary to get inside his head and play with his mind, as she had done with Stephen Christopher, Cecilia Mathews, Mark Singleton, Edwina Jacobs and even Neil Danes.

It was too easy simply extinguishing a life.

When some ominous clouds started to appear overhead, she decided the time had come to pay her visit to Dan Calder's house.

In daylight, the back of the house seemed a lot more open to view than she expected before she arrived. Even the substantial fence around it was somehow lower and through the few trees in the garden, mostly bereft of the first leaves of the new season, she could see the backs of houses in the adjoining street. Abbey took the first manageable handful of keys from her pocket and inserted one into the lock. It slid in easily but did not turn; placing it quickly in the opposite pocket she tried another with the same result.

Constable Tim O'Connor was not happy. Victims' protection patrol was not his idea of police work, or why he joined the job six years before. Checking on vulnerable persons and property was for security guards who did not have the necessary abilities to get into the police in the first place.

His duty sergeant had had it in for him for a couple of months since the accident with the prisoner wagon. O'Connor managed to convince himself that it was the fault of the drunken loud-mouth in the back; although side-swiping a brand new Mercedes by swerving and braking to throw the prisoner from one side of the rear compartment to the other was a stretch of the imagination that eluded almost everyone else.

There were at least thirty addresses to check today; he was only on number six but already completely disinterested in the task. When he got to Beach View Parade in St. Heliers he did not bother to look at the information sheet that detailed the reason for the check. It looked like it might start to rain at any time, and he considered not getting out of the car at all; when he did he gave the door a mighty slam, which made him feel a little better.

Abbey heard the car door and froze instantly. Her choices were very limited: the nearest fence was only five metres away, and she was sure she could get up and over it. As she processed the options, she pushed the key in her hand fully into the lock without thinking. She could now hear one person's heavy steps on the concrete path at the side of the house, coming towards her. Without knowing why, she knew they did not belong to Dan Calder.

She momentarily thought about confronting the owner of the footsteps—until the unmistakable crackle and metallic human voice of a radio transmission halted the walker. *Shit!*

O'Connor stopped to listen to the radio broadcast; if there was any job remotely within range, he would happily flag this bull. Unfortunately for him, the call related to something almost as tedious and he continued up the path.

The back garden lacked personality and the owner was obviously not green-fingered. A lawn, a few trees and a shed; he looked along the back elevation of the house and saw nothing amiss. He shook hands with the handles of the double French doors and also the back door and glanced in through the windows at the dark, empty interior. When he got back to the car, the rain he feared was just starting to spatter against the windscreen. On the visit sheet, he wrote, "All in order" and the time, and then initialled the entry.

"Fuckin' waste of time," he muttered as he fired up the engine and drove off to his next dead loss visit of the day.

Abbey took slow deep breaths.

The key had miraculously turned almost on its own. When the cop stopped, presumably to listen to his radio, it gave her the three seconds she needed to open the door and get inside. For a moment, she thought he must be bound to see or hear the door clicking shut as he rounded the corner of the house, but fortunately he did not. She flattened her back against the inside of the door and prayed she could not be seen from the outside.

When the footsteps retreated and finally disappeared, she started breathing again.

The house was deathly quiet. No ambient noise whatsoever gave her the feeling of being lost in outer space. She could see most of the open-plan ground floor, apart from the conservatory to her far left on the other side of the kitchen.

Being careful to stay away from the windows, Abbey navigated her way around, noting the lack of personal effects that make a house a home; however, she could feel Calder's presence in the heavy atmosphere.

When she went upstairs, she found what she was looking for.

His bedroom was purely a space to sleep and store clothes in. His wardrobe told her that he was not a follower of current fashion trends, and in fact, his interest in clothes stopped at functionality. He was very much an outdoors man with more jeans, heavy-duty shirts and fleece jackets than formal trousers, suits and ties.

She located the real Dan Calder in what had been the proper wardrobe once and was now a small study. The computer desk supported two machines, one a laptop. She smiled, thinking about how he must have spent so much time and effort compiling the J.D. Calder persona that he allowed her access to; she did not bother to turn either of them on as she knew with certainty they would be password protected. The stacks of paperwork in no particular order on the rest of the available table top space comprised of research material mostly related to her and also a manuscript. On closer examination, she saw it was the first chapters of a book.

"An author; who'd have thought? You're full of surprises, aren't you?" she said to her reflection in the larger computer screen.

The walls held an array of notes and pages that also related mostly to her. She recognised the letterhead of The Primrose Residential Care Home and also the name Clive Craddock, the conveyancer. When she saw a photocopied picture of Valerie she stopped. It was taken in the Craddock office; casting her mind back to work out it was taken from the area of the reception desk. *That useless bitch Heidi*, she thought.

There was a box on the floor. Inside she found a number of photos taken over Calder's career; surveillance courses, she noted. When she saw her own words in print again, she took the time to read the newspaper article in full one more time.

In the bottom of the box there was a well-worn envelope on which was written in faded black ink, 'John.' When she opened it she saw three small photographs, one colour and two black and whites plus a small card with writing printed on one side and small neat handwriting on the other.

Looking at the photos first she saw they were all of a boy and a woman, the same boy and the same woman in each one at different ages. The boy was unmistakably Dan Calder; the woman undoubtedly was his mother. On the back of the coloured image was a date: *Aug 1970.*

She examined the small card next, the printed side read,

There never was a woman like her. She was gentle as a dove and brave as a lioness ... The memory of my mother and her teachings were, after all, the only capital I had to start life with, and on that capital I have made my way.

—Andrew Jackson.

On the reverse side the writing was in pencil and read, *"To Mum, with all my love from John X."* It was written in a more mature hand than could have belonged to the boy in any of the photos. Abbey wondered how and when he gave his mother this small token and in what circumstances it was returned to his possession.

For a moment, she felt an affinity with Dan Calder that had nothing to do with anything else which went before; it was as if they were walking together on different sides of the same street. The moment passed, but not before she noticed a small bible on the bookshelf, on the inside of the front cover was a short inscription. *"To John. I hope you find strength in the words, with love from Mum."* Abbey put it in her pocket then selected a red marker pen from the ample supply, taking it and the envelope and it contents downstairs into the kitchen where she found a frying pan in one of the cupboards.

She put the photos and the quotation card in the pan and placed it on one of the gas rings. She heated the pan just sufficiently for the photos to start to scorch and discolour then removed it from the heat so the images remained distorted but visible. She left the pan and its contents on top of another gas

ring and sat down on one of the bench stools with the marker
and the envelope.

She wanted to get her message just right and took the time she
needed before writing in large letters across the front. PLAY
WITH FIRE, GET BURNED. THEN YOU WILL KNOW
MY PAIN.

Abbey let herself out as she had got in.

All there was to do now was wait.

CHAPTER THIRTY-ONE

Dan and Tara were behaving like honeymooners. Even if the dramatic recent circumstances had not influenced their coming together and they had instead met in a supermarket queue or on a street corner, they were sure their mutual attraction would have eventually brought them together.

During the days they walked and kayaked in the area around the lodge. In the evenings, they usually stayed at home with simple meals and good wine, none of which Dan drank as the race was just over a week out. Once or twice he talked her into going as far as Nelson for restaurant fare.

Day and night they talked, about their pasts, present and future. By the end of the first week, there was only one solitary secret he had left to himself. Apart from that, it was like discovering religion and being born again.

One evening, he told her more about his first book. "I suppose it's an attempt to make sense of the past and to try and find some closure. I changed the names and substituted the Navy for the Police, but otherwise it is all as I remember. You can read it if you like."

"I'd love to. What's the style?"

"An honest account of my feelings from childhood to when I finished the early and middle parts of my police service," he replied, thinking again about the twenty chapters he was willing to acknowledge and single sequestered one.

"Tell me a bit about it?"

"It is in the form of a story, but it is also almost completely based on personal experiences. It describes my feelings about the circumstances around my mother's death, how it affected me at the time and since. Then it talks about my life in the police and some of the people I knew in that time. Do you remember asking me if I ever talked about things?"

She nodded.

"That's how I did it. Let the words come out on the page and see what the characters have to say to me and each other. On a good day that is, when I could get some text on the page. Some days I wondered if I would ever finish. I didn't enjoy doing it. The new one is different; it's all about one particular time when I was in an obs van on my own for nearly three days. It might not sound like a good story, but I think self-examination of a person's character when they are in a confined space for so long has got possibilities."

"And you recently did the same thing again! How much have you done so far?"

"That was a much different time and place altogether. Sixty thousand words, a hundred and fifty pages or so."

"And does it help?"

"Some days I think it does. I won't be sure until I finish it."

She cuddled up close to him on the sofa in front of the log fire. "I think it's going to have a very happy ending."

"I hope you're right," Dan said not believing it altogether.

They had extended their stay by two days once already and were sorely tempted to do the same again. "How long do you think it will take before we got really bored though?" Dan asked as they swung gently in the giant hammock on the front deck. The sun was setting over the top of the hills to the west, making its exit in a flashy show of orange and red.

"That depends on how much more of this wine is left," Tara said winking and holding up her empty glass.

Dan was managing to stick to cranberry juice for the last week before the race, but comments like that tested his resolve. He reached down and pulled the bottle out of the bucket of icy water beneath them, deliberately letting a few droplets fall onto Tara's bare legs and stomach as he refilled her. She giggled, but then became serious. "I'm going to sell Neil's and Mum's old house when we get back. I have been thinking about it, and I can't think of any reason to keep them."

"No one could argue with that," he answered. "I know it might seem a bit soon, but have you given any thoughts to our living situation?"

He loved her lopsided smile. "What do you mean?" she teased.

"Please don't make me have to beg. You know I love you, and I want to be with you, not live a few miles apart and travel between two houses. How about it, the last ten days have been a pretty good trial, haven't they?"

"I think I might like to see you beg." After a pause long enough to make him suffer just a little she went on. "There is nothing in the whole world I'd rather do. Your place or mine? If we do mine, then you'll have to decorate for me, and if it's yours, you will have to let me do some interior design."

He kissed her nose. "Your house is a little bigger, but I like mine being so close to the sea. I don't really mind to be honest; so if you have a preference?"

"What about your place to start with and maybe we could start to look for somewhere new? A real new beginning."

"That sounds perfect, but it's got to be a partnership, equal shares and equal investment. I don't want you paying for everything."

"Alright—but enough about the money; if it hadn't been for you, Neil could still have been dead and all his money gone. I probably owe you."

They clinked their glasses to seal the deal and she rested back against him as the first shooting star of the evening passed overhead.

They made the following day their last day so they could be home for the weekend. That gave Dan one more week before the race. Tara was already planning with military precision moving some of her things to Dan's house; the absolutely cannot-do-withouts first, followed by the must-haves, prefer-to-haves and then the might-be-nice-to-haves. It was a list that only a woman could devise, and he could not have been happier.

At midday while Tara was sunning herself on the deck, he phoned Harry to let him know they were coming back to Auckland the next morning. They arranged to meet so the detective could update them on the aspects of the Mallinder case that directly affected them. Dan wanted Tara to see him distancing himself from the investigation process.

"How has it been down there?"

"It's lovely Harry; you should bring the wife down sometime. What's the news with you?"

There was not a lot new for Harry to pass on. Mallinder had not appeared on their investigative radar and there were no new lines of enquiry. "Her inactivity could mean she has cut her losses," Harry suggested more as filling in a break of conversation rather than a bona fide belief.

"You and I both know we won't be resting until the big metal door closes behind her, she hears her first 'Lights out' call and has to piss in a bucket," Dan said with feeling.

"How's Tara?"

"Good. When we get back we are going to move in together."

"Nice, good for both of you," Harry enthused.

They talked rubbish until Harry had to go and do some real work. "Call me when you get home. Have a good trip back."

"Will do, see you Harry."

"Nothing more to report," he said to Tara as he walked in from the deck.

"Maybe she really has just gone away."

"That's what Harry said." He replied as skilfully as a politician. It seemed to brighten Tara, which was reward enough for his economy with the truth.

Abbey and Walter were engaged in a game of speed costume change. When the job was done, she needed to be as far away as possible as soon as possible. Always in the past, she had taken her time to present as perfect as she could the intended persona of the moment. When she was at university playing a role, Katrina read all the books and watched all the movies before, if they existed, to see how her character had been portrayed.

The Stenning women were all very different from one another; however, her biggest challenge with each of them was the same, making them as unmemorable as possible for people to recall and describe. There were a dozen different Terrys; varying from the teenage youth to Walter at the other end of the age divide. In between, a homeless vagrant, truck driver, business executives, and once a driving instructor, had come and gone. Throughout it all, Walter remained a constant, the most fulfilling and the most productive. Abbey could have chosen someone else, but Walter was the only real choice for the end game. Unfortunately, he was also one of the most complex characters to create and, more importantly, dismantle.

When the time came, he needed to execute the job and melt into the crowd, then away from the crowd without drawing attention to himself. Once at a safe distance, he had to very quickly become Candice Drysdale and only then could *she* start to relax again.

Early in the afternoon the next day, Dan pulled the old VW up onto the driveway. Despite a wonderful time away, they were both glad to be home; they had a future to get started.

"I'll grab the bags, you put the coffee on," he said.

He was just behind Tara, and she had not made it as far as the kitchen when he came inside. He dropped the bags at the bottom of the stairs and grabbed her from behind, wrapping his arms around her and pulling her back into him.

"Welcome home."

She wriggled around to see Dan with a big smile all across her face. "Sounds good, doesn't it. When we get unpacked, can we go over to Shelley and Paul's? I haven't seen her since she started the new job, and I feel a bit bad about it."

"Sure, it will be good to catch up with them and tell them our news too."

They held each other in a long embrace, her head tucked in under his chin. Dan loved Tara more than he ever have thought possible; he had allowed his defences to come down, as he only did twice in the past and as he promised himself he would never do again.

Dan readily accepted he was difficult to like and held very particular views and opinions. Only to those closest had he ever tried to explain that he genuinely considered himself to be a decent human being with a set of rules which were as important to him as anything else in the world. He could not compromise them for the sake of an easier life or to placate somebody else. It was these unyielding beliefs which were his strength as well as his curse over the years.

He prayed Tara would be able to live with all his facets; as he rested his chin on her head, he gazed into the space between them and the far kitchen wall. As his focus sharpened, he found himself looking and seeing something not right.

"Have you been into the kitchen yet, honey?"

Tara sensed his tension and reacted similarly. "No, you gave me something more pleasant to do before I got there."

Dan slowly separated himself. "Stay here." He scanned around, trying to take in every detail and compare them with a memory snapshot brought to the front of his mind. The frying pan on the stove top was not supposed to be there; it was never left there, he had not left it there before they went to the South Island.

"Dan, what is it?" When he did not answer, Tara followed him across the room. "What are you doing?" She tracked his eyes to the bench top and the cast-iron pan. "That should not be there should it? Tell me what to do."

"Nothing for now, watch me and tell me if you see something which is strange." He liked that she knew enough to ask the right questions. Before he approached it, he looked around again to see if there was anything else amiss.

The pan was shallow enough for him to see what was in it. His gut twisted when he recognised the photographs. They were from a box of photos and personal effects which he usually stored in the lounge cupboard; then he remembered the box was last in the study upstairs.

He was sure they were alone in the house, knowing it if they were not, but he was not going to take the smallest chance with Tara's safety. "Come over here, honey," he said as casually as he could and took her hand when she did.

"They're photos from a box in my study. It looks like they have been burned a little. We're going to check the rest of the house together, but I'm sure there's no one here, okay?"

"Okay," Tara whispered back.

They cleared the rest of the ground floor; closing all the doors behind them as they went. There was only one possibility; he sniffed the still air as they went upstairs, in case there was any residual trace of perfume or other identifier.

Even without the photos in the kitchen, he would have known somebody had been in his study. Tara had not let his hand go since he asked for hers. "It's her, isn't it?"

"It is. Look."

He was pointing at his computer monitor where an old envelope was stuck. When Tara read the short message printed on the front, she involuntarily took in a sharp breath.

"Are you alright?" she asked.

"Yeah, fine. You?"

"I'm okay if you tell me I am," she said.

Dan took in the whole of the small room, assessing the level of Mallinder's intrusion. She had taken her time; been free to wander in and out of every room opening cupboards and drawers. He could tell she had taken a special interest in the study.

Tara watched him with the unflinching belief that she was safe so long as he was with her. He exuded calm. After a few minutes, he said, "She's taken my book."

Tara gasped involuntarily. "I'm so sorry. You must be feeling sick."

"No, I'm alright; this is her biggest mistake. Come on, let's have that coffee and then we'd better call Harry."

Downstairs again, he put on the kettle and spooned some grounds into the big plunger.

"Dan, you are being incredibly calm. It's kind of weird."

"Sorry, I was just thinking. She won't come back again, if that's bothering you. But if you prefer not to stay here, we can go to yours."

"I don't mean that. She was in your house, burned your photos and left a threatening message. You're making coffee!"

He wrapped her in his arms again and spoke to her like he was telling her the hidden secrets of the universe. "No matter what happens, I will always take care of you, and there is no one and nothing which will stop me from doing that.

"She's been here sometime while we have been away, and she is thinking she has gotten to know about me from what she found. Now she aims to use that knowledge against me."

Tara shook her head. "So how is that reassuring?"

"Because she's wrong, honey. She doesn't know me, but she has just brought herself within range. I have never been surer we are going to get her than I am right now."

"We, we?"

"I'm sorry Tara; yes it's going to be 'we' again. When we talk to Harry, you'll understand."

"Why, what are you going to say?"

"I know how to get her, but it will need the police to help me, not me helping them."

"No, Dan, no." She tried to pull herself away from him, but he held tight.

"It's the only way to finish this, to finish everything. Please, you have to believe me."

"Finish everything—what does that mean? Oh my God, it's about you again isn't it? You think you can repair all the damage that's been done to you by catching her?"

Dan looked at her, looked all the way inside her; but he did not reply, as he had no idea if she was right or not.

Harry came over, still dressed in his gardening gear. "Thanks for rescuing me. Not my idea of a day off," he said in explanation. "Where's Tara?"

Tara was sat outside, remaining in the house after her exchange with Dan proved impossible and they were still in the middle of an impasse when he walked through the door. Dan showed him into the garden and followed a minute later with a tray of coffee, the frying pan and the envelope, also brought from the kitchen.

"Are you two okay?"

Tara looked at Dan but did not answer.

"Shook up, it's not the best thing to come home to," Dan replied.

"I'm sorry; we did do twice daily checks, sometimes it's not enough."

Dan was philosophical. "It would have been a major fluke to find her here during a routine check, so don't worry about it."

Harry cut to the chase. "You mentioned a plan to catch Mallinder?"

Tara made a despairing noise of frustration and annoyance, stood, then changing her mind, sat down again with as much force as she was able to impart; Dan responded by putting an arm around her shoulder, which she immediately shrugged off.

Harry frowned. "What's going on?"

"You are only limited by your imagination, Harry."

Harry looked from Dan to Tara and back again. "I don't like the sound of it already."

Tara snatched her coffee cup off the tray. "Don't tell me; tell Mr. Death-wish!"

Abbey was thinking about Calder's book again. For the past ten years, there had not been much which surprised her, let alone shocked and amazed. It was not so much a window to the soul, as some authors described their autobiographies, more like a detailed map around it.

She could not have learned more if she sat down and asked him a series of questions under deep hypnosis. He was at least as disturbed as any one of her previous victims and much more so than most. She took out the pages once more and began to read.

Chapter One. I killed my mother. I did not pull a trigger, thrust a dagger or even swing a heavy object, but I killed her as surely as if I had done any of those heinous acts.

When she needed my help, I turned away; when she was too scared to call for assistance, I did nothing. When she died, I cried with pain, regret, remorse and sheer bloody anger.

I was an only child, son to the perfect mother and a father who probably resented the attention I received from her and made sure we both knew it.

He was an important man with an important job; he knew lots of other important men too. When I first became aware of his status, I mistook his beastliness for something which was a by-product of his work. I call it beastliness because my father was a beast; more of that in due course.

It went on and on in stark detail. Abbey sensed his emotions in the words and was drawn into turning over page after page to read more. If she had not been connected to Calder as she was, if she was a normal reader of books, she may have appreciated his style. Dan's description of the people and places which formed the background to his life was similar to how Dickens wrote of Victorian England's brutal harshness and the characters who inhabited it, figures defined by their unabashed wickedness, shining benevolence or their lack of morals.

On page sixty, there was the first introduction to what became the recurring dream the boy in the story remembered.

I woke with certainty that something was wrong in or around the house. For a terrible second, I thought I may have wet the bed, but then I realised the whole of me was soaked through. My favourite pyjamas with pictures of trains on them were so wet, I might have been able to wring them out. My sweat rapidly turned from hot to cold and made me shiver and shake as I lay in the dark.

Somewhere in the distance I could hear noises, more than one. I thought it was street animals, a couple of cats mewing and spewing for supremacy over a discarded take-away chicken, but one of the sounds was much deeper than the other, and I knew cats were mostly the same. I tried to control the shakes by hugging myself as tight as I could, making my pyjamas stick to my skinny body all the more.

The sounds weren't from outside at all.

I do not think I have ever been as scared as I was that night. I don't know if it was because it was the first time, or because I didn't know what caused me to wake up. It might have been because I did know exactly what it was.

When I closed my eyes, I hoped my ears could join them, but as I disabled my visual sense, the aural one intensified, and I could hear it all so much better. It was coming from along the hallway. I had no intention of getting out of bed, and yet before I knew it, I found myself not only out of bed but out of the bedroom. The voices of my parents were not so clear I could have written down a verbatim account of their complete conversation, but some of his words were all too easy to hear.

He was kneeling above her, straddling her like a horse with his back ramrod straight. Although he was still wearing his uniform trousers and shoes, he was bare-chested, making him look like a Native American Indian warrior. A split second after taking in the sight of them like this, it could still have been a game until I saw him raising his right arm and hand towards the lampshade above the bed. He held the buckle end of his belt in his hand and as it moved upwards so the other end slipped easily through the last of the belt loops on his trousers until it hung down in a thick strap of menacing violence.

I went from the shiny black of the belt to the shiny fear in my mother's eyes, and when I found them, she was already looking at me.

"John, oh John dear, what are you doing there? Everything is alright; you go back to bed. Please darling; go back to bed."

What happened next will shame me for the rest of my life.

I slowly withdrew my head from the gap in the doorway, until I was out in the hallway again, the door was closed and I my face was resting against its grainy surface.

I did not stand there for long, but it was long enough to hear my father again. "Are you smiling? Are you laughing at me? I'll teach you to laugh at me." The sound of his stinging voice was followed immediately by the sound of his belt being brought down across my mother's bare skin.

I ran back to my room and buried myself in the sheets and blankets, begging and crying for sleep to come again and trying to block out the animal noises I could still hear.

I never got out of bed at night-time again, no matter how many cats mewing and spewing I heard. I did hear them, so many times.

Sometimes when I woke up, it was the dream again, sometimes it wasn't.

Abbey tried to imagine the scene; one of the photos she toasted was of him in his favourite pyjamas. He looked happy, as did his mother on whose lap he was sitting; she guessed he was aged about seven or eight in the picture. Other details in the book led her to believe Calder was fifteen when she died; that was a lot of twisted memories and a lifetime of guilt.

It was late in the evening by the time she finished reading. Sitting back and looking at the sheaf of papers, she wondered what sort of man Dan Calder really was. They had met only once—and now he might be the one person in the world who could endanger her. She checked the notes made during reading and one stuck out like a mountain top beacon above all others.

Where was chapter fourteen?

"You must be joking," Tara said when Dan finished. "I've never heard anything so stupid in my life. Harry, for God's sake tell him, will you, that you're not going to do it?"

"It's the only way," Dan said.

"Not doing it is another way."

"Try and understand, Tara; she's thinking she understands me because of what I've written and because of the history of our knowing each other. She is alluding to it in her message, what she says for sure, but in what she doesn't say as well.

"I've made a career out of understanding the fine detail in a mess of information and evidence, and I can no more explain it as you can by telling me she's a 34-26-36 just by looking. She's told me more about herself than she knows about me; you cannot get close to someone without revealing part of yourself too."

"So what is it you know?" Harry asked.

"She's feeling invincible. 'Play with fire and get burned', she's the fire and the rest is self-explanatory, okay?"

"Yes."

"But she also makes the point of saying I will be burned, as if she knows I will be doing it anyway, and the burning is not total destruction, like the photos; she left them damaged but not destroyed so that I can see and feel the damage.

"I don't know exactly what she has planned, but she wants me to feel her pain and she can only do that by burning me so I can see and feel it."

Tara trembled at the thought. "It sounds horrible. She must be absolutely mad."

"Oh she is. Cold, calculating, mad."

"Why the marathon?" Harry asked, nodding.

"It has to be soon, she is already taking more risks than ever before. It's the only place she knows where I'm going to be for several hours at a time in the near future. It provides protection in numbers for her and multiple escape routes; being in public view increases the pain I'd suffer, too. There are another dozen reasons I could give you.

"The fact is I'm going to run anyway. Will you help me? Please."

When Harry was gone, Tara grabbed her car keys. "I'm going over to Shelley's for a while. You can do the rest of the unpacking."

"I thought we were going over together."

"Circumstances change don't they?" she replied sarcastically. "Don't wait up."

CHAPTER THIRTY-TWO

At breakfast on Saturday morning, Dan handed Tara a package. They had come to an impasse regarding what the best way of *dealing* with Sunday was; Tara was still desperately concerned for his safety and motives. It was their first disagreement, and Dan resolutely refused to budge. He was going to run the race in the hope of drawing Mallinder into a trap of his design and put an end to her killing career. He was sure he could keep himself one step ahead, and, with the police backup, stay safe.

"I meant to give you this the other day," he said, intending the gesture to make the situation a little better.

Before taking the package, Tara looked at him intently. "I know I'm not going to change your mind but would you consider doing something for me?"

"Anything." Dan was desperate to clear the air between them.

"When all this is over, promise me you won't just write it down as a way of bringing it to an end. Please just think about talking to someone about it, and I don't mean me."

Tara's plea was so heartfelt, Dan was silenced for a moment. He did not want to say yes or no simply as response. "I promise I will think about it. If it means that much to you. Now will you take this before I change my mind?"

"Thank you Dan, for that. And this, I love presents."

"Don't hold your breath, you may not be that excited when you see what it is," he said, handing over the package.

"What is it?" She opened the print-shop paper bag and pulled out the wad of pages. Recognising the contents, she smiled and touched Dan's arm. "You got it all done again."

"I promised you could read it if you wanted to."

"I do. Have you read it again?"

"No, I haven't been in the mood for book writing or reading lately. Let me have it back when you've finished with it, and maybe I will have to catch up with it again; it might give me the impetus to start writing again.

"I'm sorry for how I've been the last few days," he went on; it was the nearest he could come to extending an olive branch. "I suppose we don't know each other as well as we thought. I am well-intentioned but very hard work."

Tara had been waiting for days for any sort of signal; it appeared Dan had gone into his shell, like he sensed the danger and was now preparing for combat.

"What if something happens to you?" she said, sitting close to him on the sofa.

He looked at her, and she could tell he was considering the question seriously.

"It won't," he said finally; she almost believed it completely. "I have not been in a position like this one before, but I have been in other ones where there was really only one course of action to take. Sometimes you just have to get on and do what's required. What's going to happen if we just let her get away? If I didn't run on Sunday, how will you feel on Monday, or next month or next year?"

"The police will get her."

"And what if they don't or if she kills someone else? Can you live with that? Because I can't."

"I do not understand. I don't understand why it *has* to be you, and I don't understand why there can't be another way."

"I promise you if there was another way, if I could take a hundred cops, walk up to her front door and drag her out, I'd do it. This is the only way and this is the only time we'll have."

"How can you be so sure?"

He hardly wanted to say the words, but the truth was inescapable. "Because she and I are the same, that is the same but very different. Two sides of one coin; always linked in some ways but always the opposite of each other. Maybe in a way like you and Neil were inseparable but so different to each other."

"But I never understood him and look how it ended."

"You knew him better than anyone and you shared so much. I bet if you really thought about it, there are a million things you could say you knew about him that he never told you."

"Will you promise me you won't do anything too dangerous or, well, you know?" Tara hesitated to finish what she wanted to say. "I only said goodbye to my brother a few weeks ago."

"I promise to be careful. I want to finish the race and come home to you afterwards … *and* be in one piece for both."

Tara's look became defiant. "I can tell that's the best I'm going to get so; I need you to tell me what I can do to help."

"Help? I don't understand, honey." He was genuinely surprised.

"You don't honestly think I'm going to wave you off on Sunday morning and then go and sit at home and just wait for you to come waltzing back through the door some time later."

"Well I …"

"You are going to do what you do best, let me do the same. I'm the one person out of everybody who can recognise her best if she is in disguise. Put me somewhere so I can be on the lookout for her."

"No, that's out of the question."

"Dan Calder, after that little speech of yours, don't you dare try and stop me. I can help, I want to help and I'm going to whether you like it or not. All I need are your instructions; otherwise, I'm going to have to wing it. So what's it going to be?"

Tara had outmanoeuvred him; any attempt to counter her intention was going to be useless, and so Dan decided to make the best use he could of his new and unexpected resource.

"Okay, this is what I want you to do," he said.

They went out for a very early dinner, as Dan wanted to be in bed by 9:00 p.m. to try for a few hours sleep before the race. At 5:00 p.m. the restaurant was almost empty, but they still chose a dimly lit corner table.

Tara did not want to show him how nervous she was; scared out of her wits was a far better description of how she was feeling. "Are you excited about tomorrow?"

Dan hoped his nervousness over the following day was not transmitting to her, as she seemed to be coping reasonably well. Until today, the race was still not quite here and she especially tried to convince herself that something good could still happen before Sunday morning. "Yes, I checked the weather forecast earlier, and it looks like it will be dry. Maybe we can do next year's together?"

"No chance, mister. I'd see how you feel tomorrow after you finish before you plan for next year."

They both chose spaghetti, Dan requested a double helping of pasta with his bolognese while Tara settled on the carbonara; she ordered sparkling water for them both. The food and the water arrived together, and she made a toast to a good race result for him.

They smiled and began to eat, although neither really felt hungry and the smiles were forced.

When they got back at home, it was still far too early to think about bed. Dan was not in the least bit tired. Tara sat next to him on the sofa and brought up a selection of real-estate websites on the laptop. It was an excellent diversion, window shopping for houses, on which they had spent many hours already, learning the other's preferences and dislikes and beginning to work out a mutually agreeable compromise.

At 9:00 p.m. Dan went for a hot shower to try and relax and then went to bed. He was still not feeling tired, but he had to be up at 4:00 a.m. to make the ferry and every minute of sleep he could get was invaluable.

Tara stayed downstairs for a while, looking for things to do to keep her mind occupied. Dan's manuscript was still in the paper bag on one of the dining chairs and she picked it up.

As she went to pull the pages out, her cell phone rang.

"I didn't know whether you would still be awake," Harry said. "How's things?"

"We have both spent the day trying not to think about it Harry, and trying to make each other think we are not thinking about it."

"I just wanted to let *you* know that we are all set for tomorrow. Are you still going to be there?"

"Yes, definitely. Dan asked me the same again yesterday, and I'll tell you what I told him; I won't go if you don't."

"Then I guess I'll see you in the morning. Tell Dan to call me if he wants or needs anything; otherwise, just wish him good luck, for the run that is."

"I will."

Tara carried the manuscript upstairs. Dan was getting into bed as she got to the room. She put the pages down on the corner chair. "Harry just called to wish you luck; he says to call if you want anything."

"Okay, thanks."

"Are you feeling tired?"

"Not really but hopefully resting will work just as well."

Tara stretched out on the bed next to him and started to massage his neck and scalp.

"Mmm, nice," Dan said, letting his eyelids droop.

She continued to gently knead her fingers into the muscles of his lower neck. She wanted to talk, there were so many things to say, but she stayed silent and tried to concentrate on listening to anything but the voices in her head.

When she sensed Dan was asleep, she carried on, simply content to be touching him.

It was dark, very dark, unnaturally dark. The overwhelming sense that obscured all the other ones now was touch; the feel of the material clawing at his skin was claustrophobic and he was terrified beyond words.

They were always his favourite pyjamas, but at this moment, he wished he could tear them off. The sounds of voices from down the hallway had woken him again in the dream but they quickly gave way to the heat and the sweat soaking his cotton PJ's. No matter how many times he found himself inside the nightmare, Dan was consumed by fright. In the next unconscious moment, he was in the hallway again and the heat from the sweat was gone, leaving him shivering with a damp, cold fear.

He looked down to see his hand coming up to meet the door handle. Further down, he could see the toes of his bare feet screwed into tight foot-fists, every other part of him tense and out of shape too. The scene was the same as it always had been except that his hand now enveloped the handle where once it seemed so large in a young boy's hand.

Beyond the door, he could hear the familiar voices; one low and menacing, the other a higher pitched, stuttering. He could never hear the precise words until the time when he cracked the door open, until then the sounds always just formed a slow, building, rumble, like thunder with no lightning.

The lights were on inside, with the first brilliant slash he heard his father's voice overwhelming the sound of his mother's plaintive sobbing.

"Why do you always do this to me? Haven't I given you everything you could have wanted and needed?"

"Oh John, please John."

"You've become a bloody disgrace, woman. I have worked for years to get where I am today, and I'll be damned if I am going to let you ruin it for me."

Next there was slow crying, soft sobs of fear and dread. However they were not from his mother. They were from Dan once again, the boy-man at the door.

Mother craned and stretched her neck to look around the body of her husband, who was kneeling on top of her on the bed. Her face was streaked with tears, and she needed all her strength just to be able to meet then hold the eyes of her son. "It's alright, John, go back to bed. Go on John, you shouldn't be up now, please go back to bed my love."

As she spoke, the fleshy bare back of his father pivoted around, and his thick neck and head followed until he too was looking at his son. Dan never looked at him in the eye; Mother always managed to maintain the eye contact as if it might somehow refute the truth and save him from her pain.

"Please, John." She smiled like a falling angel.

As he backed out, catching the first glimpse of his father's black belt snaking through the loops of his uniform trousers, something changed. Replacing the sound of more angry words and an even angrier crack of leather on skin as he departed the scene like a thief in the night; something was different.

Still within the dream, Dan, the forty-four-year-old policeman in boy's pyjamas, pale blue with pictures of trains, checked his senses for the difference. It was the natural reaction that had always set him apart from his peers; an instinctive, inborn five-dimensional ability to gather information and evidence. The scene looked the same, smelled and tasted the same, felt the same. But it sounded different.

He made himself look again for the first time ever to see what it was that changed, and as he did, a new fear which dwarfed all others came over him, like a coffin lid closing while he was still alive.

Come on detective, detect! He thought now from somewhere just outside the dream but still in sleep.

Keeping the door open a fraction so he could see back into the room again; forcing himself to keep his eyes averted from his father, who was still turned towards him, but now had his belt hanging down from his fully extended arm, Dan entered the unknown.

Think. Concentrate. It sounded different. What was different?

She was different. Why was she different?

Her voice was different. How different?

It wasn't her. Who was it?

Someone new. Who?

He looked. The eyes still straining to peer into his own around the bulk of his father's body as he knelt and crushed down on top of the bed belonged to a different face, which belonged to a different head, which belonged to a different body.

Tara's body, Tara's head, Tara's face, Tara's eyes.

Oh dear God, no.

When he woke this time, it was with a new level of panic which no amount of rats, spiders, ghosts or any other nightmare visitors could come close to equalling.

"Oh dear God, no!" This time in his waking state he could hear himself saying it. He was back in his bed again. His eyes were wide open and looking towards the painted plaster ceiling, and yet he could still see Tara's eyes staring back at him, beseeching him for assistance.

In the silent dark, twelve thousand miles and a lifetime away from the time and place of his original suffering, he finally made the promise to Tara he had been wanting and waiting to make to his beloved mother.

"I'm coming, I'm coming."

The relief in finally taking on his father and so bringing an end to the innocent suffering of his mother was instantaneous; that chapter of his book concluding at last. For a long moment, Dan lay very still, processing what he knew to be true. Through

Tara, he had finally gone to his mother's aid. Breathing normally again, he relaxed and his brain shifted away from the nightmare for the last time. He could not know then, its next stop would be another one; Zoe, Mapperley and the missing chapter fourteen.

Reluctant to dwell on the subject, he checked the clock and saw the alarm was due to activate. Leaning across Tara, who he noticed was still fully dressed, he clicked the alarm button off and then kissed her lightly on the cheek. "Tara, time to wake up."

CHAPTER THIRTY-THREE

It was a perfect morning for running, not least because it was the last one. The sun was still more than an hour away from making an appearance when he arrived at Devonport, but there was not a cloud in the bruised sky or a breath of wind. When Tara dropped him off at the downtown ferry terminal at 4:30 a.m., they hugged as if he was leaving on a world trip.

"Be careful, okay?" she said not wanting to let go. "She's out there."

He tried to sound confident and reassuring. "I will. Don't worry about me, there will be so many people around, she will have to take a huge risk getting close, and you know how she is about taking risks. You know where you're going to go?"

"Yes, nine thirty, I'll be looking out for you from then on just like you told me."

"Listen to me, alright; *you* don't have to do this. There are going to be hundreds if not thousands of people around in the stands and on the road. I'm not sure how much either of us will be able to see."

"Now you listen, you know that has nothing to do with it. I'm not going to let you run for forty-two kilometres without doing my part. I'll be there and that's the end of it. I love you and I'm scared for you and I'm the one who has got the best chance of recognising her. So you just be careful doing your bit and I'll do mine."

"I love you too, Tara; thanks. I'll be looking out for you. Remember, I'll have people all around me so I will be well protected. Try and get some more sleep when you get home."

There were already hundreds of people milling around the quay area in various states of exercise apparel, some in large matching groups. Dan felt a part of them all, and he exchanged a dozen hellos by the time they boarded the especially rostered ferry a few minutes later. Conversation on the twenty-minute journey over was only about the race. There was an air of nervous excitement.

Dan was nervous too—but for a much more serious reason: it was impossible to scan every face to try and identify Katrina Mallinder. If she was here already, if she was going to be anywhere in the next six hours, the chances of him recognising her were ridiculously small. There was no choice: it required him to wait for her to make the first move.

He was as sure as he could be that she would not be here or at the start; it just did not fit. He made Harry agree to minimal cover up to the starter's gun, fearing blowing it all before the race even began.

Nevertheless he was still anxious as he wandered around, stopping to stretch here and there, listening to the radio station which had an outside broadcast unit working; music to suit the marathon morning and interviews with participants and race staff, taking in the atmosphere with the other twelve thousand runners.

At 6:00 a.m., the ten-minute warning got everybody moving excitedly to their final starting positions. He was somewhere in the middle, not able to see the front over the taller heads in front of him. He didn't look backwards.

At exactly 6:10, the start horn blared, loud cheers went up from participants and spectators; but Dan didn't move. It took a full minute before he was able to slowly walk forwards and another minute before he crossed the start line at a jog, the microchipped tag attached to his shoe registering his official start time.

He felt relief that the day was finally here and all the training was behind him. For the next four or so hours, he wished he would be able to forget about everything else and concentrate on the road ahead, but there were other deadly serious issues to attend to as well as running a marathon.

Tara went back to bed but did not sleep. She was reading his manuscript as Dan passed under the start line banner and was completely engrossed before he passed the one kilometre sign.

Harry had not slept much at all either over the previous few nights; he was in the race control room as he had been for hours already when the horn sounded. His preparations were as complete as he could make them. He had done all he could to secure Dan's safety during the race. The shield teams knew what they were required to do, and the radio comms with the first team were perfect.

Walter Terry selected his spot to wait. The build-up to this morning had been more intense than anything Katrina ever experienced before. The various Stenning women and Terry men were alter egos; able to create pasts and presents, a whole identity and make it be anything she wanted. In the last week, she became much more like her real self again.

For the first time in years, she was thinking as Katrina Mallinder most of the time. Although she had been known as Abbey Turner during this period, she and Katrina shared the same personality: shy daughter, unlikely drama student, Italian food junkie, 1940s and '50s music lover. She indulged her passions and got reacquainted with her former self.

The new Katrina-and-Abbey combination, however, now had the Stenning-and-Terry influences too: strong, singularly determined and as cold as hell.

With all financial incentives gone, her anger and frustrations toward Calder and Tara Danes were distilled down to pathological hatred. Today was going to be the summit of her career. She could hardly believe how formidable she felt—the ultimate incarnation; and one of which she was convinced her parents would have been so proud.

She had been over and over the final act. Once today was finished, she had the means to escape from New Zealand as Candice Drysdale and go anywhere in the world she wanted. By this time tomorrow, her last journey was going to be well under way.

As Dan ran along, he was just one of a large number of individuals all doing the same thing—nothing special to set him apart from the guy next to him or any of the other thousands of runners. Yet he was different to every one of them; he was the only one who felt he was running with a bullseye painted on his shirt.

Until Mallinder was captured, neither he nor Tara could properly move on. The circumstances of how they came together and faced their demons made them closer than either could explain. He loved her as completely as anybody could in the time they had known each other. He briefly considered telling her what happened with Zoe after the race was over, but then reminded himself, in order to do so he needed to still be alive at the end of the day.

He liked the fact he was missing her already. There were still more than thirty-five ks to the finish, but he knew the area where she should be sitting, and he couldn't wait to see that smile again as he rounded the final corner.

His pace was good; looking at the runners all around him, there was a cosmopolitan mixture of sizes, shapes and styles. The man next to him nodded and smiled, no words were necessary. Dan nodded and smiled back; he knew him, but did not know him.

The man was Sergeant Paul Price, usually a traffic and high-ways officer based on Auckland's North Shore; today he was on a completely different duty.

On the Monday before the race, Harry contacted the secretary of the New Zealand Police Athletics Association and requested assistance. Dan's suggested plan.

Two meetings later a squad of forty-five police officers, all athletes, had been selected to act as a moving physical barrier to protect Dan as he completed the forty-two kilometre event. Each sub-team of three would run with him, one behind and one to each side completing three ks before being replaced by three fresh colleagues.

The runner behind, in this case Constable Mike Rumbold was equipped with a covert radio pack under his running vest and a small wireless ear piece to liaise with the police incident room at Avondale, which was being manned by Glen Johannsen, and Harry, who was in the race coordinators' temporary building at the finish line with Phil Brown and a portable radio base station. The rest of the team were on a roving foot patrol in the area of the finish, similarly equipped to the runners with a covert radio set each.

It was all part of Dan's idea; Harry was initially sceptical and reluctant; Tara was dead set against it.

"Trust me, have I ever let you down?" worked a little with Harry; it failed completely with Tara.

"She means to do something during the marathon; if we don't get her there we may never get another chance. This is our chance to finish it on our terms," he said.

Eventually Harry acquiesced to Dan's wishes and with the scorched photos of Dan and his mother still in the frying pan, he explained to Tara and Harry what he needed to happen.

The briefing at Avondale on Friday afternoon was attended by everybody who needed be involved on race day. Dan and Harry ran through it together. Against both their wishes, Tara was there and sat to the side with a look somewhere between poorly disguised fury and disbelief.

Later, she would try to talk him out of it again and cry when he refused to.

Dan explained how a traditional 1.2.3. foot surveillance worked and ran a lesson of sorts for the entire room. Harry viewed it like watching a dramatic production; he could have sworn that half of those in attendance didn't even realise they were being taught. What did surprise him was the fact that he was no longer surprised by Dan's ability to convey information.

It took Dan forty-five minutes to finish, by which time he was as satisfied as he could be. It wasn't his best work, but it was all he could do. Afterwards, he and Tara stayed in the incident room when everybody except Harry's team had gone.

"It's probably going to change a little on the day, depending on what happens; with all those people around, it will be impossible to say with certainty how the whole thing will go."

"You're taking a big risk," Harry said.

"It's necessary and I can't think of an alternative. Not if we want to apprehend her."

"Not running is an alternative."

"I was going to run it anyway. I haven't done all this training to back out right at the end."

Tara could not hold her tongue any longer. "We are not talking about backing out of a race; we are talking about you deliberately putting yourself in harm's way and saying, 'here I am come and get me!'"

"Control from Shield 3," Rumbold said, depressing his concealed transmit button.

"Shield 3, go ahead," Phil Brown replied from his seat next to Harry.

"We are at kilometre eight, all in order."

"Roger that Shield 3. Shield 4 is ahead and waiting at kilometre ten."

"This is either medal of honour stuff or the craziest thing we have ever got ourselves into," Harry said looking at his second in command.

"If it was anybody but Dan, I'd agree with you. After what he said, can you possibly disagree that she's here today?"

Rumbold and his two colleagues flowed around Dan. Moving in and out, swapping positions but maintaining control of their subject. The normal 1.2.3. formation required the three surveillance operatives to communicate with each other, maintain visual contact with the subject and also control the space around him by occupying predetermined positions in relation to the subject. They were charged with preventing any potential attacker from getting within touching distance and also looking ahead for approaching hazards.

Foot surveillance was normally a walking activity performed by highly trained operatives. What they were currently engaged in was eight or ten times faster, surrounded by twelve thousand other runners and tens of thousands of spectators with no barriers between them and the competitors. With no disrespect to the officers working today, their priority skill was to be able to run.

Dan's instructions were particularly explicit when it came to the need to allow movement in and around the area of subject control, meaning: don't come too close to me for too long. They had to prevent Mallinder from physically attacking him, but not stay so close that he was obviously being protected. Another consideration was that of all the other runners; some slower and some faster, moving in and out of the controlled area during the normal course of the race or naturally massing in the hundred metres either side of the refreshment stations situated on the roadside every two ks.

Dan was also wearing an earpiece and could pick up on all the transmissions when one of the covert radios came within three or four metres. The reality was he received about a tenth of what was broadcast; the rest he guessed.

He knew his protectors were not able to perform like experienced officers given the lack of time and training; therefore he deliberately tailored his lesson to give them confidence. The task he was asking them to complete was not highly complex, though it was.

As he began the ninth kilometre, his mind was consumed by far more than the effort to run another thirty-four. The current team around him were doing their best. He pinged them within the first few metres of them taking over from the Shield 2 team, who he also easily spotted. They were communicating well and trying to move as he had instructed; whilst running, he also subtly moved laterally around on the road, thereby assisting them even though they did not realise he was doing it.

He was also looking around and ahead. The only way he could not see was behind; for that he had no choice but to trust his escort of experienced police athletes and woefully inexperienced surveillance operatives.

Tara read the first three chapters. By the bottom of the first page, the first tears were rolling down her face. By the fifth, she had seen enough but ploughed on anyway. She then flicked through a number of other pages, reading a paragraph here and there or simply scanning the words in front of her.

Dan said to her he thought of it as a way of hopefully finding some closure and trying to find an explanation for what happened to them all as a family. Her heart ached for him with every line; he was never afforded that luxury or able to get far enough away from his own feelings to be able to look at them dispassionately. Even as a young adult, when he followed his father into the police, he remained under his influence and that of the service, which lauded the elder Calder as a gentleman and hero. He must have seemed like a god to the vulnerable young boy.

If that was the case then Dan's behaviour corresponded to flagellation. He was the penitent soul who had to inflict harm upon himself to try and make up for his supposed sins. Tara did not think his book was looking for closure at all; it was another self-imposed punishment for a false sense of guilt.

Dan crossed the Harbour Bridge feeling more tired than he expected, drained by the other things going on in his mind. As he approached the halfway point at Westhaven, he looked at the temporary race clock on the side of the road. At one hour and fifty-five minutes, he was ten minutes behind where he wanted to be.

His latest batch of protectors, Shield 7, were doing well and he was more able to concentrate on trying to be just another runner getting from A to B in the shortest time.

The number of spectators in the marina area was bigger and more concentrated than anywhere else on the course so far. It was a challenge for Shield 7, but to their credit, they were coping. Soon he was into the familiar territory of Quay Street; when he crossed the brass ten k marker of his training route, he felt an injection of confidence and adrenaline as he was back onto his training route for one final time.

He was also pleased to find himself doing his physical checks from bottom to top. Both feet were good, no feelings of pain or soreness. Legs were strong, he could tell he had run a distance already, but it didn't feel like they were about to start giving him pain any time soon. There was slight discomfort in the back of his left knee, but that had been there for as long as he was in serious training. His breathing was a little tighter than he wanted it to be, so he tried to make himself take deep breaths, in through his nose and slowly out through his mouth.

But he could not ignore the genuine discomfort in the points of both shoulders; the bone facing forwards where his arm, neck and shoulder came together. Holding and pumping arms at the ninety degree angle as runners do strains the points of the shoulder. Without realising it and with the tension of all that was happening, he had run the first twenty ks with his fists clenched tight, not relaxed as they should be; now his shoulders were suffering the consequences.

Dan let his arms hang loose by his sides and tried to shake out the tension, starting at the hands and wrists and then all the way up. Both shoulders protested; he knew by the end they were going to be very sore, but that would have little effect for the next couple hours of running.

From the beginning, he was vaguely aware of spectators calling his name, rather disconcertingly, but like every other runner, his official race number was pinned to his vest and like every other runner he printed his name, "Dan" on the blank name panel immediately below his number. Each time he heard it, he flinched, involuntarily darting his eyes towards the source.

Tara left the house with her emotions in turmoil. Her usual determination was tempered with an unholy anxiety that made her feel sick and weak. She wished that she had been able to read Dan's book long before now. By his own estimates, he should be on Tamaki Drive at this time, about ten kilometres from her, twenty from the finish and still a million miles away in other ways. With her new insight, she felt sure she could close that gap in a flash and desperately hoped for the chance to try when today was over.

The taxi took her to Victoria Park, avoiding the waterfront area, which was closed for the race. She walked across the grass football pitches towards the back of the temporary stand erected for the day. The air was filled with the sounds of pulsating music from speakers broadcasting a radio station. It competed for supremacy with a man commentating on the race with equal verve and whipping up the crowd into a cheering mass as some of the faster racers began to cross the finish line. The excitement was palpable, even from a hundred metres away.

She and Dan had agreed on the area where she should try to reach to see him finish. Somewhere they both had the chance to see each other, and somewhere Harry would be able to see them both as well.

"I don't like it, Phil. I really don't like it. Where is he now?" Harry asked, studying the six race-cam monitors set up in the control room.

"Last call in was Shield 10 taking over, so around thirty kilometres give or take."

"Fifty minutes to an hour to go?"

"Maybe."

"Check in with everyone again."

"Harry, we only did it five minutes ago."

Harry glared at his second in command and then softened his look. "Please, Phil, just check in."

"Sure Boss. Kiri 1 from control, radio check."

A moment later, accompanied with a little electronic hiss as the encryption kicked in, Kiri responded as she had with all previous comms checks. "Control from Kiri 1, loud and clear. Kiri 1 calling around; acknowledge in sequence."

"Phil 2, loud and clear."

"Phil 3, loud and clear."

"Jerome 4, loud and clear."

Glen Johannsen completed the circle. "Avondale Centre, loud and clear."

"All units from control, you are loud and clear. No change, no change," Phil Brown said, looking at Harry.

"Thanks. Sorry about that."

"No problem. I'd rather be out there as well," Brown replied honestly.

Walter Terry picked Tara out from his vantage point.

Looking at the crowds from where he was, it was relatively easy to spot individual spectators as they slowly funnelled onto the stand. She worked her way across through several rows of mostly occupied seats towards the front right corner section. When she had passed enough vacant seats, it was clear she was aiming for a particular area. *Somewhere predetermined with a loved one*, he thought.

He checked his watch and calculated the time it would take to get where he needed to be when the time came. Beneath his gloved hands and coat, Candice Drysdale was already waiting; fresh nail polish already applied and flat rings to show her married state but not be an obstruction, thin female clothes under Walter's outer shell.

Tara hoped she was close enough to where they agreed. It gave her a good view of the last two hundred metres which included the right hand turn out of the Viaduct onto Halsey Street and the final short straight in Fanshawe.

When Dan reached the St. Heliers turnaround point, he was starting to suffer. At Mission Bay, he still had another eight ks to go, but the pain in his shoulders was becoming overwhelming. Each stride caused a needle sharp jolt that took his mind off all the things he should have been concentrating on during the last phase of the race.

He looked over to his near left, where police athlete Amanda Henare was holding position 2 in the current 1.2.3. formation. She met his look and smiled, completely unaware of how he was feeling. Dan knew he had to find a way to get his head back into the right space. Being so close to the finish, he needed to be completely focused. Somehow he knew it would be at the end, it was always going to be at the end.

Unintentionally, he started mentally reviewing the briefing he gave the previous Friday and whether some of the lesson points could be improved on. He utilised 1.2.3. because it was what he was familiar with; having run for three hours and thirty-four kilometres, he thought an adapted version, 1.2.3.4., might work better. As he was thinking about some of the finer points, it occurred to him that Phil Larson had asked an interesting question during the briefing when Harry was going over the information and intention phase.

"Mallinder referred to her suffering. Do you think she intends to use a method that will cause Dan to feel the physical pain *she* did with Stephen Christopher, or maybe cause him to feel the pain Christopher did at the time of his death?"

Harry looked at Dan to see if he wanted to answer, but he indicated for Harry to do so. "We believe she intends it to be a close quarters attack; close enough so she can see Dan's reaction and feel it. She wants it to be *that* personal."

Dan agreed; he was expecting a knife or something equally physically dramatic; he was convinced of it a week ago the instant he read the message on the envelope. Tara did not need to know that then or now.

With the thousands of people compressed into the finish, it was the obvious and best location; taking advantage of the excitement and commotion of the place and time. Because he thought of that first, it also occurred to him that Mallinder would consider exactly the same thing and therefore do something different, hence the 1.2.3. from the beginning.

There was no doubt Katrina Mallinder suffered in the way she lost her parents. He also correctly guessed the time it took her to get to know Stephen Christopher as Vanessa must have been torture for her being so close to the man responsible for their deaths. In as much as he could understand and sympathise with her, even share her drive for retribution, he drew a very thick line at subsequent multiple murder.

So she had suffered. How could she have him suffer in the same way?

His right foot came down on a raised crack in the road, sending him off balance for a second; automatically he lifted both arms up to correct his gait and a shock of electric pain hit him in both shoulders.

"Fuck and shit!" he cursed, then affirmed, "It's okay you're still here, you are still here."

Two strides later, he was fully recovered. In the following six paces, something happened—as it had months before when he knew an email address, v.stenning@theagency.org, meant something.

"You-are-still-here, you-are-still-here," he said, in time to his foot-strike on the tarmac. "You-are-st … Oh Christ."

He was one kilometre from the finish now. Five minutes: too far, too long.

Philip Te Tuke was sat reading the Sunday newspaper. He drew the short straw for today because he had not been in the room when the Detective Inspector wanted someone for bedside duty over the weekend.

The young woman, Stella Banks, was incredibly lucky to have survived the attack on the late-night train. The off-duty paramedic who got on at the next stop thought the fact she was doubled over probably saved her life by stemming the flow of blood just enough for her to receive life-saving emergency treatment before she bled to death.

Under constant police guard since she arrived at the hospital unconscious, Stella was being treated and looked after in the Intensive Care Unit but had not regained consciousness. She chose that moment to wake up.

Dan's last escort, Shield 14, comprised of the three officers most skilled and experienced in public order situations and self-defence; Harry directed that be the case the closer to the end of the race Dan got. All the members of Shield 1 to Shield 12 were collected by unmarked police cars at predetermined positions and were now at the finish area; waiting and searching with the available pictures of Katrina Mallinder on sheets of A4. Shield 13 were left to their own devices to get to the end; they were currently running together about a hundred metres behind Dan and Shield 14.

Despite the pain he anticipated accompanying the act, Dan had to raise his right arm; it was the signal to tell everyone something was happening. As he tried, his right shoulder felt like a red-hot poker was being jammed into it. He screamed, but continued to lever it up straight.

Constables Johnny Tate at 1 and Ray Malpern at 2 closed in to Dan's flanks as if pulled by magnets; neither had seen anything and both were panicking because of it. Constable Kevin Steele at 3 hit his transmit button below his vest and shouted as loud as he could "Flag up! Flag up! Shield 14 flag up! Wait for more." Like his colleagues, he did not see anyone or anything that could have caused Dan to signal an emergency. He closed in too.

Dan was calling out, still in awful pain and short of breath. Tate, Malpern and Steele desperately tried to catch what he was saying, but it was being made no easier by the fact their subject had not stopped running; in fact, if anything, he was going faster.

Katrina Mallinder's suffering was her living hell. She had not died, she had not been injured. She had to go on with the pain of losing the ones she was closest to. She never meant to injure Dan, she meant to take what he was closest to all the time and make him suffer exactly as she had suffered, and still was.

"It's Tara, it's not me! Tara, Tara, get to Tara!" The effort of trying to get the words out while speeding up his pace was agony. His chest was at the point of bursting, his legs begged for mercy at the sudden change. The relief of being able to lower his arm again helped a little but only a little. He wasn't sure if the guys at his sides understood. Kevin Steele definitely did not; however it did not stop him from doing his job and relaying the message Dan breathlessly managed to get out and was still trying to repeat.

"Control from Shield 14, control from Shield 14, message is 'It's not me it's Tara, get to Tara.' Shield 14 repeating, it's not me, get to Tara, get to Tara!"

All hell broke loose in the race control room. Phil Brown went to the microphone as Harry's attention went to the bank of monitors.

"All units from control, all units from control. Secure Tara Danes, secure Tara Danes! Secure the spectator stand at race finish!" Brown urgently transmitted.

Harry was ordering the two remote camera operators to focus everything they had on the stand and to find Tara. "She'll be somewhere in the right-hand section. Come on, get a move on," he bellowed, not caring the operators were untrained and ill-prepared volunteers not subordinate police officers.

"There!" he shouted, jabbing a thick finger at monitor number four. "Phil, there you see her?"

"Yeah, got her," Brown replied.

"I'm going out; call them all in and find that fucking woman!" Harry yelled.

Immediately following his transmission, the radio traffic was chaotic and confused. Phil Brown knew he must restore order.

When Harry's cell phone activated, he picked it out of his pocket automatically; he was on his feet but still scanning the monitors for the first sight of someone approaching Tara. It took a few seconds before he looked down at the screen and saw 'P Te Tuke mob' on the display.

He hit the decline call button and made for the door. Emerging into the natural sunlight, he covered his eyes. As he did his phone rang again.

He answered this time but only with the intention of telling Philip Te Tuke not too politely to call back later. He only got two words out.

"Harry listen, just shut up and listen will you!"

Spiller shut up.

"Harry, it's my girl, the girl who got stabbed on the train, she's just woken up. She's been able to give us a brief description."

"Philip, we have got a situation going on here at the moment."

"She was attacked by an old man Harry; an old man with glasses, a cloth hat and a walking stick!" Te Tuke went on as if he had not heard a word Harry said.

"Philip, I cannot help you now; let me call you later."

"No Harry, listen to me. The old man, he was wearing a gold watch with hands and digital numbers. She's sure, Harry, she is still very weak, but she is sure. Harry, did you hear me?"

Detective Senior Sergeant Harry Spiller heard it perfectly.

Having been in the control room, he was not equipped with a radio set. He reached the end of the stand closer to where Tara was sat and therefore well away from Phil Brown. He put his phone in his pocket again without ending the call; on the other end Philip was still talking, trying to make sure Harry understood what he was trying to say.

"Harry, boss, did you hear me? Boss, boss …"

Brown took Harry's lead and started directing the two poor camera operators, both of whom were trying their best to keep calm while the policeman leaning over them was sending out a radio message to all the staff outside, indicating where Tara was seated.

There was nothing in the operation order about an attack on anybody else. Harry had disappeared; Brown could sense fifty or so police officers waiting outside desperate for information and orders.

"All units from control, all units from control; Tara Danes is identified as a target. Secure the area of the spectator stand and secure Tara Danes. Do not allow any spectators onto the stand from this time and do not allow any existing spectator in the stand to leave.

"Kiri 1, Tara Danes is in the front right section approximately twelve rows from the front, she is wearing a thick black padded jacket and a pale blue wool hat.

"Kiri 1, locate and remain with Tara Danes. Kiri 1 acknowledge."

Brown kept his eyes fixed on the monitor. "Look for any single women approaching her from any direction," he ordered the camera operators.

The police speaker crackled and then transmitted. "Control from Kiri 1; yes, yes. I have Jerome and another officer with me. We are on the stand now. No sighting of Tara Danes yet."

"All other units; surround and secure the stand," Brown said, trying to remain calm. "Acknowledge in sequence."

"Kiri 1; yes, yes."

"Phil 2; yes, yes."

"Glen 3; yes, yes."

"Jerome 4; yes, yes."

"Avondale Centre; yes, yes."

The spectators in the stand had no idea what was happening all around them; some of the new arrivals trying to get on and find a seat found themselves turned away by police officers in plain clothes or running gear. The music continued, as did the race MC who was currently shouting in a group of army cadets along the final straight who ran the whole race in three ranks of five.

The spectators remained concentrated on the race. Kiri wildly calling Tara's name was no different to hundreds of other people calling out names of competitors as the MC identified them by name and number. She and Jerome were also studying the stand for any sign of a lone female acting suspiciously.

At that moment, Harry was the only one looking for an old man in the crowds.

Tara's eyes were fixed on the last corner; it was just too far away to be able to recognise Dan immediately, but she would be able to spot him quickly as he got closer. Following his orders she scoured the area between her and the corner, looking up and down and side to side in a grid pattern, repeating the process over and over.

The voice of the MC and the music pumped loudly from nearby speakers. She did her best to dial it out along with everything else; Dan should be coming into view anytime now. He told her to watch the area of the finish; he had known all along it must happen there, she thought.

With all the noise around her and her concentration on the task at hand, she had no chance of hearing Kiri calling her name. She was feeling hot too and took her hat off, shaking a hand through her hair to cool herself.

Parts of Dan's body were sure he was dying and if anything happened to Tara, he did not care if they were right. He felt like he was running through quicksand, and his legs were rubber. His chest was being tortuously squeezed by an invisible vice so he could not get enough air into his lungs, and his vision was so blurred by sweat which he could not reach to wipe away; like trying to see underwater. He was not capable of speech either; even if he wanted to repeat his warning regarding Tara, nothing would have happened when he tried.

All the months of marathon training, every experience of a full and busy career could not have prepared him for what his mind and body were telling him now. Only a small section of his brain was functioning properly, that which controlled his sense of guilt. He had spent a lifetime feeling sorry and at fault. With all other senses and emotions stripped away by over forty kilometres of tarmac and physical exhaustion, he was left filled with only those feelings. However, with Tara in real danger, it became a high octane fuel powering his body beyond its rational limits.

He was three hundred metres from the finish line.

Harry was in the middle of the stand. He had yet to sight Tara and the mass of heads all at the same height made the job even more difficult. He was focused on the light blue hat she was wearing rather than the mixture of hair colours and styles that coagulated into a single mass.

An old man or a woman between twenty and sixty! It was next to impossible. *What would Dan do?* he thought.

Walter moved easily through the people in the stands. He acquired an unguarded fluorescent "event steward" vest soon after arriving and had been able to move unhindered around the finish area, occasionally having to assist a spectator, but otherwise blending in effortlessly.

When Tara took her hat off, he momentarily lost sight of her but quickly regained it; she seemed totally focused out towards the final corner, obviously watching for her beloved to come into view.

He was in position now, waiting for her expression to give her away so at that exact time he could move in.

Dan could see the last corner; the left-hand into Halsey Street was followed by a natural right-hand curve that brought him onto Fanshawe Street and within the arena of the finish. In Halsey, he would be able to see the stand; Tara should be in the section of it first to come into view—it was what they had arranged. He willed it to be so.

From the depths of his soul, he maintained the spirit to put one foot in front of the other and over the last six hundred metres kept up the punishing increase in pace which was causing him pain in muscles he never knew he had; his shoulders were on fire.

He threw himself around the corner in a daze of blurred agonies and forced his left arm up so he could wipe the sweat from his eyes. None of the emotional traumas he experienced before came close to the physical agony he was enduring now.

The spectators' stand rose like a giant jury box in the near distance. Thousands of people sitting in judgement, his life now came down to what was going to happen in the next twenty seconds. He did not care about the race, he did not care about the volcanic lava of pain that recently replaced his blood; he could only think of Tara.

The detail of his view improved with every stride as he got closer; he forced his eyes to scan the stand for her trying vainly to pick her out of the thousands of smiling, cheering faces, but for once his skills failed him.

There he is. Tara's eyes widened and a tense smile cracked her face. She sat a little straighter but managed to contain the desire to shout Dan's name and instead redoubled her efforts to take in everything and everyone near to him.

The runners were mostly dressed in the official gun-metal grey T-shirts; Dan was somewhere within a loose group of ten or so athletes of varying ages and descriptions. They were all

looking forward towards the finish and all of them had a look
of tired satisfaction. All except for him.

As he came closer to her, she could see he seemed to be in a
world of pain. He was looking in her direction, obviously, without seeing her yet. His mouth was moving as if he was trying
to speak, and he was angling away from the other runners who
were following the curve of the road towards the finish line. It
looked as if he was running straight towards her.

Walter saw Tara recognise the object of her affection from the
change in her face and attitude. The time had come to end the
misery Katrina carried for so long and pass that burden over
to another. He was two rows behind Tara in an aisle that gave
him unobstructed access to her and an immediate escape route
afterwards. He moved down the aisle and into the row immediately behind her, and as he did, he slipped the top of his cane
from its body. Freeing the blade, he kept it close to his side.

The attention of all the spectators was on the constant flow
of marathon runners in front of them. Nobody paid any attention to the elderly steward politely asking to be allowed through.

Harry was no longer looking for a man or a woman. Just before,
he had finally seen Tara; she must have taken her hat off and
was the only person in the crowd who seemed not to be enjoying the entertainment unfolding in front of her.

Harry found the answer to his last question and Tara at the
same moment. Dan told him what the answer was a week or
more ago. The words crashed into his mind, when a glint of
gold in the sunlight caught his eye.

"The watch will give her away, find the watch and you will
find her."

There was an official race steward behind Tara, he was stood
to her left as she sat in an aisle seat. The steward was between
him and Tara now. Instantly Harry took in sufficient informa-

tion to determine it was a male, middle-aged or older, wearing a coat under his steward's vest and a brown flat hat.

He could also see the man was carrying a walking stick in his left hand. His right hand was not in view; his right side was closest to Tara.

In the next fraction of a second, he assimilated all the facts: the golden flash had come when the steward adjusted his left arm to bring the cane in close to his side. It was gone now and there was nothing metallic on the cane or his coat sleeve.

With a level of agility that belied his age and waistline, Harry launched himself into the air.

Dan saw Tara at the same time Harry did, and suddenly the scene around her slowed and crystallised into a brilliantly clear tableau. She was doing everything he told her to do; maintaining a systematic roving watch around him without letting herself focus on him. If she saw anything untoward, she had her mobile in her hand to call Harry.

He then saw Spiller, eyes wide and approaching her from her left.

"Please Dad, no," he gasped.

Walter kept the blade as close to his right side as he could until he was immediately behind Tara Danes, so his lowered hand was level with her neck. All the ghosts of Katrina Mallinder's past lives came into his mind for one final time; like spectators at another event, they were all there with him now, come to bear witness.

Walter leaned forward and put his left arm and stick across Danes' chest to act as a brace as he pushed the blade in. To everyone else around, it looked like an elderly steward just losing his balance momentarily.

Tara had no time to react; by the time she was aware of the arm across her, the blade was already piercing the outer layers of her jacket.

Harry crashed into the pair, knocking them both sideways with the force of a charging rhinoceros. The blade tore through the fabric of Tara's jacket and out close to the collar. The nearest spectators scattered like dropped marbles, leaving the three of them in a tangled mess across three or four seats.

Harry was shouting, "Police, police!" and grabbing for any piece of the steward he could get to.

Tara screamed and fought to try and get out from under the two men.

Walter's hat and wig came off in the initial collision and fell between seats. Candice Drysdale's new hairstyle was exposed, and it, along with the dislodged actor's putty of Walter's nose, gave him the bizarre look of a circus freak.

Harry's natural instincts took over. Mallinder still had the blade in her tightly clenched fist. He drove his own fist into her chest and followed it with another aimed at her face, which caught her squarely at the join of nose and left cheek.

As he went to grab the blade, which looked more like a highly polished skewer at that moment, a foot came down across Mallinder's wrist, pinning it to the ground and making her release it.

Harry looked up to the owner of the foot. "Kiri, glad you could make it," he grinned.

"Sorry I'm a bit late. Are you okay?"

"Fine, check Tara."

"I'm fine too," Tara said, sitting up between the seats in front of him and looking over to where Harry was.

Katrina Mallinder lay unconscious with a small spot of blood under her left eye. Harry leaned over and pulled up her left sleeve. The glass of her watch had a new crack across it and the digital time was frozen.

Tara stood up as more police arrived from all directions. She was shaken but otherwise unhurt. Leaning over the seats to see the prostrate figure of Mallinder she was numb and began to shake uncontrollably. She wanted her to be awake and to able to see her so she could spit in her face and tell her how much she hated her.

She jumped as Kiri put her arm around her shoulder. "Sorry, sorry, it's me Tara, it's all okay now."

Tara managed a smile and suddenly remembered Dan. When she turned, she could not immediately see him and so she stood up on a seat.

Dan was still running, about twenty metres from the base of the stand with his eyes glued on the area where Tara should be. Their eyes met and when they did he could not compute the reason for her being head and shoulders above all those around her. When he saw she was not just safe but was wearing a beautiful smile, what remained of his energy leaked out of his body. She was shouting.

"Finish the race, finish the race!" Tara called out with tears, laughter and relief. He was still running, albeit away from the finish line.

"Number 3891 Dan Calder from Auckland. Come on Dan, come on Dan." The sound of his name booming out of the speakers drilled into his head, and he looked around as if completely lost. The emotion that had got him to this point was gone and there was nothing left inside to propel him onwards. He looked at Tara again, she was waving and smiling and pointing towards her far left. Dan followed her extended finger and saw the big digital clock suspended over the finish line some sixty metres farther along the road; the numbers meant nothing to him; he could not remember the physical requirements needed to change direction.

He crashed into the base of the stand, sending more shards of pain around his body. With his head still facing towards the finish, he fixed his eyes on a figure standing below the clock and waving frantically.

"Dan, here, come on, come on!" Phil Brown was screaming at the top of his voice. He had come out from the control room when it was confirmed Mallinder was detained and seeing he was not going to be of any use in the stand, he stopped for a moment and found himself looking along the length of the front of the stand; he saw Dan careen into the metal structure.

"Dan, come on!"
It was Phil Brown. Dan recognised the familiar face and tried to fix his stare on him as if he was a lifebelt floating in the sea. He had a deep cut on his right knee where it struck one of the scaffold poles holding the stand upright. If he had any thoughts in his head, they were utterly battered into submission by the assorted agonies that were assaulting every limb and muscle.

As if he was being dragged along the road, he forced his broken body off the stand rail and towards the still screaming Phil Brown. Spectators who had not seen what happened before re-doubled their clapping and cheering as the MC called out Dan's name and number again.

It was all he could do to stagger forwards. He kept his eyes on the reddening face of Phil Brown who was extolling him on to still greater efforts. It took another fifteen excruciating seconds to cover the ground between them, and as he crossed the finish line, he crumpled into Phil's arms completely spent.

When he opened his eyes all he could see was a flawless sky, but there were noises all around.

Tara leaned over and filled his field of vision; he was lying flat on his back on the grass of Victoria Park; completely unaware of the time elapsed since he crossed the line at the end of the race. For a moment, he felt nothing until he blinked for the first time; even his eyelids ached, serving as the early warning system for the rest of his body.

"Hey darling, it's all over, they got her; we all got her. Just lay still for as long as you need," Tara said, stroking his forehead.

The tears that welled in his eyes stung, but Dan was powerless to stop them. "You're okay. I'm so sorry I was wrong. Are you sure you're alright?"

"I'm fine. Harry and Kiri got her, and she's been taken away."

It hurt to speak but he could not stop himself. "I was so frightened that I'd lost you, I didn't think I could get to you in time." He tried to move as his brain started to readjust, but he was still paralysed by overworked muscles, which had no intention of resuming normal function yet.

"I can't move; I can't do anything. I tried to warn you."

Other familiar voices close by joined the general cacophony of the background sounds which were the continuance of the marathon day event. He recognised Phil Brown and Jerome Brett who were talking light-heartedly.

"We got it, but only Harry knew it was a man to look for," Phil said somewhere just out of Dan's view.

"A man? She was a man?"

Jerome laughed. "She was today, but by the looks of it she was ready to change into a female again. Under the coat and hat, she was wearing women's running gear. We would have lost her in the crowd if Harry had not got to her when he did. He got a call from Philip Te Tuke just in time. I'm still not sure of the whole story, and he's gone off to the hospital." He laughed again and was joined by Phil and Tara.

Dan was missing the point of the shared joke. "What?"

"Harry might have broken his hip tackling her," said Tara.

"Hopefully, his swallow dive was recorded by the control room guys; they told me it was very funny to watch," Phil said.

Tara grinned down at Dan. "More police humour."

Dan coughed as he laughed, the pain had not subsided. "I can't wait to see it. Can someone please help me up; otherwise, I'll need the hospital too."

CHAPTER THIRTY-FOUR

The Auckland-London liaison and negotiations finally resulted in Katrina Mallinder's return to England for trial; the extradition process took four months.

Now she stood impassively in the dock, a subject of the British justice system. It took the Clerk of the Court over eleven minutes to read out the list of charges which included ten murders beginning in 2002. Walter Terry's walking stick weapon had been matched to the wounds of six unsolved killings dating back to 2003.

How many more remaining undiscovered were likely never to be known. She was interviewed a total of nine times and only ever repeated the same words.

"I will talk to Dan Calder or to the court."

As the clerk continued to speak, she looked across the courtroom to the public gallery where Dan sat, returning her gaze with equal impassiveness.

In the first week at Auckland's Remand Centre, she resolutely refused to answer any police investigators questions until her watch was repaired and returned to her.

Harry's operation to repair his broken hip and subsequent recovery took six weeks, during which time Phil Brown led the Auckland based investigation into her New Zealand crimes. When the inquiries into the circumstances leading up to Neil Danes' death and the attack on Stella Banks concluded, she was not formally charged.

Dan took two days to get over the physical effects of the race, by which time both he and Tara were emotionally recovered too. On Wednesday, Tara went to see Cathy at the shop, leaving Dan to tidy the house.

Toby McCallister was at the Coping with Grief reception desk when the outer doorbell rang. He was surprised but pleasantly so to hear who the new caller was.

"Would it be okay to come in and talk to you; I haven't made an appointment," Dan Calder asked.

"Absolutely. I have a spare session now as luck would have it. Let's go to a quieter room."

Once in his appointment room, Toby offered Dan a seat. "What brings you here Dan?"

"It's a long story. To be honest, I don't really know where to start or how much to say."

Toby crossed his legs comfortably and interlocked his fingers on his lap. "Well look at it this way; you are here and so you have started already. How are you feeling today?"

They talked for an hour and it was good. Dan told Toby about the effect Neil Danes' death had on him and Tara to begin with which led to a lengthy exchange on some of the other deaths Dan experienced. At the end of the hour, Toby thanked him for coming. "I know it's hard."

Dan breathed out slowly. "Actually it wasn't as hard as I thought it was going to be, perhaps I can come again on a more regular basis."

Later that day Dan was pleased to get a call from Phil Brown. After some discussion, they arranged to see each other the next day at Dan's house.

An application to allow him to conduct the interview travelled up and down the chain of command in Auckland and Wellington until someone from the Office of the Commissioner finally said no. So Dan schooled Kiri Ieremia and Phil secretly for two days solid.

While he desperately wanted to sit across the desk, look her in the eyes himself and ask the questions, he knew that was never going to be an option realistically. Brown was quick to make the Tactical Advisor request as a next best and had put together a reasonable argument for Dan's presence, but at the end of three days of phone calls even that was a step too far. Police interviewed suspects, not ex-police.

Tactical Advisor meant an input into preparing the interview strategy, monitoring the interview from another room, being able to communicate with the officers who were actually conducting it, suspending it in order to suggest new avenues of questioning and to debrief the interviewers. Dan explained how it worked weeks before during an afternoon when Harry asked him to talk about his past career; he soon had them all convinced. Unfortunately it was not in the armoury of current New Zealand Police interviewing tools, and Phil felt it would not become so any time soon. Dan agreed to Phil's request for the off-the-books lessons when Phil refused to let the matter go.

The refusal from Police HQ was not a surprise to Dan. The use of natural and talented interviewers was still relatively new in the UK too and it sometimes took a big man to accept direction from somebody else unconnected to the investigation or junior in rank. Phil said he had not encountered Tac Advisors or enthusiasm for the idea in New Zealand at all. However, he and Kiri were keen to make the most of Dan's special talents, and they were willing to be the first students at the Calder home school for criminal interviewing.

Dan's abbreviated lessons got the sessions pared down to two days of teaching and role plays in his lounge.

When she was brought into the room, Katrina Mallinder had been in custody for eight days already. Extensions to her continuing detention were properly sought and court-ordered; the extradition process began and two officers from NCIS in London had been in Auckland since the day before to assist with the early submission of documentation.

In all of the time she was in custody, including her first two court appearances, she did not speak more than a few dozen words, answering to confirm her name and demanding the return of her broken watch in fully working order.

She was dressed in the matching uniform of mid-blue shirt and trousers with soft, flat slip-on shoes of Auckland Prison's remand section, for suspects awaiting trial or detained for other serious reasons. She was also wearing a look of ambivalence.

"Good afternoon, please come in and take a seat," Phil Brown said.

Interview room ten at Auckland Central Police Station was identical in size, colour and furnishing to the other seventeen windowless, soulless rooms. The integrated camera and sound system meant the interviewing officer need only press two buttons to start, and at the conclusion press, the same two again to terminate the interview. When Mallinder sat in the one available chair, she took several moments to look around the room and take in all its sparse details. Only when she was completely satisfied did she turn to the officers.

"Can I have my watch back please?"

"I do have it for you, but we *must* complete the formalities of the interview introduction first," Brown said, placing an envelope on the table between them.

"No," Mallinder replied.

Kiri's heart was racing. Dan told them Mallinder would want to assume the authoritative role from the outset, and it was important for them not to allow her to do so, no matter what.

"Very well. I'm sorry we have wasted all our time then," Phil said and started to gather his belongings. In the short time it took him to put the pad and pencil in his briefcase and stand to reach around for his jacket, Mallinder remained pokerfaced and motionless. It was all Kiri could do not to look at her as per Dan's instructions.

"Alright, will you give it back after the introduction?"

Phil and Kiri paused. *Dan, you're a legend.* Phil thought.

"Yes," he said.

He clicked on the DVD recording and began to speak.

"This interview is being recorded. The time is twelve fourteen hours on Monday the 7th of November. This interview is being conducted at the Auckland Central Police Station by myself, Detective Sergeant Philip Brown and Detective Kiri Ieremia. We are interviewing Katrina Mallinder. Katrina, please identify yourself by stating your name, date of birth, place of birth and current address."

There was no noise in the sound-proofed room, even the recording equipment worked in silence. Kiri counted six of her heartbeats and each one felt like a sonic boom.

"Katrina Mallinder. 31st of May 1974. Sleeford in England. Auckland Prison."

It was like a chess match already. Phil Brown and Katrina Mallinder looked across the table at each other. Brown raised an eyebrow and moved his right hand slightly in the direction of the envelope which he put back on the writing pad when he sat down again.

Katrina Mallinder blinked slowly. "I'm sorry I misunderstood; my last residential address before I was arrested was 4 bar 12 Kohimarama Road, Auckland."

"Thank you," he said not missing a beat. "To complete the formalities and before we begin the interview properly, we need to confirm your rights to free legal advice and also confirm you understand that whatever you say during the interview may be used in subsequent court proceedings."

He read from a laminated card all interviewing police officers were given by the custody centre staff prior to interviews. When he finished, Mallinder spoke as if she was also reading from a pre-arranged script. "I do not want to be represented by a lawyer, I understand whatever I say may be given in evidence."

Phil Brown nodded, satisfied. He removed the gold watch from the envelope and checked the times on it with his own and then handed it across the table. Mallinder looked at the back of the watch first, tracing her finger over the inscribed letters and then put it on her left wrist.

"For the purposes of the interview, I have just returned Miss Mallinder's watch to her, which she was wearing at the time of her arrest and was broken at that time. Katrina, can you confirm I have given you your watch back and that it is in good working order?"

"Yes and yes," she replied, looking down through the new glass to the gold and LCD displays. "Thank you."

"Katrina, you were arrested last Sunday, that is, the 30th of October here in Auckland. I want you to tell me in your own words first, of all the events that you feel are relevant which led up to your arrest. Take as long as you want; when you have finished, I will probably have some questions to ask you."

She looked from Phil to Kiri and then to her watch again before refocusing on Phil. "I was expecting Dan Calder to be here in person," she said, crossing one leg over the other in a cat-like movement.

"Mr. Calder assisted the police during the investigation which led to your arrest in a consultative role. His dealings in this matter have been concluded."

"I doubt that. Are these your questions or his?"

"Katrina, we are here to talk about the events leading to your arrest. I am not prepared to get into a general discussion with you about Mr. Calder or anybody else. This is your opportunity to tell us in your own words what has led to you being here today."

This was crunch time now, she had her watch back, and Phil Brown had laid out the ground rules. Kiri started counting heartbeats again.

"I was not there when my parents died. They lived for me, and they died for me too. It's a very hard thing to know. I would have much rather they gave me the choice as to whether we should all carry on living together or die together in the back seat of our car. I'd probably have chosen the car.

"Do you know what the most powerful emotion is? I was surprised for a long time when I found out; it's guilt. Guilt can generate more strength or more weakness than all the others put together, but the unique quality is that it can generate them both together.

"You want me to talk about the deaths of people, you have questions about money, you want to know what I have done over the last what, two years, five, ten? As we are in New Zealand, maybe you just want to know about the last few months?"

Brown was tempted to speak, but held his tongue. More time passed during which Mallinder looked at her watch as if she were trying to make the time go backwards, all the way back to the day of her graduation when everything was good.

"No," she said. "What I have to say I'll only say once; to a court."

Silence enveloped the room apart from the feint buzz coming from the overhead lights while she sat looking at her watch, and Phil Brown looked at a typed document, which had nothing to do with the case but gave him a reason to be quiet. It was clear she meant what she said.

"Katrina, I can't understand why you do not want to speak to me. If you told me why, then perhaps I could."

"Charlotte Bronte once said, 'If all the world hated you, and believed you wicked, while your own conscience approved you, and absolved you from guilt, you would not be without friends.' I will talk with Dan Calder or what I have to say will wait until I'm in the court; after all, it's his questions you are asking. Thank you again for returning my watch."

They were to be the last meaningful words she spoke.

"That is not going to happen, Katrina. I told you Mr. Calder has nothing more to do with this investigation." Both he and Kiri tried all they could to continue without passing control over to Mallinder, but to no effect. She remained silent.

Before pressing the buttons to conclude the interview, Phil Brown said "The time is twelve twenty-five; I am now turning the recording device off."

While Katrina Mallinder was driven back to the Remand Centre; Phil and Kiri drove back to Avondale feeling miserable. It was not how they hoped the day might pan out.

The incident room was now being used for another police inquiry, and so they trudged back into their old office like defeated soldiers. To make matters worse, there was nobody there to welcome them.

The police organisation is a living entity and there are always new matters requiring manpower and resources. Phil and Kiri were all that was left of the team; Philip Te Tuke was still employed on the Stella Banks investigation, although he was due to finish soon; Phil Larson and Glen Johannsen returned to their uniform duties and Jerome Brett was now dealing with a series of burglaries where the offenders not only stole property, but also set fire to the occupants' clothes before they left.

Like it or not, things were returning to normal, or at least whatever normal was in a busy police station. Kiri called Dan to let him know the bad news while Phil called Harry at the hospital.

"Hey, don't worry; you can only do what you can do. The chances are she wouldn't have talked to anyone, including me," Dan said. "What are you going to do next?"

"I think Phil will have to talk with the Chief Inspector; the other Stella Banks investigation may well take precedence so far as local enquiries go. Don't be surprised if the NCIS guys play their serial killer trump card though, and that's a kind of difficult one to beat. What about you, any plans?"

"Well, maybe something Harry suggested a while ago; in training."

Katrina was sitting on her bed with her knees pulled up, reading her latest borrowed book. Her favourite was Dan Calder's bible, which she kept with her all the time, but the prison library was also sufficiently well stocked to keep her occupied when she wanted something else. She had not read *Children of a Lesser God* since she played Lydia in a university production.

She took to prison life with remarkable ease, and for the first time in years, she was truly herself, even though she was behind bars. The appearance of a uniformed officer at her open door halted progress, but she did not look up from the page.

"You have a visitor," the guard said.

"No thanks." It was a month since the last one, but she had seen enough of police and psychologists asking questions, trying to assess her sanity.

"He said you'd say that."

She looked up. "Hmm, what's his name?"

"Brendan Thomas."

Katrina took a moment before she marked her page and got up; slipping on her soft shoes, she hesitated. "Let me just brush my teeth," she said, suddenly aware of wanting to make just the right impression.

"Mr. Thomas, nice to see you again; it's been a long time, hasn't it?" She extended her hand, but it was not reciprocated. "So still some hard feelings then?"

Dan Calder sat on the other side of the table. "Let's talk first, please?"

"Brendan and Thomas Edrich. That takes me back; I wonder whatever happened to them." Katrina smiled.

"I expect they carried on robbing old men."

"What do you want to talk about? I have your bible, it's been a great comfort; would like it back?"

"No, you can keep it; I don't need it any more. What made you want to kill them all rather than just steal their money? Not Christopher and Mathews, but the others."

"Okay, no small talk, very well. For the same reason you did what you did. We are all products of our own experiences. What else could I have done?"

"You would have made a formidable detective."

"And you one hell of a serial killer."

They both sat forwards, he with his palms on the table and she with her elbows. They were close enough she could see the odd yellow flecks in his right eye, and he could smell her toothpaste.

He started quietly so she would have to listen hard. "I'm here using a false name and nothing is going to be admissible. I'd like to talk for my own benefit, nothing more. What have you got to lose?"

"Don't play games with me, Dan; quiet voice, authority assertion; you know what I mean. I'll talk to you, if you talk to me too."

He turned his palms up. "Fair enough. I suppose I should thank you. I haven't had a nightmare for weeks. I don't think I'll be having any more." It was total fabrication; in the last two weeks alone, Zoe and all that happened at 22 Powton Road, Mapperley visited him during sleep three times, seamlessly taking over from the nightmare about his parents which he knew was now gone forever.

"It must have been terrible for you. Did he abuse her right up to the end?"

"Yes, the week before she died, I remember a big bruise on her arm."

"I don't think my parents even had a cross word in all the time they were together," she said. "They were so busy struggling to get from one day to the next, they didn't have the time or the strength to."

"Did you have any idea they could do something as drastic as that? Drastic and brave; to do it for you."

"It's funny isn't it; how different we see the same things. They weren't brave to me, and I would have swapped them for your parents in many ways. Tell me about you and how you came to be in New Zealand."

"Your article was the beginning of the end. I got my arse kicked for speaking in the way I did. I told them to shove the job and came here six months later. Have you seen much of the country? If you have, you will understand the attraction."

"I never got the chance, but I really like it around Auckland. I've read and heard lots about the rest of the country, but something tells me I won't get the chance to see it for myself now."

They managed to exchange a smile of something like understanding. She had not been in a position like this before, unlike Dan. With the subject in custody, the rules of the chase were over now; the next job for the police officer was to disassociate himself from the crime and concentrate on the interview stage. It was not necessary to build a friendship, but a relationship of some description helped.

"After I first came here, I always wanted to come back to live one day. I've been here for three years."

"Nice little house but not very personal," she said.

He did not hold it against her. Breaking in was necessary for her at the time, and he respected her professionalism. "Yeah, I need to work on that. Where were you going to end up?"

Katrina sighed. "I never got around to deciding. My plan was to retire one day, but … well, you know."

"What happened with Mark Singleton? I think I understand the others, but I never understood the why concerning him."

"I loved him. He turned me into whatever I am in a way; I was a mouse when I first went to university, and he got me interested in acting. I fell hopelessly in love with him; I was so naïve. I got pregnant." She immediately noticed his surprise. "Oh you didn't know? I thought everything was going to be fine, but he had other ideas. We rented a house together for a while until I lost the baby, and then he dropped me like a stone. He was relieved and wanted out as fast as he could.

"He got a newspaper job and disappeared. I managed to finish my degree and tried to get work around the Yorkshire area. After two years of bad jobs, I was offered a good position but that was when my parents were told they were going to lose everything they had. I told them I'd go back to help, but they committed suicide before I did."

"I'm sorry. It wasn't your fault. I mean I'm sure there was nothing you could have done to help by that time."

"I read your book, so don't lecture me on guilt and responsibility."

"I could have helped my mother though."

"No; you were a young boy. What was it you called him? A beast; no there was nothing more you could have done."

"Now who's lecturing?"

They both smiled again. "You didn't finish telling me about Singleton."

"After the death of my mother and father, I contemplated all sorts of things. I can't remember now how it started, but there came a time when I realised I could exact revenge. It's as simple as that."

"With Stephen Christopher?"

"Yes. I got the idea from a book somewhere. One Mark introduced me to, probably, so he really did make me in a number of ways you see.

"He was a good reporter. He was the editor at Garstone as you know. When I approached him for a job and told him I was using the name of Stenning because my real one had so many issues attached to it, he believed me without question. It didn't take much to convince him to take me on."

"But that still doesn't explain why you should want to kill him."

"I told you; he was a good reporter. By that time, it was my life. I could not take the chance he might work it out one day. You did."

"That sounds like an excuse rather than a reason."

She smiled sweetly. "You would have to do it to understand how it feels."

"Didn't you ever feel like stopping?"

"Did you *want* to resign? You loved your work; only circumstances made you give it all up. We are not so different. How are things with Tara?"

Dan had no hesitation in answering. "Good. I think, or at least I hope, we can be happy. I'm trying not to screw it up."

"We met once before, a chance meeting, just like how you and Tara started. All things have a beginning, some more complicated than others. Do you wonder what might have happened if we had met in different circumstances?"

He chose not to entertain the thought; it would have troubled him if he did. "I nearly forgot. I have something for you." He reached into his pocket and took out a clear plastic photo frame. Inside was a copy of Mallinder's family portrait he took from the original in the silver frame. As he passed it over and she accepted it, she touched the back of his hand sending a shock-wave up his arm.

"Thank you," she said. "I've missed being able to look at them."

"Will you be admitting all the murders when the time comes? Ten isn't it?"

She regarded him even more intently. "Is it?"

"I'm told the British police have enough to prove six more with the cane as well as Miss Stenning's exploits."

"Why Dan, it sounds as if you have your doubts. They really should allow you back on the case."

"And you'd tell me if I was?"

"Of course; I don't want us to have any secrets."

As he got up, she held up her hand and he sat again. "No secrets Dan, tell me yours and I will tell you all of mine."

"I should be going. Is there anything else you need?"

"Chapter fourteen, what is in chapter fourteen?"

He shuddered and went so weak that he almost slumped completely off his chair. "I deleted it," he said, but it was so clearly a hopeless lie, he was embarrassed to hear the words himself.

"It's at the time just before we met; something which happened to you then. Did it affect the way you talked to me on the steps of Garstone Court?"

He tried not to confirm or deny her suspicions by looking straight ahead.

"You know you will have to tell somebody one day; not darling Tara, you would have done it by now if you were going to. Come on Dan, get it off your chest, I might be the one person who can help."

He felt claustrophobic and desperate to be away from her before she reached inside him and plucked out his heart. "No thanks."

"So you're just going to leave me here wondering. Will you come again maybe?"

"No, I just wanted to ask you what I have."

When he stood again, she got up too. "And the police are not likely to let you play with them again are they? So I suppose this is it. Sorry if I was the cause of your troubles with them."

Dan extended his hand and shook Katrina's as he replied. "Without you, I don't think I'd be in New Zealand, and I'd probably still be having nightmares, so let's call it even."

As he waited to be let out of the room, Katrina asked, "What was your marathon time?"

"Four hours and three seconds; I'm going to have to do it all over again next year to knock those three seconds off."

She watched him leave and then waited for the guard to take her back to her cell. *Sweet dreams, Dan Calder*, she thought.

EPILOGUE

Dan never considered a return to England in the time after he left, but as the star witness for the prosecution, it was essential. He and Tara travelled together, and he spent two weeks showing her around the country, during which time they visited a number of places from his past, and he made his peace with some ghosts. The only place he didn't consider visiting again was Mapperley.

The most difficult and rewarding moment was at the cemetery where the ashes of both his parents were scattered in one of the remembrance gardens years before. They walked together as the trees rustled and the birds sang, during which time Dan tried unsuccessfully to remember a happy family moment which he could take away. At the end of their circuitous route, he was content to simply say goodbye to them both. When they left, he did not look back.

Katrina Mallinder displayed the barest hint of interest in the court proceedings as the clerk came to the end of the charges list. She was five feet eleven inches tall in her heels and wore a high-end dark blue skirt-suit and matching silk shirt. Her natural light brown hair was brushed into a pleasing style which extenuated her facial features to make the most of moderate attractiveness.

Dan looked away from her when the clerk paused after completing the list of charges and then back again as the clerk continued. "Katrina Mallinder. To the charge of the murder of Stephen Lucas Christopher; are you guilty or not guilty?"

She took a small breath and then addressed the judge. "My Lord, I certainly killed him, but I have no guilt about doing so."

Turning her head few degrees to the right she looked at Dan. "It's a wonderful thing to be guilt free; let not your heart be troubled, John. You should try it."

He frowned at her choice of words and the name for him but nodded and got up. He had seen and heard enough to know it was over. By the time the next charge was read out, he was halfway down the hallway, heading for the exit and home.

It was over a week later when Katrina Mallinder's last words to Dan finally made sense. His irregular memory self-scan told him she must have called him John for good reason. When he searched the Internet for "Let not your heart be troubled," the answer beamed back immediately. She'd kept his bible and told him it was a comfort to her.

It was the first line of the New Testament Book of John. Chapter 14.

Thank you for reading *The Agency*. I have drawn on some personal experiences to try and make it believable, but rest assured, I am not Dan Calder. His next adventure is to follow; mine is just to record it.

The passage of writing I used at various times in my career remains as important today as it was on the day it was first given to me. It was at a time in my life when direction and meaning were a constant struggle.

Max Ehrmann wrote the *Desiderata* in 1927, although it was mistakenly thought to be a much older text for several decades until its real history was explained in 1965. *Desiderata* is Latin, it means desired things.

Go placidly amid the noise and haste, and remember what peace there may be in silence.

As far as possible, without surrender, be on good terms with all persons.

Speak your truth quietly and clearly; and listen to others, even the dull and ignorant; they too have their story.

Avoid loud and aggressive persons; they are vexatious to the spirit.

If you compare yourself with others, you may become vain and bitter, for always there will be greater and lesser persons than yourself.

Enjoy your achievements as well as your plans.

Keep interested in your career, however humble; it is a real possession in the changing fortunes of time.

Exercise caution in your business affairs, for the world is full of trickery.

But let this not blind you to what virtue there is; many persons strive for high ideals,

and everywhere life is full of heroism.

Be yourself.

Especially, do not feign affection.

Neither be critical about love; for in the face of all aridity and disenchantment, it is as perennial as the grass.

Take kindly the counsel of the years, gracefully surrendering the things of youth.

Nurture strength of spirit to shield you in sudden misfortune. But do not distress yourself with imaginings.

Many fears are born of fatigue and loneliness. Beyond a wholesome discipline, be gentle with yourself.

You are a child of the universe, no less than the trees and the stars;

you have a right to be here.

And whether or not it is clear to you, no doubt the universe is unfolding as it should.

Therefore be at peace with God, whatever you conceive Him to be.

And whatever your labors and aspirations, in the noisy confusion of life, keep peace with your soul.

With all its sham, drudgery and broken dreams, it is still a beautiful world. Be cheerful. Strive to be happy.

Max Ehrmann, *Desiderata*

Best wishes. Ian.

Ian Austin was born in 1963 in Southampton, England. His very unremarkable school life ended at 16. Drifting into and out of several jobs including hotel porter and photocopier salesman he eventually found his salvation in the Hampshire Police. A career as first a constable and then detective in the UK followed, where he also served as a tactical firearms officer, covert surveillance operative and National Crime Squad trainer.

He transferred to the New Zealand Police in 2003 having visited several times before and falling in love with the country and the Kiwi way of life.

He left the police in 2006 to set up a training and consultancy business.

He now lives in Auckland with his artist partner Sallie.